THOMAS MANN (1875–1955) was born in Lubeck, Germany. His first novel, *The Buddenbrooks*, appeared in 1901, winning critical acclaim. He followed this success with the novellas "Tonio Kröger" (1903) and "Death in Venice" (1912), as well as the novel *The Magic Mountain* (1924). The works established him as the leading writer of his generation and as the first twentieth-century representative of the great German literary tradition. After winning the Nobel Prize for Literature in 1929, he left Hitler's Germany in 1933, eventually settling in the United States in 1938, where he was an outspoken supporter of the Allied war effort. His most important late work was *Dr. Faustus* (1947), a novel exploring the cultural and psychological reasons for the rise of Nazism in civilized, bourgeois Germany. He eventually returned to Europe. He died in Switzerland.

JEFFERSON S. CHASE holds a doctorate in German Literature from the University of Virginia, where he was also a President's Fellow. From 1994 to 1996, he was a postdoctoral fellow at the Berlin Institute for German and European Studies. He collaborated on the English version of Gregor von Rezzori's *Oedipus at Stalingrad*, and his translations of Heine, Börne, and Saphir appear in his book *Inciting Laughter: The Rise of Jewish Humor in German Culture.* He is currently Lecturer in German at the University of Nottingham.

THOMAS MANN

Death in Venice and Other Stories

TRANSLATED AND WITH AN
INTRODUCTION BY
JEFFERSON S. CHASE

A SIGNET CLASSIC

SIGNET CLASSIC
Published by the Penguin Group
Penguin Putnam Inc., 375 Hudson Street,
New York, New York 10014, U.S.A.
Penguin Books Ltd, 27 Wrights Lane,
London W8 5TZ, England
Penguin Books Australia Ltd, Ringwood,
Victoria, Australia
Penguin Books Canada Ltd, 10 Alcorn Avenue,
Toronto, Ontario, Canada M4V 3B2
Penguin Books (N.Z.) Ltd, 182–190 Wairau Road,
Auckland 10, New Zealand

Penguin Books Ltd, Registered Offices:
Harmondsworth, Middlesex, England

Published by Signet Classic, an imprint of Dutton NAL,
a member of Penguin Putnam Inc.

First Signet Classic Printing, May 1999
10 9 8 7 6 5 4 3 2 1

Printed in the United States of America

Library of Congress Catalog Card Number: 98-50734

CONTENTS

ACKNOWLEDGMENTS

I would like to take this opportunity to thank some of the people who supported and assisted me in the long process of preparing this edition, to wit: Julia Moskin, Don Hymans at Signet, Jonathan Long, Walter Sokel, Wiebke Sievers, Julie Gregson, and Irmela Plamann. Many of my ideas about translating and reading these stories arose during enjoyable conversations with Alex Ross, a true Mann enthusiast and an insightful critic. Above all, my thanks go out to Lara Brekenfeld, to whom my translations are also dedicated.

Thomas Mann: An Introduction

"For an imaginative work of any significance to make an on-the-spot impact that is both broad and deep," writes Thomas Mann in "Death in Venice," "there must be some unspoken affinity, indeed basic agreement between the individual destiny of the author and the general one of his contemporaries and fellow citizens." Mann might well have been writing of himself. Together with Franz Kafka, Mann overshadows all other twentieth-century German authors in world fame and importance. He sold millions of books during his lifetime, exerted a literary influence to rival that of Faulkner or Joyce, functioned in American exile during World War II as the premier voice of Germany's humanist tradition, and is still read today throughout the world by both popular and academic audiences. Yet he remains a difficult, problematic figure. Unlike Kafka, whose works take place in a singular alternative nightmare world and whose name spawned an English adjective, Mann wrote in a variety of modes ranging from the everyday-realistic to the surreal, and his authorial presence always seems to hover outside his fictional creations, apart and separate from them. There is no adjective *Mannian* except among Mann scholars. Instead, there is a continuing fascination with him as a person and with the circumstances surrounding the composition of his works. No fewer than three Mann biographies appeared in 1995.

Paul Thomas Mann was born on June 6, 1875, in Lubeck, the second child of Senator Thomas Johann Heinrich Mann. The Manns had been citizens first-class of the Hanseatic trading city for over a hundred years before Thomas's birth, possessing a large import-export firm and holding office in the autonomous city-state's government. Thomas's mother, Julia da Silva-Bruhns, was of Brazilian descent: his mixed parentage would later become a subject he would explore in his semi-autobiographical "Tonio Kröger" and "Death in Venice." Success for Thomas came early, despite the swift demise of the family business after his father's death in 1892. After his father died, Thomas's family moved to Munich, where he was educated and worked as a clerk in an insurance office and served on the staff of the Munich journal *Simplicissimus* before taking up writing as a career. He published his first novella at the age of nineteen. By 1904 he had completed *The Buddenbrooks*, the novel that was to bring him international fame. In the years to follow, despite occasional financial crises brought on by the vicissitudes in Germany's political fortunes, Mann never seriously questioned his calling as an author and a public figure. Indeed, he saw his career as following in the great tradition of the twin idols of German literature, Goethe and Schiller. After he completed *The Buddenbrooks*, Mann married into a wealthy Jewish family, composed the short stories collected in this edition, and experienced his second novelistic triumph with the epic *The Magic Mountain* (1924). He was awarded the Nobel Prize in Literature in 1929.

Thomas Mann was an enthusiastic, indeed chauvinistic supporter of the German cause in World War I, which led to a prolonged estrangement from his older brother Heinrich, a successful and important novelist in his own right, with whom Thomas had worked closely in the incipient days of his career. The experience of German defeat, however, converted Mann from an adherent of Imperial monarchism to a committed, if culturally snobbish proponent of democracy. His opposition to the politics of the National Socialists, together with his wife Katia's Jewish background, led to his emigration shortly after Hitler became Chancellor in 1933, first to Switzerland, then to the United States (1938). He became a U.S. citizen in 1944, took up various academic posts, and worked closely with the U.S. State Department on scores of anti-Hitlerian essays and radio addresses. In 1947, while he was living in Los Angeles, he completed his last great novel, *Doctor Faustus*, a fictional reckoning with what the historian Friedrich Meineke was to term "the German catastrophe." He returned to Europe in 1953 and settled near Zurich, Switzerland, where he died on August 12, 1955. He was the father of the author Klaus Mann (1906–49) and the historian Golo Mann (1909–94).

Mann's works are remarkably philosophical, very much the product of the intellectual environment of their time. Though a poor student, Mann was an avid reader and absorbed a great deal of the philosophical views that were popular during his formative years, chiefly those of Schopenhauer and Nietzsche. From Schopenhauer, he incorporated the idea of an irrational, destructive will—a natural force of life described as present alternately in the world itself and deep within the human psyche—which was fundamentally opposed to the stabilizing, constructive efforts of the rational mind. From Nietzsche, he took insights concerning human psychology, especially the psychology of the artist as outsider vis-à-vis Western civilization. This view ran contrary to the popular nineteenth-century idea of the artist as a heroic representative of bourgeois society. For Mann, as well as for Nietzsche, the artist was a dubious figure, a creature of sickness and longing for death, motivated by resentment of society's stronger self-perpetuating impulses. As such, however, the artist was emblematic of a basic conflict between individual desire and civilized behavior.

Mann was also influenced by his contemporary Freud, who likewise focused on sexual desire as a nexus of frustrated individual will and likewise came to perceive a death-wish, or *thanatos*, embedded within the human subconscious. Still another, less frequently noted influence was the phenomenology of Edmund Husserl, with its methodological emphasis on descriptive perception as a means of insight into the human condition. Some of Mann's maddeningly detailed, at times seemingly hair-splitting prose can be understood as an attempt to do in fiction what the phenomenologists of his day pursued in philosophy.

Surprisingly, Mann's thematic interests are rather narrow—although he did often quote from outside sources, he was not the writer to be inspired by newspaper curiosities or second-hand anecdotes. First and foremost among his favorite themes is the relationship between the artist and bourgeois society. This topic had long been a literary preoccupation before Mann, but no writer had ever depicted the entwined impulses toward integration and rebellion characteristic of the artist with quite the complexity that Mann did. The artists in Mann's works are not Romantic bohemians who sacrifice themselves in struggle against bourgeois constraints. More often than not, they are profoundly bourgeois souls who long for complete integration into the everyday world of the warm-hearted and the banal. Their central dilemma, which Mann treats both tragically and comically, is that the very artistic talent that earns them social acclaim also makes them creatures of anti-emotional irony, musical frenzy, or destructive passion. Mann challenges traditional conceptions of the artist as a heroic figure by portraying the creative impulse as a compensatory mechanism for individual weakness, for the artist or art-lover's inability to fit into a "normal," healthy world. Mann pursues this theme most satirically in "Tristan," whereas the writer-protagonists of "Tonio Kröger" and "Man and Dog" (two directly autobiographical works) reconcile their social and destructive impulses in much the same fashion as Mann did in real life. In "Death in Venice," it is debatable as to whether Gustav Aschenbach's fatal lapse into forbidden passion represents ridiculous foible or tragic triumph.

Mann is not a "political" writer in the typical sense of the word. He largely eschews depictions of class conflict, political events, and technological transformations of society in his works. Yet his treatment of the individual-versus-society theme does have broad relevance. For Mann, the destructive, antisocial impulses at work within the artistic psyche reveal the potential for violence and warfare latent in civilized society, of which art is a major institution. Public attitudes toward war during Mann's time differed markedly from our own. World War I was greeted by some as a positive development that would cleanse Europe of the torpor and malaise into which it was perceived to have fallen at the turn of the century. Mann lived through both of the great European wars and witnessed the near destruction of the culture with which he identified most. It is not surprising, then, that references to war are scattered throughout his late works: the evocation of the politically explosive atmosphere of the early 1910's in the beginning of "Death in Venice," for example, or allusions to war-time privation in "Man and Dog." In these and other passages, Mann suggests that individual "artistic" antipathy toward civilization is indicative of a self-destructive impulse at work within European culture at large. He would develop this view with unambiguous reference to fascism in later works such as "Mario and the Magician" (not included here because of copyright constraints) and *Doctor Faustus*. For Mann, European society, like the artist, was sick.

A third major theme in Mann's work is homoeroticism. As his recent biographer Anthony Heilbutt points out, Mann repeatedly developed crushes on attractive young men of the sort depicted in the first chapter of "Tonio Kröger." Aschenbach's obsession with Tadzio in "Death in Venice," too, had its origins in a real-life fascination to which Mann succumbed while on vacation with his brother and wife. However, there is no reliable evidence to suggest that Mann consummated any of these relationships sexually. What seems more probable is that, like Tonio Kröger, Mann restricted his homosexual leanings to fiction and led a life of heterosexual "normality." In any case, his exploration of homosexuality enabled him to develop a unique understanding of the situation of the social outsider. In drawing the connection between artists and homosexuality, Mann directly confronted an issue that had been lurking scandalously within German literature at least since the Heine-Platen feud of 1828. Mann does not take up a clear moral position in regard to homosexuality in his works. Aschenbach's feelings for Tadzio are described in sympathetic detail, but at the same time Mann's overall depiction of his protagonist is ironic and therefore calls Aschenbach's sensibilities—artistic as well as erotic—into question. It was thanks to this ironic distance from his subject matter that Thomas Mann—who otherwise placed enormous value on respectability—could create one of the most frank depictions of homosexual desire the world has ever known.

Mann's distanced perspective as author is reinforced by the style in which he writes. The first and perhaps most obvious feature of his style is parataxis—long-windedness. Owing to its syntactic structure, German is a "long" language, but even so Mann constructs mammoth sentences. Contrary to initial impressions, though, Mann's long-windedness is motivated by a desire to be as precise as possible. True to the phenomenological belief in the intrinsic worth of descriptive perception, Mann leaves no impression about his subject matter unrecorded. It is a signature move of Mann's, for instance, to juxtapose two or more seemingly synonymous adjectives or verbs in order to point out the subtle differences in meaning and perception they entail. He also exploits syntactic vagaries to create revealing ambiguity: this occurs most prominently in "Death in Venice," in which ambiguously referring relative pronouns are employed to depict Aschenbach's own confused and conflict-ridden thought process. Even when its sense does eventually emerge without ambiguity, the typical Mann sentence is not necessarily immediately comprehensible. It is a puzzle that one has to put together, and this putting together is an important part of the pleasure and the profit of reading Mann.

A second major aspect of Mann's style is the protean

quality of his narrative voice. Much like his contemporary Alfred Döblin, the author of *Berlin Alexanderplatz*, Mann was a great lover of found material, and his writing often takes on the character of quoted pastiche. "Death in Venice," for example, contains strategically altered citations from Plato, Cicero, Homer, Xenophon, Plutarch, and August von Platen, as well as an encyclopedia entry on Asiatic cholera. This penchant for quotation feeds into two other stylistic idiosyncrasies: an inscrutable authorial perspective and periodic ruptures of hermetic fictionality. Because Mann's narrators so often speak through the voice of a quoted source, authorial opinion is placed at double remove, filtered through narration that is itself filtered through the material on which it is based. It is thus very difficult to determine, in any definitive way, what Mann may have thought about his characters—readers are left to judge them for themselves. Moreover, Mann's quotations also direct readers' attention outside the fictional universe of the actual story at hand. His stories are set in real places and at real times. They occasionally even modulate into the present tense, as in the graveyard scene in the first chapter of "Death in Venice," to emphasize that the fictional events are taking place in actual locations that readers can, if they choose, go and see for themselves. Both in its intertextuality and its willful rupturing of fictional illusion, Mann's work anticipates the postmodern impulses characteristic of contemporary fiction.

It is a tribute to Mann's compositional talent that his works are anything but postmodern exercises in the arbitrary and the contingent. On the contrary, they are structured to a remarkable degree, with motifs recurring and connecting in a way that has often been described as symphonic. Thinking of music is appropriate when reading Mann: he was a great admirer of Richard Wagner and Gustav Mahler, and he used Mahler as the physical model for Gustav Aschenbach. As in a symphony, scarcely a phrase goes by in Mann's writing without echoing, or being echoed by, another phrase. There are other echoes as well. The list of citations from "Death in Venice" reveals the extent of Mann's familiarity with Greek literature and myth, and the complex network of allusions in that novella rivals that in *Faust* by Goethe. Any assertions about Mann's classicism must be tempered, however, by an appreciation of ironic context. The classical allusions in "Death in Venice," after all, reflect the decidedly ambiguous consciousness of Aschenbach. Even in his greatest creative triumph, Mann remains impossible to pin down.

Mann's ironic, disengaged but precise treatment of the most personal and explosive subject matter is the basis of his literary achievement. His importance to both German and world literature—as well as the status of the former within the latter—can hardly be overestimated. Unlike its English, French, Russian, and American counterparts, nineteenth-century German literature, with its emphasis on poetry and ornate novellas, produced no monumental novels of lasting international reputation. In fact, if we ignore the existence of several excellent and innovative writers (Heinrich Heine, Annette von Droste-Hülshoff, Theodor Fontane), Mann can be said to have rescued German literature from a relatively fallow period. In scope and stylistic mastery, though not in content, *The Buddenbrooks* can be compared to the great novels of Balzac and Flaubert, Dickens and Eliot, Dostoyevsky and Tolstoy. Yet in *The Buddenbrooks* and in his remarkable series of short stories, Mann progresses beyond the bourgeois concerns and mimetic techniques of Realism to expose the precarious psychological foundations of Western civilization, uncovering in the process the often dubious aspects of literary creativity itself. In doing so, he was perfectly attuned to what the social theorist E. J. Hobsbawm calls "The Age of Extremes," the twentieth century—a century of rupture between the individual and society, a century of unprecedented improvement in Western standards of living and almost unthinkable bureaucratized destruction.

The present edition has been selected and translated with this connection between author and society in mind. "Death in Venice" is, of course, a natural selection and among Germans "Tonio Kröger" and "Tristan" also have the status of classics in their own right. "Man and Dog," one of Mann's most everyday, realistic works, is also one of his most underrated—valuable for its mastery of parataxis and as a companion piece to "Death in Venice," its immediate predecessor. The remaining three short stories have been included because they contain themes also found in Mann's longer works. "The Child Prodigy" is a quasi-clinical case study of the conflict between commercialism and art in twentieth-century cultural production. "Hour of Hardship," narrated from Schiller's point of view, reveals Mann's fascination with the role of sickness and self-transcendence in artistic genius. Finally, "Tobias Mindernickel" introduces Mann's strange preoccupation with house pets (specifically dogs) as mirrors of mankind's ambiguous attitudes toward the unthinking, amoral vitality of the Schopenhauerian will. All three reflect and interact with Mann's "major" works and shed considerable light on his creative development.

My translations focus not only on content but also seek to render the complexity of Mann's style into contemporary American English. For all his stylistic elegance, Mann writes anything but standard German literary prose and is therefore among the most difficult writers to translate. Because Mann's long, complex sentences are written to be puzzled out, I have retained his paratactic syntax, rather than broken up the German into easily digestible units. I have also tried to preserve Mann's often idiosyncratic emphasis within sentences, which is crucial to our ability to follow their sense. This is not just a question of following original word order. Owing to the differences between English and German, reproduction of emphasis often involves reformulation, the insertion of introductory, emphatic phrases, for instance, or the use of dashes to capture the interjectory character of the German relative clause. At the same time, the syntactic differences between German and English occasionally require the shortening, even elision of phrases to avoid overloading individual sentences—

Mann's prose is ponderous, but rarely clumsy. Rhetorical techniques such as assonance, alliteration and rhyme are also crucial to reproducing the literary quality of Mann's work. In order to compensate for inevitable translation loss in this regard, I have not shied away from pursuing occasional felicitous opportunities in English for typically Mannian effects. In terms of word choice, I have sought to compensate for the drift caused by inexact vocabulary equivalents by striking a balance between the particularizing and the general. Moreover, I have made a distinction between those multipurpose German words like *Geist* (mind, spirit, imagination) which need to be rendered by various English equivalents and recurring terms like *Zügellosigkeit* (abandon) in "Death in Venice," which function as quasi-symphonic motifs and therefore must be signaled with one and the same English word. In general, I have opted for a temporally neutral vocabulary, avoiding words not in currency during Mann's day but resisting deliberate archaism, which inevitably rings precious and false. Temporal neutrality of course itself entails distortion, but it is, I believe, the most acceptable approach to a work foreign to its audience not only in language but in time.

All these strategic decisions have been made with one ultimate goal: to allow the contemporary American reader to experience Mann much as a contemporary German reader would. The reader should not approach Mann—in translation, or in German for that matter—expecting to experience anything immediately obvious. Puzzling out Mann is an intrinsic part of reading his work. I hope the present edition is one that helps the reader to do this and contributes in some way to a deeper appreciation of Mann's uniquely enigmatic work.

—Jefferson S. Chase
Nottingham, 1998

Tobias Mindernickel

1

Among the streets that head up the rather steep hill from the quayside to the middle of town, there is one called *Grauer Weg.* About halfway along on the right, if one is walking from the river, comes number 47, a narrow, drab-gray building utterly indistinguishable from its neighbors. The ground floor is home to a small shop, where, along with the usual, one can find galoshes and castor oil. Past the main hall, which looks out on a small courtyard populated by cats, a narrow wooden staircase with footworn treads and an unspeakably dank, seedy smell leads to the upper floors. On the second-floor left is a cabinetmaker; second-floor right, a midwife. On the third-floor left is a cobbler; third-floor right, a lady who immediately starts up a loud singing whenever she hears footsteps on the stairs. The fourth-floor left is empty, but on the fourth-floor right lives a man by the name of Mindernickel, who, on top of that, is called Tobias. An intriguing story is connected to this man that just has to be told, for it is both intriguing and scandalous beyond measure.

Mindernickel's appearance is eye-catching, quite odd, indeed ridiculous. If you see him, for example, out on a walk, hauling his gaunt frame up the hill with the help of a cane, he will invariably be dressed in black, from head to toe. He always wears an old-fashioned coarse top hat with a curved brim, a threadbare overcoat that fits too tightly and an equally shabby pair of trousers, frayed at the cuffs and so short you can see the rubber trim of his boots—though it should also be noted that he keeps his attire immaculately brushed. His haggard neck, jutting out of a low turn-down collar, looks even longer than it actually is. His hair is gray and slicked back severely at the temples, and the wide brim of his hat casts a shadow upon a pale clean-shaven face with sunken cheeks, swollen eyes that rarely lift from the ground and two deep, sullen lines that connect his nose and perennially frowning mouth.

Mindernickel seldom leaves his room—with good reason. No sooner does he appear on the street than a large group of children gathers, trailing at his heels for some distance, laughing, jeering, singing "Hah, hah, Tobias," often tugging at his coattails, while people emerge from their houses to make jokes at his expense. Undeterred, he proceeds on his walk, putting up no resistance, just timorously glancing around, his head pressed into his shoulders and his neck craned, like a person hurrying through a downpour without an umbrella. And although they're all laughing in his face, these people standing at their front doors, he still greets the odd one with humble courtesies. Further on, after the children have run back home, in streets where he's unknown and rarely attracts a second glance, his behavior doesn't alter significantly. He continues to glance around in fear and scurry along his way, huddled, as though he felt a thousand scornful stares upon him, and when he does timorously and hesitantly lift his gaze from the ground, one notices something strange. He's unable to *look* with any steadiness or determination at other people or even at inanimate objects. As strange as this may sound, he seems to lack that natural sovereignty of sensory perception that allows the individual to gaze out upon external phenomena. He seems to feel a sense of inferiority toward any and all such outside presence, and his aimlessly wandering eyes can't help but grovel before man and thing . . .

How to explain this person, who is so constantly alone and seems so extraordinarily sad? His decisively bourgeois attire, along with his genteel habit of delicately rubbing his chin, would indicate that he rejects any affiliation with the class of society in whose midst he lives. God only knows what hardships he has had to endure. From his face, it looks as though life itself had reared back in contemptuous laughter and punched him with all its might . . . On the other hand, it's quite possible that he's never suffered any such blows of fate, that he's simply unequal to the task of being a man. The tortured submissiveness and vacuity of his appearance convey the disagreeable impression that nature has denied him the strength, equilibrium and spine necessary to exist with his head held upright.

Having completed his huddled walk on his black cane to the center of town, he will make his way home to *Grauer Weg* to be received by the howling children. He'll climb up the musty stairs to his room, which is poorly furnished and void of decoration, the only object of any value or beauty being the sturdy Empire commode with the heavy metal handles. In front of his lone window, whose view is abruptly cut off by the gray wall of the neighboring house, there is a flowerpot full of soil in which nothing at all grows. Nonetheless Tobias Mindernickel will occasionally go over and examine it, sniffing at the barren soil. — Off to the side is a dark little sleeping alcove. — Back in his room, Tobias will lay his hat and cane atop the table, sit down upon his dusty-smelling sofa with its green upholstery, put his hand to his chin and stare with raised eyebrows at the ground in front of him. This would seem to be his sole purpose on earth.

As far as Mindernickel's character is concerned, it's difficult to say, although the following incident appears to speak in his favor. One day, as the odd little man left the house with the usual gang of children trailing behind him, laughing and shouting out insults, a boy of about ten tripped over another's foot and fell so hard on the cobblestones that he bloodied his nose and cut his forehead. He lay there in tears. Tobias immediately turned, hurried back to the fallen child, crouched down and began to comfort him in a mild, quavering voice. "You poor boy," he said. "Have you hurt yourself? Why, you're bleeding! Just look at the blood running down his forehead! How miserable you look lying there! Of course when it hurts so, the poor child starts crying! How I feel for you! It was your own fault, but let me bandage your head with my handkerchief . . . So, there we are! Now let's pull ourselves together and stand on our feet . . ." And having spoken these words of consolation and indeed made a bandage from his very own handkerchief, he gently lifted the boy and continued on. At that particular moment, however, he seemed utterly transformed in both posture and expression. He walked firm and upright, taking deep breaths, his chest swelling under his tight-fitting overcoat. His eyes were wide and had begun to twinkle, gazing at people and things with assurance, while a contented smile of sorrow played over his lips . . .

This incident had the short-term result that the denizens of *Grauer Weg* relented somewhat in their gleeful insults. After a little while, however, they forgot about the surprising behavior of this errant, huddled man, and a chorus of healthy, cheerful, cruel young throats again sang out behind him: "Hah, hah, Tobias!"

2

One sunny morning around eleven, Mindernickel left the house and proceeded across town to the *Lerchenberge*, that gradual slope that provides the best grounds in the city for an afternoon stroll and that, even before noon, was well visited by a number of carriages and pedestrians out to enjoy the excellent spring weather. Beside the broad main esplanade stood a man under a tree with a young game dog on a leash. He was displaying it to all passers-by, obviously in hope of finding an interested buyer. It was a handsome, healthy little animal, yellow in color, approximately four months old, with one black ear and a black ring around one eye.

When Tobias first saw them, at ten steps' remove, he

stopped short, rubbed his chin repeatedly and stared thoughtfully at the owner and the little dog, who was alertly wagging his tail. A moment later, with the handle of his cane pressed to his mouth, he started out again. He made three circles around the tree where the man was leaning, then finally approached and asked, never taking his eyes off the animal, in a soft and flustered voice: "How much is the dog?"

"Ten marks," answered the man.

At first Tobias said nothing. Then he repeated, hesitantly, "Ten marks?"

"Yes," said the man.

With that, Tobias removed a leather pouch from his pocket, took out a five-mark note together with one three- and one two-mark coin, and hastily handed the money to the seller. He then grabbed the leash, this huddled man, timorously glanced around as several witnesses to the transaction broke out in laughter, and began to pull the whimpering, struggling animal urgently along behind him. The dog put up a fight for the entire duration of their way, digging its front paws into the ground and looking up with frightened, searching eyes at his new master. The latter, however, continued to pull at the leash, mute and insistent, and managed to proceed back through town and start down the hill.

The street kids of *Grauer Weg* gave a terrific noise when Tobias appeared with the dog, but he lifted the animal and, cradling him in his arms, hurried through the mockery, the insults, the laughter and the tugging at his coattails up the three flights of stairs to his room. There he set the still whimpering creature on the ground, patted him affectionately and said in a condescending tone: "There, there, there's no reason to be afraid of me, you silly thing. That's not necessary."

With that, he pulled out a commode drawer, removed a plate of boiled meat and potatoes and tossed some to the animal, which ceased its whining and devoured the meal, happily wagging its tail and slobbering.

"By the way, your name is Esau," said Tobias. "Do

you understand? Esau. The simple sounds should be easy for you to remember . . ."

And pointing to the ground before him, he called out in a tone of command: "Esau!"

The dog, probably expecting something more to eat, did in fact come, and Tobias patted his side in approval, saying, "Well done, my friend. You've earned my praise."

Then he took a couple of steps back, once more pointed to the floor and called out: "Esau!"

And the animal, whose spirits had perked up, again sprang forward and licked his master's boot.

Tobias, tireless in his joy at issuing commands and seeing them executed, must have repeated this exercise thirteen or fourteen times. The dog, however, did finally get tired. It seemed he wanted to stop and digest his food. He lay down on the floor in the typically graceful, alert pose of a game dog, both of his long and delicately formed front paws stretched out beside one another.

"Again!" ordered Tobias. "Esau!"

But Esau turned his head and remained where he was.

"Esau!" Tobias repeated, imperiously raising his voice. "You must come at my command, even if you're tired!"

But Esau rested his head on his paws and gave no sign of coming at all.

"Listen here," said Tobias in a quiet but terribly menacing tone. "Obey my commands, or you'll find out how unwise it is to challenge me!"

The animal hardly moved its tail.

At that Mindernickel was seized by anger, a boundless, disproportionate, fully irrational anger. Beside himself with indignant rage, he grabbed his black cane, lifted Esau by the scruff of the neck and gave the yowling animal a thrashing, repeating over and over in a terrible hiss: "So you refuse to obey? You dare to disobey *me*?"

Finally he tossed his cane aside, set the whimpering dog back on the ground and began to pace the room in long strides, his hands behind his back, drawing deep breaths, occasionally casting a proud and angry glance down at Esau. After parading about for some time, he stopped before the animal, which lay on its back making pleading motions with its front legs. He folded his arms across his chest and spoke with the horribly cold, hard gaze and tone Napoleon had used in confronting the regiment that had lost its standard in battle: "How have you conducted yourself, if I may ask?"

Happy for even this bit of reconciliation, the dog crawled nearer, pressed himself against his master's leg and looked up at him with bright beseeching eyes.

For a long while Tobias looked down without a word, observing the humble creature; but then, with the warmth of Esau's body against his leg tugging at his heart, he picked him back up.

"All right, I'll take pity on you," he said. And as the good-natured animal began to lick his face, his mood swung full round, becoming melancholy and sentimental. He hugged the dog to his chest with a love full of sorrow, tears flooding his eyes, and repeated, his voice faltering, never finishing the sentence, over and over:

"You see, you're my only . . . my only . . ." Then he laid Esau gently on the sofa, sat down beside him, put his hand to his chin and gazed at the animal, his eyes calm and mild.

3

From then on Tobias Mindernickel left the house even less often than previously, for he felt no desire to show himself in public with Esau. He devoted all his attention to the dog: morning, noon and night Tobias did nothing but feed him, wipe his eyes, issue commands, scold him and talk to him like a human being. The only thing was that Esau didn't always conduct himself as his master would have wished. As long as the dog, lethargic from the lack of fresh air and freedom, lay on the sofa staring up at his face with melancholy eyes, Tobias had no complaints. He would sit there, calm and content, patting Esau's back and consoling him: "Why do you look up at me with such sorrow, my poor little friend? Yes, indeed, the world is a sad place, you feel it, too, even at your young age . . ."

Sometimes, however, the animal's playful game-dog instincts would whip him up into a blind frenzy. He would scamper frantically throughout the room and vent his enormous energy tussling with a slipper, jumping on the furniture and doing somersaults across the floor. Tobias, keeping his distance, followed such activity with a hapless, disapproving, uncertain look and a smile that was both ugly and full of irritation. Finally, laying down the law, he would bring the animal to heel: "Quit the rambunctiousness. There's no reason to be waltzing around."

Once, it even happened that Esau escaped his master's quarters and sprang downstairs into the street, where in a fit of delight he immediately began chasing a cat, eating horse dung and playing with the children. And when Tobias, his face twisted with sorrow, arrived on the scene—to the applause and laughter of half the street—the sad truth was that the dog fled from his master in long leaps . . . Tobias gave him a long and bitter thrashing for that.

One day at feeding time—the dog had been in his possession for several weeks—Tobias took a loaf of bread from the commode drawer. With the long bone-handled knife he always used for such purposes, the hunched little man began to cut off small pieces and drop them on the ground. Esau, however, heedless in his hunger and frivolity, leapt headlong toward his master, ramming his right shoulder into the clumsily held knife. He fell to the floor, twisted and bleeding.

Shocked, Tobias tossed everything aside and crouched over the wounded animal. Suddenly, however, his face was transformed; truth be told, a shimmer of happy relief flitted across it. He gently carried the whimpering dog over to the sofa, and you can't imagine the devotion with which he began to nurse his patient! During the day, Tobias never left his side for a minute, and at night, he let him sleep on his very own bed. He washed and bandaged him, patted and consoled him, and never tired in his gleeful expressions of sympathy and concern.

"Does it hurt a lot?" he would ask. "Yes, indeed, your suffering is bitter, my poor little creature! But lie still! We must endure it!" His face was calm, melancholy and glad as he said this.

Yet the more Esau gained in strength, the more he took heart and began to recover, the more agitated and resentful Tobias became. From that point on, he found it best no longer to fuss over the wound itself, ministering to the dog instead with pitying words and caresses. The dog's recovery, however, was quite well advanced. He had a strong constitution and soon began to move about the room again. And one day, having lapped up a plate of milk and white bread, he jumped down from the sofa in full health and began to race through the room with his former abandon, happily yelping, clawing the bedspread, chasing a potato across the floor and performing a series of gleeful somersaults.

Over at the window, beside the flowerpot, stood Tobias, twirling a lock of severely slicked-back hair in one of those hands that protruded so long and gaunt from their frayed sleeves. His frame loomed dark and eerie against the gray backdrop of the neighboring house, his face was pale and twisted by hate, and he followed every movement with a resentful, desperate, jealous and malevolent glare. Suddenly, though, he came to. He approached Esau, stopped him and took him slowly in his arms.

"My poor little creature," he started to say in a melancholy voice—but Esau, full of energy and in no mood to tolerate any further such treatment, took a playful bite at the hand attempting to pat him, wriggled from Tobias's arms, leapt to the ground, sprang mischievously to one side, yelped, then ran off happily.

What followed was something so incomprehensible and dastardly that I refuse to recount it in detail. Inclined slightly forward, Tobias Mindernickel stood, his arms hanging at his sides, his lips pressed together and his eyeballs trembling eerily in their sockets. Suddenly, with a kind of crazed leap, he had taken hold of the animal. A long bright object gleamed in his hand and the dog crashed to the floor, a knife wound running from his right shoulder deep into his chest. He didn't make a sound. He just fell on his side, bleeding and quivering . . .

A second later he was lying on the sofa, Tobias kneeling over him, pressing a handkerchief to the wound and stammering: "My poor little creature! My poor little creature! How sad this all is! How sad for both of us! Are you in pain? There, there, I know you are—how pitiful you look lying there! But I'll, I'll stay by your side! I'll comfort you! I'll take my best handkerchief . . ."

But Esau just lay there and groaned his last. His dim searching eyes were directed at his master, all innocence and accusation, unable to comprehend—then he straightened his legs out slightly and died.

Tobias, however, remained in his position, not moving. He had laid his face down upon Esau's body and was crying bitterly.

Tristan

1

This is "Einfried," the sanitarium. The long main building with its straight white lines and side wing stands amidst the spacious garden, which is delightfully appointed with grottos, arbors and little tree-bark pavilions, while behind its slate-tiled roof, pine-green mountains, massive and delicately fissured, tower toward the heavens.

Now as always the director of the institution is Dr. Leander. With his double-pointed black beard, which is as hard and frizzy as upholstery horsehair, with his thick eyeglasses that shine with reflected light, and with the aspect of a man whom science has made cold and hard, this quiet, thoughtful pessimist holds sway over the patients. Yes, in his curt, close-to-the-vest manner, he holds absolute sway over all these individuals who, too weak to set and follow their own rules, relinquish their fortunes in return for permission to abandon themselves to his strict regimen.

Miss von Osterloh, for her part, runs the household with tireless devotion. Lord, what a busy woman she is, hurrying up and down the stairs, from one end of the institution to the other. She lays down the law in the kitchen and the stock room, climbs around in the linen closets, issues orders to the servants and sets a house menu of economy, nutrition, taste and external elegance, managing everything with frantic conscientiousness. Concealed within this extreme efficiency is a standing reproach against men, against men everywhere, none of whom have succumbed to the idea of taking her for a wife. Nonetheless, in the two round, crimson spots on her cheeks, the inextinguishable hope still burns of someday becoming Mrs. Leander, the doctor's wife . . .

Ozone and calm, calm air . . . For sufferers of lung ailments, Einfried is, whatever Dr. Leander's jealous colleagues and rivals might say, to be warmly recommended. Not that consumptives are the only ones who check themselves in here. All sorts of patients—gentlemen, ladies, and even children—check in as well, for Dr. Leander has triumphs to report in the widest of areas. There are stomach cases here—Mrs. Spatz, for example, the magistrate's wife, who also has an ear problem—heart patients, paralytics, rheumatics and people with various nervous conditions. There's a diabetic general, constantly grumbling as he uses up his pension. There are a number of gentlemen with emaciated faces whose legs twitch in that spastic way from which nothing good ever comes. There's a fifty-year-old lady—Mrs. Höhlenrauch, the pastor's wife—who lost her wits after bringing nineteen children into the world and yet is still unable to find any peace. For a year now she has been driven by some absurd restlessness to wander on the arm of her private nurse, staring and silent, aimless and uncanny, throughout the entire household.

Now and then there is a death among the "serious cases," who are confined to their beds and appear neither at meals nor in the sitting room, but no one, not even the patient in the next room, hears anything of it. In the still of night the waxlike guest is laid aside, and Einfried's normal activities—the massages, shocks and shots, the showers, baths, exercise, steam cures and inhalations—continue on undisturbed in the various modern, technologically up-to-date treatment areas . . .

Yes, things are lively in these parts. The clinic is flourishing. The porter at the entrance to the side wing sounds the great bell every time new guests arrive, and with all the formalities both Dr. Leander and Miss von Osterloh accompany those departing to their carriages. And Einfried certainly has welcomed all types within its walls! There is even a writer, who has a name that sounds like a mineral or a precious stone, whiling away the days here . . .

Moreover, in addition to Dr. Leander, there is a second physician in residence for the minor cases and the terminally ill. But his name is Müller, and he's of no concern.

2

At the beginning of January the wholesaler Klöterjahn—of the firm A. C. Klöterjahn & Co.—brought his wife to Einfried. The porter sounded the bell, and Miss von Osterloh greeted the guests after their long journey in the ground-floor reception room, which, like almost everything else in the grand old house, was decorated exclusively in wonderful authentic Empire style. Scarcely a second passed before Dr. Leander too appeared. He bowed, and an introductory conversation was held for the orientation of both parties.

Outside, the wintertime garden lay with its flowerbeds covered in matting, its grottos snowed under and its little shrines abandoned. Two house employees lugged in the new guests' suitcases from their carriage, which, since there was no direct access to the house itself, had pulled up by the wrought-iron gate.

"Slowly, Gabriele, take care, my angel. Keep your lips closed," Mr. Klöterjahn had said as he led his wife through the garden. No one who had witnessed them could have helped but silently join, heart atremble, in the phrase "take care," which Mr. Klöterjahn had said, without any particular reason, in English.

The coachman who had brought the worthy couple from the station to the sanitarium, a rough, simple man of corresponding sensibilities, had practically bitten his tongue in helpless concern as the wholesaler helped his wife down from the carriage. Indeed, even the team of bay horses, their breath steaming in the frigid stillness of the air, seemingly strained to follow this harrowing procedure, their eyes rolled back in their heads, full of concern for such fragile grace and delicate charm.

The young woman had a throat condition, something in the trachea, as was unequivocally stated in the letter announcing their arrival that Mr. Klöterjahn had addressed from the Baltic coast to Einfried's director. Thank God it wasn't the lungs. Had it been the lungs, however, the new patient could hardly have looked fairer and more delicately refined, more sublime and ethereal than she did now, seated beside her burly husband in her whitewashed, straight-backed armchair, leaning back weak and tired as she followed the conversation.

Her beautiful pale hands, devoid of all jewelry except for a simple wedding ring, rested in her lap amid the folds of a heavy, dark cloth skirt, and she was wearing a silvery gray connecting bodice with a stiff standing collar and layers of arabesque patterns in raised velvet. These warm, heavy materials only rendered her indescribably delicate, charming, weary little head all the more moving, unearthly and delightful. Secured in a knot at the bottom of her neck, her light brown hair was brushed back flat, one single loose curl falling near her right temple, not far from the spot just over her clearly defined eyebrow where a strange little vein branched out, pale blue and sickly, across the otherwise unblemished perfection of her nearly transparent forehead. This little blue vein above the eye loomed unsettlingly over the entire fine oval of her face. It stood out all the more whenever the woman spoke, indeed whenever she as much as smiled, and gave her face the expression of exertion, even strain, which was the cause of considerable indefinite alarm. Nonetheless, she did talk and did smile. She talked openly and amicably, in a slightly husky voice, and she smiled both with her somewhat tired eyes, which now and then displayed a slight tendency to lose focus and whose interior corners lay in the shadows of her narrow nose, and with her beautiful wide mouth, which seemed to shine despite its pallor, probably on account of her lips being so clearly and distinctly outlined. Frequently she would clear her throat. On such occasions she would bring her handkerchief to her mouth, inspecting it immediately thereafter.

"Don't clear your throat, Gabriele, darling," Mr. Klöterjahn said. "You know that Dr. Hinzpeter back home expressly forbade it—it's simply a matter of self-control, my angel. As the doctor said, it's just the trachea," he repeated. "When it began, I really thought it was the lungs. That was, God knows, quite a shock. But it's not the lungs, no, the hell with that, we won't have any of that, will we, Gabriele? Oh no!"

"Of course not," said Dr. Leander, his glasses reflecting light in their faces.

Mr. Klöterjahn then ordered some coffee, coffee with buttered rolls. He had such an animated Northern accent—pronouncing the c in "coffee" all the way back in his throat, and saying "bottered" rolls—that everyone present felt suddenly hungry too.

He was given what he requested, then also given rooms for himself and his wife, and they settled in.

Moreover, Dr. Leander personally took over her treatment, not consulting Dr. Müller about the case.

3

The personability of the new patient caused an unusual stir at Einfried, and Mr. Klöterjahn, accustomed to such triumphs, accepted every compliment she was paid with self-satisfaction. The diabetic general momentarily ceased grumbling when he first caught glimpse of her, the gentlemen with the emaciated faces smiled and did their best to control their spastic legs whenever she came near, and Mrs. Spatz, the magistrate's wife, immediately attached herself as the young woman's mentor. She certainly made an impression, this woman who had taken Mr. Klöterjahn's good name! A certain writer who had been staying at Einfried for a couple of weeks now—an unpleasant oddball whose name sounded like a precious stone—almost blushed when she first passed him in the hallway. He stopped cold and stood as though rooted to the spot long after she had gone.

Before two full days had passed, the entire clinic community was familiar with her story. She came from Bremen—a fact obvious from certain charmingly pronounced vowels when she spoke—and that was where, twenty-four months ago, she had given the wholesaler Klöterjahn her lifelong "I do." She had followed him to his hometown, up there on the Baltic coast, and about ten months ago had, after an extraordinarily difficult and dangerous labor, borne him a child, blessing her spouse with a son and heir of astonishing vigor and magnificence. Since those terrible days, however, she had never regained her strength, assuming, that is, that she'd ever had any. She had barely left the maternity bed, when, extremely exhausted, extremely low on vital energy, she had coughed up a little blood. Oh, not much, an insignificant drop. It would have been better, though, if it had never happened, and even more worrisome was the recurrence of this disturbing little incident not long afterward. There were treatments for this sort of thing, of course, and Dr. Hinzpeter, the family physician, availed himself of them. Complete rest was ordered, bits of ice taken internally, morphine prescribed for the cough and the pulse calmed whenever possible. But her recovery just wouldn't take, and while the child, Anton Klöterjahn, Jr., a jewel of a baby, took possession of and asserted his place in the world with energetic disregard, his young mother seemed to fade, gently and silently, like a dying ember. It was, as they knew, the trachea, a word which in Dr. Hinzpeter's mouth had a surprisingly comforting, calming, almost uplifting effect on everyone's spirits. But even though it wasn't the lungs, the doctor had concluded that the influence of a milder climate and a stay in a clinic would be desirable in order to speed her recovery. The reputation of Einfried and its director had done the rest.

That was how things stood; Mr. Klöterjahn himself would tell the whole story to anyone who revealed an interest in it. He spoke in the loud, coarse, cheerful voice of a man whose digestion is as sound as his finances, with prominently flanging lips and the broad yet clipped accent typical of Northern coastal denizens. He blurted out a good portion of what he said, each syllable resembling a tiny discharge, and laughed at his own words as at a good joke.

He was of average height, broad-shouldered, strong and short-legged, possessing a full red face, aquamarine eyes shadowed by very light blond brows, wide nostrils and moist lips. He sported English whiskers, dressed in the English style and was delighted to discover at Einfried an English family—father, mother and three darling children together with their nurse—who were staying here simply and solely because they didn't know where else to stay. With them he enjoyed an English breakfast every morning. Above all else he loved food and drink, in both fine quality and great quantity. Indeed he proved to be a genuine connoisseur of kitchen and wine cellar, entertaining the clinic society with the most fascinating stories about dinners back home among his circle, replete with descriptions of certain select, hereabouts unknown dishes. Engaged in such descriptions, his eyes would squint congenially and his voice would take on a gummy nasal quality, accompanied by a slight smacking in the back of the throat. He also demonstrated his lack of aversion to other worldly pleasures: one night a patient at Einfried, a writer by trade, witnessed him in the hall jesting most freely with a chambermaid—a minor, comic incident that the writer in question greeted with a ridiculously disgusted expression.

As for Mr. Klöterjahn's wife, it was plain to see that she was devoted to him with all her heart. She followed his every word and gesture with a smile, displaying none of the patronizing indulgence many invalids show toward the healthy, but rather benevolently enjoying and sharing the excitement of others, as good-natured patients do when confronted with confident outbursts of vitality from those who have no complaints from life.

Mr. Klöterjahn did not stay long at Einfried. He had escorted his wife there, but after a week had passed, after he saw that she was well housed and in good hands, his time was up. Equally important duties—his bouncing baby boy, his likewise booming business—called him back home, obliging him to depart. He left his wife behind to enjoy the best of care.

4

Spinell was the name of that writer who had for some weeks now been living at Einfried—Detlev Spinell—and his appearance was rather remarkable.

Picture a dark-complected man in his early thirties, of stately frame, whose hair has begun to go noticeably gray at the temples and whose round, white, somewhat bloated face is without a trace of beard. It wasn't just clean-shaven—one would have been able to see some stubble. On the contrary, it was soft, bleary and boyish, nourishing only the occasional patch of down. And that looked very odd. The expression in his glassy, doe-brown eyes was mild, his nose squat and a bit too fleshy. What's more, this Mr. Spinell had an arched Roman-looking upper lip that was perished like leather, big decaying teeth and feet of unusual dimensions. One of the gentlemen with the spastic legs, a cynical joker, had dubbed him, behind his back, the "Rotten Infant," but that was spiteful and less than accurate.—He went around in fine, stylish clothes, always with a long black jacket and a colorful spotted vest.

He was unsociable, sharing nothing of himself with a single soul. Only occasionally a congenial, affable, even exuberant mood could steal over him: this happened invariably when Mr. Spinell was in an aesthetic frame of mind, when the sight of something beautiful—the harmony of two colors, an exquisitely sculpted vase or the sunset shining over the mountains—inspired him. His amazement on such occasions often turned vocal. "How beautiful," he'd say, tilting his head to one side, raising his shoulders, spreading his fingers and crinkling his nose and lips. "Lord, just look how beautiful!" He was capable of blindly hugging the most dignified personages, ladies as well as gentlemen, when he got carried away in such moments . . .

On the table in his room, permanently on display for anyone caring to visit, was the book he had written. It was a novel of moderate length, complete with an utterly inscrutable cover illustration. It was printed on a kind of paper like that used to filter coffee, in a typeface whose every letter looked like a Gothic cathedral. Miss von Osterloh had looked through it once during an idle fifteen minutes and pronounced it "quite sophisticated," which verdict was her euphemism for "inhumanly boring." It was set in chic salons and luxurious boudoirs crammed with precious objects—Gobelin tapestries, ancient furniture, exquisite china, priceless materials and *objets d'art* of every sort. Loving care had been lavished on the descriptions of these things, and upon reading them you could picture Mr. Spinell crinkling his nose and exclaiming "How beautiful! Lord, just look how beautiful!" . . . Incidentally, it was remarkable that he hadn't published any other books besides this one since he appeared to be an avid writer. He spent the better part of every day writing away in his room and had an extraordinary number of letters posted, one or two almost every day—the absurd and amusing fact being that he rarely received any himself . . .

5

Mr. Spinell was seated across from Mr. Klöterjahn's wife at dinner. During the first meal the couple attended, he arrived a bit late in the large dining room, which was located on the ground floor of the side wing. He murmured a soft greeting to all present and took his seat, whereupon Dr. Leander, without much ceremony, introduced him to the newly arrived guests. He bowed, then began to eat, apparently somewhat self-conscious, for the movements of the large, well-formed white hands that poked out from his extremely tight sleeves while maneuvering knife and fork were rather affected. Later on he relaxed and, by turns, calmly observed Mr. Klöterjahn and his wife. Mr. Klöterjahn addressed him during the course of the meal with several questions and remarks concerning the layout and climate at Einfried, and his wife interspersed two or three words in her charming way, which Mr. Spinell returned politely. His voice was mild and quite pleasant, although he had a rather cumbersome, slurping manner of speech, as if his teeth were getting in the way of his tongue.

After dinner, the party having adjourned to the sitting room and Dr. Leander having specially inquired as to whether the new guests had enjoyed their meal, Mr. Klöterjahn's wife asked about her opposite at table.

"What was the gentleman's name?" she asked . . . "Spinelli? I couldn't make it out."

"Spinell . . . not Spinelli, madam. He's not Italian, not at all. Born in Lemberg, as far as I know . . ."

"A writer you say? Is that right?" Mr. Klöterjahn asked; his hands were thrust in the pockets of his comfortable English trousers, and he turned his ear toward the doctor and opened his mouth, as some people do, when listening intently.

"Well, I don't know—he writes . . ." Dr. Leander answered. "He has, I believe, published a book, some kind of novel, but I don't really know."

This repeated "I don't know" was meant to indicate that Dr. Leander didn't think much of the writer and disclaimed any responsibility for him.

"But that's very interesting!" Mr. Klöterjahn's wife said. She had never met a writer face to face.

"Oh, indeed," Dr. Leander responded amiably. "He supposedly enjoys something of a reputation . . ." After that nothing more was said about the writer.

A bit later, when the new guests had retired and Dr. Leander too was ready to leave the sitting room, Mr. Spinell stopped him and made inquiries of his own.

"What was the name of that couple?" he asked . . . "Of course I couldn't understand a word."

"Klöterjahn," Dr. Leander said, trying to leave.

"*What* is the man's name?"

"Their name is *Klöterjahn*!" said Dr. Leander, brushing past him. — He didn't think very much at all of the writer.

6

Have we gotten to the point when Mr. Klöterjahn returned home? Yes, indeed, he was back on the Baltic coast with his business and his baby, that selfish and vigorous little creature who had cost his mother much suffering and a minor tracheal condition. She, the young wife, however, stayed behind at Einfried, and Mrs. Spatz immediately attached herself as her mentor. That didn't prevent Mrs. Klöterjahn, however, from enjoying good relations with the other patients at the clinic. This was the case, for example, with Mr. Spinell, who, right from the start and to everyone's amazement (since he had shared nothing of himself with a single soul), proved extraordinarily helpful and devoted, and with whom she, for her part, during the few free hours she had in her strict daily regimen, didn't object to chatting.

He would approach her with extreme delicacy, like a supplicant, never speaking except in carefully hushed tones, so that the magistrate's wife, who had an ear condition, could rarely make out anything of what he said. He would tiptoe on his immense feet over to the chair where Mr. Klöterjahn's wife leaned back, fragile and smiling. There he would stand at two steps remove, one leg behind the other, bent over at the waist, talking in his rather cumbersome, slurping manner, speaking softly but urgently, prepared at any moment to withdraw and disappear should any sign of fatigue or annoyance cross her face. But he didn't annoy her at all; she encouraged him to sit with her and the magistrate's wife. She would ask him some question or other, then listen with an inquisitive smile, for he often gave such amusing and strange answers as she had never before heard.

"Why exactly are you at Einfried?" she asked. "What treatments do you need, Mr. Spinell?"

"Treatment? . . .Oh, I'm getting a little electricity. It's not worth mentioning, though. I'll tell you, madam, why I'm really here—because of the decor."

"Ah!" said Mr. Klöterjahn's wife, bracing her chin in her hand and turning toward him with the sort of exaggerated enthusiasm people show toward children who have something to tell.

"Yes, madam. Einfried is pure Empire. It used to be an estate, a royal summer residence, I'm told. This side wing is certainly a later addition, but the main building is authentic. There are times when I simply cannot do without Empire, when I absolutely must have it, if I'm to feel even moderately well. Clearly one feels one way amidst furniture that is sinfully soft and comfortable, altogether differently amidst the austere lines of these tables, chairs and draperies . . . This brightness and severity, this cold, blunt simplicity and reserved exactitude—they impart composure, madam, and dignity. The result is an inner cleansing and convalescence, a moral elevation. Of that I'm absolutely sure . . ."

"Yes, it's strange how that is," she said. "I think I can understand what you mean, if I try."

Here he responded that it wasn't worth the effort, and they shared a laugh. Mrs. Spatz, the magistrate's wife, laughed too and agreed that it was strange, but she didn't say she understood what he meant.

The sitting room was spacious and well furnished. The tall white French doors to the adjacent billiard room were wide open, beyond which the gentlemen with the spastic legs and others were amusing themselves. On the other end of the sitting room, a glass door looked out on the broad terrace and the garden. Off to the side stood a piano. There was also a card table with green felt, at which the diabetic general and a couple of the other gentlemen were playing whist. Ladies sat reading and doing needlework. A cast-iron stove supplied the room's heat, but over in front of the stylish decorative fireplace, its imitation coals pasted over with red-hot strips of paper, were the comfortable places to sit and chat.

"You're an early riser, Mr. Spinell!" said Mr. Klöterjahn's wife. "Two or three times now I've noticed you leaving the house at seven-thirty in the morning."

"An early riser? Alas, not as you mean it, madam. The truth is that I get up early because I'm actually a late sleeper."

"You must explain that, Mr. Spinell!"—Mrs. Spatz, too, wanted it explained.

"Well now . . . true early risers, it seems to me, have no need of getting up so early. Conscience, madam . . . conscience is a terrible thing! I and my kind, we battle it our entire lives wherever we go and have enough trouble deceiving it now and then, occasionally letting it seem to have its way. We're useless creatures, my kind and I. Except for our few good hours, we wear ourselves ragged and drive ourselves sick just thinking how useless we are. We hate all that is useful, we know how base and ugly it is, and we defend this piece of wisdom in the way people only defend those pieces of wisdom they absolutely require. Still, bad conscience gnaws away at every square inch of us. What's more, the whole tenor of our inner existence, our world-view, our work habits . . . have a terribly unwholesome, undermining and exhaustive effect, exacerbating the situation. There are minor palliatives of course—without them we simply couldn't endure. For many of us, a well-regulated, hygienically strict regimen is an absolute necessity. An early start, horrifically early, a cold bath and a walk out in the snow . . . Then we can perhaps feel a tiny bit content with ourselves for an hour or so afterward. But if I gave in to my true nature, I'd lie in bed until afternoon, you can believe me. It's actually hypocrisy for me to get up so early."

"Not at all, how so? I'd call it self-discipline . . . isn't that right Mrs. Spatz?" —Mrs. Spatz, too, called it self-discipline.

"Hypocrisy or self-discipline, madam, take your pick.

I have such terrible predisposition toward the honest truth that I . . ."

"But that's exactly it. Surely you plague yourself too much."

"You're right, madam, I do plague myself a lot."

The good weather continued. The landscape—mountains, house and garden—lay white, hard and clear in the windless air and light frost, the dazzling brilliance and blue-colored shadows, while a delicate blue sky, in which a myriad of twinkling little particles and glowing crystals seemed to dance, arched flawlessly over everything. During this time Mr. Klöterjahn's wife felt tolerably well; she had no fever, hardly coughed at all and felt only the mildest aversion to food. She would sit for hours, as per doctor's orders, on the sunny frost of the terrace. She would sit in the snow, tightly bundled in blankets and furs, optimistically inhaling the pure icy air, doing all she could for her ailing trachea. While there she would sometimes notice Mr. Spinell, also dressed warmly, wearing fur-lined boots that gave his feet surreal dimensions, as he strolled across the garden. He would walk tentatively through the snow, feeling his way forward, his arms set in a cautious and rigidly graceful position, and upon approaching the terrace, he would offer his supplicant's greetings and ascend the bottom steps for a short conversation.

"This morning on my walk I saw a beautiful woman . . . Lord, she was beautiful!" he said, tilting his head to the side and splaying his fingers.

"Really, Mr. Spinell? Do describe her to me!"

"No, I can't. If I did, I would give you a false picture. I only glanced at the lady out of the corner of my eye as we passed; I never saw her really. But this fleeting shadow was enough to excite my imagination, so that I took away an image of her that is very beautiful . . . Lord, how beautiful!"

She laughed. "Is that how you look at beautiful women, Mr. Spinell?"

"Certainly, madam, and better I should do that than

stare them crassly in the face, ogling reality, to ingrain upon myself the impression of a flawed actuality . . ."

"Ogling reality . . . what a strange turn of phrase. Just the sort of thing a writer would say, Mr. Spinell! But it's made an impression on me, I must tell you. There's much in it that I too can halfway understand. There's something independent and free, announcing its disregard for reality, even though reality is what's most respectable. Indeed reality is the very essence of respectability . . . And I sense also that there's something beyond grasping, something more delicate . . ."

"I know of only one face," he said suddenly with an unusual joyous lilt in his voice, raising his clenched hands to his shoulders and displaying his rotten teeth in an exalted smile . . . "I know of only one face whose reality is so glorious that it would be a sin for my imagination to try to improve upon it, a face I could look at, could contemplate, not for minutes or hours, but my whole life through, losing myself entirely in it and forgetting everything on earth . . ."

"Yes, certainly, Mr. Spinell. Only Miss von Osterloh does have awful jug ears."

He gave no reply and bowed deeply. When he stood upright again, his eyes came to rest, with a pained and sorrowful look, on the strange little vein branching out, pale blue and sickly, across the otherwise unblemished perfection of her practically transparent forehead.

7

An oddball, a true oddball! Mr. Klöterjahn's wife would occasionally reflect. And she had plenty of time for reflection. Perhaps it was that the change of climate had begun to lose its effect, or perhaps she had come under some directly pernicious influence. Whatever the reason, her health had worsened and full tracheal convalescence seemed a long way off, for she felt weak and tired, had no appetite and often ran a fever. Dr. Leander had most urgently recommended rest, quiet and caution. So, even when she was not required to lie down, she would sit, disregarded needlework in her lap, in the company of Mrs. Spatz, keeping still and pursuing this or that line of thought.

He certainly made her think, this peculiar Mr. Spinell, but strangely, not so much about him as about herself. For some reason, he brought out in her an unusual curiosity, a heretofore unknown interest in her own person. One day in conversation he had remarked:

"Yes, indeed, women are a true riddle . . . although it's hardly an original thought, you can't help but stand back and wonder. You take a marvelous creature, a sylph, a mere wisp, a fairy-tale figure from a dream. And what does she do? She goes out and gives herself to some young marketplace Hercules or butcher's apprentice. She walks with him arm in arm, maybe even leans her head on his shoulder and looks around with a sly smile, as if to say: go ahead and rack your brains over this latest development! — And we do indeed rack our brains."

This remark preoccupied Mr. Klöterjahn's wife on more than one occasion.

On another day, to Mrs. Spatz's astonishment, the following exchange took place between them.

"Pardon me if it's somewhat forward, but may I ask you a question? What's your name, your real one?"

"But my name is Klöterjahn, Mr. Spinell!"

"Hmm—I know that. Or better yet: I refuse to accept it. I mean of course your own name, your maiden name. In all fairness you'll have to admit, madam, that anyone who thinks you should be called 'Mrs. Klöterjahn' deserves a good flogging."

She laughed so heartily that the little blue vein above her eyebrow stood out with alarming prominence, giving her sweet, delicate face a certain deeply unsettling expression of strain and exertion.

"No, I don't. Really, Mr. Spinell! A flogging? Do you find Klöterjahn so terrible?"

"Yes indeed, madam. I've hated this name with all my heart from the moment I heard it. It's ridiculous, terribly ugly. It's a vile practice to insist on convention so strictly as to call you by your husband's name."

"Well now, and 'Eckhof'? Is Eckhof any better? My father's name is Eckhof."

"There, you see! Eckhof is something else entirely! There was even once a great actor named Eckhof. Eckhof passes muster. — But you spoke only of your father. Is your good mother . . ."

"Yes. My mother died when I was young."

"Aha. Do tell me a little more about yourself, if I may be so bold. Should you find it tiresome, you're under no obligation: you can just rest, and I'll go on with those stories about Paris from the other day. But you could speak very softly. In fact, if you whisper, it would only make everything even more beautiful . . . You were born in Bremen?" And he asked her this question almost silently, with an expression of profound reverence, as if Bremen were an incomparable city full of untellable adventure and secret delights, which cloaked anyone born there in a mysterious aura of majesty.

"Yes, imagine," she said involuntarily. "I'm from Bremen."

"I was there once," he remarked contemplatively.

"My God, you've even been *there*? No, really, Mr. Spinell, I believe you've seen everything from Tunis to Spitzbergen!"

"Yes, I was there once," he repeated. "For a couple of brief hours one evening. I recall an old, narrow street with the moon shining down oblique and strange upon the gabled rooftops. Then I was in a cellar that smelled of wine and mildew. I have a vivid memory of that . . ."

"Really? Where might that have been? You see, it was in just such a gray-gabled house, an old merchant's house with an echoing wooden hallway and a white-washed gallery that I was born."

"So your good father is a businessman?" he asked with some hesitation.

"Yes. But he's an artist too; actually he's first and foremost an musician."

"Aha! Aha! Of what sort?"

"He plays the violin . . . but that doesn't tell the whole story. *The way* he plays it, Mr. Spinell, that's the thing! There are certain notes I cannot so much as hear without feeling the extraordinary sting of tears in my eyes. Nothing else affects me this way. You wouldn't believe it . . ."

"I believe it! Oh, to think I wouldn't believe it! Tell me, madam: your family must be an old one? Surely there have been many generations that have lived, worked and passed on under that gray-gabled roof?"

"Yes. But why do you ask?"

"Because it is not uncommon for an ancient family with a background in mundane, middle-class practicality to transcend its origins in art during its final days . . ."

"Is that so?—Well, as far as my father is concerned, he's certainly more of a musician than most who go by the name and earn their keep from it. I only play a little piano. Nowadays they have expressly forbidden me to play; but back then, at home, I still did. My father and I, we played together . . . Yes, I have fond memories of all those years, especially of the garden, our garden behind the house. It was pathetically weed-infested and overgrown, and its walls were crumbling and covered by moss, but that was precisely its charm. In its center was a fountain with a thick ring of irises around it. Every summer I spent many a long hour there with my friends. We would all sit on little garden stools around the fountain . . ."

"How beautiful!" said Mr. Spinell, hunching his shoulders. "Did you sit and sing?"

"No, mostly we crocheted."

"Nonetheless . . . nonetheless . . ."

"Yes, we crocheted and gossiped, my six friends and I . . ."

"How beautiful! Lord, do you hear, how beautiful!" exclaimed Mr. Spinell, his face quite distorted.

"What do you find so beautiful *about that*, Mr. Spinell?"

"Oh, just this, that there were six beside you, that you weren't included in their number, but instead stood out from amongst them as the obvious queen . . . that you were distinguished from your six friends. A small golden crown, utterly inconspicuous but deeply significant, sat on your head and sparkled . . ."

"But that's nonsense. There was no crown . . ."

"Yes there was. It sparkled there, hidden. I would have seen it, seen it sitting clearly on your head, had I been lurking in the bushes . . ."

"God only knows what you would have seen. But you weren't lurking there; it was my current husband who one day emerged with my father from those bushes. I'm afraid they heard all sorts of gossip . . ."

"So it was there that you first met your husband, madam?"

"Yes, that was where I first met him!" she said in a loud and happy voice, and as she smiled, the little blue vein over her eyebrow stood out, strained and uncanny. "He was visiting my father on business, you see. The very next day he was invited to dinner, and just three days later he asked for my hand."

"Is that so! Did everything happen that quickly?"

"Yes . . . well, from that point on, things went a bit more slowly. My father was firmly set against it, you see, and insisted on more time to think things over. In the first place, he would have rather kept me by his side, and he had other objections as well. But . . ."

"But?"

"But I truly *wanted* to," she said with a smile, and again the little pale-blue vein, together with an expression of strain and sickness, dominated her sweet face.

"Aha, you wanted to."

"Yes, and I showed him that my mind was firmly made up and that my intentions were honorable, as you see . . ."

"As I see. Certainly."

". . . So that my father finally had to give in."

"So then you left him and his violin, left the old house, the overgrown garden, the fountain and your six friends, to follow after Mr. Klöterjahn."

" 'Follow after' . . . what a strange way you have of

expressing yourself, Mr. Spinell! It's almost biblical! — Yes, I left it all, just as nature intends."

"Indeed, as nature intends."

"And then there was also my happiness to think about."

"Of course. You found it, happiness . . ."

"I found it, Mr. Spinell, in that hour when little Anton was first brought to me, that hour when our little Anton cried out at the top of his little lungs, strong and healthy as he is . . ."

"This isn't the first time I've heard you describe little Anton as healthy, madam. He must be the veritable picture of health?"

"He certainly is. And it's comical how much he resembles my husband!"

"Aha! — Yes, and so it came to pass. And now your name is no longer Eckhof but something else, and you have little Anton and a minor tracheal condition."

"Yes. — And *you* are a thoroughly puzzling individual, Mr. Spinell, I assure you . . ."

"Yes, so help me God, you are that!" said Mrs. Spatz who, incidentally, was still present.

This conversation also internally preoccupied Mr. Klöterjahn's wife. As trivial as it had been, it concealed something at its core that fueled her reflections about herself. Was *this* the pernicious influence under which she had come? She grew weaker and often ran a fever, a quiet heat that surrounded her with a feeling of gently being borne upward and left her in a meditative, fragile, complacent, somewhat prickly frame of mind. In those moments when she wasn't confined to her bed, when Mr. Spinell would tiptoe over with the utmost care on his immense feet, stand at two steps' remove and talk in his supplicant's hushed tone, one leg behind the other, bent over at the waist, as if he were lifting her aloft, gently, with timid reverence, to lay her down on a bed of cloudy pillows, where no shrill sounds or earthly contact could reach her . . . she would always remember the way Mr. Klöterjahn always said "Careful, Gabriele, take care, my angel, keep your lips closed!" It was like a hard and well-meaning clap on the shoulder. But she would then shrink back from the memory of him and rest, high aloft in her weakness, on the cloudy pillows that Mr. Spinell had dutifully prepared her.

One day, without occasion, she returned to the brief conversation she had had with him about her family and her childhood.

"So is it really true, Mr. Spinell," she asked, "that you would have seen the crown?"

And even though their little chat had taken place fourteen days earlier, he knew immediately what she meant and passionately reassured her that, back then, as she had sat around the fountain amidst her six friends, he would have seen the little crown sparkling, seen it secretly sparkling on her head.

A few days later, out of politeness, another patient inquired how everything was with little Anton back at home. She shot a nimble glance at Mr. Spinell, who was nearby, and answered, in a slightly bored tone of voice:

"Very well, thanks. What could be wrong with him? —He and my husband are both fine."

8

At the end of February, on a frosty day purer and brighter than any that had come before, Einfried was ruled by high spirits. The heart patients jabbered amongst themselves with flushed cheeks, the diabetic general was humming tunes like a schoolboy and the gentlemen with the spastic legs were beside themselves with glee. What was going on? Nothing less than the undertaking of a communal excursion, consisting of a sleigh ride in the mountains, with several vehicles, under the jingle of bells and cracking of whips. Dr. Leander had ordered it for the amusement of his patients.

Of course the "serious cases" had to remain at home. Poor "serious cases!" The others concurred in this decision and agreed not to let on about the whole business; it felt uncommonly good to be in the position of showing a little pity and consideration. But even among those who could well have taken part in the fun, there were several who opted not to. Miss von Osterloh, for her part, was immediately excused. No one as overburdened with duties as she was could seriously consider going on a sleigh ride. The maintenance of the house absolutely required her presence, and to make a long story short, she stayed behind at Einfried. Moreover, there was universal disappointment among those concerned when Mr. Klöterjahn's wife announced that she, too, wished to stay at home. In vain Dr. Leander argued for the benefits of a refreshing trip; she declared that she wasn't in the mood, that she had a migraine and felt exhausted, and he finally gave in. The cynical joker, however, took the opportunity to remark:

"You watch, now the Rotten Infant won't come either."

And he was proven right, for Mr. Spinell let it be known that he intended to work that afternoon—he was quite fond of using the word "work" for his dubious activity. Not a single soul mourned his absence, and equally little regret was expressed when Mrs. Spatz decided to keep her young friend company since, as she said, sleigh rides always made her seasick.

Immediately after the main meal, which had been moved forward that day to around twelve o'clock, the sleighs pulled up in front of Einfried, and the patients, wrapped up warmly, full of curiosity and excitement, made their way in lively groups through the garden. Mr. Klöterjahn's wife stood with Mrs. Spatz behind the glass door leading to the terrace, Mr. Spinell at the window of his room, to watch their departure. They saw how the guests laughed and argued briefly with one another over the best seats, saw how Miss von Osterloh ran with a fur boa around her neck from one sleigh to the next, shoving baskets of provisions under the seats, saw how Dr. Leander, a fur hat pulled over his forehead, his glasses reflecting the sunlight, surveyed the situation one last time, then too took his seat and gave the signal to depart . . . The horses started, a couple of ladies shrieked and toppled backwards, the bells jingled, the short-handled whips cracked and their long lashes dragged in the snow behind the runners. Miss von Osterloh stood at the garden gate waving her handkerchief until the party glided out of sight around a bend in the road and their gleeful shouts died away. Then she went back through the garden to catch up with her duties. The two ladies left the glass door, and almost simultaneously Mr. Spinell stepped back from his point of vantage.

Silence prevailed at Einfried. The expedition was not expected to be back before nightfall. The "serious cases" lay in their rooms, suffering. Mr. Klöterjahn's wife and her mentor went on a short walk, after which both returned to their quarters. Mr. Spinell stayed in his room as well, occupying himself in his own way. At around four o'clock the ladies were each brought a half-liter of milk, while Mr. Spinell took his usual weak tea. A short time later, Mr. Klöterjahn's wife tapped on the wall separating her room from Mrs. Spatz's and said:

"Should we go down to the sitting room, Mrs. Spatz? I just don't know what to do with myself any more up here."

"Just a second, dear!" answered the magistrate's wife. "I'll just put on my boots, if you don't mind. I've been lying on my bed, you see."

As was only to be expected, the sitting room was empty. The ladies sat down by the fireplace. Mrs. Spatz stitched flowers on a piece of evenweave, and Mr. Klöterjahn's wife, too, completed a couple of stitches, whereupon she let her needlework drop into her lap and sat staring out over the armrest of her chair, daydreaming. Finally she made a remark hardly worth her opening her mouth for, and to her dismay, Mrs. Spatz asked "What?" and she had to repeat the entire sentence. Mrs. Spatz asked again, "What?" At that moment, however, steps could be heard in the outside foyer. The door opened, and Mr. Spinell came into the room.

"Am I disturbing?" he asked softly, still on the threshold, looking exclusively at Mr. Klöterjahn's wife and bowing at the waist in a kind of gentle, hovering way . . . The young woman answered:

"Oh, why not at all! In the first place this room is a designated open port, Mr. Spinell, and secondly, there's nothing to disturb. I have the distinct impression I'm boring Mrs. Spatz . . ."

He had nothing to say to this, so he smiled instead, baring his decayed teeth, and under the eyes of the ladies walked over to the glass door, his steps extremely self-conscious. There he stopped and stared outside with his back rather impolitely toward them. Then he turned halfway around, continuing to stare out into the garden, and said:

"The sun has disappeared. The sky has clouded over little by little. It's already beginning to get dark."

"Yes, there are shadows everywhere," answered Mr. Klöterjahn's wife. "It seems our sleigh riders will get their snow after all. Yesterday at this time it was still broad daylight, but today it's already getting dark."

"Oh," he said, "after the extreme brightness of these past weeks, the darkness is good for the eyes. I'm almost grateful to this sun, which lights up the beautiful and vulgar with the same obtrusive clarity, for finally hiding its face a bit."

"You're not fond of the sun, Mr. Spinell?"

"Well, I'm not a painter . . . People turn inward in the absence of sun. — There's a thick pale gray line of clouds. Perhaps that means a thaw tomorrow. In any case, I wouldn't recommend straining your eyes on your needlepoint all the way over there, madam."

"Oh, don't worry. I'm in no danger of that. But what is there to do?"

He had sat down on the rotating stool in front of the piano, one arm resting on the instrument's lid.

"Music . . ." he said. "If only we had some music now! Sometimes the English children sing little Negro songs, but that's about it."

"Yesterday afternoon Miss von Osterloh thrashed her way through 'The Monastery Bells,' " Mr. Klöterjahn's wife remarked.

"But you play, madam," he said in a pleading tone, standing up . . . "You used to play duets every day with your father."

"Yes, Mr. Spinell, but that was then. In the days of the fountain, you know . . ."

"Do it now!" he requested. "Play a few bars just this once! If you only knew how I long . . ."

"Both our family doctor and Dr. Leander have expressly forbidden it, Mr. Spinell."

"They're not here, either of them! We're free . . . You're free, madam. A few meager chords . . ."

"No, Mr. Spinell, you won't get anywhere with that. Who knows what kind of miracles you expect from me! I've forgotten everything, believe me. There's hardly a thing I still know by heart."

"Oh, then just play this 'hardly a thing'! And besides, there's some sheet music here somewhere. Here it is, on top of the piano. No, this is nothing. But here's some Chopin . . ."

"Chopin?"

"Yes, the nocturnes. The only thing left is for me to light the candles . . ."

"Don't get the idea I'm going to play, Mr. Spinell! I'm not allowed to. What if it damages my health?" —

He fell silent. He stood with his immense feet, his long black jacket and his gray-haired, weak-jawed, beardless face in the light of the two candles on the piano, letting his hands dangle at his sides.

"I won't ask you again," he said at last, softly. "If you're afraid of damaging your health, madam, then let the beauty that might have sounded under your fingers remain dead and mute. You weren't always so reasonable, at least not conversely when it came to renouncing beauty. You didn't worry about your health and showed much more daring and determination about following your will, when you forsook your childhood fountain and laid aside the little golden crown. . . . Hear me out," he said after a short pause, lowering his voice even further. "If you sit down here and play as you did before, when your father stood beside you drawing those notes from his violin which always made you cry, then maybe it will appear once more, secretly sparkling on your head, the little, golden crown . . ."

"Really?" she asked with a smile . . . By chance, her voice failed her when she said this word, so that the first half came out hoarse and the second was utterly toneless. She cleared her throat and then said:

"Are those truly Chopin's nocturnes you have there?"

"They truly are. They're open and everything is ready."

"Well, then, by God, I will play one of them," she said. "But only one, you hear? You'll have heard enough of me then forever, anyway."

With that, she got up, laid her needlepoint down at her side and walked over to the piano. She took a seat on the stool, which had a couple of bound volumes of music on top, adjusted the candelabras and flipped through the sheet music. Mr. Spinell had pulled up a chair and sat there next to her like a music teacher.

She played the Nocturne in E-flat Major, op. 9, no. 2. If it was true that she had forgotten some of what she once knew, her performing skills back then must have been truly first-class. It was only a mediocre piano, but after the first few chords she knew how to handle it with control and taste. She displayed a tensely attuned sensitivity to timbre and a joyful command of rhythm that bordered on the fantastic. Her touch was both sure and delicate. Under her hands, the melody yielded every last bit of sweetness, and her embellishments nestled around its main lines with restrained grace.

She wore the same dress as on the day of her arrival: the dark, heavy bodice with the thick-cut velvet arabesques that made her head and hands look so unearthly and delicate. Her facial expression remained unchanged while she played, but her lips seemed to become more clearly defined, and the shadows in the corners of her eyes seemed to deepen. After she had finished, she put her hands in her lap and continued to gaze at the music. Mr. Spinell sat silent and still.

She played another nocturne, then a second and a

third. Then she stood up, but only in order to look for more music on the top of the piano.

Mr. Spinell had the idea of investigating the volumes in black cardboard on the piano stool. Suddenly he made an incomprehensible sound, and his immense white hands fumbled excitedly with one of those discarded books.

"Impossible! . . .It can't be," he said . . . "Do my eyes deceive me? No! . . .Do you know what this is? . . .What was lying here? . . .What I'm holding here?"

"What is it?" she asked.

Without a word he showed her the title page. Quite pale, he lowered the book and stared at her with trembling lips.

"Really? How did that get there? Let me see it," she said simply. She propped it up on the stand, sat down and after a moment's silence began with the first page.

He was sitting at her side, leaning forward, his hands folded between his knees, his head down. She played the beginning at an extravagantly, torturously slow tempo with unsettlingly long pauses between the individual phrases. The *Sehnsuchtsmotiv*, a lonely and wayward voice in the night, softly made its fearful question heard. Silence and waiting. And look: the answer. That same timid and lonely sound, only a bit brighter and more tender. Renewed silence. Then, in that wonderful hushed sforzando, came the *Liebesmotiv* that is so like passion stirring and arising in sacred revolt. It ascended, climbed ecstatically upward toward sweet entanglement, than sank back, disengaging itself, as the cellos emerged with their deep song of heavy, anguished rapture to carry the melody . . .

With not inconsiderable success, the pianist strove to suggest on this poor instrument the effects of an orchestra. The violin runs of the great crescendo sounded with shining precision. Playing with keen reverence, she lingered piously over every theme and emphasized each individual passage with humble insistence, like a priest raising the Holy Communion over his head. What was happening? Two forces, two enraptured beings reached out in suffering and bliss toward one other and embraced in the ecstatic, frenzied pursuit of the eternal and the absolute . . . The prelude blazed, then died down. She concluded at the parting of the curtains and continued to gaze silently at the music.

Meanwhile, in Mrs. Spatz, boredom had reached that point where it distorts the human countenance, causing the eyes to bulge and giving the face a hideous, corpselike look. This sort of music upset the nerves in her stomach, filling the dyspeptic magistrate's wife with such anxiety that she feared an attack of cramps.

"I'm afraid I must go to my room," she said weakly. "Farewell, I'll be back . . ."

With that she left. The light had grown much dimmer. Outside you could see the snow falling thick and silent on the terrace. The two candles gave off a close, flickering light.

"The second act," he whispered, and she turned the pages and began the second act.

The horns died away in the distance. Or was it the rustling leaves? The gentle murmuring of the fountain? Already night's silence had swathed hedge and house, and pleading admonitions could no longer check the sway of passion. The sacred mystery was consummated. The torch was extinguished, the *Todesmotiv* descended with an unearthly, suddenly muted timbre, and restless with impatience, longing waved her white veil at the beloved, who was approaching, arms outspread, through the darkness.

O torrential and unquenchable exultation at union in the eternal realm beyond things! Liberated from agonizing delusion, delivered from the bonds of space and time, thou and I, thine and mine melted together in sublime bliss. Though the day's thievish illusions might still divide them, those nocturnal seers could no longer be blinded by its pompous lies, for the love philter had initiated their vision. For him who had lovingly gazed into death's night and its secret, there remained in the madness of day but one desire, the longing for that sacred night, unending and true, that unifying . . .

O fall upon them, night of love, grant them the oblivion they crave, wrap them wholly in your bliss and free them from the world of deception and division. Behold the last torch extinguished! Reason and supposition founder in the sacred twilight that spreads out, world redeeming, over the agonies of madness. Then, when the illusions fade, when mine eye bursts with delight, and that from which the day's lies have excluded me, that which it has falsely and to my eternal agony pitted against longing—then I, o miracle of fulfillment! then *I myself* am the world. And there followed, during Brangäne's dark song of warning, that ascending violin phrase that surpasses all reason.

"I don't understand it all, Mr. Spinell; a lot of it I can only sense. This part 'then—I myself am the world,' what does that mean?"

He explained it to her, softly and in a few words.

"Yes, so it is. — How is it that you, who understand it so well, can be unable to play it?"

Strangely enough, he was at an absolute loss in the face of this harmless question. He blushed, wrung his hands and sank into his chair.

"The two rarely coincide," he said finally, looking pained. "No, I cannot play. — But you please continue."

And they continued with the drunken songs of the mystery ritual. Has love ever died? Tristan's love? The love of thine and mine Isolde? O, the strokes of death cannot touch love eternal! What is there to perish in death except that which plagues us, that which deceptively divides beings that are one? Love joined them with a sweet *and*. If death tore them asunder, could it be other than that, in destroying the individual life of the one, death would be given to the other as well? And a duet, full of mystery, united them in the ineffable hope of the *Liebestod*, of eternal undivided immersion in night's miracle realm. Sweet night! Eternal night of love! All-encompassing land of bliss! Once one has had an inkling glimpse of you, how could he reawaken without horror into the barren day? O fair death, banish their fears! Free these lovers forever from the desperation of waking! O, unbound storm of rhythms! O upward-struggling chromatic ecstasy of metaphysical realization! How to seize it, how to leave it, this great bliss, far from the divisive agonies of the light? Gentle longing, fearless and real; dying embers, exalted and painless; twilight beyond sublime, immeasurable! Thou Isolde, Tristan I, no longer Tristan, no longer Isolde—

Suddenly, something startled them. The pianist broke off the music and put her hand to her eyes to peer through the darkness, and Mr. Spinell swung around quickly in his chair. The door behind them leading to the hall had opened, and a shadowy figure entered, leaning on the arm of a second. It was one of Einfried's guests, who had likewise been unprepared to accompany the others on the sleigh ride and who was now passing the hour on one of her sad unthinking walks through the clinic, that sick woman who had lost her wits after bringing nineteen children into the world—Mrs. Höhlenrauch, the pastor's wife—on the arm of her nurse. Without looking up she proceeded with groping, erratic steps through the rear of the room, then disappeared through the opposite door—silent and blank, straying and unconscious. — There was silence everywhere.

"That was Mrs. Höhlenrauch, the pastor's wife," he said.

"Yes, poor Mrs. Höhlenrauch." Then she turned some pages and played the end of the entire composition, the *Liebestod*, Isolde's final song.

How pallid and clear her lips were! How deep the shadows had grown in the corners of her eyes! Above the brow, in the transparent skin of her forehead, that little pale-blue vein emerged, strained and unsettling, with ever increasing prominence. Under her busy hands the incomparable crescendo arose, interrupted by that almost ruthless, sudden pianissimo, which is like a yanking of ground from under the feet, a drowning in sublime lust. The effusion of a massive release and resolution erupted and was repeated insatiably, a deafening thunder of satisfaction beyond dimension, retreating, then regrouping like a wave, seeming about to breathe its last before interweaving the *Sehnsuchtsmotiv* one last time into the orchestration. Then it exhaled, died, faded, drifted away. Profound silence.

Both of them listened, pricked their ears and listened.

"Those are bells," she said.

"It's the sleighs," he said. "I'm going."

He stood up and walked across the room. At the rear door he stopped and turned around, shifting his weight restlessly for a moment from one foot to the other. And then, lo and behold, fifteen or twenty paces from her, he sank to his knees, sank silently to his knees. His long black coat spread out on the floor around him. He held his hands folded over his mouth, and his shoulders twitched.

She sat there, her hands in her lap, leaning forward away from the piano, gazing at him. A vague smile of distress lay upon her face, and her eyes peered pensively, so intently into the gloom that they succumbed to their tendency to wander.

In the distance the jingling of sleigh bells, the crack of whips and the confusion of human voices drew nearer.

9

The sleigh ride, which long remained a topic of conversation for all, had taken place on February the 26th. On the 27th, a day of thaw, when everything softened and began to drip, splash and flow, Mr. Klöterjahn's wife felt splendid. On the 28th she coughed up a little blood . . . oh, nothing serious, but it was blood. At the same time she felt weaker than ever before and had to remain in bed.

Dr. Leander gave her an examination, his face remaining stone cold throughout the entire procedure. Then he ordered exactly what was prescribed by science: little bits of ice, morphine and complete rest. Moreover, on the following day, citing his excessive workload, he gave up responsibility for her case and transferred it to Dr. Müller, who in his gentle way dutifully and contractually took over her care. He was a quiet, pale, insignificant, melancholy man whose unassuming and thankless ministrations were directed at the quite nearly recovered and the terminally ill.

The opinion he expressed above all was that the Klöterjahn couple had been separated for too long. It was highly advisable that, if his booming business would allow, Mr. Klöterjahn should pay another visit to Einfried. He could be written, perhaps a short telegram could be sent . . . And it would certainly bolster the young mother's spirits and strength, if he brought little Anton along—not to mention that it would be extraordinarily interesting for the doctors to make healthy little Anton's acquaintance.

And behold, Mr. Klöterjahn appeared. He had received Dr. Müller's short telegram and had come down from the Baltic coast. He got out of his carriage and ordered some coffee and buttered rolls, looking quite annoyed.

"Sir," he said. "What's going on? Why have I been summoned to my wife's side?"

"Because I felt it would be advisable," Dr. Müller answered, "for you to be near your good wife at present."

"Advisable . . . Advisable . . . But is it necessary? I'm thinking of the expense, sir. Times are tough, and trains cost a lot. Couldn't this day's traveling have been avoided? I wouldn't say a word if it were the lungs; but since, thank God, it's only the trachea . . ."

"Mr. Klöterjahn," said Dr. Müller gently, "first of all the trachea is a very important organ . . ." He said "first of all" by mistake, despite the fact that no "second of all" was to follow.

Arriving along with Mr. Klöterjahn at Einfried, despite expense, was a curvaceous thing dressed entirely in red, tartan and gold, and it was she who carried in her arms Anton Klöterjahn, Jr., healthy little Anton. Yes, he was here, and there was no denying that he was indeed the absolute picture of health. Rosy and white, dressed in clean fresh clothes, fat and fragrant, he weighed heavily on the bare red arm of his gold-braided nanny, devouring great quantities of milk and diced meat, howling and indulging his every instinct.

From the window in his room the writer Spinell had witnessed the arrival of the baby Klöterjahn. With a strange, veiled, but nonetheless sharp look, he had stared at the infant as the latter was brought from the carriage to the clinic and had maintained his position for a long time afterward with no change of expression.

From then on he avoided crossing paths with Anton Klöterjahn, Jr. as best he could.

10

Mr. Spinell sat in his room and "worked."

It was a room like all the others at Einfried: old-fashioned, simple and elegant. Its massive chest of drawers was mounted with metal lions' heads; its high wall mirror consisted not of a single smooth surface, but numerous little square pieces held together by lead; and its blue-painted stone floor, into which the stiff legs of the furnishings extended in the form of transparent shadows, had been left uncarpeted. A large desk stood next to the window, in front of which the novelist had drawn a yellow curtain, probably for the sake of turning inward.

In the yellowish twilight he was bent over the surface of his secretary writing—working on one of those many letters he had posted every week, letters to which, humorously enough, he usually received no answer. A large, thick sheet of paper was stretched out in front of him, in whose upper left-hand corner, under an intricate sketch of a landscape, the name Detlev Spinell was written in the latest newfangled lettering. He was in the process of covering it with his small, carefully formed, exceedingly legible hand.

"Sir," stood written there. "I am addressing the following lines to you because I cannot help it, because what I have to say fills me, fills me to the brim with anguished trembling, because the words come flooding with such force that I would choke on them, if I weren't allowed to unburden myself in this letter . . ."

To tell the truth, the bit about "flooding" simply wasn't the case, and God only knows what had inspired Mr. Spinell to write it. Words certainly didn't seem to come flooding into his head. For a man whose livelihood was writing, he was pathetically slow off the mark—no one could have watched him without becoming convinced that an author is a person to whom writing comes more difficult than to everyone else.

For fifteen minutes at a time he would sit pinching one of the strange downy hairs on his cheek between his fingertips, twirling it round as he stared off into empty space, making not a line's progress. Then he would write out a couple of decorous words before once again faltering. On the other hand, it must be admitted that what finally emerged did seem polished and dynamic, though in terms of content it was bizarre, dubious, often even incomprehensible.

"It has become," the letter went on, "an inescapable need of mine to make you see what I see—this indelible vision that I've had before my eyes for weeks now—to make you view it through my eyes, illuminated by the same words that illuminate it for my inner eye. I'm accustomed to following this impulse, which compels me, in unforgettably and scorchingly well-placed words, to transform personal experiences into those of the world. Thus hear me out.

"I only want to put into words what was and what is. I will simply tell a story—a very short, unspeakably scandalous story—without commentary, without making accusations or passing judgement, just expressing things in my own way. It is Gabriele Eckhof's story, sir, the woman whom you call your own. Take heed! It was your experience, but it is my words that will first allow you truly to appreciate its, *her* significance.

"Do you remember the garden, sir, the old, overgrown garden behind the gray patrician house? Green moss thrived in the fissures of the weather-beaten walls around this dreamy wilderness. Do you remember the fountain in the center? Purple lilies drooped over that crumbling disk, and its white stream babbled mysteriously as it splashed down upon the cracked stonework. A summer's day was almost at an end.

"Seven innocent girls sat in a circle around that fountain; and yet only in the hair of the seventh, the leader, the one, did the setting sun seem to weave a shimmering emblem of supremacy. Her eyes were like fearful dreams, and yet there was a smile on her flawless lips . . .

"They were singing. Their slim faces were lifted toward the fountain's stream, toward that point in its weary yet noble cycle where it begins its descent, and their soft clear voices hovered around its nimble dance. Perhaps their tender hands were folded upon their knees as they sang . . .

"Can you recall the scene, sir? Did you see it? You did not. Your eyes were not made for it, just as your ears weren't made to take in the chaste sweetness of that melody. Had you seen it, you wouldn't have dared breathe, you would have stopped your heart from beating. You would have had to flee, return to life, to your life, and guard for the rest of your earthly days what you witnessed as a sacrosanct, inviolable relic in your soul. But what did you do?

"This scene was an ending, sir. Did you have to come along and destroy it, in order to give the story a continuation of vulgarity and unsightly suffering? It was a moving and peaceful apotheosis, bathed in the transfiguring twilight of decline, dissolution and extinction. An ancient family, already too weary and too noble for action and life, stands at the end of its days, and its last utterances are musical sounds, a couple of notes from a violin, full of that wise melancholy which signals readiness for death . . . Did you see those eyes, tear-stained from those notes? It may be that the souls of the six playmates belonged to life; that of their sisterly queen, however, belonged to beauty and to death.

"You saw it, this deathly beauty, looked upon it that you might lust for it. No reverence, no awe moved your heart in the presence of such holiness. It wasn't enough to look. You needed to possess, consume, defile . . . And how well you chose! You are a gourmand, sir, a plebeian gourmand, a peasant with taste.

"Please rest assured that I intend you no offense whatsoever. What I'm saying is not an insult, but the formula, the basic psychological formula of your simple, aesthetically quite uninteresting personality. I only write of it because I feel compelled to enlighten you a bit as to your pursuits and pastimes, because it is my never-ceasing vocation on earth to call things by their true names, to let them speak, to illuminate what remains unconscious. The world is full of what I call 'the unconscious type': I simply can't bear the thought of all these unconscious types! I can't bear the thought of all this dull, ignorant, unconsidered living and doing, this world of irritating naiveté all around me! I am driven by a torturously irresistible urge to comment on all human life around me—as far as it lies within my power—to articulate it and make it conscious, be the end result positive or negative, consolation and relief, or pain.

"You, as I said before, sir, are a plebeian gourmand, a peasant with taste. Although you are actually quite crude of constitution, typical of primitive development, your wealth and settled life have led to a sudden, historically reversed, barbaric corruption of the nervous system, resulting in a certain lecherous refinement of the appetites. It's entirely likely that the muscles in your throat began to smack, as at the sight of some delicious soup or rare dish, when you decided to make Gabriele Eckhof your wife . . .

"And in the end you succeed in misdirecting her half-dormant will, you lead her out of the overgrown garden into life and its ugliness, you give her your vulgar name and transform her into spouse, housewife and mother. You demean the weary, reserved beauty of death, which can only flourish in sublime obsolescence, making it serve common everyday life and that ridiculously clumsy and contemptible idol called 'nature,' without an inkling of the profound vileness of what you've undertaken stirring in your peasant conscience.

"And again, what happens? The girl with the eyes that are like fearful dreams bears you a child; she gives to this little life, a mere continuation of the crude existence of the man who begot it, all the blood and vitality she possesses, then dies! She's dying, sir! And if, despite everything, she passes away in something other than baseness, if in her final hour she has lifted herself from the depths of her degradation and dies proudly and joyously, beneath a final deathly kiss of beauty, it has been *my* doing. Yours, meanwhile, has been to pass the time with chambermaids in deserted corridors.

"Your child, however, Gabriele Eckhof's son, grows, flourishes and lives on in triumph. Probably he will lead his father's life and become a solid citizen, doing business, paying taxes, eating well. Perhaps he will become a general or a politician, an ignorant and reliable pillar of the nation, in any case a philistine, normally functioning creature, ruthless and confident, strong and stupid.

"I must confess, sir, that I hate you, you and your child, as I hate life itself, this vulgar, ridiculous yet triumphant life you represent, the eternal antithesis and enemy of beauty. It would be wrong to say that I despise you. I can't. I'm too honest. Of the two of us, you are the stronger. I have only one thing to use against you in our battle, the sublime weapon of the weak, their tool for revenge: imagination and words. Today I have used this weapon. For this letter—here too I must be honest, sir—is nothing but an act of revenge. And if one single word in it is sharp, shining and beautiful enough to affect you, to make you feel an alien force, to shake the foundations of your robust equanimity for even one moment, I shall rejoice.

Detlev Spinell."

And Mr. Spinell enclosed this missive in an envelope and affixed postage, then furnished it with an ornately written address and had it posted.

11

Mr. Klöterjahn rapped on the door to Mr. Spinell's room. In his hand he was holding a large sheet of paper covered with neat handwriting, and he had the look of a man determined to proceed forcefully. The postman had done his duty, the letter had gone on its way, making the strange journey from Einfried to Einfried, and had arrived in the hands of its addressee. It was four o'clock in the afternoon.

When Mr. Klöterjahn entered the room, Mr. Spinell was seated on his sofa reading his own novel, the book with the inscrutable drawing on the cover. He stood up with a surprised, inquisitive look as he recognized his visitor, blushing noticeably.

"Good afternoon," said Mr. Klöterjahn. "Excuse me for disturbing you when you're busy. But may I ask whether you wrote this?" He held up the large sheet of paper in his left hand and slapped it with the back of his right so that it rustled loudly. Then he immediately stuck his right hand in the pocket of his comfortably wide-cut trousers, tilted his head to one side and opened his mouth to listen, as some people do.

Strangely, Mr. Spinell smiled; it was an obliging smile, a little puzzled, half-apologetic. Then he put his hand to his forehead as if to think things over and said:

"Ah, correct . . . yes . . . I took the liberty . . ."

The situation was this: on that particular day he had given in to his true nature and slept until around noon. Consequently he was suffering from a bad conscience and a light head, feeling jumpy, little capable of self-defense. Added to this was the hint of spring in the air that filled him with exhaustion and despair. All of which must be mentioned as an explanation for why he acted so haplessly during the whole scene to follow.

"So! Aha! That's nice!" said Mr. Klöterjahn at the settlement of this formality, pressing his chin into his chest, raising his eyebrows, stretching out his arms and intimating with a number of similar gestures that he was going to come mercilessly to the point. He was so pleased with himself that he took things a little too far; what followed afterward didn't entirely measure up to the elaborate threat carried by his pantomime preparation. Nonetheless, Mr. Spinell had grown extremely pale.

"That's nice!" repeated Mr. Klöterjahn. "Then allow me to answer your letter face to face, dear fellow, since I find it idiotic to write long letters to someone you can talk to at any time . . ."

"Well now . . . idiotic . . ." Mr. Spinell said, smiling apologetically, almost meekly . . .

"Idiotic!" repeated Mr. Klöterjahn, shaking his head vigorously to show how unassailably sure he was of his position. "And I wouldn't dignify this scrap of paper with a single word, to be frank, I wouldn't use it as bread wrap, if it hadn't cleared up certain things I hadn't previously understood, certain changes . . . In any case, these don't concern you. They are beside the point. I'm a busy man and have better things to worry about than your ineffable visions . . ."

" 'Indelible visions' is what I wrote," said Mr. Spinell, straightening up. It was the only moment during this whole scene when he displayed a modicum of dignity.

"Indelible . . . ineffable . . . !" countered Mr. Klöterjahn, staring at the manuscript. "Your handwriting is pathetic, dear fellow. I wouldn't have you in my office. At first glance it seems clear enough, but when you look at it in the light, you see it's full of gaps and wavering. But that's your problem, one which doesn't concern me. I have come to tell that you are first of all a fool—hopefully you're aware of this already. And secondly, you are a genuine coward—I doubt I need to give you any great proof of that either. My wife once wrote me that when you meet women you never stare them straight in the eye but just sneak a look in order to take away a mere glimpse of beauty—out of fear for what the truth might hold. Unfortunately she stopped mentioning you in her later letters or I would know more stories about you. But that sums you up pretty well. Every third word of yours is 'beauty,' but at bottom you're just a fearful old biddy, cowering and jealous—hence, no doubt, your insolent comment about 'deserted corridors,' which was obviously supposed to cut me to the quick. In reality, it only made me laugh. Made me laugh it did! Does that now clear things up for you? Have I 'enlightened you a bit' about your . . . your 'pursuits and pastimes,' you miserable fool? Although it's not my 'incessant vocation.' Hah! Hah!" . . .

" 'Never-ceasing' was what I wrote," said Mr. Spinell, but he gave up immediately. He stood there, helplessly dressed down like a great big miserable gray-haired schoolboy.

"Never-ceasing . . . incessant . . . You're a despicable coward, let me say that to your face. Every day you see me at the dinner table. You say 'hello' and smile, you pass things to me and smile, you wish me *bon appetit* and smile. And then one day you attack me with this piece of paper full of idiotic insults. Hah, sure, you have courage on paper. And as if this ridiculous letter were the only thing! You've conspired against me, conspired against me behind my back, I see that very clearly indeed . . . although you shouldn't imagine it's done you any good! If you were even vaguely hoping to give my wife ideas, you're on the wrong track, my dear sir. She's too reasonable a person for that! And if you even think that she treated me differently than usual, either me or our child, when we arrived, that's just the crowning touch to your contemptible audacity. She may not have kissed the little one, but that was for safety's sake. Recently the theory has been advanced that it's not the trachea but the lungs, and you can never tell in that case . . . although it's yet to be proven, that it is the lungs, and you, with your 'she's dying, dear sir,' you're an ass!"

Here Mr. Klöterjahn tried to bring his breathing under control. He had worked himself into a rage, repeatedly stabbing the air with his right index finger and punching most violently at the manuscript in his left hand. A terrible redness of face had spread between his blond, English-style whiskers, and swollen veins ran across his protruding forehead like angry lightning bolts.

"You hate me," he went on, "and would despise me if I weren't the stronger of us . . . Yes, I am that, damn it all. I've got heart, heart in the right place, while yours is no doubt in your pants, and I would wipe the floor with you and your 'imagination and words,' you treacherous imbecile, if it weren't forbidden by law. But that doesn't mean, dear fellow, that I am simply going to swallow your insults lying down, and when I show my lawyer back home that part about my 'vulgar name,' we'll see if you know what's hit you. I have a good name, sir, and I've earned it. I leave you to ask yourself whether anyone would give you a plugged nickel for yours, you rotten little interloper! Legal means are the only recourse against you! You're a menace to society! You cloud people's minds! . . .Though don't imagine that you've succeeded this time, you insidious upstart! I'm not going to let myself be pushed aside by someone like you. I've got heart . . ."

Mr. Klöterjahn had now really lost control of his temper. He was shouting, saying repeatedly that he had heart . . .

" 'They were singing.' Period. They weren't singing at all! They were knitting! What's more, they were talking, as far I could tell, about a recipe for potato pancakes, and if I show my father-in-law what you write about 'decline' and 'dissolution,' he'll lodge his own complaint against you, you can bank on that! . . . 'Did you see the scene, did you see it?' Of course I saw it, but I fail to understand why I should have held my breath and run away. I don't just steal a glance when I meet women. I look them in the face, and if I like them and they want me, I take them for my own. I've got h . . ."

Someone knocked—knocked nine or ten times in very rapid succession on the front door, raising an urgent, frightened little commotion that cut off Mr. Klöterjahn's tirade. A voice, completely beside itself, stumbling with panic, said in great haste:

"Mr. Klöterjahn, Mr. Klöterjahn, oh, is Mr. Klöterjahn there?"

"Don't come in," said Mr. Klöterjahn brusquely . . . "What is it? I'm busy here."

"Mr. Klöterjahn," said the trembling, faltering voice. "You must come . . . the doctors are there too . . . oh it's so terribly sad . . ."

He reached the door in a single step and tore it open. Mrs. Spatz, the magistrate's wife, was standing outside. She held her handkerchief to her mouth, and two sets of large, elongated tears rolled down into it.

"Mr. Klöterjahn," she blurted out, ". . . it's so terribly sad . . . She coughed up so much blood, it was terrible . . . she lay there very still in her bed and hummed some music, and then it came, dear God, such an incredible amount . . ."

"Is she dead?" shouted Mr. Klöterjahn . . . He grabbed the magistrate's wife by the arm and shook her back and forth upon the threshold. "No, it can't be true, is she? Not yet, she can still see me . . . ? Cough up a little blood again, did she? From the lungs, was it? All right, I see now, it probably was the lungs . . . Gabriele!"

He cried out with tears in his eyes, and you could see a warm, good, humane, honest emotion spread over him. "Yes, I'm coming." he said, and with long strides he dragged the magistrate's wife out of the room and down the hall. From a remote part of the corridor you could still hear his voice, quickly growing more and more distant: "It can't be true. Is she? . . . From the lungs, was it?"

12

Mr. Spinell remained standing on the exact spot where he had stood throughout Mr. Klöterjahn's so abruptly terminated visit, staring at the open door. Finally he took a couple of steps forward and listened into the distance. But all was quiet, so he shut the door and returned to his room.

For a while, he observed his reflection in the mirror. After that he went to his desk, took out a small flask and a glass from a drawer and drank a brandy, something for which no one could have blamed him. Then he stretched out on the sofa and shut his eyes.

The upper window latch was open. Outside in Einfried's garden, birds chirped, and the whole of spring was expressed subtly and profoundly in this delicate, bold little noise. Once, Mr. Spinell said out loud: "incessant calling . . ." Then he shook his head side to side and drew air between his teeth as though suffering from an exposed nerve.

He found it impossible to calm down and collect himself. People simply weren't made to endure such crudities as this just now! — After a bit of soul searching, which would lead too far from the subject to analyze, Mr. Spinell decided to get up and move about some, to take a short walk outdoors. He picked up his hat and left the room.

As he stepped out of the house into the mild fragrant air, he turned his head and slowly scanned up the side of the building until he reached one of the windows, a window with drawn curtains. He stared at it for quite some time, his eyes serious, fixed and dark. Then he put his hands behind his back and walked along the gravel path. He walked, lost in thought.

The flowerbeds were still covered with matting, and the trees and bushes were still bare, but the snow was gone, and the paths revealed only the occasional damp patch. The spacious garden with its grottos, arbors and little pavilions was bathed in the marvelously colored afternoon sunlight, and the dark tree branches stood out sharply and delicately defined against the bright sky.

It was around the hour when the sun takes on form, when that shapeless mass of light becomes a visible sinking disc whose richer and milder glow admits the human gaze. Mr. Spinell did not see the sun; where the path led him, it remained hidden and obscure. He walked, head down, humming a bit of music, a short run of notes, a timidly and plaintively ascending phrase, the *Sehnsuchtsmotiv* . . . Then suddenly, with a start—a short, convulsive gasp—he halted as if chained to the spot. From under their sharply knitted brows, an expression of horrified aversion on his face, his staring eyes peered straight ahead . . .

The path had wound round; it was now heading into the setting sun. Streaked by two narrow, illuminated bands of clouds with gilded edges, it loomed large and oblique in the sky, setting the tips of the trees aglow and bathing the garden in its yellowish-red rays. And standing tall on the path, in the middle of this golden transfiguration, with the burning sphere's mighty halo at her head, was a curvaceous thing dressed entirely in red, gold and tartan. She braced her right hand against her hip and rocked an elegantly designed baby carriage back and forth. And inside this baby carriage sat Anton Klöterjahn, Jr., sat Gabriele Eckhof's bouncing baby son!

There he sat on his cushions, clad in a white jacket of yarn and an oversized white hat, chubby-cheeked, magnificent and robust, so that his eyes, cheery and unabashed, met those of Mr. Spinell. The novelist was about to gather himself. He was a grown man. He had the strength to walk past this unexpected apparition, resplendent in sunshine, and continue on his way. But then something horrific happened: Anton Klöterjahn began to laugh and cry out in jubilation, shrieking with inexplicable joy. It was unnerving.

God knows what had set him off. Perhaps it was the dark figure opposite that had brought on this mood of wild hilarity, or maybe some fit of animalistic well-being had seized him. He held a teething ring of bone in one hand and a tin rattle in the other. These he exultantly thrust up into the sunshine, shaking them and banging them together, as if contemptuously shooing someone away. His eyes were almost shut with glee, and his mouth gaped so wide that the whole of his rosy gums was visible. He even tossed his head back and forth in exultation.

At that, Mr. Spinell did an about-face and hurried off. He walked, pursued by the little Klöterjahn's jubilation, along the gravel path, his arms set in a certain tentative, rigidly graceful posture, forcibly hesitating with every step, like someone trying to disguise the fact that, internally, he is running away.

Tonio Kröger

1

The winter sun appeared as but a weak spot of brightness over the cramped city, milky-white and dull behind layers of clouds. It was wet and drafty in the narrow gable-lined streets, and a kind of soft hail, neither ice nor snow, fell intermittently.

School was done for the day. Throngs of liberated schoolchildren streamed out over the cobblestone schoolyard and through the iron gate, scattering and hurrying off in various directions. The older ones proceeded with dignity, their bookbags pressed high against their left shoulders, their right arms flailing in the wind as they steered their way home for their afternoon meal. The younger population broke into a happy trot, spraying icy slush all around, while the paraphernalia of knowledge rattled in their sealskin knapsacks. Here and there, however, they all stopped to gaze up with pious eyes and doff their caps before the Wotan's hat and Jove's beard of a deliberately striding master teacher . . .

"Are you ready yet, Hans?" said Tonio Kröger, who had been waiting for some time on the curb. Smiling, he walked over to his friend, who was on his way through the gate. He was talking to some other classmates and was about to leave with them.

"Huh?" he said, looking at Tonio . . . "Oh yes, that's right! Well, sure, let's take a little walk."

Tonio said nothing, and his eyes clouded over. Had Hans forgotten, had he only just remembered that they wanted to take a short walk together that afternoon?

And here he had been looking forward to it practically nonstop from the moment they had made their plan!

"All right, adieu, fellows!" Hans Hansen said to his classmates. "I'm going to go a ways with Kröger." — And the two of them turned left, while the others ambled off to the right.

Hans and Tonio had time for an after-school walk because they both came from households where the family didn't sit down to its main meal until four o'clock. Their fathers were important businessmen who held public office and were very influential in the city. For many generations the Hansens had owned the great timber yards down by the river, where giant mechanical saws hissed and spat as they cut tree trunks into lumber. Tonio, on the other hand, was the son of Consul Kröger, whose sacks of grain with the big black firm insignia could be seen being transported through the streets, day in, day out, and whose large ancestral home was the most magisterial in the entire city . . . Such was the number of their family acquaintances that the two friends constantly had to doff their caps; in fact, many people rushed up to pay first respects to this pair of fourteen-year-olds.

Both had their schoolbags slung over their shoulders, and both were warmly dressed in fine clothes: Hans in a short fisherman's jacket with the wide blue collar of his sailor suit folded down over the shoulders and back, Tonio in a gray belted peacoat. Hans wore a Danish sailor's cap with short ribbons from which a shock of raffia blond hair poked out. He was extraordinarily handsome and well built, broad in the shoulders, thin at the waist, with incisive steely blue eyes set wide apart. Underneath Tonio's round fur hat, two dark, delicately shadowed eyes with heavy lids peered out drowsily and somewhat timidly from his brunet face with its sharply defined, Mediterranean-looking features . . . The cast of his mouth and chin was unusually soft. He walked listlessly and unevenly, while the Hansen boy's trim black-stocking-clad legs marched along in nimbly unerring step.

Tonio didn't speak. He was in pain. Knitting his rather crooked brows, holding his lips pursed in a whistle and his head at an angle, he stared into the distance. This was his typical carriage and demeanor.

Suddenly Hans locked arms with Tonio and looked sideways over at him, for he understood quite well what this was all about. And although Tonio said nothing as they took their next steps, his anger instantaneously melted.

"I hadn't forgotten, you know, Tonio," said Hans, staring down at the pavement before him. "I just thought our walk today would be off because it's so cold and windy. A bit of cold and wind doesn't bother me, though, and I think it's fabulous that you waited for me. I was getting annoyed because I thought you had gone home . . ."

At these words, everything inside Tonio leapt with joy.

"Yes, well then let's walk along the levees!" he said, emotion in his voice. "Along *Mühlenwall* and *Holstenwall*, and then I'll walk you home . . . I don't mind going on alone from there, not at all. Next time we can go my way."

At heart, he didn't really believe what Hans had told him, and he felt quite sure that this private walk was only half so important to his companion as it was to him. But he saw too that Hans rued his forgetfulness and was trying hard to make it up to him. And the last thing he wanted was to forestall their reconciliation . . .

The fact was that Tonio was utterly smitten with Hans Hansen and had already suffered quite a bit on his account. The one who loves most becomes subordinate and must suffer—his fourteen-year-old soul had already learned this simple yet hard lesson from life. And it was in his nature to record experiences like this, making mental notes and savoring them somewhat, although he never applied them to his own person or benefited from them in any practical way. It was also in his nature to find these sorts of lessons much more important and interesting than any of the knowledge forced on him in school. Indeed, he spent most of his classroom hours under those vaulted Gothic arches plumbing the emotional depths of such insights, thinking them through to their logical conclusion. This pursuit gave him a feeling of satisfaction much like the one he got wandering around his room with his violin (for he played the violin), producing the softest notes he could to accompany the rippling water of the fountain, which danced its way skyward under the branches of the old walnut tree down in the garden . . .

The fountain, the old walnut tree, his violin and the sea in the distance, the Baltic Sea, whose summer dreams he was permitted to listen in on every vacation—these were the things he loved, the things he surrounded himself with, the things amidst which his inner life played itself out. They were all things with names that could be used to good effect in poetry and that did indeed keep recurring in the actual poems Tonio Kröger wrote from time to time.

This—the fact that he had written a notebook full of poems—had through his own negligence become public knowledge and had greatly harmed his reputation among his classmates and teachers. On the one hand, Consul Kröger's son found it stupid and vulgar to be put off by poetry, and he despised them accordingly, both his classmates and his teachers, whose ill manners in other areas repulsed him too and whose own personal shortcomings he perceived with unusual penetrating clarity. On the other hand, he also found something extravagant and actually unbecoming in the writing of poetry and had to agree partially with all those who considered it a dubious activity. That alone, however, wasn't enough to make him desist . . .

Since he squandered his free time after school, was slow and disinterested in the classroom and possessed a poor reputation among his teachers, he always brought home the most miserable report cards. These drew the ire and consternation of his father, a tall, meticulously attired gentleman with thoughtful blue eyes, who always wore a wildflower in his buttonhole. With Tonio's mother, his beautiful, dark-haired mother, it was different. Her first name was Consuelo, and she was unlike the other ladies of the city in every respect, having been brought there by his father one day long ago from somewhere at the very bottom of the map. She could have cared less about his grades . . .

Tonio loved his dark, fiery mother, who played piano and mandolin so marvelously, and was glad that she didn't fret about his dubious standing in society. On the other hand, he sensed that his father's anger was much more respectable and decent and, though constantly scolded by him, ultimately saw everything through his father's eyes, whereas he found his mother's cheerful indifference a bit disreputable. His thoughts often ran something like: I have gone on long enough being the way I am—negligent, contrary, fascinated by things no one else thinks about—with no desire or capacity to change. At least, it's only natural that people scold and punish me seriously for it, instead of looking past the problem with kisses and music. We're not gypsies in some green wagon; we're respectable people, Consul Kröger's family, *the* Krögers . . . On more than one occasion he had also thought: why am I so obstinate, so quick to contradict, so at odds with my teachers and outcast from the other boys? Just look at them, the students at the head of the class and the good, solid average ones. They don't find the teachers ridiculous; they don't write poems; they only think about things that people do think about, things that can be said out loud. How proper they must feel, existing in harmony with everything and everyone around them! That must be nice . . . What's wrong with me? What end will this come to?

This way of looking at himself and his position in life played a major part in Tonio's love for Hans Hansen. He loved him first of all because he was handsome, but also because he appeared in every respect to be the reverse and opposite of himself. Hans Hansen was an excellent student and a fun-loving fellow to boot, who rode horses, played sports, swam like a champion and enjoyed universal popularity. The teachers doted on him with something approaching tender fondness, addressing him by his first name and giving him every encouragement. His classmates vied for his favor, and on the street gentlemen and ladies would stop him, tug the shock of raffia blond hair that poked out from his Danish sailor's cap and say: "Good day, Hans Hansen, with the nice shock of hair! Are you still *primus*? Say hello to Papa and Mama, my fine young man . . ."

That was Hans Hansen, and ever since they had known each other, the mere sight of him had filled Tonio Kröger with longing, a jealous longing that sat somewhere above the breast and burned. Oh, to have your blue eyes, he thought, to live as peacefully and happily with the entire world as you do! You are always doing something respectable and generally considered worthwhile. After your homework, you take riding lessons or make something with your fretsaw. Even during vacation by the sea, your time is spent rowing, sailing and swimming, while I lie around in the sand, idly daydreaming and staring at the mysterious shifting expressions that flit across the face of the ocean. That's why *your* eyes are so bright. Oh, to be like you . . .

He made no attempt to become like Hans Hansen, and perhaps this wish was never meant very seriously. But he felt an anguished desire to be loved by him for what he was, and he vied for such love in his own way, in slow, heartfelt, solicitous, long-suffering melancholy, although it was a melancholy that could burn more brightly and more intensely than any of the impetuous passion one might have expected from his foreign appearance.

And his overtures were not entirely in vain, for Hans, who incidentally respected Tonio for a certain mastery, a skill with words that allowed him to express complicated things, clearly understood that an extraordinarily strong and tender affection was alive for him. He did his best to show his gratitude and was the cause in Tonio of much delight at reciprocated interest, but also of much jealous dismay and disappointment at his ultimately fruitless efforts to establish a deeper bond between them. For the strangest thing was that Tonio, who envied

Hans Hansen and the life he led, was nonetheless constantly trying to convert him to his own ways, an enterprise that could succeed at best for isolated moments and even then only superficially . . .

"I've just been reading something wonderful, something splendid . . ." said Tonio Kröger. They walked along sharing a bag of fruit drops they had bought for ten pfennigs at Iversen's store on *Mühlenstraße*. "You must read it, Hans. It's Schiller's *Don Carlos* . . . I'll lend it to you, if you want . . ."

"Oh no," said Hans Hansen. "Forget it, Tonio. That's not for me. I'll stick to my horse books. There are some fabulous illustrations in them, I tell you. Sometime when you're at my house, I'll show them to you. They have stop-action photographs where you can see the animals at a trot, a gallop or a jump, in all the positions too fast to be made out with the naked eye . . ."

"In all the positions?" Tonio asked, to be polite. "That's swell. But *Don Carlos*, now that beats everything. There are parts, you'll see, that are so beautiful they send a chill up your spine. At the same time they're like a small explosion . . ."

"An explosion?" asked Hans Hansen. "How so?"

"Well now, there's the part where the king breaks down because he's been betrayed by the marquis . . . although the marquis has only betrayed him out of love, you see, because he's sacrificing himself for the prince. And then the news makes its way from the royal cabinet into the anteroom that the king is in tears. 'In tears?' 'The king in tears?' None of the courtiers know what to say, and it's really moving because the king is such a terribly strict, strong man. You can easily understand why he breaks down and cries, though, and I actually feel sorrier for him than the prince and the marquis put together. He's always so alone and unloved, and just when he thinks he's found someone, that person betrays him . . ."

Hans Hansen looked him sideways in the eye, and something he saw must have won him over, for he suddenly hooked arms again with Tonio and asked:

"So what sort of a betrayal is it, Tonio?"

This roused Tonio's excitement.

"Yes, well you see," he began, "the thing is that all the letters to Brabant and Flanders . . ."

"Look, here comes Erwin Jimmerthal!" said Hans.

Tonio fell silent. Why, he thought, I wish the earth would just open up and swallow him, this Jimmerthal! Why does he have to come along and bother us? Please don't let him walk the whole way with us and talk about riding lessons . . . for Erwin Jimmerthal also took riding lessons. He was the son of a bank director and lived just outside the city walls. With his crooked legs and slits for eyes, he was coming, already rid of his schoolbag, up the avenue.

"Hi, Jimmerthal," said Hans. "I'm on a little walk with Kröger . . ."

"I have to go into town to get something," said Jimmerthal, "but I'll walk with you a little ways . . . Hey, are those fruit drops you have there? Sure, thanks. I'll have a couple. So we have lessons again tomorrow, Hans." — Riding lessons were meant.

"Fabulous!" said Hans. "My parents are buying me leather gaiters, you know, because I got top marks on the *exertitium* the other day . . ."

"You probably don't take riding lessons, do you, Kröger?" Jimmerthal asked, his eyes nothing more than a pair of blank slits.

"No . . ." answered Tonio in an uncertain tone.

"You should ask your father," Hans Hansen chipped in, "to let you take lessons too, Kröger."

"Sure . . ." said Tonio both quickly and indifferently. He was choked up for a moment because Hans had addressed him by his last name. Hans seemed to sense this, adding by way of explanation:

"I have to call you Kröger because your first name is so strange. No offence, but I just don't like it. Tonio . . . what sort of a name is that? It's not your fault, but . . ."

"No, you were probably given that name because it's got something foreign and exceptional . . ." said Jimmerthal, acting as if he were putting the best face on the matter.

Tonio's lips trembled. He collected himself and said:

"Yes, it's a silly name. God knows I'd rather be called Heinrich or Wilhelm, you can believe me. It's because I was named after my mother's brother, who's called Antonio; my mother's from abroad, you see . . ."

Then he fell silent, letting the other two boys talk on about horses and leather riding gear. Hans had hooked Jimmerthal by the arm and was speaking with a lively enthusiasm that could have never been awakened in him for *Don Carlos* . . . From time to time Tonio felt an urge to cry making its way upward and tickling his nose; he also had difficulty controlling his chin, which was on the verge of twitching . . .

Hans just didn't like Tonio's name—what could be done about it? His own was Hans, and Jimmerthal's was Erwin, fine, those were normal names that no one found alienating. "Tonio," however, was something foreign and exceptional. Yes, there was always something exceptional about him, regardless of what he might have wanted himself; he was isolated, outcast from normal everyday people, despite the fact that he was Consul Kröger's son, one of *the* Krögers, not some gypsy in a green wagon . . . But why did Hans call him Tonio so long as they were alone together only to be ashamed whenever someone else appeared? At times he was so close to him, won over, no doubt about it. What sort of a betrayal, Tonio? Hans had asked and then took his arm. Nonetheless he had breathed a sigh of relief when Jimmerthal had showed up. He had abandoned him, throwing his alien name in his face for no reason. How painful it was to have to see through it all! . . . In his heart, he knew that, as long as they were alone, Hans Hansen was somewhat fond of him. But as soon as a third person appeared, he would feel ashamed and give him up. And he would be alone again. He thought of King Philip. The king in tears . . .

"Jesus," said Erwin Jimmerthal, "now I really have to get going! Adieu, fellows, thanks for the fruit drops."

With that he jumped on a bench by the side of the avenue, ran with his crooked legs along its surface and trotted off.

"I don't mind Jimmerthal one bit," said Hans emphatically. He had a spoiled way of self-consciously announcing his likes and dislikes, as if generously conferring them . . . Then, since he was already warm on the subject, he went on talking about his riding lessons. They weren't far from the Hansens' residence; the walk along the levees didn't take all that long. They held on tightly to their caps and bent their heads against the strong, damp wind creaking and groaning among the bare branches of the trees. Hans Hansen kept on talking, Tonio adding only an occasional forced "Aha" and "I see" and feeling no pleasure when Hans, carried away by his monologue, again took him by the arm, for this was only a semblance of intimacy, without significance.

Then, not far from the train station, they turned away from the levees to watch a train puff by in unceremonious haste, idly counting the number of cars and waving to the man who sat wrapped in fur atop of the very last one. And when they arrived at *Lindenplatz*, they stopped before the timber wholesaler Hansen's villa, and Hans gave an extensive demonstration of the fun that could be had swinging back and forth on the bottom rail of the iron gate so that its hinges squeaked in that special way. After this he said goodbye.

"Well, I have to go in now," he said. "Adieu, Tonio. Next time I'll walk you home, you can count on it."

"Adieu, Hans," said Tonio. "It was a nice walk."

Their hands, as they shook them, were wet and covered with rust from the iron gate. As Hans looked Tonio in the eye, however, something like thoughtful regret came over his handsome face.

"By the way, I'll read *Don Carlos* soon!" he said hastily. "All that about the king in his cabinet sounds fabulous!" Then he tucked his schoolbag under his arm and ran across the front yard. Before disappearing into his house, he turned around and nodded once more.

Tonio Kröger walked away from that spot thoroughly

transfigured and elated. The wind was pushing him from behind, but that was hardly the only reason for the wings on his heels.

Hans was going to read *Don Carlos*, and then they would have something to talk about just between the two of them, without Jimmerthal or anyone else! How well they understood each other! Who knew, maybe he could even get Hans to write poems? . . . No, no, he didn't want that! Hans must never become like Tonio; he should stay as he was, so bright and strong, beloved by all, Tonio more than anyone! But it wouldn't hurt for him to read *Don Carlos* . . . And Tonio passed through the squat old city gate, walked along the ships' landing, up the steep, drafty, damp, gable-lined little street until he reached his family's house. His heart was alive then; there was longing in it and somber jealousy and a tiny bit of contempt and an utterly innocent sense of bliss.

2

Blonde Inge—Ingeborg Holm, the daughter of Dr. Holm who lived by the marketplace, near the tall Gothic fountain with its many spires—she was the one whom Tonio Kröger loved at the age of sixteen.

How did it happen? He had seen her a thousand times; but one evening he saw her lit up a certain way, saw how in conversation with a friend she gave her head a certain exuberant toss sideways as she laughed, and how she lifted her hand—the not especially slender or delicately formed hand of a mere girl—to the back of her head so that her sleeve of white gauze slid up from the elbow. He also heard how she pronounced some word, some meaningless word, so that a certain warm music entered her voice, and his heart was filled with delight far greater than that which he had occasionally felt earlier at the sight of Hans Hansen, back when he had still been a foolish little boy.

On this particular evening he took away her image—

her thick blonde ponytail, her long horizontal blue eyes full of laughter and the faintly outlined bridge of freckles at her nose—and was unable to sleep. Still hearing the musical quality in her voice, he tried softly to imitate the way she had pronounced that meaningless word, shuddering as he did. Experience told him that this was love. And although he knew only too well that love would invariably bring him great pain, hardship and humiliation, that it would moreover destroy his peace of mind and flood his heart with melodies, without bringing the composure necessary to form something well-rounded and calmly forge it into a whole, he nonetheless gladly accepted this new love. He abandoned himself to it and nourished it with every strength in his disposition, for he knew that it enriched and inspired, and he longed to be enriched and inspired, instead of calmly forging something whole.

The site where Tonio fell head over heels for carefree Ingeborg Holm was the empty salon of Mrs. Husteede, the Consul's wife, whose evening it was to host the dance lessons. It was a private course, attended only by children from the best families, and they assembled in each one of their parents' houses in turn to receive instruction in dance and etiquette. To these ends Mr. Knaak, the ballet instructor, came every week specially from Hamburg.

Francois Knaak was his name, and what a man he was! *"J'ai l'honneur de me vous representer,"* he would say, *"mon nom est Knaak* . . . This is not to be said as one bows, but rather after one is again standing upright—not too loudly but still audibly. It's not every day that one is called upon to introduce oneself in French, but if one can do it correctly in that language, one can be sure it will never fail one in German either." How magnificently his black silk tails clung to his corpulent hips! The soft folds of his trousers tumbled down on his patent leather shoes, which sported wide satin bows, and his brown eyes glanced around with weary satisfaction at their own beauty.

Everyone was overwhelmed by his more than ample self-assurance and his command of form. He would walk up to the lady of the house—as no one else *could* walk, nimbly striding and swaying like a king—then bow and wait for her to extend her hand. When he had received it, he would thank her in a soft voice, skip back and turn on his left foot, kicking his right up to the side, tip down, and strutting away with undulating hips.

Upon taking one's leave, one walked backwards in an extended bow, and if one brought up a chair, one didn't grab it by the leg or drag it across the floor but carried it by the back and set it down silently. When standing, one didn't fold one's hands over one's belly and let one's tongue loll in the corner of one's mouth—if one did do so, Mr. Knaak had such a talent for mimicry that for the rest of one's life one couldn't witness such behavior without feeling slightly ill . . .

So much for etiquette. In dancing, Mr. Knaak had attained, if possible, an even higher degree of mastery. In a salon emptied of furniture, gaslights burning in the chandelier, candles flickering on the fireplace, the pupils stood around on a floor strewn with talcum powder in a silent semicircle. In the adjoining room, beyond the *portières*, mothers and aunts sat on upholstered chairs and watched through their lorgnettes as Mr. Knaak, gracefully inclined, took up the ends of his tails between two fingers and skipped about demonstrating the various steps of the mazurka. When he really wanted to impress his audience, he would kick himself suddenly and inexplicably up from the floor, twirl his legs around in the air with blinding speed and trill his lips in time, coming down to earth with a muffled thud that shook everything where it stood . . .

Look at him, making a monkey of himself, Tonio Kröger thought. He couldn't help noticing, however, that Inge Holm, carefree Inge, often followed Mr. Knaak's movements with a faraway smile, and that wasn't the only reason that such displays of magnificent physical prowess ultimately wrung something like admiration from him. How calm and imperturbable Mr. Knaak's eyes were! They never penetrated the surface, never reached the point where things became complicated and sad; they knew only that they were brown and beautiful. And that was precisely the reason for his proud demeanor! You had to be stupid in order to strut around like that; you were loved for it because you were indeed loveable. He understood only too well why Inge—sweet, blonde Inge—looked at Mr. Knaak the way she did. But did that mean no girl would ever look at him that way?

Oh, it did happen. There was Magdalena Vermehren, the daughter of Attorney Vermehren, with her gentle lips and large, dark, glassy eyes that were so serious and romantic. She often fell while dancing, and it was she who approached him during the ladies' choice. She knew that he wrote poems, she had asked him twice if he would show them to her, and she often stared up at him from afar, head held low. But what good was that? *He* loved Inge Holm—carefree, blonde Inge—who surely despised him for writing bits of poetry . . . He stared at her long horizontal blue eyes, which were full of happiness and mockery, and a jealous longing, a bitter and insistent pain at being isolated from her as an eternal stranger, sat in his breast and burned . . .

"First couple, *en avant!*" said Mr. Knaak, and words cannot describe how magnificently the man pronounced these nasal vowels. They were practising the quadrille, and to Tonio Kröger's profound horror, he found himself in the same square as Inge Holm. He avoided her as best as he could, yet he was always near her; he refused to let his eyes seek her out, yet his gaze constantly encountered her . . . Here she came, gliding hand in hand with redheaded Ferdinand Matthiessen, running Tonio's way, where, throwing back her ponytail and panting, she took up position. Mr. Heinzelmann, the pianist, placed his bony hands on the keys, Mr. Knaak issued instructions and the quadrille began.

She swayed from side to side in front of him, forward and backward, stepping and turning, her hair—or maybe it was the delicate white material of her dress—giving off an aroma that sometimes drifted over to him. Sorrow increasingly clouded his eyes. I love you, dear sweet Inge, he said to himself, putting into these words all the hurt he felt because she was eagerly and happily concentrating on her dance steps and took no notice of him at all. He thought of a beautiful poem by Theodor Storm—"I would sleep, and yet you must dance"—and was tortured by the humiliating senselessness of having to dance when one was in love . . .

"First couple, *en avant!*" said Mr. Knaak, as a new figure was begun. *"Compliment! Moulinet des dames! Tour de main!"* And there were no words for the elegant way he swallowed the silent *e* in *de*.

"Second couple *en avant!*" Tonio Kröger and his lady were next. *"Compliment!"* Tonio bowed. *"Moulinet des dames!"* And Tonio Kröger, head down, countenance dark, touched hands with each of the four ladies, with Inge Holm, and danced the *moulinet.*

All around there was giggling and laughter. Mr. Knaak assumed a ballet position of stylized horror. "Oh no!" he cried. "Stop, stop, Kröger has fallen in with the ladies! *En arrière*, Miss Kröger, get back, *fi donc!* Everyone has gotten it except you. Be off with you! Away! Back you go!" And he took out a yellow silk handkerchief and waved it at Tonio Kröger, shooing him back to his place.

Everyone was laughing, the boys, the girls, even the ladies behind the *portières*, for Mr. Knaak had made something just too comical out of the incident—a vaudeville routine couldn't have been more entertaining. Only Mr. Heinzelmann maintained a sober, businesslike expression as he waited for the signal to resume playing, for he was immune to Mr. Knaak's devices.

Then the quadrille continued. And then there was a break. The serving girl brought in a silver tray full of wine jellies in clinking glasses, and the cook followed in tow with a load of plum cake. Tonio Kröger, however, slipped away unnoticed and stood in the outside hallway before a window with drawn Venetian blinds, his hands behind his back, not considering that since nothing could be seen through the blinds it was ridiculous to stand there pretending to look out.

He was looking not out, but inside himself, where

there was so much grief and longing. Why, oh why was he here? Why wasn't he in his room, sitting by the window reading Storm's *Immensee*, occasionally glancing down into the evening garden where the old walnut tree ponderously creaked? That was his place. The others could dance and get as lively as they wanted while they practiced their skills! . . . No, no, his place was here, in Inge's vicinity. He was standing alone, apart from the group, trying to distinguish her voice with its musical sound of warm life from the general hum, the tinkling of glasses and the laughter inside, but she was near. Your long horizontal blue eyes full of laughter, blonde Inge! No one who has read—not to mention tried to imitate—*Immensee* could ever be as beautiful and sunny as you! That's the real tragedy . . .

She had to come! She had to notice he wasn't there, had to sense how it stood with him, had to follow him secretly, if only out of pity, had to lay her hand on his shoulder and say: "Come back inside and join us, don't be sad, I love you." And he listened for her voice behind him and waited with irrational anticipation for her to come. But she didn't come, of course. Things like that just don't happen in reality.

Had she laughed at him too, like all the others? Yes, of course she had, as much as he would have liked to deny it for her sake and his own. It was only because of her presence distracting him that he had joined in the *moulinet des dames*. But what did it matter? One day they'd stop laughing! Hadn't one of his poems recently been accepted by a magazine, albeit one that had folded before his work had had a chance to appear? The day would come when he was famous, when everything he wrote would be published, and then he would see whether Inge Holm would be impressed . . . No, she would *not*, that was precisely it. Magdalena Vermehren, who was always falling down, sure, she would be impressed. But never Inge Holm, never blue-eyed, carefree Inge. Therefore was it not all in vain? . . .

Tonio Kröger's heart shrank painfully at this thought. To feel a miraculous, playful and profound creativity stirring within and yet know that the people whose admiration you most crave will greet it only with cheerful indifference—that causes great pain. Yet even while he stood alone, outcast and hopeless, pretending in his distress that he could see out the drawn Venetian blind, he was happy. For in those days his heart was alive. It beat warmly and sadly for you, Ingeborg Holm, and his soul embraced your blonde, bright, ardently normal little existence in blissful self-negation.

More than once he stood with flushed cheeks in some lonely corner where music, the scent of flowers and the clinking of glasses were only faintly discernible, trying to distinguish the melody of your voice from the festive noises in the distance; more than once he stood suffering in your vicinity and was happy. More than once it grieved him that he was able to talk to Magdalena Vermehren, who was always falling down. It was she who understood him and shared his sense of humor and took him seriously, whereas blonde Inge seemed distant, alien and suspicious whenever he sat next to her, for his language was not hers. Yet nonetheless he was happy. For happiness, he told himself, isn't being loved; that was just a slightly nauseous satisfaction of vanity. Happiness is loving and perhaps seizing a few short illusory moments of intimacy with the object of one's love. And inwardly he took note of this idea, thought it fully through and plumbed its emotional depths.

Fidelity! thought Tonio Kröger. I will be faithful and love you, Ingeborg, so long as I live! So good were his intentions. And yet a soft voice of fear and sadness whispered within him that he had utterly forgotten Hans Hansen, even though he saw him on a daily basis. And the ugly, wretched truth was that this quiet, faintly malevolent voice would be proven right, that time passed and days came when Tonio Kröger was no longer so unconditionally prepared to die for carefree Inge as before, for deep within he felt the desire and the ability to achieve, after his own peculiar fashion, a host of things that would attract the world's attention.

And he cautiously circled the sacrificial altar where

the pure and chaste flame of his love was ablaze; he knelt down before it and did all he could to fan and tend it in his efforts to keep the faith. And yet after a certain interval, imperceptibly, without noise or spectacle, it went out nonetheless.

Tonio Kröger stood for some while before that cold altar, incredulous and disappointed at the fact that fidelity was impossible on earth. Then he shrugged his shoulders and went on his way.

3

He went the way he had to go, a little carelessly and unsteadily, whistling and gazing into the distance, head angled, and if he went astray, it was because for many people a right way just doesn't exist. When asked what in the world he wanted to become, he gave various answers, for he liked to say (and had already put in writing) that he carried within him a thousand existential possibilities, together with the secret conviction that they were all impossibilities . . .

Even before he departed the cramped city that was his home, it had quietly released the shackles and ties with which it had held him bound. The ancient Kröger family had little by little succumbed to a state of disintegration and collapse, and people had good reason to count Tonio Kröger himself among its symptoms. His father's mother, the matriarch of the family, had died, and not long afterward his father—the tall, pensive, meticulously attired gentleman with the wildflower in his buttonhole—had followed her to the grave. The grand house of the Krögers with all its distinguished history was put up for sale, and the firm was liquidated. Tonio's mother, his beautiful fiery mother, who played such marvelous piano and mandolin and who was so indifferent toward everything, married again immediately after her year of mourning, indeed married a musician, a virtuoso with an Italian name whom she followed into the wild blue yonder. Tonio Kröger found this a bit disreputable;

but it was hardly *his* place to forbid anyone anything. He wrote poems and couldn't even answer the question about what in the world he wanted to become . . .

So he left his childhood city with its nooks and crannies and damp wind whistling through the gables, left the fountain and the walnut tree in the garden, those trusty friends of his youth, left the sea, too, which he loved so passionately, and felt no pain as he did. After all, he was grown-up and clever; he understood the reasons behind everything and had nothing but contempt for the crude and primitive existence that had held him so long in its midst.

He gave himself over entirely to that power he felt to be the most sublime on earth, which he felt himself called to serve and which promised him elevated status and accolades: the power of imagination and word, which gleefully thrones above all unconscious, inarticulate forms of life. With the passion of youth he gave himself over to it, and it rewarded him with everything it has to give and pitilessly took from him everything it habitually demands as compensation.

It sharpened his eye and allowed him to see through the great-sounding words that inflate people's chests; it revealed to him the souls of other men, as well as his own, gave him vision, and showed him the world's interior working and all that ultimately lurks behind word and deed. What he saw, however, was this: comedy and despair—comedy and despair.

And along with the trials and exhilaration of such insight came solitude, for he could not endure the company of harmless people with their cheerfully dim minds, and, conversely, the mark upon his forehead always set them on edge. But his delight in word and form grew sweeter and sweeter, for he liked to say (and had already put in writing) that deep acquaintance with the soul, by itself, would invariably lead to depression, if the pleasures of the well-turned phrase didn't entertain and lift our spirits . . .

He lived in large cities and throughout Southern Europe, where he hoped the sun would more fully ripen his art; perhaps it was his mother's blood that drew him there. But because his heart was dead and loveless, he succumbed to pursuits of the flesh, plunging deep into lust and carnal sin, suffering unspeakably because of it. Perhaps it was an inheritance from his father—the tall, pensive, spotlessly attired man with the wildflower in his buttonhole—that caused him to suffer so down south and occasionally stirred a weak, nostalgic memory in him of a desire of the soul that he had once known and never found again amidst all his other desires.

A disgust for, a hatred of the senses took hold of him, along with a thirst for purity and respectable peace of mind, yet he continued to inhale the air of art, the mild, sweet fragrant air of eternal blissful spring, in which fertility is ever at work, secretly fermenting and germinating. Thus it came about that he was ceaselessly thrown back and forth between crass extremes, between icy intellectualism and the all-consuming fever of the senses, causing him to lead an exhausting life, tormented by conscience, an exemplary, extravagant, extraordinary life, which he himself, Tonio Kröger, ultimately detested. How very astray! he would sometimes think. How is it that I have fallen into all these eccentric adventures? I'm not some gypsy in a green wagon, not by birth . . .

But just as his health weakened, his artistic talent increased, becoming selective, discriminating, sumptuous, refined, impatient with all banality and hypersensitive in matters of tact and taste. When he was first published, applause and cries of joy went up from the *cognoscenti*, for it was a worthy and well-wrought thing he had produced, full of humor and intimately known sorrow. And rapidly his name—the same one his teachers had called out in tones of opprobrium, the same one with which he had signed his first verses in honor of the walnut tree, the fountain and the sea, this combination of Mediterranean and Nordic sounds, this exotically tinged bourgeois name—became a synonym for excellence, for the painful clarity of his vision was augmented by an unusual, bitterly unremitting and ambitious work ethic, which in its struggles with the discriminating impatience of his aesthetic judgement gave rise, under great torment, to works of remarkable quality.

He worked, not like someone working in order to live, but like someone who, because he places no value on himself as a living person, wants only to work, someone who seeks recognition solely as a creative artist and otherwise goes around gray and anonymous, akin to an actor without make-up, who is nothing so long as he has nothing to act out. He worked in silence, isolated, invisible and contemptuous of those insignificant rivals for whom talent was a social ornament, who, whether rich or poor, whether they went about wild and dishevelled or in monogrammed-tie luxury, were basically concerned with living happy, loveable, bohemian lives, not seeing that good work only arises under the strain of a miserable life, that he who lives cannot work, and that only after having undergone death can one completely become a creator.

4

"Am I intruding?" Tonio Kröger asked in the doorway of the atelier. He held his hat in his hands and even bowed slightly, although Lizaveta Ivanovna was a friend of his, from whom he had no secrets.

"Spare the formalities, Tonio Kröger, and come inside!" she answered in her skipping accent. "It's common knowledge that you had a proper upbringing and know what's proper form." In the process, she laid her brush on the palette, which she held in her left hand, extended her right and looked up at him, laughing and shaking her head.

"Yes, but you're working," he said. "Let me see . . . Oh, you're making progress." And he examined by turns the colorful sketches leaning against the stools on either side of the easel and the large canvas with its square-lined drafting grid on which the first patches of color were beginning to appear within a crude, indefinite charcoal outline.

It was in Munich, in a courtyard building on *Schellingstraße*, several floors up. Outside, beyond the wide north-facing windows, the sky was blue, birds were chirping and the sun was shining. Newly arrived spring's sweet breath streamed in through an open casement and mingled with the smell of bonding agent and oil paints that filled the spacious studio. Unobstructed, the golden light of the bright afternoon flooded the expansive emptiness of the atelier, boldly illuminating the rather uneven floor, the unvarnished windowside table with its little bottles, tubes and brushes, the unframed studies on the bare walls, the torn silk tapestry cordoning off a small, stylishly furnished living and relaxation area near the door, the nascent work on the easel, and the painter and author before it.

She looked to be about the same age as he was, namely a bit over thirty. Clad in a dark-blue, well-splattered painter's apron, she sat on a low stool resting her chin in her hand. Her brown hair, rigidly sculpted and already beginning to gray a bit at the sides, covered her temples in gentle curves and set off her dark, Slavic, infinitely likeable face with its button nose, prominently protruding cheekbones and small, black, glassy eyes. Tense, mistrustful and yet excited, she took stock of her work with a narrow sidelong gaze . . .

He stood beside her, pressing his right hand to his hip and rapidly twirling his brown moustache with his left. His slanting eyebrows were knitted together, gloomy and strained, and he whistled softly to himself, as was his habit. He was quite meticulously and excellently attired in a sober gray suit of conservative cut. A nervous twitch ran through his wrinkled forehead, over which his dark hair was parted with extraordinary simplicity and exactitude, and his Mediterrean features were already quite sharply defined, as if someone had gone over and emphasized them with a slate pencil. The outlines of his mouth and his chin nonetheless remained soft and weak. After a while he brushed his hand over his forehead and his eyes and turned away.

"I shouldn't have come," he said.

"Why shouldn't you have, Tonio Kröger?"

"I've just come from work, Lizaveta, and in my head it looks just like this canvas: a bit of framework, a faint sketch smudged with corrections and a couple patches of color. And now I come here and see the exact same thing. I even find the exact same conflict and contradiction here," he said, sniffing the air, "that was bothering me at home. It's odd. When an idea has you in its sway, you'll find manifestations of it everywhere, you'll even *smell* it in the wind. Bonding agent and the aroma of spring, am I right? Art and—well, what is the antithesis? Don't say 'nature,' Lizaveta. 'Nature' doesn't cover it. I should have gone for a walk—though I doubt I would have felt any better if I had. You see, five minutes ago, not far from here, I ran into my colleague Adalbert, the short-story writer. 'God damn the spring!' he said in that aggressive way of his. 'It will always be the most horrible season of the year! How can one come up with even a single reasonable idea, Kröger? How can one be relaxed enough to work out the tiniest epiphany or effect with the blood itching indecently and the attention distracted by a million irrelevant feelings, the sort that always turn out on reflection to be utterly trivial, entirely useless garbage? I'm off to a café. That's neutral territory, you know, untouched by change of season, one which represents, you might say, the well-removed and elevated sphere of the literary, where a person is only capable of more distinguished forms of inspiration . . .' And he went to a café; maybe I should have gone with him."

Lizaveta looked amused.

"That's good, Tonio Kröger, especially the bit about 'indecent itching.' And he's partially right: spring isn't especially well suited to getting work done. But now stand back. Despite everything I'm going to take care of this tiny detail here, this tiny epiphany and effect, as Adalbert would say. Afterward we'll step into the 'salon' and have some tea and you can tell me what's on your mind; I can see something's eating you today. In the meantime, please congregate somewhere else, perhaps over by that crate, if you care about your noble vestments . . ."

"Oh spare me, please. Vestments, Lizaveta Ivanovna! Would you rather I went around in a ragged velvet jacket or a red silk vest? As an artist, one is adventurous enough on the inside. On the outside one should dress properly, damn it, and behave like a respectable person. No, nothing's eating me," he said, watching her mix some colors on her palette. "You heard me: it's just a problem, a conflict that's been on my mind, that's been holding up my work . . . What were we talking about just now? About Adalbert, the writer, and about what a proud and determined man he is. 'The spring is the most horrible season of the year,' he said, then fled to a café. You have to know your own mind, isn't that right? You see, spring makes me jumpy too. I also get confused by the fair, if trivial memories and feelings it awakens. The difference is that I can never bring myself to curse and condemn spring itself, for the fact is that I feel ashamed of myself because it's so pure and natural and triumphant in its youth. And I don't know whether I should envy Adalbert or look down on him for lacking any such sensibility . . .

"It's hard to work in spring, true enough. Why? Because one feels. And only the rank amateur believes that a creative artist is allowed to feel. That's the naivest of beginner's mistakes, one which would raise a smile from any genuine and honest artist—a smile of melancholy perhaps, but smile nonetheless. The main point is never what you want to say. Quite on the contrary, what you want to say is nothing more than the essentially indifferent raw material from which the aesthetic work is put together, with distance, playful but calmly aloof. If you care too much about what you're saying, if you have too soft a heart for it, you're assured of a total fiasco. You become mawkish, you become sentimental, the product of your hands will turn out clumsy, ponderous, ungainly, unironic, bland, tedious and banal, and nothing but your audience's indifference and your own disappointment and heartbreak will be the result . . . That's the way it is, Lizaveta: emotion—warm, sincere emotion—is always banal and useless. It's not artistic. The only things that are artistic are the thrills and cold ecstasies that act upon our corrupt artists' nerves. You have to be both inhuman and extrahuman, you have to maintain a strangely remote, detached relationship toward humanity in order to be able, or indeed even tempted, to try this game, to play at the creation of vivid, artistic depictions of human life. A talent for style, composition and turns of phrase requires this sort of cool, discriminating relationship toward humanity; in fact it presupposes a certain human impoverishment and stultification in the artist himself. For healthy, strong emotion has no taste, and never will. The artist is finished as soon as he becomes a human being and begins to feel. Adalbert knew this and that's why he took refuge in a café, in his 'well-removed sphere,' yes indeed!"

"Well, God be with him, *batushka*," said Lizaveta, washing her hands in a tin basin. "You don't have to follow him."

"No, Lizaveta, I'm not going to follow him, if only because now and then, in the face of spring, I'm still capable of feeling slightly ashamed of my artistic pursuits. You know, sometimes I receive letters from strangers, words of praise and gratitude from my readers, admiring messages from people who have been deeply moved. I read these messages, and my heart is stirred at the warm, ungainly human emotion that has been elicited by my work. A kind of pity comes over me for the enthusiastic naiveté speaking from the lines, and I blush at the thought of how disillusioned these upright citizens would be if they could ever peek behind the curtains, if they in their innocence ever grasped that the last thing a proper, healthy, respectable person does is write, act or compose music . . . none of which prevents me from using their admiration of my genius for encouragement and inspiration, from treating it with massive seriousness, from putting on the face of the ape pretending to be the great man . . . Oh, don't interrupt, Lizaveta! I'm telling you that I'm sick and tired of depicting humanity without sharing in it . . . Is an artist even a man? Ask any woman! It seems to me that to some degree we artists share the lot of those specially equipped papal choirboys . . . We sing with heartrending beauty. But—"

"You should feel a little ashamed, Tonio Kröger. Now come have some tea. The water will be boiling any minute, and here are some *papirosi*. You were talking about soprano singing; please continue. But you should be ashamed. If I didn't know how proud you were of your career, how passionately dedicated . . ."

"Don't say a word about my 'career,' Lizaveta Ivanovna! Literature is anything but a career; it's a curse—there you have it. When does it first make itself felt, this curse? Early on, terribly early on. At an age when you could easily still be living in peace and harmony with God and the world. You start to feel marked out, mysteriously opposed to the others, the ordinary ones, the normal ones, the gulf of irony, skepticism, disagreement, insight and sensitivity separating you from everyone else gapes ever wider, you grow isolated, and from then on communication becomes impossible. What a fate! Assuming your heart still has enough life and *love* left in it to comprehend the horror! . . . Self-consciousness swells up in you like an infection. Alone among thousands, you feel the mark upon *your* forehead and sense its unmistakable obviousness to all. I once knew an actor of great genius, who had to struggle against pathological shyness and insecurity in real life. A hyperactive sense of ego made this man, who was both an accomplished artist and an impoverished human being, into a neurotic whenever he lacked a role, whenever he had nothing to depict . . . Anyone who can see two feet in front of his nose can look into a crowd and pick out the artist—a genuine one, that is, not someone whose societal profession is art, but someone called and condemned to it. The feeling of being separate, of not fitting in, of being the center of attention, a simultaneously regal and embarrassed expression, sits in the face. Something similar can be observed in the features of a prince walking in civilian clothing through the masses. Civilian clothing is of no use, Lizaveta! Disguise yourself, wrap yourself completely, dress yourself like a diplomat or an off-duty guards lieutenant: you can hardly look up and speak a single word, before everyone knows that you aren't a human being, but something strange, alien, different . . .

"So *what is* an artist, then? No question has more bitterly demonstrated humanity's complacency and intellectual laziness than this one. 'That sort of thing is a gift,' good people will say, humbly, when they're under an artist's spell. And because in their benevolent opinion whatever has an uplifting and edifying effect must naturally have uplifting and edifying origins, no one objects that they are talking about an extremely limited, extremely dubious 'gift.' . . . Everyone knows artists are easily offended—well, everyone also knows that this tends not to be the case for people with a clear conscience and a solid foundation of self-confidence. You see, Lizaveta, at the bottom of my soul—to transfer things to that realm—I have the same basic *suspicion* of the artist as a human type that any of my honorable forefathers in our cramped city up north would have had toward a traveling minstrel or vagabond entertainer who happened to intrude upon his house. Listen to this. I know a banker, a gray-haired businessman, who has a talent for writing short stories. He indulges this talent in his spare time, and what he writes is often quite excellent. In spite—I say 'in spite'—of this sublime ability, the last thing this man possesses is a clean record; on the contrary, he at one time had to endure a long and indeed justified stretch of incarceration. It was in prison that he first became aware of his artistic gift, and the experience of being a prisoner is the basic theme of all his works. You might draw the somewhat impudent conclusion that you have to have done some sort of hard time in order to become a writer. But don't you also suspect that his experiences in that house of correction might have had less in common with the roots and origins of his artistic talent than *whatever it was that put him there in the first place*?—A banker who writes short stories, that's a rarity, right? But a non-felonious, utterly reputable banker who writes short stories—*there's no such thing* . . . You laugh, but I'm only half joking. There is no question, no question in the world, more agonizing than that of artistic talent and its influence on human beings. Take the most remarkable creation of the most representative and therefore most influential artist. Take one as morbid and as profoundly ambiguous as *Tristan and Isolde,* and watch the effect this work has on a young, healthy person with decidedly normal sensibilities. You will observe edification, renewal, warm, honest enthusiasm, perhaps inspiration for his own 'artistic' pursuits . . . the good dilettante! What actually goes on inside us artists, however, is entirely different than anything the dilettante with his 'warm heart' and 'honest enthusiasm' might imagine. I've seen artists swarmed by admiring women and youngsters, while I *knew* . . . One is always making—as far as the origin, symptoms and conditions of artistic talent go—the strangest discoveries . . ."

"About others, Tonio Kröger—you'll pardon me for asking—or not just about others?"

He didn't respond. He knitted his slanting brows and whistled to himself.

"Give me your cup, Tonio. It's not strong. And have another cigarette. Besides you're well aware that you don't have to see things that way . . ."

"That's the answer Horatio gave, dear Lizaveta. 'Twere to consider too curiously to consider so.' That's it, isn't it?"

"What I'm saying is that you can see things just as curiously from another perspective. I'm just a stupid woman who paints, and if I'm at all capable of responding, of defending your own profession against you, what I come up with won't be anything new, but only a reminder of what you already know yourself . . . Things like the cathartic and enobling effect of literature, the taming of the passions through knowledge and words, literature as a means to understanding, tolerance and love, the liberating power of language, the literary imagination as the most exalted manifestation of the human spirit and the writer of literature as fully realized human being, as saint—isn't it to consider curiously enough to consider *so*?"

"You have a right to say such things, Lizaveta Ivanovna, considering the work of your national writers, the astonishing literature of Mother Russia, which to a great degree actually does represent the sacred literature of which you speak. But your objections aren't new to me; on the contrary they are part of what is on my mind today . . . Look at me. I hardly look overly exuberant, do I? A little old and craggy and tired, right? Well—and here we return to the question of 'knowledge'—it's easy to imagine someone innately credulous, gentle and benevolent, perhaps a little sentimental, who would simply be worn down and destroyed by psychological insight. Not to let yourself be overwhelmed by the sadness of the world; to observe, to register, to take account of even that which is most painful and keep your spirits, your confidence in your own moral superiority over all the horrible things this life invents—very well and good. But occasionally, despite all the joys of the well-turned phrase, it gets to be too much. To understand is to forgive? I'm not so sure. There is something I call knowledge-sickness, Lizaveta: the condition in which no sooner does a person see to the bottom of something than he feels sickened to death by it and is not at all inclined toward reconciliation. This was the case with Hamlet, Prince of Denmark, that typical writer of literature. He knew what it meant to be called to knowledge without actually being born to it. To see things clearly despite an emotional veil of tears, to have to recognize, observe and then discard with a smile, even during those moments when hands are being held, lips are finding one other, and the human gaze, blinded by emotion, is failing—it's shameful, Lizaveta, it's contemptible and outrageous. But what's the use of outrage?

"Another equally charming side of the matter, of course, is blasé indifference, ironic exhaustion with truth itself. The fact speaks for itself that nowhere in the world is human society more silent and hopeless than in a circle of intellectuals who have been through the works. To them all knowledge is old hat and boring. If you should share some truism in whose acquisition and possession you have perhaps taken a certain youthful enthusiasm, your vulgar enlightenment will raise nothing more than a brief snort . . . Oh yes, literature causes fatigue, Lizaveta. In ordinary human society it can happen, I assure you, that your skepticism and intellectual reticence can be mistaken for stupidity, whereas you are actually just too high and mighty, and too dispirited, for opinions . . . So much for 'knowledge.' As for 'words': aren't they less a matter of unburdening yourself than of cooling yourself off and putting your feelings on ice? In all seriousness, there's something chilling and outrageously presumptuous about the brusque and superficial way that literary language deals with feelings. If your heart is too full, if you feel too moved by a certain sweet or sublime experience, nothing could be simpler! You just go to the writer of literature, and in no time everything will be taken care of. He'll analyze your situation, formulate it, call it by name, articulate it, make it explicit; he'll deal with the whole thing for you once and for all, turn it into something of utter indifference and not even accept your thanks in return. You'll go home relieved, cooled off and clearheaded, wondering what it was that could ever have disturbed you and caused such sweet confusion. Do you seriously want to defend this cold, conceited old witch doctor? Whatever is made explicit, in his articles of faith, is dealt with. If the whole world is made explicit, it's been dealt with, resolved, disposed of . . . Very well! But I'm no nihilist . . ."

"You're no . . ." said Lizaveta . . . She had been lifting a small spoonful of tea to her mouth but had stopped, frozen in this position.

"Not at all . . . not at all . . . come to your senses, Lizaveta! I'm not, I tell you, not where living emotion is concerned. You see, the writer of literature is incapable of understanding that life might just go on living, without shame, even after it has been made explicit and 'dealt with.' Just look! It persists in its sins, despite being resolved by literature, undeterred. But then all action is sin in the eyes of the literary imagination . . .

"I'm almost finished, Lizaveta. Hear me out. I love life—this is a confession. Receive and preserve it—I've never shared it with anyone else. It's been said, it's even been published that I hate and fear and despise and abhor life. I liked hearing this—it was flattering—but that doesn't make it any less false. I love life . . . You smile, Lizaveta, and I know why. But I implore you: don't mistake what I'm saying for literature! Don't think of Cesare Borgia or any philosophy of intoxication that lifts him upon its shield! He means nothing to me, Cesare Borgia. I put no stock in him whatsoever and will never understand how something extraordinary, even demonic can be worshipped as an ideal. 'Life'—the eternal antithesis of human imagination and art—reveals itself to us, the unconventional, not as a vision of bloody greatness and wild beauty, not as anything unconventional itself. The normal, the respectable and the affable are the realm of our longing, are life itself in all its seductive banality! It is no artist, not by a long shot, dear friend, who is ultimately most excited by the sophisticated, the eccentric and the demonic, who knows no longing for innocence, simplicity and vitality, for a bit of friendship, indulgence, intimacy and human happiness—the covert and all-consuming longing for the joys of ordinariness! . . .

"A human friend! Would you believe that I would be proud and happy to possess a single human friend? Thus far all my friends have been demons, kobolds, subterranean monsters and ghosts of silent knowledge—in other words, writers of literature.

"Occasionally I end up on some podium before a room full of people who have come to hear me speak. And do you know what? It happens in such situations that I catch myself glancing around the audience, discreetly searching the auditorium with a question in my heart: who is it who has come here, whose grateful applause is making its way to my ears, with whom has my art forged this idealistic bond? . . . I never find what I seek, Lizaveta. I find that herd and congregation with which I'm already so familiar, ever reminiscent of an assemblage of early Christians, the clumsy of body and the fine of soul, those who are always, so to speak, falling down, you understand what I mean, those for whom poetry is a form of gentle revenge on life. It's always the sufferers, the longers and the poor folks, never any of the others, the clear blue-eyed ones who have no need for the literary imagination . . .

"And in the end would it not be terribly inconsistent to wish it otherwise? It's a contradiction to love life and yet to try with all of your wiles to convert it to your own side, to win it over for the refinements and melancholies, for the whole sick aristocracy of literature. The realm of Art on earth is expanding, while that of health and innocence is shrinking. What's left of it should be most carefully conserved, and one should not try to seduce those who like stop-action photographs of horses into reading poetry!

"For, ultimately, could there be a more pathetic sight than that of life having a go at art? We artists despise no one more than the dilettante, the man of life who thinks that in his spare time, on top of everything else, he can become an artist. I assure you I have experienced this sort of contempt personally. Let's say I'm invited to a high-society party. There, amidst the eating, drinking and idle conversation, everyone getting along as well as can be, I find myself happy. I'm grateful for the chance to disappear for a while among harmless and upstanding people. Then suddenly (I've actually experienced this) an officer gets up—a lieutenant, a good-looking, solid man whom I would never consider capable of any action disgracing his uniform—and asks straight out for permission to share with those assembled some poems he has written. The host smiles uneasily and gives permission, and he carries out his plan, reading his work from a scrap of paper he has kept hidden in his coat pocket, something in homage to music and love, in short, something as deeply felt as it is unaffecting. Now I would ask anyone: a lieutenant! A gentleman of the world! Is it really necessary? Well, the inevitable follows: long faces, silence, a bit of strained applause and deep discomfort all around. The first thing I sense in myself is that I am also to blame for the disruption that this rash young man has brought upon the assembled company. There's no doubt that their contemptuous and suspicious glances are also aimed at me, for it is my trade that has just been botched. But the second thing is that this man, whose character and way of life have until just now elicited my utmost respect and admiration, is suddenly sinking down, down, down in my eyes . . . I'm seized by compassionate goodwill. I, along with a few other courageous and warm-hearted gentlemen, go over and offer him a few words. 'My congratulations, Lieutenant!' I say. 'What a marvelous talent you have! Yes, that was just delightful!' And I'm not far from patting him on the back. But are you supposed to feel patronizing in the presence of a lieutenant? . . . No one to blame but himself! There he stands, embarrassed, doing penance for the mistake of plucking even one single laurel from the tree of Art without paying for it with his life. No, there I'll stick with my colleague, the banker with the criminal record. — Well, don't you think I'm positively Hamletesque in my eloquence today, Lizaveta?"

"Are you finished, Tonio Kröger?"

"No. But I won't say another word."

"You've said enough already. — Are you waiting for an answer?"

"Do you have one?"

"I believe so. — I've listened to you closely, Tonio, from beginning to end, and I want to give you the response that fits everything you've said this afternoon, that solves the problem that has gotten you into such a state. Here it comes. The solution is that you, as sure as you're sitting there, are simply a bourgeois."

"Am I?" he asked, somewhat crestfallen.

"You see, it hits you hard, as it should. So let me soften my judgement somewhat, since that is possible. You're a bourgeois who's gotten off track—Tonio Kröger—a bourgeois who's gone astray."

—No reply. Then he stood up decisively and grabbed his hat and cane.

"I'm grateful to you, Lizaveta Ivanovna; I can now go home, comforted. *I've been dealt with.*"

5

At the beginning of autumn, Tonio Kröger said to Lizaveta Ivanovna:

"Well, Lizaveta, I'm off for a while. I've got to air myself out, get away and seek some wide open spaces."

"Well, where then, old man? Are you deigning to return to Italy?"

"Lord, don't give me any Italy, Lizaveta! Italy is of no interest at all to me—I almost despise it! It's been a long time since I imagined that was where I truly belonged. Art, right? Blue velvet skies, warm wine and sweet sensuality . . . The simple truth is I don't like it. I'll pass. The whole *bellezza* makes me nervous, and I can't stand all those terribly lively people down there with their dark animal way of looking at you. These Latins have no conscience at all in their eyes . . . On the contrary, I'm taking a short trip to Denmark."

"To Denmark?"

"Yes. And I have high hopes. It so happens that I never made it up there, despite spending my entire boyhood so close to the border. Nevertheless, I've always known and loved the country. I must have gotten this Nordic inclination from my father, since my mother was actually more one for the *bellezza*, inasmuch as she cared about anything at all. Think of the books written up there, those profoundly lucid books full of good humor—there's nothing better, I just love them. Think of Scandinavian cuisine, that incomparable cuisine, which can only be taken in strong salt air. I don't know whether I'll still be able to take it, even though I know some of it from my childhood since people where I'm from eat similar sorts of food. Think of the names they have! They're like adornments—many of them were also common where I'm from. Think of a name like 'Ingeborg'—it's like three notes plucked on harpstrings, it's pure poetry! And then there's the sea—they have the Baltic Sea up there! . . . In a word, I'm going *upward*, Lizaveta. I want to see the Baltic again and hear those names again and read those books in the places where they were written; I also want to stand on the terrace at Kronborg, where the ghost came to Hamlet and brought death and anguish upon the poor young prince . . ."

"How are you getting there, Tonio, if I may ask? Which route are you taking?"

"The usual one," he said, shrugging his shoulders and visibly blushing. "Yes, I'll be passing through my—my point of origin, Lizaveta, after thirteen years. That promises to be amusing."

She smiled.

"That's what I wanted to hear, Tonio Kröger. God be with you. Don't forget to write, you hear? I expect an eventful letter describing your trip to—Denmark . . ."

6

And Tonio Kröger traveled north. He traveled in style (since he liked to say that anyone whose internal problems were so much more taxing than those of other people had a right to a little external comfort), and he didn't rest until the spires of the cramped city where he had started out rose before him in the gray sky. There, he had a visit that was short and odd . . .

A dreary afternoon was already fading into evening when his train pulled into the narrow, sooty, so strangely familiar terminus; the smoke still condensed into clouds under the filthy glass roof and drifted back and forth in long wisps, just as it had long ago when Tonio Kröger, with nothing but scorn in his heart, had originally left this place. — He checked his luggage, arranged for it to be brought into his hotel and left the station.

Lined up outside were those black, two-horse city broughams which are so disproportionate in both width and height. He made no move to hail one; he only stared at them, as he stared at everything—the narrow gables and pointed spires that greeted him from above the adjacent roofs, the blond, naturally coarse people with their broad yet rapid accent all around—and there arose within him a nervous laughter that bore secret affinity to a sob. He proceeded on foot, walking slowly, fighting the damp wind that blew relentlessly in his face, crossed the bridge with the statues of mythological creatures on its balustrade and continued along the harbor for a stretch.

Good God, how tiny it all looked with its nooks and crannies! Had the narrow gable-lined streets here always risen at such a quaintly steep angle toward the city center? Ships' smokestacks and masts rocked softly in the windswept dusk over the dreary river. Should he go up that street, that one there, which led to the house that was foremost on his mind? No, tomorrow. He was too sleepy right now. His head felt heavy from traveling, and his mind was preoccupied by sluggish, nebulous thoughts.

Occasionally during the past thirteen years, especially when he had an upset stomach, he had dreamt of being at home again in the old, echoing house on that crooked little street and of his father, too, going on at him about his decadent way of life—a judgement that he could have only seconded. And his present situation was indistinguishable from one of those enchanting and indivisible dream tissues that can be difficult to identify as either illusion or reality, where one may even settle on the latter, if forced to decide, only to awaken after all in the end . . . He walked through the largely deserted, drafty streets, bending his head against the wind, plodding like a sleepwalker toward the hotel, the best in the city, where he intended to spend the night. Up ahead of him, a bowlegged man with a swaying sailor's gait carried a staff with a small flame at its tip and lit the gaslights.

What was with him? What was all that which smoldered so obscurely and painfully under the ashes of his fatigue without ever igniting into a clear flame? Silence, silence, not a word! No words! He would have liked to walk on further like that, in the wind, through the dusky, dreamily familiar streets. But everything was so cramped and close. In no time he was at his destination.

The upper part of the city had arc lamps, which at that very moment were switched on. There was the hotel, and lying in front of it were the two black lions that had put such fear into him as a child. They were still staring at each other with those strange sneezelike expressions on their faces; they seemed to have shrunk, however, in the intervening years. — Tonio Kröger passed between them.

Since he arrived on foot, he was greeted without much ceremony. The porter and a very elegant gentleman dressed in black who took care of the formalities and whose small fingers were constantly poking his cuffs back into his coat sleeves looked him over critically from head to toe, mustering his appearance, visibly endeavoring to determine his approximate social status, categorize him in terms of class and wealth and decide how much respect he was due. Unable to arrive at a satisfactory conclusion, they settled for a moderate level of courtesy. A waiter, a demure man with flaxen wisps for sideburns, a frock coat shiny with age and rosettes on his soft-soled shoes accompanied him two stories up to his quarters. It was a neatly furnished, grandfatherly room with windows affording a picturesque, medieval view in the twilight over courtyards, gables and the fantastic spires of the church, in whose vicinity the hotel was located. Tonio Kröger stood for some time in front of this window, then sat down with folded arms on the spacious sofa, knitting his brows and whistling to himself.

Light was brought up, and his luggage arrived. At the same time, the demure waiter laid a registration form on the table, and Tonio Kröger, head angled sideways, wrote out something resembling his name, occupation and home address. Then he ordered a small supper and continued to stare out from the corner sofa into nothingness. When his food was delivered, he left it sitting untouched for a time, finally ate a couple of bites, and then spent an hour pacing in his room, occasionally stopping and standing with his eyes closed. After that, in a series of slow movements, he undressed and went to bed. He slept late and had a number of jumbled, odd dreams full of longing.

When he awoke, he found his room suffused with bright sunshine. In confusion and haste, he figured out where he was, got up and opened the curtains. The already somewhat pale blue of the late-summer sky was streaked by thin, wind-stretched wisps of cloud, but nonetheless the sun was shining over his hometown.

He took more care getting ready than usual, washing up and shaving quite meticulously, trying to look fresh and neat, as though paying a visit to a well-bred, proper household where it was imperative to make a tidy, irreproachable impression, and as he rummaged around getting dressed, he listened to the anxious beating of his heart.

How bright it was outside! He would have felt more at ease if yesterday's dusk had still lain upon the street; now he would have to walk in broad daylight under the eyes of the people. Would he run into old acquaintances, would they stop him on the street and ask questions, would he have to tell them how he had spent the past thirteen years? No, thank God, no one knew him anymore, and anyone who did remember wouldn't recognize him, for he really had changed a great deal in the meantime. He examined himself carefully in the mirror and suddenly felt safer behind his mask, behind the prematurely overworked face that looked older than its years . . . He ordered breakfast and then went out, went out under the appraising eyes of the porter and the elegant gentleman in black, through the lobby, between the two lions and into the open air.

Where was he going? He hardly knew. It was the same as yesterday. No sooner did he find himself surrounded by this curiously dignified, ancient amalgamation of gables, spires, arcades and fountains, no sooner did he feel the wind blowing in his face again, that strong wind which carried with it a delicately sharp aroma from distant dreams, than a veil and tissue of fog seemed to befall his senses . . . The muscles in his face relaxed, and with suddenly calm eyes, he observed people and things. Maybe over there, on that corner, he would finally wake up . . .

Where was he going? It seemed to him that the direction he took had something to do with his sad, strangely rueful dreams of the night before . . . He entered the main square, passed through the curved arches of the town hall, where butchers with bloody hands weighed their wares, into the marketplace proper, where the tall, Gothic fountain with its many spires was located. There he stopped in front of a house—a plain, narrow house like many others, with an openwork bell gable and stood lost in thought at the sight of it. He read the nameplate beside the door and let his eyes rest a short while on each of the windows. Then he slowly turned away and went on.

Where was he going? Toward home. But first he made a detour, strolling out past the city gate, because he had time. He walked along *Mühlenwall* and *Holstenwall*, holding on firmly to his hat against the wind that rustled and creaked among the trees. Then, not far from the train station, he forsook the levees to watch a train puff by in unceremonious haste and idly counted the number of cars, his eyes following the man who sat atop the very last one. Arriving at *Lindenplatz*, he stopped before one of the handsome villas, peered for a long while into the yard and up at the windows and finally hit upon the idea of swinging the iron gate back and forth on its hinges so that it squeaked. For a moment he stared at his hand, which was cold and covered with rust, then went on his way, proceeding through the squat old city gate along the ships' landing and up the steep, drafty little street to his family's house.

There it stood, surrounded on all sides by the neighboring ones, over which its great gable towered, as gray and somber as it had been for three centuries, and Tonio Kröger read the pious maxim carved in half-obliterated letters over the entrance. Then he took a deep breath and walked in.

His heart was pounding anxiously, for as he passed the doors on the ground floor, he could imagine his father, in a bookkeeper's jacket, with a pen behind his ear, emerging, stopping him and strictly demanding an explanation for his extravagant way of life—a demand that he would only have seconded. But he made it past these doors unmolested. One in front of him, which kept out the drafts, wasn't truly shut, only pushed closed. This he found objectionable, yet he also had the sensation, common in certain shallow dream states, of all impediments giving way of their own accord, allowing one to press forward unhindered, abetted by some fabulous string of luck . . . The large, square stonework in the front hallway echoed with his footsteps. Opposite the kitchen, where all was still, several unusual, crudely fashioned but neatly stained wooden cubicles still protruded as in the old days a considerable distance up the wall: the maids' quarters, accessible from the floor only by a kind of exposed ladder. The large cabinets and the carved chest that had stood on this spot were no longer here . . . The son of the house climbed the massive staircase, steadying himself with his hand on the whitewashed wood of the openwork railing, raising it with one step, then letting it gently drop with the next, as if bashfully testing to see whether his former intimacy with the solid old banister could be reestablished . . . He paused, however, on the landing in front of the entrance to the mezzanine. On the door was a white sign with black letters reading "Public Library."

Public library? Tonio Kröger thought, musing that neither literature nor the public had any place here. He knocked on the door . . . A voice said, "Come in," and Tonio Kröger obeyed. Tense and grim, he looked into the room and saw a most unbecoming transformation.

The mezzanine extended through three rooms, whose connecting doors all stood open. The walls were covered almost up to the ceiling with identically bound volumes arranged on dark shelves in long rows. In each one of the rooms, behind a kind of shop counter, sat a miserable-looking person, writing. The furthest two merely turned their heads toward Tonio Kröger, but the first hastily stood up, braced himself with both hands on the counter, craned his neck, pursed his lips, raised his eyebrows and took in the visitor with eagerly blinking eyes . . .

"Pardon me," said Tonio Kröger, not taking his eyes off the many books. "I'm a stranger on a tour of the city. So this is the public library? Would it be allowed to take a quick look at your collection?"

"With pleasure!" said the librarian, blinking even more rapidly . . . "Certainly, it's open to everyone. Do you just want to have a look around . . . Do you require a catalogue?"

"No, thank you," answered Tonio Kröger. "I'll get my bearings soon enough." With that he began to walk slowly along the walls, pretending to study the titles on the spines of the books. Finally he took down a volume, opened it and sat down by the window.

This had been the morning room. This was where they had eaten breakfast every day, not in the large dining room upstairs with the white statues of gods emerging sharply from the blue-background wallpaper . . . The next room had served as a bedroom. His father's mother had died there, struggling to the bitter end despite her age, for she was a pleasure-loving lady of the world who clung to life. That was where his father too had breathed his last, that tall, correct, somewhat melancholy and pensive gentleman with the wildflower in his buttonhole . . . Tonio had sat at the foot of his deathbed, his eyes burning with tears, genuinely and completely overcome by an inarticulate but powerful emotion, overcome with love and anguish. His mother had also knelt down by the bed, his beautiful, fiery mother, and had broken out in passionate weeping, only to go off not long thereafter with that Mediterranean musician into the wild blue yonder . . . And the third room there in the back, the smaller one, now likewise full of books guarded by some miserable-looking person, had for many years been his own. There was where he had returned after school, after one of those walks like just now. Against that wall, the desk had stood in whose drawer he had stored his first, heartfelt, hapless attempts at poetry . . . The walnut tree . . . A stab of melancholy ran through him. He glanced off to the side out the window. The garden lay in a state of neglect, but the old walnut tree still stood where it always had, creaking ponderously and rustling in the wind. And Tonio Kröger allowed his eyes to wander back to the book he was holding in his hands, an outstanding literary work he already knew quite well. He glanced down at the black lines and groups of sentences, followed the artful rhythm of the words for a while as they swelled with vivid passion toward epiphany and effect, then likewise successfully receded . . .

"Yes, that's nicely done," he said, laying aside the literary work and turning around. He saw that the librarian was still standing there blinking his eyes, partly from eagerness to be of service, partly from speculative mistrust.

"I see you have an excellent collection," said Tonio Kröger. "I already feel I have an overview. I'm much obliged. Adieu." With that he went toward the door, but his departure was hesitant, and he clearly sensed that the librarian, made uneasy by his visit, would continue to stand there blinking for some minutes to come.

He had no desire to press any further. He had been home. He could see that strangers now lived in the large rooms upstairs behind the columned hall, for the landing was closed off by a glass door that had not been there before, with some name printed on the attached sign. He turned away, went down the stairs, passed through the echoing main hall and left his boyhood home. Alone with his thoughts in the corner of a restaurant, he ate a heavy, rich meal and then returned to his hotel.

"I'm finished here," he said to the elegant gentleman in black. "I'm leaving this afternoon." He ordered his bill, as well as a cab to bring him to the landing where the steamer was to sail for Copenhagen. He then returned to his room and sat down at the table, sat silent and stiff, resting his chin on his hand, gazing with unseeing eyes at the tabletop. Later he settled his bill and packed his things. At the appointed hour his cab was announced, and Tonio Kröger, ready to depart, descended the staircase.

On the ground floor, at the foot of the stairs, the elegant gentleman in black was waiting for him.

"Forgive the interruption!" he said, his little fingers poking his cuffs back into their sleeves . . . "Pardon me, sir, but I must take up a minute of your time. Mr. Seehaase—the owner of the hotel—has asked to have a word or two with you. A formality . . . He's back there . . . Would you please be so good as to follow me . . . It's just Mr. Seehaase, the owner of the hotel."

And with a number of encouraging gestures, he led Tonio to the rear of the lobby. There indeed stood Mr. Seehaase—Tonio Kröger recognized him from the old days. He was short, fat and bowlegged. His closely cropped whiskers had turned white, but as always he wore a wide-cut frock coat and a little velvet cap embroidered with green. What's more, he wasn't alone. Next to him, behind a small lectern attached to the wall, stood a helmeted policeman, his gloved right hand resting before him on a document covered with various notations, his honest soldier's face peering at Tonio Kröger as if he expected the traveler to sink into the ground under his stare.

Tonio Kröger glanced from one to the other and decided to wait for them to begin conversation.

"You come from Munich?" the policeman finally asked in an amiable, if coarse voice.

Tonio Kröger reaffirmed this.

"You're on your way to Copenhagen?"

"Yes, I'm taking my vacation at a resort on the Danish coast."

"Coast?—Yes, well, you must have some identification you can produce," said the policeman, pronouncing the word with special satisfaction.

"Identification . . ." He had no identification. He took out his billfold and looked through it, but there was nothing inside except some banknotes and the proofs of a short story he had planned to check over once he'd reached his ultimate goal. He disliked all contact with postmasters and had never been issued a passport . . .

"I'm very sorry," he said, "but I don't have any identification with me."

"Is that so?" said the policeman . . . "None at all?—What's your name?"

Tonio Kröger answered him.

"Is that your real name?!" asked the policeman, who straightened up and suddenly flared his nostrils as wide as he could . . .

"Certainly," answered Tonio Kröger.

"What are you then?"

Tonio Kröger swallowed and stated his occupation in a firm voice. — Mr. Seehaase raised his head and looked up at him with curiosity.

"Hm!" said the policeman. "So you claim that you are not the same person as a certain indivigial named—" He pronounced the word "indivigial," spelling out from the document with the various notations a bewilderingly exotic name, which seemed to be an experimental syllabic compound of various national languages and which Tonio Kröger would have been hard pressed to reconstruct a second later. "—an indivigial," the policeman continued, "of unknown origin and no fixed address who is sought by the Munich police in connection with a number of frauds and other offenses and is believed to have taken flight for Denmark?"

"I don't just claim it," said Tonio Kröger with a nervous motion of his shoulders. — That made a definite impression.

"What? Oh yes, I see, sure!" said the policeman. "But you can't produce anything to confirm it!"

Attempting to disarm the situation, Mr. Seehaase interposed.

"The whole thing is just a formality," he said, "nothing more! You must realize that the officer is just doing his duty. If you could only prove somehow that you are who you say. A single piece of identification . . ."

No one said a word. Should he put an end to the matter by introducing himself, by revealing to Mr. Seehaase that he was not some con artist with no known address, not some gypsy in a green wagon by birth, but the son of Consul Kröger, of the Kröger family. No, he had no desire to do that. And weren't they right in a way, these representatives of bourgeois law and order? In one sense he completely agreed with them . . . He shrugged and said nothing.

"What do you have there then?" asked the policeman. "There in the portfoolio?"

"Here? Nothing. Just a proof," answered Tonio Kröger.

"Proof? Huh? Let me see."

And Tonio Kröger handed him his work. The policeman spread it out on the surface of the desk and began to read through it. Mr. Seehaase walked over and joined him in this activity. Tonio Kröger looked over their shoulders to see where they were in the story. It was a good passage, one he had successfully worked through, a moment of real epiphany and literary effect. He felt satisfied with himself.

"Look," he said. "There's my name. I wrote this, and now it's going to be published, you understand?"

"Well, that's good enough!" said Mr. Seehaase emphatically, scooping up the pages, folding them and giving them back. "That must be good enough, Petersen!" he repeated curtly as he surreptitiously shut his eyes and shook his head to close the issue. "We must not cause the gentleman any further delay. His cab is waiting. Please forgive this little interruption, sir. The officer was just doing his duty, though I told him right off that he was on the wrong track . . ."

Is that so? thought Tonio Kröger.

The policeman didn't seem fully satisfied; he objected, saying something about "indivigial" and "identification." But with repeated expressions of regret Mr. Seehaase led his guest back through the lobby, escorted him through the two lions to his cab and insisted with profuse displays of respect on personally closing the door behind him.

And then the ridiculously disproportionate brougham cab began to roll, shaking, rattling and raising a din, down the steep narrow streets to the landing . . .

Thus ended Tonio Kröger's odd visit to his hometown.

7

Night had fallen with a swimming silvery glow, and the moon was on the rise as Tonio Kröger's ship gained open sea. He stood at the bow, wrapped in his overcoat against the gathering wind, and stared down into the dark drifting and rolling of the smooth muscular bodies below, as they circled one another, slapped together, then sprang back in unexpected directions with a sudden glimmer of froth . . .

He was suffused with swaying, silent bliss. He had been somewhat dejected at the thought of being mistaken for a con man in his own hometown—although in one sense he could only second the thought. But later, on board, he had watched the cargo being loaded, just as he and his father had done when he was a boy, had heard the men shouting out in a mix of Danish and Lowland German dialects while filling the ship's deep hold and had also seen them lowering down, along with the usual bales and crates, two thick-barred cages containing a polar bear and a king tiger, which had no doubt been shipped up from Hamburg, to be forwarded on to some Danish zoo. This had taken his mind off his sadness. By the time the ship had begun to glide downstream along the flat embankments, he had forgotten his interrogation by Officer Petersen, and everything that had come before—the sweet, sad, regretful dreams of the previous night, his walk, the sight of the walnut tree—once again grew strong within his soul. And in the distance, now that the banks were opening up, he recognized the beach where as a boy he had been permitted to listen in on the sea's summer dreams, saw the shine of the lighthouse and the lamps of the resort in which he had stayed with his parents . . . The Baltic Sea!

He bent his head against the strong salt wind that blew in free and unobstructed, that whipped around his ears and produced a gentle vertigo, a vague numbness, which submerged the memory of everything bad—pain and confusion, desire and ambition—in lethargic bliss. And amidst the whistling, slapping, frothing and sighing all around him, he thought he could make out the rustling and creaking of the old walnut tree, the squeaking of a garden gate . . . It was getting darker and darker.

"The staahs, Lord, just look at the staahs," a voice said suddenly in a Northern accent and a ponderous singsong rhythm that might have issued from a large, empty barrel. He recognized it immediately. It belonged to a reddish-blond, plainly dressed man with red eyelids who looked damp and cold, as if he had just come in from a swim. At dinner in the ship's mess he had sat next to Tonio Kröger, where, with a series of modest, unassuming maneuvers, he had consumed an extraordinary quantity of lobster omelet. Now he stood beside him, leaning on the railing and looking up at the heavens, his chin pinched between his thumb and index finger. No doubt he found himself in one of those extraordinary, solemnly tranquil moods in which the barriers between people are lowered, in which the heart opens up to strangers and the mouth utters sentiments it would otherwise find embarrassing . . .

"Look, sir, just look at the staahs. All aglitter, by god, the whole sky's full of them. Let me ask you: looking up at the sky, knowing that many of these staahs are supposedly a hundred times bigger than the earth, how does it make you feel? We human beings have invented the telegraph and the telephone and so many newfangled scientific wonders, to be sure, we've done that. But when we look up at the sky, we are forced to recognize and understaand that we are still worms, pathetic little worms and nothing more—am I right or am I wrong, sir? Indeed, we're nothing but worms!" he said, answering himself as he nodded, humble and contrite, at the firmament above.

Oh please . . . no, this man doesn't have an ounce of

literature in him, thought Tonio Kröger. And in that instant he was reminded of something he'd recently read, an essay by a famous French writer comparing cosmology and psychology. That had been a really fancy bit of palaver.

He gave the young man something resembling an answer to his heartfelt remark, and then they continued their conversation, leaning out over the railing and staring into the uneasy evening, lit by turbulent waves. It turned out that his companion was a young businessman from Hamburg, who was using this cruise as a vacation . . .

"You should take a little steamaah trip to Copenhagen," he said. "No sooner do I think this than I'm standing here. So far, so good. But lobstaah omelet, that was a mistake, you wait and see, sir: this will be a staahmy night, the captain said it himself, and with such heavy food in your staamach, it's not going to be an easy trip . . ."

Tonio Kröger listened to all this solicitous nonsense with concealed affection.

"That's true," he said. "The food up here is altogether too heavy. It makes one listless and depressed."

"Depressed?" the young man repeated, giving him a dumfounded look . . . "You're a stranger here then?" he asked suddenly . . .

"Oh yes, I come from a long way off!" Tonio Kröger answered with a vague, evasive arm motion.

"Anyway you're right," said the young man. "God knows, what you said about depressed is exactly right. I'm almost always depressed, but especially on nights like this when the staahs are in the sky." And he rested his chin once more on his thumb and index finger.

Surely he writes poems, thought Tonio Kröger, honest, heartfelt businessman's poems.

It was getting late and the wind had now grown so powerful that it impeded further conversation. Therefore they decided to catch a bit of sleep and wished each other good night.

In his berth Tonio Kröger stretched out on the narrow

bunk but couldn't drift off. The strong wind and its sharp aftertaste had left him extremely flushed, and his heart was restless, as though he were anxiously awaiting something sweet. Moreover, the vibrations from the ship sliding down a steep ocean swell and the propeller as it emerged sputtering from the water made him terribly queasy. He got dressed again and climbed up onto the open deck.

Clouds raced past the moon. The sea was dancing. No longer were smooth, even waves rolling at regular intervals; instead, at some distance in the pale, flickering light, the sea was torn, whipped, churned into a frenzy. Gigantic, sharp-crested tongues licked up like flames, leaping skyward, hurling spray and spitting out jagged, unlikely shapes between froth-filled chasms, as though somewhere below monstrous tentacles were playing some crazy game. The ship's passage was slow. Pounding, swaying and sighing, it worked its way through the tumult, and at times the polar bear and the tiger could be heard growling in the hold, for the ship's motion made them ill. A man in a slicker, his hood pulled up over his head and his lantern strapped around his waist, walked back and forth on deck. His feet were set wide as he struggled to maintain his balance. There in back, bent far over the ship's side, was the young man from Hamburg getting sick. "Lord," he said in a hollow, trembling voice, as he spotted Tonio Kröger, "just look at the elements. All in an uproar, sir!" But then he was interrupted and hastily turned away.

Tonio Kröger held tight to the nearest taut line and gazed out into the unfettered exuberance. A cry of jubilation gathered inside him that almost felt strong enough to drown out the wind and the waves. A hymn to the sea, inspired by love, began to sound in his soul. *Untamed friend from when I was young, now again we are as one . . .* but that was as far as it went. The poem had never been finished, never been roundly formed or calmly forged into a whole. His heart was alive . . .

For a long time he stood there like that; then he stretched out on a bench beside the small ship's housing and gazed up at the sky, where the stars flickered. He even dozed off a bit. And when the cold froth occasionally sprayed in his face, it seemed, in his half-sleep, like a caress.

Vertical limestone cliffs, ghostly in the moonlight, came into view and approached; that was Moen Island. And again he dozed off, roused periodically by salty showers of spray that stung at his face and numbed his features . . . By the time he was completely awake, it was already morning, a light gray, refreshing morning, and the green sea had calmed down. At breakfast he again saw the young businessman, who turned quite red, apparently embarrassed at having uttered, under the cover of darkness, such shamefully poetic sentiments. He brushed his small red moustache with upward strokes of all five fingers and barked out a brisk morning greeting, like a soldier, only to avoid his companion anxiously thereafter.

And so Tonio Kröger landed in Denmark. He arrived in Copenhagen, giving a tip to anyone who acted as if he had a claim to one, and explored the city from his hotel for three days, holding his guidebook open before him and behaving like a genteel foreigner wishing to enhance his knowledge. He took in the Kongens Nytorv with the horse in the center, gazed respectfully at the pillars of the Fruekirke, stood for a long time before Thorwaldsen's noble and charming sculptures, climbed to the top of the Circular Tower, visited castles and spent two lively evenings in the Tivoli. But this was not really what he saw.

Many of the houses had exteriors with openwork bell gables exactly like the older ones in his home town, and on their doorplates he recognized many of the names from those days, names that seemed to signify something delicate and priceless to him, yet nonetheless also brought a kind of recrimination, reproach and longing for what had been lost. And everywhere he went, inhaling the damp sea air in deliberate, pensive breaths, he saw eyes that were as blue, hair that was as blond, and faces that were of exactly the same type and shape as those he had glimpsed in his unusually tormented, remorseful dreams during that one night in his home town. It happened several times that, in the middle of the streets, a glance, a melodic word, a peal of laughter cut him to the quick . . .

He didn't hold out for long in this cheerful city. Unrest—sweet and foolish, part recollection and part expectation—drove him on, along with the need to lie peacefully on the beach rather than to play the role of the avid sightseer. So one gloomy day (the sea turned black) he boarded another ship and sailed north along the coast of Zealand toward Elsinore. There he continued his journey without delay by carriage, traveling three quarters of an hour along the main coastal road, never more than a short distance above the sea, until he reached his final and true destination amidst a small settlement of low-lying houses, the small white beachfront hotel with green shutters, whose shingled tower looked out upon the sound and the Swedish coastline. He disembarked, took possession of the sunny room reserved for him, filled the shelves and cupboards with the things he had brought along and prepared to live for a while in the place.

8

September was almost over, and there were not many visitors left at Aalsgaard. Meals were taken in the large, ground-floor dining room with its open crossbeams and its tall windows looking out on the enclosed veranda and the sea. The proprietress headed the table, an elderly spinster with white hair, colorless eyes, faintly rosy cheeks and an uncertain warble of a voice, who constantly twiddled her red hands, trying to find a somewhat advantageous pose for them on the tablecloth. Also present was an old gentleman with a short neck, an icy gray sailor's beard and a dark bluish face, a fish merchant from the capital who spoke German. He seemed to be afflicted with congenital congestion and suffered periodic sinus attacks, for he would occasionally put a ringed index finger up to one of his nostrils, press it shut and snort vigorously through the other to clear the passages. This didn't prevent him, however, from constantly addressing the aquavit bottle that was kept in front of him at lunch and dinner, even at breakfast. Lastly there were three tall American boys together with a chaperon or tutor who always tugged at his glasses, never said anything and spent his days kicking around a ball with them. Their reddish blond hair was parted in the middle, and their faces were long and expressionless. "Please give me the *wurst*-things there!" one of them would say in English. "That's not *wurst*, that's *schinken*!" one of the others would reply—that was all they and their tutor ever contributed to mealtime conversation. Otherwise they just sat mute, drinking warm water.

Tonio Kröger could not have wished for better company. He enjoyed the peace and quiet: he would take in the guttural consonants and bright, sorrowful vowels of the Danish language during the brief conversations between the fish merchant and the lady of the house, occasionally exchange a couple of words with the man about the current state of the barometer and then excuse himself, walking through the veranda down to the beach, where he spent many an idle morning hour.

Sometimes it was still and summery there. The sea lay lazy and smooth in blue, bottle-green and reddish streaks, with sparkling reflections of silvery light playing over its surface, as the seaweed withered to hay in the sun and jellyfish dried out in the sand. It always smelled slightly of decay and also slightly of tar from the fishing boat against which Tonio Kröger leaned so as to have the open horizon, not the Swedish coast, in view while he sat in the sand. But the gentle breath from the sea nonetheless swept pure and fresh over everything.

And then there were gray, stormy days. The waves lowered their heads like bulls preparing their horns for the charge and ran furiously at the beach, awash and covered with dripping-wet seaweed, mussels and driftwood. Between the long swells great troughs formed, pale-green and frothy under the overcast sky, while there beyond the clouds, where the sun was shining, a bright velvet gleam blanketed the water's surface.

Tonio Kröger stood surrounded by the roaring of the wind and surf, absorbed by this timeless, profound, deafening din he loved so very much, and when he turned to go, everything around him suddenly seemed so calm and warm. But at his back he always sensed the sea, calling out its greetings, tempting him. And he smiled.

He walked inland across the solitude of fields and was soon swallowed by beech forest, such as stretched out for miles over this hilly region. He sat down on a bed of moss and leaned against a tree, so positioned that a strip of ocean was visible through the other trunks. Now and then the wind carried over the noise of the surf, a sound like distant wooden planks falling against each other. Crow caws above the treetops, hoarse, desolate and forlorn . . . he held a book propped upon his knees but didn't read a single line. He savored a deep oblivion, floating weightlessly over space and time, and only occasionally did his heart shudder with sorrow, pierced by a short stab of longing or regret, whose name and origin he was too lethargic and distracted to question.

Many a day passed like this, although he couldn't have said how many and felt no need to find out. Then, however, came a special day when something different took place. It took place under sunny skies and in the presence of others, and Tonio Kröger wasn't even particularly amazed.

The day even began as something festive and delightful. Tonio Kröger awoke very early, quite abruptly, his sleep broken by a delicate, indefinite anxiety, to the sight of a miracle, a display of light conjured up by magic fairies. His room, which had a glass door, a sound-facing balcony and a thin white gauze curtain between the living and sleeping areas, was papered in delicate colors and decorated with small, cheery furniture: thus it always looked bright and hospitable. But at that moment, it had been supernaturally transfigured and illuminated before his sleepy eyes, dipped again and again in an ineffably fair and misty rose-colored light that gave the walls and furniture a golden tint and made the gauze curtain glow in mild pink . . . For a long time Tonio Kröger couldn't comprehend what was happening. But as soon as he went to the glass door and looked outside, he saw that it was the sun on the rise.

It had been overcast and rainy for several days, but now the sky was spread out like tightly spanned, pale-blue silk, shimmering and clear, over land and sea. The sun, streaked and bordered by clouds shining red and gold, rose solemnly above the flickering ripples of the water, which seemed to shudder and begin glowing beneath it . . . That was how the day began, and, dumbfounded with joy, Tonio Kröger threw on his clothes, ate breakfast before everyone else downstairs on the veranda, swam for some distance in the sound in front of the small wooden changing hut, then took an hour's walk on the beach. When he returned to the hotel, several omnibus carriages stood out front, and from the dining room he could see, both in the adjacent piano parlor and on the terraced veranda, great numbers of people in basic middle-class attire sitting at round tables consuming buttered bread and beer and carrying on animated conversations. There were whole families present, with older and younger members, even a few children.

At his second breakfast—the table was heavy with cold dishes, smoked goods, salted foods and pastries—Tonio Kröger inquired what was going on.

"Guests!" said the fish merchant. "Visitors from Elsinore on an excursion, ball guests. Yes, God help us, we won't get any sleep, not tonight! There'll be dancing, dancing and music, and you have to think it will go on for quite some time. It's a family gathering, a country outing followed by a reunion back here, essentially a package deal, or something similar, to take advantage of the nice weather. They've come by boat and carriage, and now they're eating breakfast. Later they're going on a bit further by land, but they'll return this evening for dancing and other amusements here in the dining room.

Yes, damn it all to hell, we won't be able to sleep a wink . . ."

"It's a nice change," said Tonio Kröger.

After that nothing more was said for quite some time. The proprietress fidgeted with her red fingers, the fish merchant snorted through one nostril to clear the passages and the Americans drank warm water and stared with their long faces.

Then all of a sudden it happened: *Hans Hansen and Ingeborg Holm walked through the dining room.* —

Tonio Kröger, pleasantly tired from his swim and brisk walk, was reclining in a chair eating smoked salmon on toast—he sat facing the veranda and the sea. Suddenly the door opened, and the two of them entered, hand in hand, leisurely strolling. Ingeborg—blonde Inge—was dressed in bright colors, just as she usually had been during Mr. Knaak's dance lessons. She wore a lightweight floral dress above the ankle, and around her shoulders was a broad white tulle collar with a low neckline that exposed her soft, supple throat. Her hat was dangling from its two tied ribbons from one of her arms. She had perhaps gotten a bit larger since then, and her fabulous ponytail was now braided around her head, but Hans Hansen was the same as ever. He was dressed in his fisherman's jacket with the golden buttons, its wide blue collar folded back over the shoulders, and in one hand he held his sailor's cap by its short straps, swinging it back and forth at his side without a care. Ingeborg kept her long horizontal eyes averted, probably vaguely embarrassed at the stares of the diners. Hans Hansen, however, turned toward the breakfast buffet, his head straight and defiant, his steel blue eyes measuring each of the guests in turn, mustering them with a certain contempt. He even let go of Ingeborg's hand so that he could swing his cap back and forth more vigorously, to demonstrate what kind of a man he was. Thus, against the backdrop of the calm sea growing ever bluer, the two of them passed before Tonio's eyes. They walked the length of the dining room and disappeared through the opposite door into the piano parlor.

This happened at around eleven-thirty in the morning, and while the regular hotel guests remained seated over their breakfast, the party in the next room and on the veranda got up and departed. They left the hotel by the side door, which also served as an entrance and exit, not one of them setting foot in the dining room proper. They could be heard getting into their carriages, joking and laughing, and then came sounds of one vehicle after another beginning to grind its way down the gravel road and into the distance . . .

"So they're coming back?" asked Tonio Kröger.

"That they are!" said the fish merchant. "And it's a crying shame. They've arranged for music, I should point out, and I sleep directly above the dining room."

"It's a nice change," Tonio Kröger repeated. Then he stood up and went.

He spent the day as he had spent all the others, on the beach and in the woods, propping a book on his knees and squinting into the sun. He thought of only one thing, that they would return and that there would be dancing and other amusements in the dining room, as the fish merchant had promised. He did nothing else but look forward to it with the sort of anxiously sweet anticipation he hadn't once felt in all these long lifeless years. At one point that day, thanks to some chain of associations, he briefly recalled a distant acquaintance, the writer Adalbert, who had known what he wanted and had taken refuge in a coffeehouse to escape the spring air. And he shrugged his shoulders at the memory . . .

Both dinner and the small evening supper were served earlier than usual, the latter in the parlor, since preparations for the dance were already underway in the dining room itself. In this festive way the normal order of things was disrupted. Then, after it had gotten dark and Tonio Kröger had returned to his room, there was activity once more on the road and in the lobby. The day guests were returning from their excursion; in fact, new visitors were arriving by bicycle and carriage from the direction of Elsinore, and downstairs one could already hear a violin being tuned and a clarinet running through its nasal-toned exercises . . .

From all indications it was going to be a splendid ball.

The small orchestra now struck up a march: though muted, the music with its steady tempo drifted upstairs. Dancing was commenced with a polonaise. Tonio Kröger sat quietly for a while and listened. But as soon as the march rhythm gave way to a waltz, he got up and slipped silently from his room.

From the hallway on which it was located, a second flight of stairs led to the side entrance of the hotel where, without passing through any of the ground-floor rooms, one could reach the glass veranda. This was the route he took, quietly and surreptitiously, as if traveling down forbidden paths, feeling his way carefully through the darkness, irresistibly attracted by the unthinking, divinely swaying rhythm of the music, whose tones already sounded loud and distinct in his ears.

The veranda was empty and unlit, but the glass door was open to the dining room, where the two large paraffin lamps with the polished mirrors cast a bright glare. He crept forward on tiptoe, and his skin prickled with furtive thrill at standing there in the dark observing the people as they danced in the light. He glanced all around frantically, his greedy eyes searching out the two of them . . .

Although the ball was only a half an hour underway, it was already in full swing. The ice had been broken, no doubt, and the guests' communal enthusiasm whipped up, even before they arrived by a whole day spent, carefree and happy, in one other's company. In the parlor, which Tonio Kröger was able to survey whenever he ventured forward a little, several older gentlemen had taken their drinks and cigarettes and had gotten up a game of cards. Other men sat with their wives on upholstered chairs in front and along the dining-room walls and watched the dancing. They rested their hands on outspread knees and puffed out their cheeks in well-being, while their female counterparts stared with folded arms into the whirling mass of young people, their bonnets high on their angled heads. A platform had been set up along one of the side walls, and on it the musicians were giving their best. There was even a trumpet, which sounded undeniably hesitant and wary, as though the instrument were afraid of its own constantly breaking and cracking voice . . . Couples were swaying and spinning, circling each other, while others promenaded through the room, arm in arm. The company wasn't formally attired, but rather dressed for a summer Sunday outing in the country: the gentlemen in suits of rustic cut obviously reserved for weekends, the young ladies in bright, thin dresses with wildflower garlands on their bodices. There were also a few children present, dancing amongst themselves in their own way even when the music stopped. A long-legged fellow in a sparrow-tailed evening jacket—some provincial bigwig with a monocle and sun-bleached hair, a junior postmaster or something similar, not unlike a stock comic figure from a Danish novel come to life—seemed to be the master of ceremonies and the king of the ball. Assiduous, perspiring and wholeheartedly on the job, he was everywhere at once. He scurried with an excess of industry throughout the room with the most elaborate of walks—putting his weight first on the toes, then on the balls of the feet, which were encased in polished military half-boots with pointed tips and which he set down one outside the other in crisscross pattern. He waved his arms in the air, issued orders, called for music and clapped his hands, with the ribbons of a large, colorful sash fluttering in his wake. It had been pinned to his shoulder as a sign of his special office, and he often turned his head to gaze at it lovingly.

And they were there, the couple who had passed by Tonio Kröger earlier that day in the sunlight. He saw them again and trembled with delight as he took them both in with almost one gaze. Here stood Hans Hansen, quite nearby, beside the door. With his body inclined slightly forward and his legs apart, he was methodically tearing off bites from a large piece of sponge cake, holding one hand cupped under his chin to catch the crumbs.

And over there along the wall sat Ingeborg Holm—blonde Inge—who was at that very moment being asked to dance by the junior postmaster, who skipped up to her with a cultivated bow, placing one hand behind his back and clutching the other gracefully to his breast. She shook her head, however, indicating that she was too short of breath and would have to rest for a bit, whereupon the junior postmaster sat down beside her.

Tonio Kröger stared at them, at the two people for whom in olden days he had suffered love: Hans and Ingeborg. It was them—not so much because they possessed certain individual characteristics or wore similar clothing as because they belonged to the identical breed and species, that bright species of steel-blue eyes and blonde hair which automatically called to mind purity, unspoilt innocence, good cheer and a simultaneously proud and simple, ultimately unapproachable superiority . . . He watched them, watched Hans Hansen stand there as smart and handsome as ever in his sailor suit, broad in the shoulders and thin at the waist, watched Ingeborg toss her head sideways in a particular exuberant way as she laughed and then characteristically lift her hand—the not especially slender or delicately formed hand of a mere girl—to the back of her head so that her thin sleeve slid up from the elbow. And suddenly his heart trembled with such intense homesickness that he instinctively retreated a bit into the darkness to hide his twitching face.

Had I forgotten you two, he asked himself. No, never! Not you, Hans, nor you, blonde Inge! You were the ones for whom I labored, and whenever I received applause, I always looked around discreetly to see if you were among my admirers . . . Have you read *Don Carlos* yet, Hans Hansen, as you promised by your garden gate? Don't bother! I no longer require it of you. What do you have to do with the lonely, tearful king? Don't dull your bright eyes. Don't cloud them with dreams by staring at melancholy poems . . . Oh, to be like you! To start again and grow up as you did, upright, happy and simple, correct, ordinary and in harmony with God and the world. To be loved by harmless, happy people, to make you my wife, Ingeborg Holm, to have a son like you, Hans Hansen—to live untouched by the curse of knowledge and the torment of creativity, to live and love and laud in blessed ordinariness! . . . Start over? It wouldn't help. It would still be the same—everything would turn out just the same. Many people go astray because, for them, there is no right way.

The music stopped. There was a break, and then refreshments were served. The junior postmaster himself scurried around with a tea tray full of herring salad, offering it to the ladies. When he got around to Ingeborg Holm, however, he also sank to one knee as he extended the dish, causing her to blush with delight.

Those in the dining room had begun by now to notice the observer by the glass door, and he was met by alienated looks from their handsome, flushed faces. Nevertheless, he held his ground. Ingeborg and Hans glanced briefly over at him too, almost simultaneously, with that attitude of absolute indifference which almost has the appearance of contempt. Suddenly, however, he became aware of another gaze from somewhere else that had searched him out and was now upon him . . . He turned his head, and immediately his eyes encountered those whose contact he had sensed. Standing not far away was a young girl with a pale, narrow, fragile face, whom he had already noticed before. She had hardly danced, the gentlemen hadn't paid her much attention, and he had watched her sit alone against the wall, her lips pressed bitterly together. She stood alone now too. She wore a bright, frilly dress like the others, but beneath its transparent material, her bare shoulders stood out miserably and bony, and her scrawny neck was sunk so deep between these pathetic shoulders that the quiet girl almost seemed slightly deformed. She held her hands in their thin short gloves before her flat chest so that their fingertips gently touched. Her head bowed, she looked up at Tonio Kröger with dark, watery eyes. He turned away . . .

Here, quite near him, were Hans and Ingeborg, together. He had sat down next to her—she was probably his sister—and surrounded by the other rosy-cheeked youngsters, they ate and drank, chatted and joked, teased each other and laughed out loud in bright peals. Could he not approach them briefly? Could he not address one or the other with a spontaneous witty remark, which would require at least a smile in answer? It would thrill him, and he longed for it. He could then return to his room with greater satisfaction, happy in the knowledge that he had established a bit of common ground with them. He thought of something he could say, but he didn't have the courage to say it. Here too it was the same as ever: they wouldn't understand him, they would only listen to what he had to say in embarrassed silence. For their language was not his.

The dancing seemed ready to resume. The junior postmaster was in full industrious swing. He scurried around, made everyone present choose a partner, helped the waiter clear away chairs and glasses, issued instructions to the musicians and pushed at the backs of several greenhorns who didn't know where to go. What were they planning? Every four couples formed a square . . . A horrible memory made Tonio Kröger blush. They were dancing the quadrille.

The music commenced, and the couples bowed, advanced and swapped partners. The junior postmaster called out instructions. Good heavens! He called them out in French, pronouncing the nasal vowels with peerless sophistication. Ingeborg Holm was dancing right in front of Tonio Kröger in the square beside the glass door. She was swaying side to side before him, stepping and turning, forward and backward. Her hair—or maybe it was the delicate white material of her dress—gave off an aroma that occasionally reached him, and he closed his eyes to savor an emotion he knew so well from the past, whose scent and sharp aftertaste he had for many a day now been vaguely able to sense. It flooded him again in this moment with all its sweet duress. What was it? Longing? Tenderness? Envy? Self-contempt? . . . *Moulinet des dames!* Did you laugh, blonde Inge, did you laugh at me when I danced the *moulinet* and made such a wretched fool of myself? And would you still laugh today, now that I've become something of a famous man? Indeed you would, and it would be entirely right of you to do so! Even if I had composed the Nine Symphonies, written *The World as Will and Representation* and painted *The Last Judgement*—you would be eternally right to laugh . . . He stared at her, and a line of poetry occurred to him, which he hadn't thought of in a long time yet which remained so familiar and close to his heart: "I would sleep and yet you must dance." He knew it so well, the Nordic melancholy, the introverted and awkward depression that spoke from this line. To sleep . . . To long for the possibility of living simply, wholly according to the feelings that lay sweet and idle within one's heart, not responsible for transforming them into action, into dance. And yet being forced to dance, to perform, nimbly and quickwittedly, the ever-so-difficult sword dance of art, never entirely forgetting the humiliating senselessness of having to dance when one was in love . . .

All of sudden everything began to speed up, becoming pure movement, giddy and reckless. The squares had dissolved, and everyone was running in leaps and bounds: the quadrille was to be concluded with a *gallopade*. The pairs raced past Tonio Kröger to the music's frantic tempo, sashaying, rushing, tripping over each other's heels with gasps of breathless laughter. One pair was coming his way, swept along by the whole chase, spinning and howling forward. The girl had a pale, delicate face and bony protruding shoulders. And suddenly, right in front of him, someone stumbled, slipped, then dropped . . . The pale girl fell down. She fell with a hard, heavy thud that almost looked dangerous, and the gentleman came down with her. The latter must have suffered such serious injury that he forgot all about his partner, since after getting halfway up he began to grimace and rub his knee, leaving the girl still lying on the floor, seemingly quite stunned from her fall. At this point Tonio Kröger stepped forward, grasped her gently under the arms and helped her up. Exhausted from the chase, confused and distraught, she looked up at him, and suddenly a dull red blush spread across her cheeks.

"Tak! O mange Tak!" she said, head down, staring up at him with dark, watery eyes.

"You should take a break from dancing, Miss," he said gently. Then he looked around once more for *them*, for Hans and Ingeborg, and departed, quitting the veranda and the ball and going upstairs to his room.

He was euphoric from the festivities, in which he had taken no part, and exhausted with jealousy. It had been like before, just like before! He had stood in the shadows with a flushed face, suffering because of you—you blond, vivacious, happy types—and then had left, alone and lonely. Someone had to come. Ingeborg had to come now, had to notice that he wasn't there, had to follow him secretly, lay her hand on his shoulder and say: "Come back inside and join us, don't be sad, I love you!" But she didn't come, of course. Things like that just don't happen in reality. Yes, it was like before, and he was happy like before. For his heart was alive. What had been going on the whole time he'd spent becoming who he now was? — Petrifaction, desolation, ice and imagination! And art! . . .

He got undressed, lay down in bed and turned off the light. He whispered the two names into his pillows, those few chaste Nordic syllables which signified for him his own particular innate form of loving, suffering and being happy—signified life itself, simple heartfelt emotion, the feeling of home. He looked back on all the years leading up to this day. He considered the barren adventure of sense, nerve and thought he had undergone, watched himself being eaten away by irony and imagination, stultified and hobbled by knowledge, erased in part by the fevers and frosts of creativity, helplessly beset by crises of conscience and tossed back and forth between crass extremes, between saintliness and lust, overrefined, impoverished and exhausted by cold, arbitrary moments of ecstasy, lost, ravaged, martyred, ill—and he sobbed with regret and homesickness.

All around him it was quiet and dark. But from downstairs the sweet, banal waltz of life drifted up to him, muffled and lilting.

9

Tonio Kröger sat up north writing, as promised, to his friend Lizaveta Ivanovna.

"Dear Lizaveta, down there in Arcadia, to which I shall soon be returning," he wrote. "Here is something resembling a letter, one that will no doubt disappoint you, for I intend to keep it on the general side. Not that I don't have anything to tell or haven't had a few experiences in my own way. Back where I come from, in my hometown, they even tried to place me under arrest . . . but you should hear about that from me in person. I have days now when I prefer to speak in well-chosen generalities than to tell stories.

"Do you still recall how you once called me a bourgeois, a bourgeois gone astray? You called me that at a time when, carried away by other confessions that I had let slip, I told you of my love for what I call 'life.' I wonder whether you knew then how right you were. My bourgeois nature and my love of life are indeed one and the same—this trip has given me the opportunity to reflect on that fact . . .

"My father, you know, was of Nordic temperament: deliberate, thorough, puritanically correct and inclined toward melancholy. My mother was of indefinite exotic blood, beautiful, sensuous, naive, at once reckless and passionate, capable of impulsive, disreputable behavior. Without doubt this was a combination that harbored extraordinary possibilities—and also extraordinary dangers. What came out of it was a bourgeois gone astray in art, a bohemian homesick for his boyhood room, an artist with a bad conscience. For it is my bourgeois conscience that makes me see in everything artistic, extraordinary and brilliant something deeply ambivalent, suspicious and dubious. It is that which fills me with love-smitten weakness for the simple, faithful and pleasantly normal, for the uninspired and the respectable.

"I stand between two worlds, feel at home in neither and as a result face great difficulties. You artists accuse me of being a bourgeois, and the bourgeois would just as soon put me under arrest . . . I don't know which hurts worse. The bourgeois may be stupid; but you devotees of beauty who dub me phlegmatic and passionless should consider that there is a form of artistic talent so profound, so innately and inalterably fated, that no longing seems sweeter and more worthy than that for the joys of an ordinary existence.

"I admire those proud, cold adventurers who wander the paths of magnificent, demonic beauty and despise 'humanity'—but I don't envy them. For if there is anything capable of turning a writer into a poet, it is this bourgeois love of mine for the ordinary, the life-affirming, the human. It is the wellspring of all warmth, all goodness and all humor; I even fancy that it is that very love, without which, it is written, one can speak with the tongues of angels and men and still be nothing more than a sounding brass or tinkling cymbal.

"What I have done so far is nothing, not much, next to nothing. I will do better, Lizaveta—that's a promise. As I write, the sea rushes up to me and I shut my eyes. I gaze into an unborn, as yet sketchy world that longs to be organized and shaped. I look upon a great mass of shadows with human form that motion for me to capture them and set them free. Some are tragic, some comic, some are both at once—and it's to these I'm greatly drawn. But my deepest and most secret love belongs to the blonde-haired and blue-eyed, the bright life-affirming ones, the happy, the likeable and the ordinary.

"Do not scorn this love, Lizaveta; it is good and fruitful. There is longing in it and somber jealousy and a tiny bit of contempt and an entire paradise of innocence."

The Child Prodigy

The child prodigy enters—the ballroom goes silent.

It goes silent, then the people start applauding because somewhere off to one side a born commander, a leader of the pack, has decided to put his hands together. Although they have yet to hear a thing, they applaud with approval, for a powerful advertising machine has been promoting the child prodigy, and the people are already under its spell, whether they know it or not.

The child prodigy walks out from behind an elegant Chinese screen embroidered with Empire-style wreaths and fantastically large flowers. He climbs nimbly up the steps to the podium and enters into the applause as one enters into a bath, shivering a bit, chilled by a slight shudder, but nonetheless recognizing it as a friendly element. He advances to the edge of the podium, smiles as though about to be photographed and acknowledges the applause with a brief, bashful, charming curtsy, although he's a boy, not a girl.

He's dressed entirely in white silk, which sends a small thrill throughout the ballroom. He wears a small white silk jacket of the most incredible cut with a sash underneath; even his shoes are made of white silk. In stark contrast to his white silk knickers, however, the skin of his short legs stands out deep brown: the boy is Greek.

He's called Bibi Saccellaphylaccas. He actually is. Which Christian name corresponds to "Bibi" no one knows except the impresario, and he considers it a trade secret. Bibi has dark, flat hair, which hangs down to his shoulders but which is nonetheless parted to the sides, kept back from his small, brownish, protruding forehead by a thin silk ribbon. He has the face of a child with a half-defined nose and an innocent mouth, as guileless as anything in the world; the area under his jet-black mouselike eyes alone is somewhat dull, bordered by two character-providing wrinkles. He looks about nine but in reality is only eight and is advertised as being seven. The people themselves don't really know whether to believe his announced age. Probably they know better and believe it anyway, as people are accustomed to do in so many situations. A little lying is part of beauty. What, they think, would become of the personal edification and elevation that follows the everyday grind, if they weren't willing to show a bit of indulgence and let two plus two equal five. And in their everyday minds, they're entirely correct!

The child prodigy keeps on curtsying until the introductory clamor settles down. Then he proceeds to the piano, and the people cast one last glance at the program. First comes *marche solennelle,* then *reverie* and then *le hibou et les moineaux*—all by Bibi Saccellaphylaccas. The entire program is by him: they are his own compositions. He can't actually write them out in musical notation, but they are all contained within his extraordinary little head, and their artistic value is undeniable, as is asserted, seriously and objectively, on the fliers the impresario has had made up. It would seem that the impresario has only wrung this admission from his critical nature after a long struggle.

The child prodigy sits down on the piano stool, his little feet fishing around for the pedals, which thanks to a clever mechanism have been positioned much higher than normal so that Bibi can reach them. It is his personal piano, which he takes along wherever he goes. It stands on wooden sawhorses, and its polish is quite scratched from the constant transport, but all that only makes for a better show.

Bibi places his white silk-clad feet on the pedals; then he makes a small, exacting face, stares straight ahead and raises his right hand. It is the brownish, naive little hand of a child, but the wrist is strong, its well-practised bones not at all childlike.

Bibi makes this face for the people, knowing that he has to entertain them a bit. For his part, he also takes pleasure in this act, a pleasure that he could never describe to anyone else. It is the prickling happiness, the secret shudder of delight that comes over him every time he sits in front of an open piano—he will never lose it. Once more the keyboard offers itself up to him, these seven black-and-white octaves among which he has lost himself so many times before, in adventure and thrilling tests of fate, octaves that nonetheless appear again as pure and as untouched as a well-erased chalkboard. It is music, the whole of music, that lies before him! It lies spread out before him like an inviting ocean: he can dive in and swim to his liking, let himself be borne up and swept away and submerged in storm, yet still retain control, keeping everything in his own firmly governing and ruling hands . . . He holds his right hand suspended in the air.

A breathless silence falls over the ballroom, the moment of anticipation before the first note . . . How will it begin? This is how it begins: Bibi's index finger draws the first tone from the piano, a middle-register tone of entirely unexpected power, reminiscent of a trumpet blast. Others then join it, an introduction takes shape—the people relax their limbs.

It's a splendid ballroom, situated in a stylish hotel of the best sort, with rosy, flesh-filled paintings on its walls, proud columns, mirrors in scrollwork frames and a myriad, a virtual solar system of electric lights that protrude on all sides in umbels, in whole bunches, and bathe the ballroom in a tremulous, brighter-than-day light, thin, golden, heavenly . . . There is not a single empty seat—people are even standing in the aisles and at the back. Up front, where the seats cost twelve marks (the impresario being a firm believer in prices that impress), high society sits in rows, for among the highest circles there is a lively interest in the child prodigy. Uniforms are everywhere, as is fine taste in cosmetics and *accoutrements* . . . A number of children are also present, sitting well-behaved, their legs dangling from their chairs, eyes gleaming as they watch their small gifted colleague in his white silk . . .

The mother of the child prodigy—an extremely corpulent lady with a powdered double chin and a feather on her head—sits up front on the left next to the impresario, an Oriental-looking gentleman with large gold buttons on his wide-cut sleeves. In the middle of the front row sits the princess. She is a small, wrinkled, shrunken old princess, but also a reliable patron of the arts, so long as they are delicate in sensibility. She sits in a deep velvet *fauteuil*, with Persian rugs spread at her feet. Her hands folded tightly at the breast over her gray-striped silk evening gown, her head angled to one side as she watches the child prodigy at work, she is the very picture of noble tranquility. Next to her sits her lady-in-waiting, herself clad in a green-striped silk evening gown—although she's only a lady-in-waiting and isn't even allowed to relax in her chair.

Bibi brings the piece to a splendid rousing conclusion. The little squirt handles the piano with such force! You can hardly believe your ears. The march theme, a lively and enthusiastic melody, emerges once more in full accompaniment, broad and boasting, and with every beat Bibi throws back his chest and shoulders, as though marching triumphantly in a parade. Then he finishes powerfully, pushes himself sideways off his stool, bowing, and awaits the applause with a smiling face.

And the applause erupts, unanimous, impressed, enthusiastic: just look what dainty hips the child has, performing his little curtsy up there. Clap, clap! Wait, let me take off my gloves. Bravo, little Saccophylax or whatever your name is—! What a brilliant little devil!

Bibi must reappear three times from behind the Chinese screen before the applause subsides. A few stragglers, late arrivals, push their way through the back rows and, with some difficulty, take their places in the packed ballroom. Then the concert resumes.

Bibi rattles through his *reverie*, which consists entirely

of arpeggios, a fragment of melody occasionally rising on weak wings; then he plays *le hibou et les moineaux*. The number is a resounding success and ignites the audience. It is wonderfully vivid, in the best tradition of children's music. In the bass you can picture the owl sitting, sullenly blinking his filmy eyes, while in the treble sparrows buzz around in skittish insolence trying to irritate him. Four times after this piece Bibi is brought out by applause. A hotel servant with shiny buttons carries three large laurel wreaths up to the podium and presents them to him from the side, while Bibi acknowledges the audience's applause. Even the princess joins in, bringing her open hands together so delicately that they make no sound at all . . .

This well-trained little creature sure knows how to get applause! He makes the public wait for him behind the Chinese screen, lingers a bit on the platform steps, feigns childish delight at the colorful satin ribbons on the wreaths (although long sick of them), acknowledges his audience with adorable bashfulness and allows the people time to clap themselves out, wasting none of the precious sounds produced by their hands. *Le hibou* is my crowd-pleaser, he thinks, using a favorite expression of his impresario. Still to come is the *fantaisie*, which is actually far superior, especially the part where it goes to C-sharp. You're all such fools for this *hibou*, my dear audience, even though the first and most infantile of my compositions. And he acknowledges the applause in his adorable way.

He plays a meditation and then an etude—it is a respectably varied program. The meditation sounds quite similar to the reverie, which is no criticism, and in the etude Bibi displays his technical proficiency, which incidentally lags somewhat behind his gift for composition. Finally the moment of the *fantaisie* has arrived. It's his favorite piece. He plays it a bit differently each time, treating it with a free hand, occasionally, when he's having a good night, surprising himself with new inspirations and turns.

Quite small and gleaming white before the huge black

piano, he sits and plays, alone, singled out on the podium above the indistinct mass of humanity with its single, dull, sluggish soul, upon which his privileged individual one is supposed to make an impression . . . His fine dark hair has fallen, together with the white silk ribbon, over his forehead, his strong-boned, well-exercised wrists are furiously at work, and you can see the muscles quivering through the baby fat on his brownish cheeks.

Occasionally there are moments of forgetting and remoteness when his unusual mouselike eyes with their dull rings drift off to one side, away from the audience and toward the painted ballroom wall, staring through it and beyond, losing themselves in a lively horizon filled with vague activity. But then he glances from the corner of one eye back into the ballroom, and he is once again in front of the people.

Lament and jubilation, hope and deep despair—my *fantaisie*! Bibi thinks lovingly. Listen, here comes the part where it goes to C-sharp! And he lets the shift in key to C-sharp resonate. Do they notice? No, of course not! And since they don't, he acts it out, gazing handsomely up at the ceiling, so they at least have something to see.

The people sit in long rows, watching the child prodigy. And in their everyday minds they think all kinds of things. An old gentleman with a white beard, a signet ring on his index finger and a bulbous growth on his bald head that might be called a deformity thinks to himself: Puts one to shame actually. Never got past "Three Hunters from Kurpfalz" myself, and here I sit, an old coot amazed by the things this little tyke can play. But you have to keep in mind that it comes from above. God distributes such gifts, there is nothing you can do about it, and there's no disgrace in being an ordinary person. It's much the same thing with the baby Jesus. One is allowed to bow down before a child and not feel any shame. How uncommonly good it feels! — He doesn't dare to think: how sweet! — "Sweet" would be shameful for a powerful old man to think. But that's how he feels. That's how he feels nonetheless.

Art . . . thinks the businessman with the parrot nose. I'll admit it gives life a bit of luster, a little do-re-mi and white silk. Besides, he's not doing too shabbily. There are at least fifty twelve-mark seats: that alone makes six hundred—and then all the rest. When you subtract the cost of renting the ballroom, the electricity and the programs, there must at least be a thousand marks left over. I'd bend over to pick that off the street.

That was Chopin he was playing just now! thinks the piano teacher, a needle-nosed woman at the age when hopes begin to slumber and judgement becomes sharper. One might well say he isn't very spontaneous. I'll remark afterward, "He's hardly spontaneous." That sounds good. Besides his hand position is utterly amateurish. One must be able to balance a silver dollar on the backs of one's hands . . . I'd correct that with a ruler.

A waxen-looking young girl, at that tender age when adolescents are often beset with awkward thoughts, thinks to herself: But what's this? What's he playing there? It's passion he's playing. But he's only a child! If he kissed me, it would be like my little brother kissing me—it wouldn't be a real kiss. Is there such a thing as emancipated passion, passion in and of itself, without any worldly object, a passion that is merely the ardent play of a child? . . . Enough! If I said this aloud, they'd get out the cod-liver oil. That's the way of the world.

An officer leans against a column. He observes Bibi in his triumph and thinks: you're something, and I'm something, each in his own way! He clicks his heels together, too, paying the child prodigy the same respect he pays all authorities.

On the other hand, the critic—an aging man in a threadbare black jacket and rolled-up, mud-splattered trousers—sits in his complementary seat and thinks: Just look at him, this Bibi, this little brat. As an individual he's only half-grown, but as a type he's already complete. He's a born artist. He already possesses the artist's superior airs and his lack of dignity, his love of swindle and his divine spark, his high-handed contempt and his private intoxication. I'm not allowed to write anything like that, though; it's too good. Oh, believe me, I would have become an artist myself, had I not seen through the whole charade so clearly.

The child prodigy is now finished, and a true storm begins to brew in the ballroom. Again and again he is compelled to emerge from behind the Chinese screen. The man with the shiny buttons drags over more floral arrangements, four laurel wreaths, a lyre of violets and a bouquet of roses. He doesn't have enough arms to hand over all the tributes to the child prodigy, so the impresario personally approaches the podium to help him. He hangs one of the laurel wreaths around Bibi's neck, affectionately tousles his dark hair, and suddenly, as if overwhelmed, bends down and gives the child prodigy a kiss, an audible kiss, directly on the lips. At that the storm swells into a true hurricane. This kiss traverses the ballroom like an electric shock, running through the crowd like a nervous shudder. The people are swept away by a crazed need for noise. Loud cheers mix with the wild clamor of hands. Several of Bibi's little comrades down below wave their handkerchiefs . . . But the critic thinks, of course there's a kiss from the impresario. A time-honored trick. Lord yes, if only I didn't see through the whole charade so clearly!

And then the child prodigy's concert comes to an end. It began at seven-thirty; at eight-thirty it's over. The platform is buried in wreaths; two small vases of flowers stand atop the lamp boards of the piano. Bibi's encore is his *rhapsodie grecque,* which eventually turns into the Greek national anthem, and his countrymen in attendance would be sorely tempted to sing along, if it weren't an elegant concert! They compensate with a mighty roar when it ends, a hot-blooded racket, a patriotic demonstration. Of course, thinks the aging critic, there had to be the national anthem. The whole thing is transferred to another level, with no means of exciting the audience left untried. I'll write that it isn't artistic. But maybe it is precisely artistic. What's an artist? A fool. Criticism is the highest pursuit. I'm not allowed to write that, though. The critic then departs in his mud-stained trousers.

After taking nine or ten bows the now red-faced child prodigy no longer ducks behind the Chinese screen, but proceeds directly to Mama and the impresario in the ballroom below. The people stand amidst the disarray of pushed-back chairs, applauding and surging forward to get a closer look at Bibi. Some also want to see the princess: two crowded circles form before the podium, one around the child prodigy, one around the princess, and it's impossible to tell which of the two is actually holding court. However, the lady-in-waiting, following orders, makes her way over to Bibi; she tugs gently at his silk jacket, smoothing it so that he is presentable, then leads him by the arm up to the princess and gravely signals for him to kiss Her Royal Majesty's hand. "How do you do it, child?" the princess asks. "Does it just appear in your head when you sit down?" — "*Oui, madame*," Bibi answers. But to himself he thinks, oh, you stupid old princess . . . ! Then he turns around, bashfully, without the proper courtesies, and goes back to his family.

Outside by the coatrooms a crowd throngs. People are holding up their numbers, and furs, shawls and galoshes are passed over the tables into their outstretched arms. Somewhere the piano teacher is standing among acquaintances offering her opinion. "He's not very spontaneous," she says loudly, glancing around . . .

In front of one of the large wall mirrors an elegant young lady allows her two brothers, both lieutenants, to help her on with her evening coat and fur-lined boots. She's fantastically beautiful with her steel-blue eyes and clear, purebred face: a genuine young noblewoman. When she's finished, she waits for her brothers. "Don't stand so long in front of the mirror, Adolf!" she says with quiet irritation to one of them, who can't seem to part from the reflection of his handsome, simple-looking face. Well, that's rich. Lieutenant Adolf will nonetheless—by her gracious indulgence—be permitted to button up his greatcoat before the mirror! Then they leave, and outside in the street, where the arc lamps shimmer gloomily in the snow and fog, Lieutenant Adolf begins to assert himself, doing a little Sambo's dance against the cold atop the solidly frozen snow, his collar turned up, his hands in his coat pockets.

A child! thinks the girl with the unstyled hair who, accompanied by a downcast young man, is walking along behind them, her arms swinging freely. An adorable child! What went on in there was a wondrous . . . And in a loud monotone voice she says, "We're all child prodigies, all of us who create."

Well now! thinks the old gentleman who has never gotten past "Three Hunters from Kurpfalz" and whose deformity is now concealed by a top hat. What do we have here? A kind of Pythia, it seems to me.

But the downcast young man, who understands her to the letter, nods slowly.

They then fall silent, and the girl with the unstyled hair stares ahead at the three aristocratic siblings. She despises them, but she stares after them until they have disappeared around the corner.

Hour of Hardship

He got up from the desk, from his rickety little *escritoire*, got up as though at the end of his wits and crossed the room with his head hung to the corner stove, which was as tall and thin as a pillar. He put his hands to its tiles, but they had nearly gone cold, for it was long past midnight. So, without having found the small comfort he had sought, he leaned back against it, coughed, drew together the tails of his house robe, its faded lace ribbon dangling from the lapels, and arduously snorted a little air through his nose to clear the passages. As usual, he was congested.

It was a special, ominous kind of congestion that almost never cleared up entirely. His eyelids were swollen and the edges of his nostrils sore, and throughout his body and head this congestion weighed down like a heavy, painful drunkenness. Or was it the tiresome routine of being confined to his room that was responsible for his lethargy and heaviness of limb? The doctor had again imposed this fate upon him some weeks ago, and God only knew if he had been correct to do so. His incessant catarrh and the cramps in his chest and lower body may have necessitated such confinement, and for weeks now—whole weeks, that was the truth—Jena had been suffering bad weather: miserable, despicable weather, weather you could feel in every nerve, desolate, dark and cold, weather that set the December wind howling in the stovepipe, abandoned and godforsaken, sounding of nocturnal heath in storm and madness, as well as irremediable anguish of soul. But it was no good, this close confinement, either for the thoughts or for the rhythm of the blood from which thoughts came . . .

The hexagonal room was sparse, sober and uncomfortable, with a whitewashed ceiling that trapped gentle wraiths of tobacco smoke, a tapestry of diagonal plaid against which oval-framed silhouettes hung, and four or five pieces of spindly furniture. It was lit by the two candles burning at the head of the manuscript atop the *escritoire*, and red curtains covered the upper frames of the windows, nothing more than little ship's flags of calico gathered up symmetrically on either side, but nonetheless red, a warm, rich red. He cherished them and would have bitterly regretted their absence, for they introduced the only hint of sumptuousness and sensuality into the unfeeling asceticism of the room . . .

He stood by the stove and directed a fleeting, strain-tormented squint over at the work from which he had fled, this burden, this weight, this stabbing of conscience, this sea to be swallowed, this terrible task that was his pride and his misery, his heaven and his damnation. It straggled along, it stumbled, it stopped—not again, not again! Surely the weather was at fault, or perhaps also the catarrh and his fatigue. Or was it the work itself? Or his work upon it? Was this a star-crossed conception, predestined to yield nothing but despair?

He had stood up in order to gain some objectivity, for spatial distance from the manuscript often gave him perspective, a more expansive view of the material, making it possible to take the appropriate measures. Indeed, there were instances when his feeling of relief at departing the arena of battle revitalized him. It was a more innocent form of revitalization than liquor or strong black coffee . . . His little cup was on the table. Could it help him overcome his block? No, no, no more! Not only the doctor, but a second, even greater authority had gently cautioned him against such things: it was none other than his counterpart over in Weimar, whom he loved with a rival's ardent enmity. *He* was wise. *He* knew both how to live and how to create, didn't abuse himself, treated himself with consideration . . .

Silence prevailed in the house. The only sounds were the whistling of the wind down the narrow *Schloßgaße* and the tapping of the rain being driven against the window. Everyone was asleep, the landlord and his family, Lotte and the children. And he stood lonely and awake by the cold stove, squinting with a tormented expression over at the work in which his own unhealthy perfectionism prevented him from believing . . . His white neck protruded starkly from his collar, and between the two tails of his house robe one could see his inwardly bowed legs. His red hair was brushed back from his delicate high forehead, exposing two pale-veined indentations at the temples, before falling in thin locks over his ears. At the base of his large Roman nose with its abrupt whitish tip, two thick, nearly connected eyebrows emerged, darker than the hair on his head, which made his sore, sunken eyes look as though they were tragically peering into the distance. Forced to breathe through his mouth, he held his thin lips continually parted, causing his cheeks, freckled and wan from stale indoor air, to slacken and sag . . .

No, it was a failure—it was all in vain! The army! The army would somehow have to be depicted! The army was the basis of everything! And it couldn't appear upon the stage—could one even conceive of the artistry gigantic enough to impress it upon the imagination? Moreover, the hero wasn't a hero at all; he was petty and cold! The basic conception was wrong, the language was wrong, and the whole thing was a dry, monotonous history lesson, diffuse, passionless, utterly unsuitable for the stage!

Very well, the game was up. A defeat. A misguided undertaking. A total bankruptcy. He felt the urge to write Körner and tell him, good old Körner, who believed in him, who subscribed with a child's faith to his genius. He would scoff, plead and rant—his friend. He would remind him of *Don Carlos*, which had also been born of doubt and hard work and revisions, and which had turned out, after all the torment, to be a thoroughly excellent work, a glorious achievement. But that was different. Back then he had still been the man to seize a problem with a happy hand and wring victory from it. Misgivings and struggle? Oh certainly. And he had been sick, probably even more so than now: a starveling, a fugitive, an outsider to the world, oppressed and destitute as a man. But young, still young! Every time, no matter how bent and bowed, his spirit had snapped back, resilient, and after the hours of woe had come others of faith and inner triumph. Those hours came no longer, came hardly at all. A single night of kindled enthusiasm in which he could glimpse in sudden brilliant illumination what could be, if only he were always so blessed, had to be paid for with a week of darkness and paralysis. He was tired, only thirty-seven years old yet already at the end. His faith was no longer alive, his faith in the future, the guiding light in his misery. That was the desperate truth: the years of privation and nothingness, which he had seen as his years of trial and tribulation, had actually been quite rich and fruitful, and now that a little luck had come his way, now that he had escaped his life as a literary pirate into some legitimacy and bourgeois recognition, now that he had obtained an official position and been awarded various honors, now that he had a wife and children, now he was used up and exhausted. Defeated and deflated—that was all that was left.

He groaned, pressed his hands to his eyes and paced as if pursued throughout the room. That thought just now had been so terrible that he could not bear to remain on the spot where it had occurred to him. He sat in a chair along the wall, dangling his folded hands between his knees, and stared gloomily down at the floorboards.

Conscience . . . how loudly his conscience cried! He was a sinner. He had sinned against himself all these years, sinned against the delicate instrument that was his body. The extravagances of bold youth, the nights worked through and the days spent in the smoky indoors, wantonly intellectual, heedless of body, the stimulants he had used to spur himself on to his labor—all of them were now coming back, coming back to exact their revenge!

But if revenge *was* being exacted, then he would spite the gods who assigned blame, then imposed punishment. He had lived as he had to live: he had no time for being wise, for being prudent. Here, in the chest, whenever he breathed, coughed or yawned, this pain, always in the same spot, this tiny, diabolical, stabbing, piercing reminder that had never once subsided in the five years since Erfurt, when he had contracted the catarrh, that raging chest fever: what was it trying to tell him? Truthfully, he knew only too well what it meant—the doctor could say what he would. He had no time to compromise on strategic abstinence, to mend his ways and become economical. Whatever he wanted to do, he had to do it soon, today even, quickly . . . Mend his ways and live right? Why was it that precisely his sin, his inclination toward the harmful and ruinous seemed more ethical to him than any wisdom or cold-blooded discipline? Living right wasn't a matter of wisdom or discipline, or the contempt-bringing practice of good conscience, but rather struggle and despair, passion and pain!

Pain . . . What a horizon this word opened in his chest! He stretched, arms folded, and from under the reddish, almost connecting eyebrows, his gaze came to life in gorgeous lament. He was not yet wretched, not utterly at least, as long as it was possible to name his wretchedness in proud and noble words. One thing was needed: the spirit to give his life great and beautiful names. Not to blame his suffering on smoke-filled rooms and constipation! To be strong enough for healthy *pathos*, to see, to feel something beyond the physical world! To be naive in this one respect, while knowing in all others! To have faith, have faith in pain. . . . And he did indeed have faith in pain, a deep, personal faith according to which nothing born of pain could be either useless or inferior. His glance flitted over to the manuscript, and his arms folded more tightly across his chest . . . Talent—was talent not itself pain? And if *that* there, that star-crossed project, caused him to suffer, was it not just as well, was it not almost a positive sign? Nothing had ever just poured out, and his mistrust would first commence in earnest if it did. Words only ever poured out of amateurs and dilettantes, the easily satisfied and the uninformed, those who didn't live under the strain and discipline of talent. For talent, ladies and gentlemen way back there in the cheap seats, talent isn't something light and trifling. It's not just pure, unadulterated ability. It is, at root, *need*, a critical awareness of the ideal that could be, a discontent that creates and hones its ability only in anguish. And for the greatest and most discontent, talent itself is the sharpest scourge . . . No complaining! No boasting! To think deferentially, patiently about what one bore! And if not a single day or hour of the week was free of suffering—what of it? To think little of the loads and labors, the demands, troubles and strains, to see them as *minor*—that was the essence of greatness!

He stood up, took out his snuffbox and inhaled greedily, then put his hands behind his back and paced so demonstratively through the room that the flames of the candles flickered in the draft . . . Greatness! Distinction! World success and the immortality of one's name! What was all the happiness of the forever unknown compared to this great goal? To be known—known and loved by the peoples of the world! Go ahead, talk of the addictive demands of the ego, you who know not the sweetness of this dream and compulsion! Such demands are common to all extraordinary talent, insofar as it suffers. Just you wait and see, talent says, those of you without a life's mission, those of you who have it so much easier on earth! And ambition, too, speaks: is my suffering to have been in vain? It must ensure my greatness!

His nostrils flared beneath his large nose; his eyes glowered and swept the room. His right hand was jammed deep in the lapel of his house robe, while his left dangled down, clenched. A fleeting redness had come over his haggard cheeks, pelted up like the tan of leather by the embers of his artistic ego, by that passion of self that burned unquenchably in the depths of his being. He knew it well, the secret intoxication of this love. Occasionally he only needed observe his hand in order to be suffused with enthusiastic affection for himself, in the service of which he vowed to employ those weapons of talent and art at his disposal. This was allowed, for there was nothing ignoble about it. Deeper still than egotism, there existed an awareness of being in the service of something greater, of consuming and sacrificing himself, admittedly out of necessity, not virtue, but selflessly nonetheless. And this was his most jealously defended point: that no one should be greater than he was without suffering more deeply for such lofty heights.

No one! . . . He stood still, his hand over his eyes, his upper body partially turned, evasively, as though trying to escape. Already he felt a certain unavoidable thought sting his heart, the thought of him, his counterpart, that bright, sure-handed, sensuous, divinely naive one, *that man* there in Weimar, whom he loved with a rival's ardent enmity . . . And again, as always, in profound agitation, in haste and zeal, he felt the beginning of that internal labor which followed from this thought: the assertion of his autonomous existence and artistic identity, separate from that of his counterpart . . . Was he then the greater? In what respect? Why? Would it be a Pyrrhic victory, if he triumphed? Would it make a tragic scene, if he succumbed in the end? A god, perhaps—a hero, he was not. It was easier, too, to be a god than a hero! — Easier . . . His counterpart had it easier! A wise and happy hand to distinguish knowledge from creativity might well make one cheerful and invulnerable and prodigious. But if creativity was divine, then knowledge was heroic, and that man who created knowingly was both: a god and a hero!

The will to hardship . . . Did anyone suspect how much discipline and self-control a single sentence, a single rigorous thought cost him? For ultimately he was ignorant and ill-educated: an obscure romantic dreamer. It was harder to write a single one of his *Philosophical Letters* than to construct the best of scenes. Was therefore the former not also perhaps the loftier? From the first rhythmic demand of inner art for material, subject matter, the possibility of effusion, to the thought, the image, the word, the line—what a battle! What a path of suffering! Miracles of longing, such were his works, longing for form, shape, limit, embodiment, the distant longing for the bright, clear world of his counterpart, who simply called the sunlit objects of that world by name, without mediation, speaking directly with the mouth of God.

Nevertheless, never mind his counterpart. Where was the artist, the poet, who was *his* equal? Who created from nothingness, as he did, from his own heart? Was it not as music, as pure primeval being, that a poem was born in his soul, long before it ever borrowed likeness and costume from the world of appearances? History, world knowledge, passion: resources and pretexts, nothing more, for something that had little to do with them, that had its home in the Orphic depths. Words, concepts: mere keys for his artistic talent to play upon so as to sound a hidden chord . . . Did anyone know of this? They showered him with praise, these good people, for the strength of purpose with which he played this or that key. And his motto, his ultimate *pathos*, the great bell he used to beckon the highest battlements of the soul—it lured many . . . freedom . . . In truth, he understood both more and less by it than they did in their celebrations. Freedom—what did that mean? A modicum of middle-class dignity—surely not!—in the presence of princely thrones? Do you even allow yourselves to dream of all that a creative mind ventures to mean by the word? Freedom from what? What ultimately from? Perhaps even happiness, human happiness, this silken restraint, this fair and gentle obligation . . .

Happiness . . . His lips trembled; it was as if his gaze were shifting inward, and slowly he let his head sink into his hands . . . He was in the adjoining room. Bluish light was shining from the lamp, and the floral curtain veiled the window in silent folds. He stood beside the bed and bent down over that sweet head on its pillows . . . A strand of dark hair curled down over that cheek, which shone with the pale shimmer of pearls, and those childlike lips were parted in sleep . . . my wife. Beloved! Did you take note of my longing? Did you come to me to be my happiness? That you are, rest easy! And sleep! Don't open your eyes in the long shadows of their sweet lashes just yet, don't let them stare at me as they sometimes do, so large and dark it seems you're questioning, seeking me. By God, by God, how I love you! It's just that occasionally I can't find my feelings because I'm often so very exhausted from suffering, from battling with that task assigned to me by my self. I can never be entirely yours or be wholly happy in you, for the sake of that which is my mission . . .

He kissed her, then tore himself away from the precious warmth of her sleep, took a look around and went back. The bell reminded him of how far along night was, but at the same time it was as if that bell were benevolently tolling the end to an hour of hardship. He took a deep breath, pressed his lips firmly together, then walked over and picked up his quill . . . No brooding! He was too deep to be permitted to brood. No descending into chaos, or at least no lingering there! To raise, instead, out of the chaos that is fullness whatever is ripe and ready for form and hold it up to the light. No brooding: get to work! Limit, delete, shape, get finished . . .

And eventually it was finished, that work of suffering. It may not have been any good, but it was finished. And now that it was finished—behold!—it was good after all. And from his soul, from Music and Idea, new works struggled forth, lyrical, shimmering creations in divine form that gave wondrous intimation of their own unfathomable place of birth, just as the shell contains the rushing of the sea from which it is fished.

Death in Venice

Chapter One

Gustav Aschenbach, or von Aschenbach, as had been his legal name since his fiftieth birthday, had begun a long solitary walk from his apartment on Munich's *Prinzregentenstraße* during a spring afternoon in 19—, a year that had for months glared so menacingly at our European continent. Even after lunch, overstimulated by many morning hours of difficult work, full of pitfalls and especially now demanding the greatest caution, judiciousness, probing insistence and exactitude of will, the writer had been unable to put a halt to the relentlessly running machine within him—that "motus animi continuus" which for Cicero is the essence of eloquence—and had been denied the relief of the nap so increasingly necessary at some point each day with the progressive decline in his stamina. Therefore, not long after tea, he had sought the outdoors, hoping that a little fresh air and exercise might revive him and help him put his evening to worthwhile use.

It was the beginning of May and after weeks of damp and cold, a false summer had set in. Though the leaves were hardly out, the *Englischer Garten* had nonetheless felt late-summer sultry, and its city end had been teeming with carriages and strollers. In front of the Aumeister, where paths of increasing solitude had led him, Aschenbach had paused a short while to survey the crowded restaurant garden, which had a few idle brougham cabs and equipages at its edge. Then, with the sun beginning to set, he had started home via the open field outside the park, stopping, on account of fatigue and storm clouds over Föhring, by the north cemetery to await the tram that would take him via the direct route back to the city.

As it happened, the tram stop and surrounding area were deserted. Neither on the paved *Ungererstraße*, with its train tracks stretching solitary and gleaming toward Schwabing, nor on the old *Föhringer Chaussee* was a single vehicle to be seen. Nothing stirred behind the fences of those stonemasons' yards where the crosses, headstones and other monuments on display make up a second, unoccupied graveyard. Across the way, the funeral chapel with its Byzantine architecture stood silently in the reflected light of the dying sun. To thc fore, said chapel, which is decorated with Greek crosses and brightly colored hieratic ornamentation, bears symmetrically arranged inscriptions in gold lettering, selected Biblical sayings concerning life in the afterworld, things like "They shall enter the house of God" or "May the Eternal Light suffuse them." For some time the waiting Aschenbach had been deriving solemn pleasure in reading those formulae and allowing his mind's eye to wander about in their shimmering mysticism, when, awakened from his dreamy musings, he noticed a man in the portico, above the pair of apocalyptic beasts that guard the outside stairs, a man whose not entirely everyday appearance turned his thoughts in a completely new direction.

It was unclear whether he had just emerged from inside the chapel through the bronze door or whether suddenly, out of nowhere, he had climbed up there from the outside. Without being especially absorbed by the question, Aschenbach was inclined toward the former. Of moderate height, skinny, unwhiskered and possessing a remarkably snub nose, the man was one of those redheads with milky-white, freckled skin. To judge from external details, he was not of Old Bavarian stock: the wide, straight-brimmed raffia hat on his head, at least, made his appearance seem alien and faraway. Nonetheless, he was wearing the indigenous rucksack around his shoulders and a yellowish belted suit of what seemed to be loden, with a gray overcoat slung over his left forearm, which he held tightly pressed just below the ribs, and a metal-tipped cane in his right hand, against whose handle he leaned, feet crossed, with his hip. Head held high, so that his Adam's apple emerged stark and bare from the wiry neck protruding from his loose tennis shirt, he peered with sharp, colorless eyes under red lashes out into the distance. Between them, there were two vigorous, perpendicular furrows that matched oddly with his short, upturned nose. Standing there like that—perhaps being elevated contributed to this impression—he had the imperious bearing of someone gazing down from on high, bold or even savage. Whether because he had to squint against the blinding effects of the setting sun or because his features were permanently distended, his lips seemed not to reach far enough down. Indeed they were so completely retracted from his teeth that the latter, bared to the gums, flashed out long and white.

It could have been that, in taking stock of this alien figure in his half-distracted, half-inquisitive way, Aschenbach had overstepped the bounds of polite restraint. He suddenly became aware of the man staring back at him, so militantly, so directly and so obviously intent upon escalating the matter and forcing the opponent to avert *his* eyes, that he turned away, smarting, and began to walk along the fences, resolving as he did to take no further notice of the fellow. A minute later he had forgotten him. Nonetheless, be it that the traveler-like aspects of the alien figure's appearance had worked upon his imagination, or that some other physical or mental influence was at play, he suddenly became conscious, to his surprise, of a strange expansion within him, a kind of roving unease, a youthful thirst for distance. This was so vital and new—or at least so long ago outgrown and forgotten—that he stopped in his tracks with his head down and his hands behind his back to ponder what this sensation was and where it was heading.

It was the desire to get away, nothing more, though it veritably attacked him in the form of a visual longing, a near hallucination. Craving had gained the power of sight, and his imagination, which had still not calmed down after his hours of hard work, was creating for itself a single emblematic scene, laboring to picture all the wonders and terrors of the multifarious world at one and the same time. He saw . . . saw a landscape, a tropical swamp under a sky thick with vapor, damp, lush and monstrous, a kind of primeval wilderness of islands, bogs and sediment-carrying channels . . . saw hairy trunks of palm trees pushing up near and far from fecund tangles of fern and beds of oily, swollen, outlandishly blooming flora . . . saw bizarrely deformed trees with roots growing down through the air into the earth, into the green shadows reflected in sluggish floodwaters where, between floating, milky-white flowers the size of plates, birds of some alien species stood in the shadows with hunched shoulders and clumsily shaped beaks and stared immovably off to one side . . . saw through the knotted shoots of a bamboo thicket the glint from the eyes of a crouching tiger . . . and felt his heart pound with horror and inexplicable longing. Then the tiger vision dissolved, and, shaking his head, Aschenbach resumed his deliberate walking along the stonemasons' fences.

He had, at least since gaining the means to enjoy the advantages of global travel whenever he wanted, always considered vacationing to be nothing other than a health measure, which had to be taken now and again, contrary to his own sensibilities and inclinations. Too occupied by the tasks set for him by his own ego and the European soul, too burdened with a sense of duty toward his output, too contemptuous of distraction to ever qualify as much of an enthusiast for the colorful world around him, he had been entirely content to have viewed that much of the earth's surface which anyone can experience without departing the immediate circle around his homeland. He had never even been tempted to leave Europe. Now that his life had begun its slow ebb, his artist's fear of not finishing everything—this special anxiety that the clock might run out before he'd completed his appointed part and given his all—had become impossible to dismiss as a mere humbug. Thus Aschenbach had restricted his existence almost exclusively to the lovely city that had become his home and to the country house that he had built for himself in the rugged mountains, where he spent the rainy summer.

Whatever it was that had come over him so suddenly at this late stage, it too was quickly moderated and corrected by reason and by the self-discipline that he had practiced from youth on. He had intended to reach a certain point in the work for which he currently lived before resettling to the country, and the thought of tramping halfway around the world seemed all too carefree and disruptive of his plans. It would take him away from his work for months and was therefore beyond serious consideration. Still, he knew only too well why this temptation had arisen so suddenly out of nowhere—he had to be honest with himself. The urge to flee was what this was, this yearning for distant lands and new sights, this desire for liberation, forgetting and relief from burden, the urge to get away from his great work, from the day-to-day stations of his rigid, cold, passionate duty. He loved his duty. There was no doubt about that. He could even almost bring himself to love the emotionally exhausting, daily renewed battle between his tenacious, proud, so often tested will and this growing fatigue, which no one could be allowed to suspect and which the finished product could not be permitted to betray in any way, not even through the slightest sign of inadequacy or relaxed concentration. Nonetheless, it was only sensible not to span the bow too tightly—he didn't want to be obstinate and suppress a need that had emerged in such vivid form. He thought about what he was working on, thought about the point at which he'd been forced to break off, today the same as yesterday, the point which still seemed unwilling to yield either to patient cultivation or to a sudden stroke of genius. He tested it once more, tried to break through or somehow unravel the resistance, before giving up with a shudder of aversion. There was nothing extraordinarily difficult here. What paralyzed him were his scruples about not wanting what he should, which manifested itself in a no longer appeasable fastidiousness. Even as a young man, he had valued fastidiousness as the essence and innermost core of talent, and its demands were the reason he had reined in and cooled off his emotions, for he knew that emotions tend to be satisfied with happy approximates and half-realized success. Could it be that his subjugated feelings were now exacting their revenge by abandoning him, refusing as of today to pick up his art and carry it aloft, taking away all his desire, all his delight in form and expression? Not that he was producing bad work: one advantage of his years at least was that he could rest absolutely assured of his own expertise, confident in it at every moment. Yet while the nation honored him for his talent, this talent no longer gave him any happiness. As far as he could see, what his present work lacked were those characteristic signs of an incendiary, playful spirit which, more than any intrinsic content, being the product of joy itself—a much greater blessing—creates joy in the appreciative audience. He dreaded the summer in the country, alone in that small house with the maid who cooked his food and the servant who brought it to him. He dreaded the familiar faces of the mountain peaks and cliffs that would once more surround him as he worked, dissatisfied and slow. A sudden switch was needed—happy-go-lucky living, idle days, exotic air and an infusion of new blood—so that he might bear his summer and so that his summer might bear fruit. Very well, he'd go away somewhere—he'd thought long enough. No such great distance, not all the way to the tigers. One night in a sleeper car and a three- or four-week siesta at some international vacation spot on the romantic Mediterranean . . .

Such were his thoughts as the noise from the tram on its wire advanced up *Ungererstraße*, and upon getting in, he decided to devote that evening to the study of maps and train schedules. On the tram steps, it occurred to him to look around for the man in the raffia hat, his companion during what had certainly been a most momentous wait. The man's whereabouts, however, remained a mystery, for he was to be found neither in his previous location nor anywhere on the platform nor within the streetcar itself.

Chapter Two

The author of that lucid and majestic prose epic based on the life of Frederick the Great, the patient artist and painstaking weaver of that densely populated novelistic tapestry known as *Maya*, which managed to subordinate so many individual human destinies to a single basic pattern, the creator of that powerful narrative which bears the title "A True Wretch" and which showed an entire grateful generation of youth the possibility for moral resolution more profound than any intellectual knowledge, and finally (to complete the short catalogue of his mature works) the author of that passionately argued treatise "Mind and Art," whose analytic force and dialectic eloquence had led serious critics to place it on par with Schiller's great meditation "On Naive and Sentimental Poetry"—Gustav Aschenbach was born the son of a ranking district court official in L., a county seat in provincial Silesia. His ancestors had been military officers, judges and bureaucratic functionaries, men who had dedicated their strict, respectably austere lives to the service of crown and state. More inwardly directed spirituality had manifested itself within the family ranks but once, in the person of a preacher; more sensual, passionate blood had been introduced during the previous generation, by the writer's mother, the daughter of a Bohemian *Kapellmeister*. The foreign traits in his appearance came from her. It was the marriage of the servant's sober devotion to duty with darker, more fiery impulses that had allowed an artist—this *particular* artist—to develop.

With the whole of his existence attuned to fame, Aschenbach had proven to be, if not genuinely precocious, then—thanks to a decisiveness and personal pregnance of tone—without doubt precociously mature and clever enough for the public eye. He had made a name for himself while still practically an academy boy. In the ten years that followed, he had learned how to make public appearances from behind his desk, how to manage his fame, how to seem gracious and distinguished in letters that had by necessity—for the demands are numerous on the time of the successful and the respected—to be kept short. By the time he was forty, exhausted by the strain and vicissitudes of his actual work, he was obliged to deal on a daily basis with correspondence postmarked from every corner of the globe.

Equally removed from the banal and the eccentric, his was a talent that could both impress a broad audience and command the appreciative, demanding interest of those with taste. Even as a young man, he had been under universal pressure to achieve, to achieve nothing short of greatness at that, and had known neither the idleness nor the blithe carefree days of youth. Once, in Vienna, around his thirty-fifth birthday, he had fallen ill. A keen observer had remarked at a party, "Aschenbach, you see, has only ever lived like *so*"—clenching the fingers of his left hand into a tight fist—"never like *so*"—unclenching it and letting it dangle relaxed from the arm of his chair. That hit the mark, and what made Aschenbach's life such an example was the fact that he did not by any means possess a robust constitution and was thus only called, not born, to such constant exertion.

Medical considerations had kept the adolescent Aschenbach from attending school and required him to be educated at home. He had grown up in solitude, without companionship, and had been forced to recognize himself early on as belonging to that breed of men who lacked, not talent, but the necessary physical foundation for the utmost development of talent—a breed of men who tend to do their best work when young and whose abilities rarely make it very far along in years. "To persevere through all," however, had always been his motto. In his Frederick the Great novel he saw nothing less than the apotheosis of this imperative, which for him represented the essence of long-suffering, ever-toiling virtue. Moreover, it was one of his most passionate wishes to grow old, for he had always believed that the only artistic talent that could be deemed truly great, sweeping, indeed truly admirable, was that given the chance to bear characteristic fruit every step of the way throughout a human lifetime.

In order to carry the burdens talent had loaded upon his frail shoulders and to travel the great distances he wanted with them, he needed discipline. This he was lucky enough to inherit from his father's side of the family. As a forty- or fifty-year-old, at that age when others begin to squander, daydream and self-contentedly postpone the execution of great plans, he would start his morning off early, with splashes of cold water across his chest and down his back. Then he would work for two or three ardently conscientious hours by the light of a pair of tall candles in silver holders at the head of his manuscript, sacrificing to art all the strength he had gathered from sleep. It was pardonable—in fact it was actually a mark of the great triumph of his work ethic—that noninitiates often mistook the world of his *Maya* or the epic blocks in which Frederick's heroic life unfolded for products of coiled strength and a massive wind. In reality such lofty edifices had been built up piecemeal, layer for layer, from hundreds of isolated inspirations, the whole and each of its parts only attaining such excellence because their creator possessed an iron-willed tenacity such as had once conquered his native Silesia and had endured the strain of year-long labor on one lone project, devoting exclusively his strongest, worthiest hours to the actual production process.

For an imaginative work of any significance to make an on-the-spot impact that is both broad and deep, there must be some unspoken affinity, indeed basic agreement between the individual destiny of the author and the general one of his contemporaries and fellow citizens. People don't know why they celebrate a particular work of art. Far removed from any expert knowledge, they convince themselves of having uncovered a hundred different examples of its superiority, which then serve to justify their enthusiasm. But the real reason for their praise is something incalculable—sympathetic attraction.

Once, in a relatively obscure passage, Aschenbach had stated as much outright, writing that practically everything great that exists does so in spite, having come into existence in spite of worry and anguish, of poverty, isolation, physical weakness, vice, overheated passions and various thousands of other obstacles. This was more than a remark. It was personal experience; it was almost the magic formula for his life and fame, the key to his work. Can there be any wonder, then, that it was also the personal ethos, the public comportment of those characters most idiosyncratically his own?

Commenting on the novel type of hero favored by this writer—one that recurred in various guises—an early but insightful dissector of his work had written that the Aschenbachian protagonist embodied "a kind of intellectual and youthful masculinity, gritting its teeth, proud in its degradation, standing firm as swords and spears pierced its flesh." That was a nice way of describing things, precise and perceptive, despite the seemingly too-passive formulation. After all, composure in the face of destiny—grace under fire—involves more than just endurance: it must be actively achieved, positively won. That is why the figure of St. Sebastian is the most beautiful image, if not in all of art, then certainly in all art relevant to this discussion. If you were to look deeply enough into Aschenbach's fictional world, you could find its equivalent: the sort of elegant self-control that kept its inner decrepitude and biological decay hidden from the eyes of the world until the last possible moment; sallow ugliness that overcame physical disadvantage to ignite its own smoldering lust into pure flame and achieve absolute mastery in the realm of beauty; pale impotence that summoned enough strength from the glowing depths of the human spirit to make an entire proud people kneel at the foot of the Cross and at *its own* feet as well. Amiable steadfastness in the empty and strict service of form, the life of falsehood and risk, the rapidly self-consuming desire and artistry of a born swindler—if you were to ponder just these few examples of heroic destiny, you could come to doubt the existence of any other type of heroism besides that of weakness. And what type of heroism, after all, could have better suited the times? Gustav Aschenbach was the poet of all those working on the brink of exhaustion, the overburdened, wornout yet nonetheless unbowed apostles of achievement who, though slight of stature and slim of resource, get by with ecstatic bursts of will and clever allocation, managing, for however short a time, to give the appearance of greatness. They are many; they are the heroes of the age. All of them found their image mirrored in his work, found themselves upheld and exalted, their praises sung, and they knew how to express their gratitude. They heralded his name.

He had been young and raw along with the times and, poorly guided by them, had publicly stumbled. He had blundered, embarrassed himself, violated tact and good judgement in both word and work. Nevertheless, he had also achieved the goal of dignity, toward which, in his way of thinking, all great talent possessed an inborn drive and impulse. Indeed you could say his entire development had been a conscious and hard-nosed climb toward dignity, to the ultimate abandonment of any inhibiting skepticism and irony.

Easily comprehensible fiction that is filled with lively figures and does not unduly tax the reading mind may delight the middle-of-the-road masses, but youth, with its uncompromising passion, can only be captivated by what is problematic. Aschenbach had certainly been problematic, and as uncompromising as any boy. He had indulged the imagination, strip-mined the intellect, pulverized promising seeds, revealed secrets, incriminated talent and exposed art itself. Indeed, even as his verbal sculptures had entertained, exalted and inspired the devout enthusiasts, the young artist had also held the twenty-year-olds breathlessly enthralled with his cynical pronouncements about the dubious nature of art and the artist himself.

There seems to be nothing, however, to which unalloyed imagination, conscious of its duty, becomes more quickly inured than to the stinging, bitter lure of the intellect. There can be no doubt that the apprentice's most dourly conscientious labor proves shallow against the experienced master's profound resolve to reject intellectual knowledge, to dismiss it, to step over it with head held high, insofar as it serves in the least to lame, discourage or derogate his own will, his capacity for action, his feelings or even his passion. How else could that famous short story "A True Wretch" be understood except as an outburst of contempt for the vulgar pseudo-psychology of his age, embodied in that ridiculous weakling, that half-pint scoundrel, who, inspired by moral velleity, weakness and turpitude, attempts to glorify his own pathetic existence by driving his wife into the arms of a fresh-faced boy, telling himself that plumbed depth justifies despicable deeds? The brunt of those words, in which dissipation was disdained, signalled Aschenbach's own repudiation of moral relativism, of all sympathetic attraction to the abyss. It announced his rejection of that all-forbearing maxim which says that to know is to forgive: what was being prepared, indeed realized here was that "miraculous rebirth of unfettered innocence," to which the talk returned, explicitly and not without a portentous emphasis, in one of his interviews shortly thereafter. Strange coincidences! Was it not a creative consequence of this "rebirth," this new dignity and rigor, that readers then began to notice in him an almost hypertrophic increase in aestheticism, that aristocratic purity, simplicity and formal symmetry which would henceforth give his entire output an unmistakable, surely intended stamp of classical mastery of technique? And yet moral conviction beyond the realm of knowledge, of all-unravelling and all-inhibiting intellect—did this not amount to a simplification in its own right, a moralistic reduction of the world and the human soul? And did it not also entail an encouragement of what was evil, forbidden, ethically indefensible? Does not form have two faces? Is it not simultaneously moral and amoral—moral, insofar as it is the ultimate expression of discipline; amoral, even immoral, insofar as it automatically entails ethical indifference, aspiring to make all that is ethical bow down before its own proud, unchecked scepter?

Be that as it may. Development is destiny—and how could one unfolding to the applause and mass faith of a broad popular audience not be different from one transpiring without the luster and gratitudes of fame? Only the eternal vagabond yawns and tries to scoff when a great talent outgrows its libertinistic incubation period, expressly affiliates itself with the dignity of the human imagination and claims the court privileges attending a lonely existence full of solitary, unshared suffering in battle, which has brought societal influence and accolades. How much playfulness, spite and sheer pleasure is there anyway in talent in its formative stages? With time, something official, pedagogical, crept into the public Gustav Aschenbach. His style dispensed in later years with boldfaced audacities, subtle and original nuances, to become paradigmatic and solid, polished and familiar, conservative, formal, even formulaic. Moreover, like the Louis XIV of historical record, the older he got, the more he purged his vocabulary of words with vulgar associations. At this point it happened that the ministry of education adopted select passages from his work as mandatory school reading. His own inner sense of himself was confirmed—and he did not demur—when a newly crowned German prince wished to honor the creator of Frederick by bestowing upon him, on the occasion of his fiftieth birthday, the title of personal nobility.

Early on, after a few unsettled years trying out various locations, he selected Munich as his permanent residence and lived there enjoying a position of the highest bourgeois respect, the sort of respect that is occasionally granted to men of intellect in certain exceptional cases. The marriage he concluded while still a young man, to a girl from an academic family, ended after a few short years of happiness with her death. He was left with a daughter, already married. He had no son.

Gustav von Aschenbach was slightly below average height, clean-shaven and brunet. His head looked a bit too large for the almost delicate figure he cut. His brushed-back hair, thinning on top, quite thick and heavily gray at the temples, framed a high, lined, perhaps even scarred forehead. The bow from a pair of rimless gold glasses dug into the base of his stout Roman nose. He had a wide mouth equally wont to droop and suddenly tense up and purse, a set of cheeks gaunt and furrowed, and a clearly defined chin with a delicate cleft. Great moments of destiny seemed to have passed over this head, which he usually held at somewhat of an angle, as though in pain. It had been art, though, that had taken over the work, otherwise associated with a difficult and stormy life, of wringing these physiological changes. Behind these brows had been born the lightninglike exchanges between Voltaire and the king as they debated war; these eyes, gazing with such weary depth through those glass lenses, had seen the bloody inferno of the *lazaretti* during the Seven Years' War. Art—understood as personal experience, too—is life raised to a higher power. It gives a deeper pleasure and exacts a quicker toll. It etches the real traces of the imaginative mind's adventures onto the face of its servant and produces, though that servant may lead an external existence of monastic calm, nerves that in the long run are overindulged, hypersensitive, exhausted and perennially craving, such as a lifetime of dissipate passions and pleasures can hardly equal.

Chapter Three

Several matters, literary and practical, kept the eager traveler in Munich for an additional fortnight after that fateful walk. He finally ordered that his country house be made ready for habitation within four weeks' time and departed one day between the middle and the end of May, taking the night train to Trieste, where he delayed only twenty-four hours before embarking for Pola the following morning.

He was looking for something exotic and disconnected, but within quick reach, so he took up residence on an Adriatic island not far from the Istrian coast, highly praised of late, with natives in colorful rags babbling wild sounds and beautiful sets of jagged cliffs wherever there was access to the sea. But the rain, the humidity, a self-contained hotel clientele of provincial Austrians and the lack of that peacefully intimate contact with the sea which only a soft, sandy beach can provide conspired to oppress his mood and never allowed him to feel as though he had found the place he was meant to be. Some impulse within—toward what he didn't know—made him restless. He began studying ship schedules and inquiring around when, suddenly, the surprising but obvious destination materialized before his eyes. Where did you go when you wanted to arrive, overnight, somewhere incomparable, somewhere fairy tale–like and exotic? It was clear as day. What was he doing here? He'd gotten off track. He'd wanted to go there all along. He wasted no time canceling his ill-made reservations. A week and a half after his arrival on the island a speedy motorboat was carrying him through the early morning mists back to that wartime harbor. He only stepped foot on land long enough to walk up the gangplank onto the damp deck of a passenger ship waiting under steam to depart for Venice.

It was an aged vessel flying an Italian flag, decrepit, sooty and grim. No sooner was Aschenbach on board, than an unwashed, smirkingly polite hunchback of a deckhand ushered him into a claustrophobic, artificially lit compartment in the ship's interior. There a goateed man sat behind a table with a face like that of an old-fashioned circus impresario, his hat slanted down over his brow, the tail end of a cigarette stuck in the corner of his mouth. He was checking passengers' identification and writing out tickets with the gesticulating flair of a salesman. "Venice!" he said, parroting Aschenbach's request and jabbing his pen into the thickening dregs of a sharply tilted inkwell. "First class to Venice! You're all taken care of, sir." He scratched out a few giant letters, scattered blue sand from a box upon them, shook the paper out over a clay bowl, folded it in his bony yellow fingers and resumed writing. "A well-chosen destination!" he chattered while doing so. "Ah Venice! A lovely city! A city no cultured person can resist, be it for its history or its present-day charms!" There was something hypnotic and distracting about the slickness and rapidity of his movements and the accompanying empty phrases, almost as though he were worried that the traveler might have second thoughts about Venice. He hastily took Aschenbach's money and, with the dexterity of a croupier, tossed the change on the stained cloth covering the table. "Enjoy yourself, sir," he said with a theatrical bow. "It's a privilege serving you . . . Next!" he called out, immediately raising one arm as if doing the briskest of business, although there was no one else who needed to be served. Aschenbach went back up on deck.

One arm on the handrail, he stared at the idle quayside crowd dawdling around to watch the ship's departure and at the other passengers on board. Those traveling second class, men and women, crouched on the foredeck, using crates and packed bundles for seats. His company on the upper deck was a group of young people, evidently clerks from Pola, who had decided on the spur of the moment to take a day trip to Italy. They were attracting considerable attention to themselves and their little excursion, jabbering, laughing, fatuously enjoying their own exaggerated gestures and leaning over the rail to shout glib taunts at busy, briefcase-toting colleagues who walked down along the harbor street and who shook their walking sticks back at the celebrants above. One fellow in particular, all done up in a bright yellow summer suit of extravagant cut, a red tie and a boldly cocked Panama hat, screeched louder than all the others in his merriment. Yet no sooner had Aschenbach gotten a somewhat closer look at him than he realized with horror that this youngster was a fake. He was old—no doubt about it—for wrinkles surrounded his eyes and mouth. The dull flush on his cheeks was mere rouge, the brown hair under his colorfully woven straw hat a wig, his neck a gnarl of sinews, his affectatious moustache and imperial a dye-job, the toothy yellow grin whenever he laughed a cheap set of dentures, and his hands, signet rings on both index fingers, those of a geriatric. Unnerved, Aschenbach watched him moving in the company of these young friends. Didn't they know he was old? Didn't they notice the deceit of his wearing the same foppish, festive attire they did, of his pretending to be one of them? As a matter of course, out of habit, so it seemed, they tolerated him among the group, treating him as an equal and responding without disgust when he playfully elbowed them in the ribs. How was this possible? Aschenbach put his hand upon his forehead and shut his eyes, which burned from lack of sleep. He felt as though not everything were getting off to exactly its usual start, as though a dreamlike strangeness were beginning to expand and engulf the world, a bizarre metamorphosis to which a stop might be put if he could briefly shade his eyes, then take another look around. At that moment, however, a sensation of swimming began and he glanced up in unthinking panic, only to discover the ship's grim hulk moving slowly away from the stone wall of the harbor. Inch by inch, as the engine alternated between forward and reverse, the slick of oily water between the quay and the side of the ship widened, and after some clumsy maneuvering, the steamer turned its prow toward the open sea. Aschenbach walked over to the starboard, where the hunchback had unfolded a deck chair for him and a steward in a stained jacket asked if there was anything he required.

The sky was gray, the wind damp. The harbor and the islands were quickly left behind, and soon all land was lost to view in the fog. Heavy flecks of coal ash, soaked with mist, fell on the freshly scrubbed deck, which seemed as if it would never dry off. An hour into the trip, it was already necessary to unfold a canopy, for it had started to rain.

Wrapped in an overcoat, with a book in his lap, the traveler relaxed, not noticing the hours that passed. It had stopped raining, and the canvas awning was folded back up. The horizon was absolute and infinite. Under the gloomy dome of the sky an eerily immense surface of desolate sea stretched in every direction. When space is empty and undivided, we have no measure of time either and begin to lose ourselves in the sheer infinity. Strange shadowy figures, the old fop and the goateed man from the ship's interior, passed through the resting Aschenbach's mind, indistinctly gesturing and speaking some scrambled dream language. He fell asleep.

At noon he was required to assemble below with the others in the ship's mess, a mere corridor to which one gained access via connecting doors from the sleeping berths. There he ate at the head of a long table, directly across from the clerks, old fop included, who had since ten o'clock been drinking toasts with the gregarious ship's captain. The meal was wretched, and he finished it quickly. The open air beckoned. He wanted to check the sky: perhaps it was clearing over Venice.

He hadn't even considered the possibility of it being otherwise, since the city had always greeted him in full splendor. But today the sky and the sea remained gloomy and leaden, misty rain fell intermittently, and he found himself approaching a different Venice by sea than he had ever encountered on land. He stood by the foremast, gazing expectantly into the distance, trying to spot the coastline. He thought of that melancholy, overexcitable poet, whose vividly dreamt domes and church bells had long ago arisen from these waters, and he silently recited several of the carefully metered verses into which reverence, joy and sadness had so long ago been wrought. Being easily moved by passion already thus sculpted, he checked his grave, exhausted heart to see if some new enthusiasm and excitability, some late emotional adventure, might be in store for an idle traveler like himself.

There, to his right, the flat coastline began to emerge, fishing boats dotted the sea, and the island resort appeared. The steamer passed it on the left, sailing at reduced speed into the narrow port of the same name. Then it came to a full stop in the Lagoon in front of some picturesque ramshackle structures to await the quarantine authorities' skiff.

An hour passed before it appeared. They had arrived and yet not arrived. There was no reason to hurry, yet they felt driven by impatience. The young clerks from Pola had had their usual patriotism excited by the bugle calls carrying across the water from the vicinity of the public gardens and had come up on deck. There, bolstered by *asti spumante*, they cheered on the *bersaglieri* exercising on the opposite shore. It was repulsive to observe the effect upon the aged fop of falsely kept company with youth. His old head had not stood the wine as those younger and hardier ones had, and he found himself in a lamentable state of drunkenness. Bleary-eyed, his cigarette trembling between his fingers, he swayed as he stood, struggling to maintain his balance against the back-and-forth pull of intoxication. He dared not take a step for fear of falling down, yet he still behaved with appalling presumption, grabbing at all who passed, babbling, winking, giggling, raising a wrinkled index finger and signet ring with each inane jest, his tongue flicking at the corners of his mouth all the while in a disgustingly suggestive manner. Aschenbach scowled at him and once again felt dazed, as if the world were subtly but relentlessly beginning to warp toward the bizarre and fragmentary. It was a feeling that external circumstances prevented him from pursuing, for at that very moment the engine resumed its pounding, and the ship, having stopped so short of its ultimate destination, started once more up the San Marco Canal.

Thus he saw it again, that most awe-inspiring port, that dazzling arrangement of fantastic architecture with which the Republic has perennially greeted the reverent eyes of approaching seafarers: the easy majesty of the Palace of the Doges, the Bridge of Sighs, the pillars of the lion and saint by the Lagoon, the magnificent projected arm of the magical San Marco Basilica, the view beyond the gateway to the city and the giant clock. And he realized as he took this all in that arriving in Venice by land via the train station was like entering a palace through one of the back doors, that this most unlikely of cities should only be approached by ship, over high sea, as he was now doing.

The engine stopped, gondolas pulled alongside them, the gangway was let down, customs officials came on board and performed their duties, and at long last they were able to begin disembarking. Aschenbach let it be known he wished to hire a gondola to take him and his luggage to the landing of those small steam boats, or *vaporetti*, which shuttle between the city and the Lido, for he intended to take a room there on the ocean. His plans meet with approval, and someone shouts down to the water, where a number of gondoliers are quarrelling in dialect. Still, he is blocked from disembarking, blocked by his own luggage, which is being half dragged, half carried down the ladderlike gangway. Consequently, for some minutes, he finds himself unable to avoid the intimacies of the horrific old fop, who has been moved by some obscure drunken impulse to pay his courtesies to this complete stranger. "We hope you have a most pleasant stay," he bleats, bowing and scraping. "We trust you won't forget us! *Au revoir*, *excusez*, and *bon jour*, your Excellency!" Drooling, the old fop shuts his eyes and licks at the corners of his mouth, and the dyed imperial on his age-worn lower lip jerks upward. "Our best," he babbles on, slurring his words and raising two fingertips to his mouth. "Give our best to your sweetheart, the sweetest, prettiest little sweetheart of them all." Suddenly his upper denture falls out of his jaw onto his lower lip. At that point Aschenbach was able to escape. "Your sweetheart, your tender little sweetheart." He could still hear the old man's vapid, alcohol-impaired cooing over his shoulder as he climbed down the gangway, clinging tightly to the ropes.

Who among us would not have to suppress a momentary shudder, a second of unspoken anxious dread, upon first stepping or first restepping after years into a Venetian gondola? Unchanged since the days of yore and of that special black possessed by no other earthly objects save coffins, this extraordinary means of conveyance calls to mind furtive criminal adventures undertaken on soggy nights. Still more, it evokes death itself, the bier, the solemn rites and the final silent voyage. Has it been duly noted that the typical seating arrangement in such a gondola—its polish coffin- and its upholstery matte-black—is the softest, plushest, most sleep-inducing armchair in the entire world? This thought impressed itself upon Aschenbach as he settled back at the gondolier's feet, facing his bags, which had been tidily arranged in the prow. The gondoliers were still quarrelling in their coarse, incomprehensible dialect, making hostile gestures all the while. The characteristic stillness of the watery city, however, seemed to envelop, disembody and scatter their voices over the tides. It was hot here in the harbor. Feeling the warm breath of the sirocco, leaning back into the cushions and floating atop that soft and forgiving element, the traveler closed his eyes to savor a moment of self-indulgence, as unfamiliar as it was sweet. This trip will not last long, he thought. If only it could last forever! Gently rocked by the water, he sensed himself gliding away from the crowd and the confusion of the voices.

How quiet it was growing around him! Nothing could be heard except the soft splash of the oar, the dull slap of the waves against the prow—which stuck up from the water, stiff, black and spiked like a halberd—and a third sound as well, a murmuring, a muttering: the hissing of the gondolier through his teeth. He was talking to himself in spasmodic phrases muted by his laboring arms. Aschenbach opened his eyes and was rather startled to find the lagoon growing wider and the boat heading out toward the open sea. It seemed he couldn't relax too much; some attention was required to ensure that his requests were indeed carried out.

"See here, to the *vaporetto* landing," he said over his shoulder. The muttering ceased, but he received no answer.

"To the *vaporetto* landing, I said!" he reiterated, turning fully around and staring up into the face of the gondolier, who towered behind him imposingly against the pale sky on his raised plank. The man cut an unforgiving, even brutal figure. He was dressed in sailor's blues, with a yellow sash for a belt and a fraying straw hat of no particular style cocked insolently on his head. His face, with its curled blond moustache under a faintly upturned nose, made him look very un-Italian. Though comparatively slight of stature, so that he might have been considered ill-suited for his career, he rowed with great energy, putting his whole body into every stroke. Once or twice, the exertion made him grimace, exposing his white teeth. Wrinkling his reddish eyebrows, he peered over his passenger's head into the distance and answered in a firm, almost rude tone:

"You go to the Lido."

Aschenbach responded:

"Yes indeed. But I only hired the gondola to take me over to San Marco. I wish to take the *vaporetto*."

"You cannot take the *vaporetto*, sir."

"And why not?"

"Because the *vaporetto* does not allow luggage."

That was true, as Aschenbach now recalled. He fell silent. Nonetheless, the brusque arrogance the man displayed toward his foreign guest, so unlike Italy, struck him as intolerable. He said:

"That's my affair. Perhaps I want to store my luggage. You'll turn around immediately."

Silence ensued. The oar splashed, and the water lapped dully against the prow. And the murmuring and muttering began again: the gondolier had resumed talking to himself through his teeth.

What was there to do? Alone, swept along by the current with this oddly insubordinate, eerily determined man, the traveler could see no way to enforce his will. And anyway, how very comfortable he could make himself, so long as he didn't cause a fuss! Hadn't he wished that the trip would take longer, that it would go on forever? It was wisest and, more to the point, most agreeable to let things take their course. A spell of lethargy seemed to emanate from his seat, from this low-slung, black-upholstered armchair that was gently rocked by the oar strokes of the all-powerful gondolier behind him. The idea of having fallen into criminal hands flashed through Aschenbach's mind like a dream but was incapable of rousing his conscious mind to any act of self-defense. The more irritating possibility was that it was all just an attempt at petty extortion. Some feeling related to duty or pride—akin to the suddenly remembered necessity of taking heed, lest one or the other flare up—allowed Aschenbach to gather himself once more. He asked:

"What do you charge for the trip?"

Staring into the distance above his head, the gondolier answered:

"You will pay."

His response was prescribed. Aschenbach said mechanically:

"I'll pay nothing, nothing at all, if you insist upon taking me where I don't want to go."

"You go to the Lido."

"But not with you."

"I take you well."

That's the truth, thought Aschenbach, giving up. You are taking me well, no doubt about that. You may just be out for the money I'm carrying, you may clobber me from behind with your oar and send me to Pluto's dark domain, but you'll have taken me well.

Only nothing of the sort happened. On the contrary, they even had company, a boatload of musical pirates, both men and women, singing to guitar and mandolin. They pushed their way hard alongside the gondola and shattered the silence on the water with profit-hungry tourist lyrics. Aschenbach threw some money into their outstretched hat, and they ceased playing immediately and moved off. Once again the gondolier could be heard, talking to himself in spasmodic, panting breaths.

Thus, after a time, they arrived, bobbing in the wake of a city-bound steamship. Two municipal policemen paced along the banks with their hands behind their backs and their faces toward the lagoon. Aschenbach got out of the gondola, assisted by that old man with a hook you find on every boat landing in Venice, and, seeing that he had only large bills, walked over to the adjacent hotel to get change in order to pay the gondolier what he felt he owed. He does this in the lobby, returns and finds his luggage loaded onto a cart on the quay. Gondola and gondolier have vanished.

"He cleared out," said the old man with the boat hook. "A bad man, a man without a license, good sir. He is the only gondolier with no license. The others phoned over. He saw that he was expected. So he cleared out."

Aschenbach shrugged.

"The gentleman has gotten a free ride," the old man said, holding out his hat. Aschenbach threw some coins in. He instructed the man to take his luggage to the beach hotel, then followed the cart down the avenue, that white-blossomed avenue lined on both sides with taverns, bazaars and *pensioni* that runs straight across the island to the beach.

He entered the grandiose hotel through the garden terrace in the back, passing through the main parlor and lobby into the reception office. He had reserved his quarters in advance, so registration was quick, a mere formality. One of the managers—a small, soft-spoken, sycophantically polite man with a dark moustache and a French frock coat—accompanied him in the elevator up to the third floor and showed him to his room, a pleasant place furnished in cherrywood and enlivened by strongly scented flowers. Its tall windows overlooked the open sea. He walked over to one of them after the manager had withdrawn and, with his back to the room where the luggage was being delivered and arranged, stared down at the largely deserted afternoon beach and the sunless sea at high tide, whose long, low-breaking waves lapped peacefully and regularly against the shore.

The observations and chance encounters of the solitary and silent are more blurred, yet at the same time more probing than those of social beings. Their thoughts are deeper and weirder, and never without a tinge of sorrow. Images and perceptions that might otherwise be easily dispensed with by a glance, a laugh or an exchange of opinion excessively occupy the lone individual, gaining depth in silence, taking on meaning, becoming personal experience, adventure and emotion. Solitude yields the original, the boldly and shockingly beautiful, the poem. Yet solitude also yields the perverse and disproportionate, the ridiculous and the beyond-the-pale. Thus the attending apparitions of his arrival in Venice, the horrible old fop babbling about his sweetheart and the pariah gondolier cheated of his pay, still weighed upon the traveler's spirits. Without being difficult to account for or providing any real food for thought, these events were nonetheless, it seemed to him, deeply strange and—precisely in the contradiction—unsettling. At the same time, his eyes welcomed the sea, and his heart lifted with the knowledge that Venice was so nearby and easily accessible. Finally, he turned away from the window, washed his face, left detailed instructions for the maid as to how to make his room most comfortable and ordered the Swiss elevator boy in the green uniform to take him to the ground floor.

He drank his tea on the seaside terrace, then went down to the promenade and followed the waterfront a good stretch in the direction of the Hotel Excelsior. When he returned, it already seemed time to get dressed for dinner. He did this slowly and deliberately, as always, for it was his habit to work while making himself ready. Nevertheless, he still arrived a bit early in the parlor, where he found a considerable number of other hotel guests assembled, unacquainted with one another and affecting mutual indifference, yet united by their common anticipation of dinner. He picked up a newspaper from the reading table, sank back into a leather armchair and observed the company, which differed from that of the earlier hotel in one particularly pleasant respect.

A broad horizon spread before him, tolerantly encompassing great diversity. Muffled sounds from all the major languages mingled with one another in the air. Evening attire, recognized the world over as the official uniform of civilized society, lent a properly homogenous exterior to the spectrum of variations on the human form. The long dry face of the American, the extended Russian family, typically English ladies and German children with French nannies were all represented, but the Slavic contingent seemed to predominate. Polish was being spoken in his immediate vicinity.

A group of young people, halfway into and just shy of adulthood, stood assembled around a small wicker table under the watchful eye of a tutor or governess: there were three young girls who appeared to be between fifteen and seventeen and a long-haired boy of around fourteen. To his astonishment Aschenbach realized that the boy was absolutely beautiful. Pale and elegantly reserved, with ringlets of honey-colored hair, a straight sloping nose, a lovely mouth and an expression of divinely blessed solemnity, his face called to mind Greek sculptures of the best period. And to complement this physical perfection, he possessed such a unique aura of personal charm that the gazing Aschenbach couldn't recall having ever encountered anything, in either nature or art, so flawlessly realized. What also struck him was an obviously fundamental contrast in the pedagogical philosophy governing how the siblings were dressed and reared. The outfits of the three girls, the oldest of whom could have passed for an adult, were so austere and chaste as to distort their appearance. The same slate-grey, cloistral uniform, cut gravely below the calf, intentionally unflattering of design, with a white turned-down collar as its sole bright spot, suppressed and negated any hint of attractiveness in the girls' figures. Their hair, slicked back flat against their skulls, gave their faces the empty, taciturn look of nuns. One thing was clear: it was a mother who laid down the rules here, one who wouldn't have dreamt of treating her son with the same pedagogic strictness deemed appropriate for the girls. His existence was one of visible softness and gentility. Care had been taken that scissors not touch his beautiful head of hair; like that of *Il Spinaro*, it curled in ringlets over his forehead and ears and down the back of his neck. His English sailor's suit with its lanyards, stitching and embroidery—its puffy sleeves tapered down to fit tightly around the fine wrists of his still childlike yet slender hands—made his delicate figure seem somewhat rich and spoiled. He sat in semiprofile across from the observing Aschenbach, one patent-leather-clad foot before the other, his elbow propped on the armrest of the wicker chair, cheek glued to a closed hand. It was a posture of relaxed dignity without a trace of the almost subservient stiffness to which his female siblings seemed accustomed. Did he suffer from something? The skin on his face gleamed white as ivory against the golden shadows of the surrounding locks. Or was he simply a pampered darling, indulged by a capricious love showing its favoritism? Aschenbach was inclined toward the latter. Almost every artistic nature is born with a revealing connoisseurial tendency that appreciates injustice so long as it results in beauty and that applauds, even worships aristocratic privilege.

A waiter made the rounds and announced in English that dinner was served. Gradually the company moved through the glass door into the dining room. Late arrivals hurried past, emerging from the lobby and the elevators. Inside, dinner was already being laid out, but the young Poles remained seated around the little wicker table. Aschenbach waited with them, comfortably ensconced in his deep chair, beauty before his eyes.

Finally the governess—a small, corpulent, red-faced lady of mixed family—signalled for the party to get up. Brows arched, she pushed her chair back and bowed as a tall woman wearing a light gray evening gown and a rich set of pearls entered the parlor. The woman's manner was cool and measured, her lightly powdered hair arranged and her gown designed with that simplicity of fashion to be found wherever piety represents an essential component of nobility. In Germany she could have been the wife of an important governmental officer. The only element of the extraordinary or the luxurious in her appearance was her jewelry, a pair of dangling earrings and three very long strands of gently shimmering pearls, as big as cherries, all of which were literally priceless.

The children were on their feet at once. They bent and kissed their mother's hand, while she stared off over their heads with a reserved smile on her well-kept, but nonetheless somewhat weary and drawn face. She addressed a few words in French to the governess, then approached the glass door. The children followed her, first the girls in order of age, then the governess, then finally the boy. For some reason he looked back as he crossed the threshold, so that, since no one else was waiting in the parlor, his peculiar twilight-gray eyes met those of Aschenbach, who had let his newspaper sink to his knee and, enraptured, was staring at the group.

As far as the details were concerned, there was nothing particularly remarkable about what he had witnessed. One doesn't sit down at table before mother has arrived; one waits for her, greeting her respectfully before going to dine, in observance of correct etiquette. Yet the whole ceremony had been performed so decisively, with such a strong accent of good breeding, devotion to duty and self-respect, that Aschenbach found it strangely arresting. He lingered a few moments longer. Then he, too, entered the dining room and was shown to his table, which, he noticed with a fleeting pang of regret, was quite far from the one where the Polish family was seated.

Fatigued, yet with fired imagination, he entertained himself during the tedious dinner with abstract, even transcendental thoughts. He contemplated the mysterious bond that must be concluded between the individual exception and the rule if human beauty is to arise, before proceeding on to general questions of form and art. But he discovered in the end that his thoughts and inspirations were like the intimations of a dream, which always seem inspired at the time but prove utterly shallow and useless to the waking mind. After dinner he passed some time smoking in a chair, then wandered around in the evening scents of the garden. He retired early and slept deeply throughout the night, although his sleep was animated by various dream images.

The weather did not get off to any better start the

following day. A land wind was blowing. Under the pale overcast sky, the sea lay in dull silence, looking almost shrunken, the horizon sobering and close, the tides so far back from the beach that long rows of sandbars had been exposed. Upon opening the window, Aschenbach thought he could smell the stale odor of the Lagoon.

His mood was bleak. He was already thinking about leaving. Once, years ago, following several bright weeks of springtime, he had been subjected to this sort of weather, with such adverse effects on his health that he had had to flee Venice like a refugee. Was this not the same listless fever, the same pressure behind the temples, the same heaviness in the eyelids? Changing locale again would be a bother, but if the wind didn't shift, his stay was up. To play it safe, he didn't unpack completely. At nine o'clock he ate breakfast in the buffet room between the parlor and the main dining area.

The air there was dominated by the solemn quiet great hotels pride themselves on. The waiters tiptoed back and forth serving the guests, and nothing could be heard beyond a rattle of the teapot and a half-whispered word. In a corner, diagonally across from the door, two tables down from his own, Aschenbach spotted the Polish girls with their governess. Bolt upright, their ash-blonde hair freshly slicked back, they sat with bloodshot eyes in stiff blue linen frocks with tiny white turndown collars and cuffs and passed around a jar of preserves. They had almost finished their breakfast. The boy was nowhere to be seen.

Aschenbach smiled. So, my little Phaeacian. It seems you alone enjoy the privilege of sleeping in. And cheering up suddenly, he recited to himself the line: ". . . changes of dress, warm baths and repose."

He ate a leisurely breakfast, took some forwarded mail from the porter, who deferentially entered the buffet room with braided cap in hand, and opened a couple of letters while smoking a cigarette. As a result, he was there to witness the arrival of the late sleeper whom they awaited over in the corner.

The boy entered through the glass door and passed

silently across the room to his sisters' table. In everything from the carriage of his upper body to the bend in his knees to the tread of his feet in their white shoes, his walk was extraordinarily graceful. It was quite light, delicate yet proud, and was made more beautiful still by the childlike modesty with which he twice batted his eyes and turned his head toward the dining room as he went along. Smiling, murmuring something half-audible in his softly liquid native tongue, he took his seat. At that moment the boy's full profile was facing in his direction, and the observing Aschenbach again marveled, indeed shuddered at the truly godlike beauty of this mortal child. Today the boy was wearing a thin blue-and-white stitched-blend uniform with a red silk breast-knot finishing at the neck in a simple white standing collar. Though this collar did not set off the rest of the outfit with particular elegance, his head floated atop it with incomparably charming beauty, like a flower in bloom. It was the head of Eros, its skin the lustrous yellow of Parian marble, its eyebrows well defined and earnest, both temples and one ear gently silhouetted by a perpendicular ringlet of hair.

Well done, well done, Aschenbach thought with the calculated professional approval that artists often use to mask their rapturous delight in the presence of a masterwork. Furthermore he thought, if the sea and the beach weren't waiting outside, I'd stay here as long as you did. With that, however, he left the buffet room, passing through the parlor, where the staff offered their courtesies. He crossed the large terrace and descended the stairs to the planks laid down on the sand for hotel guests to reach the reserved section of the beach. Inside the entrance, a barefoot old man in linen pants, a sailor's shirt and a straw hat, who turned out to be the lifeguard, showed him to the changing hut that came with his room. The man set up a table and a reclining beach chair on the hut's sandy wooden deck, and Aschenbach made himself comfortable, shoving the chair out onto the wax-yellow sand to be nearer the sea.

The beach scene—the sight of human culture frolicking carefree at the edge of that great element—uplifted his spirits and entertained him as much as ever. The shallow gray ocean was already well populated with wading children, swimmers and assorted colorful figures lying on the sandbars, their heads resting upon their folded arms. Others rowed around in little keelless boats painted red and blue, laughing whenever they capsized. The extended row of *capanne* with their miniature decks, where people sat as though on tiny verandas, provided a backdrop to the playful activity and the lazy sprawling relaxation, the visitations and the chatter, the proper morning elegance alongside the naked flesh taking bold yet casual advantage of the local liberties. Further on, individuals in white bathrobes and billowing, brightly dyed beach shirts strolled over the packed damp sand. To the right, some children had built a multitiered sandcastle crowned by a circle of tiny flags bearing a complete set of international colors. Vendors selling mussels, baked goods and fruit knelt down and spread out their wares. To the left, a Russian family was camped out in front of one of the huts that had been arranged in a row, perpendicular to the others and to the sea, so as to form a boundary at that end of the beach. There were bearded men with enormous teeth, women grown soft with inactivity, a Baltic girl behind an easel who kept crying out in frustration as she tried to paint the ocean, two cheerfully homely children and an old servant in a bandana with the mild, compliant mannerisms of a serf. They inhabited the beach, gratefully enjoying it all, patiently calling out the names of their disobediently rambunctious offspring, using what Italian they knew to joke a bit with the amusing old man from whom they bought candy and kissing each other on the cheeks, and didn't seem to care if anyone was watching. It was a thoroughly human troupe.

I'll stay then, Aschenbach decided. Where could it be better? And with his hands folded in his lap, his eyes drifted over the expanse of the sea, his gaze slipping away, blurring and ultimately disintegrating in the monotone haze of desolate space. He had a profoundly motivated love of the sea. As an artist, burdened by an artist's intense labors, he needed rest and longed to turn away from the taxing multiplicity of the external world, to bury his face in the breast of something simple and immense. At the same time, personally, he also felt a forbidden attraction—seductive precisely because it so directly contradicted his life's mission—toward everything unstructured, excessive and endless, an attraction to nothingness. Every overachiever's dream is the stasis of perfection. And is not nothingness a form of perfection? But as Aschenbach sat dreaming into the void, a human figure suddenly intersected with the horizontal of the shore's edge. When he withdrew his eyes from the limitless distance and refocused them, there to the left the beautiful young boy passed before him in the sand. His pants were rolled up to his knees for wading, and his thin legs were exposed. He walked by slowly, but with graceful pride, as though quite accustomed to going around barefoot, staring over at the perpendicular row of huts. Yet hardly had he noticed the Russian family gratefully and peaceably going about their business, than a storm cloud of angry contempt passed across his face. His expression darkened, he grimaced, his mouth tensed, his lips bitterly curled to one side so that a wrinkle ran through his cheek, and his brows furrowed deeply enough for his eyes to appear sunken beneath their weight. They were dark and malevolent, speaking the language of hatred. He looked at the ground, then glanced back again menacingly, before an emphatically dismissive gesture of rejection with his shoulders ended the matter, and he turned his back upon his enemies.

A sudden pang of delicacy or scandalization, something between respect and shame, caused Aschenbach to turn away as though he had seen nothing, for it goes against the grain of any mature person to exploit, even for private consumption, an accidentally observed moment of passion. Nevertheless, Aschenbach was simultaneously heartened and surprised, that is to say, delighted. This childish extremism, which had been directed against such a good-natured embodiment of life, humanized the boy's divine impenetrability. It made an exquisite natural sculpture, which until now had been merely a feast for the eyes, suddenly seem worthy of a deeper interest. It gave this half-grown adolescent, already remarkable for his beauty, an external layer that allowed him to be taken more seriously than his years.

Eyes still averted, Aschenbach strained to discern the boy's voice, a bright but somewhat weak one, which was struggling to announce its owner's arrival from a distance. He greeted his playmates at work on the sandcastle, and they answered by repeatedly shouting his name, or some nickname. Aschenbach listened with special curiosity without being able to make out anything more distinct than two melodic syllables, "Adgio" or more often "Adgiu," with a drawn-out *u* like a call at the end. He was happy about the sound of the name—he found that the pleasant vowels suited the object to which they referred—and repeated it to himself *sotto voce*. Then he returned, satisfied, to his letters and papers.

With his portable escritoire on his knees, he took up his fountain pen and started to work on some odds and ends of correspondence. However, after only fifteen minutes, he felt it was a shame to squander his present situation, the most enjoyable one he knew, mentally abandoning it in favor of some insignificant activity. He tossed his materials aside and returned his attention to the sea. Before long, distracted by the young voices from the sandcastle, he had inclined his head to the right, resting it comfortably on the back of his beach chair in order to investigate once more the various pursuits of the excellent Adgio.

He located him at once—it was impossible to miss the red knot on his chest. Busy with some others laying down an old plank for a bridge across the castle's damp moat, he called out instructions, nodding his head now and then. In addition to him, there were about ten other children, boys and girls, his own age and younger, who jabbered in tongues, mixing Polish, French and even Balkan languages. His name, however, was the one that was heard most often. Obviously he was coveted, courted, admired. One boy in particular, a fellow Pole called something like "Yashu," seemed to be his highest vassal and closest friend: he was a strapping young lad with black pomaded hair in a linen jumpsuit. When work on the sandcastle had been temporarily completed, they walked arm in arm the length of the beach, with the one called "Yashu" kissing his beautiful friend.

Aschenbach was sorely tempted to shake a finger at him. "And you, Critobulos," he thought with a smile, "spend a year traveling. You'll need at least that long to recover." And then he ate a second breakfast, some large, perfectly ripe strawberries bought from a vendor. It had grown very hot, though the sun had never managed to break through the thin layer of mist in the sky. Laziness overcame his mind as his senses reveled in the vast, hypnotic spectacle of the sea. To guess or otherwise ascertain the Christian name corresponding to "Adgio" seemed like a perfectly appropriate and satisfying way for this serious man to spend his time. Thanks to some recollections about the Polish language, he succeeded in determining that the name had to be "Tadzio," a shortened form of "Tadeusz" inflected to "Tadziu" as a form of address.

Tadzio was swimming. Aschenbach, who had lost sight of him, spotted his head, then his arm, one hand waving with a paddling motion, far out in the water. The sea obviously remained shallow for some distance. Nonetheless, there was already concern for his safety, already women's voices were calling out to him from the huts, repeatedly crying out that name, whose soft consonants and final drawn-out *u* dominated the beach almost like a battle cry, possessing something both sweet and wild: "Tadziu! Tadziu!" He turned and ran back against the current, his head thrown back, his legs beating the resisting water to foam. And to watch this mortal figure, boyishly fair yet precociously dour, emerge sprinting from the element with dripping locks, beautiful, like a tender young god born of the depths of air and sea—the sight conjured up mythic images. It was like something from a poetic saga about the dawn of time, when the universe was originally given form and the gods were born. Aschenbach shut his eyes and listened to the song playing within him, and once more he thought that it was good where he was and that he wanted to stay.

Later on, Tadzio lay in the sand resting from his swim, a white towel drawn under his right shoulder, his head on his bare arm. Even when Aschenbach stopped staring at him to read a few pages of his book, he hardly ever forgot that the boy was lying there, that it only cost him a slight rightward turn of the head to glimpse that sight which was so worthy of admiration. He could almost imagine himself sitting there for the resting boy's protection, busy with his own matters, yet ever watchful over the fine visual representation of humankind to his right, not far from him. And his heart was filled and moved by a kind of paternal pride, by the sentimental affection of the self-sacrificing creative mind that produces beauty toward someone who simply possesses it.

After twelve he left the beach, returned to the hotel and took the elevator up to his room. Inside, he stood before the mirror for some time gazing at his gray hair, at his weary and drawn face. He was thinking just then about his fame, about the people who recognized him on the street and stared with reverent awe, out of respect for his unerring, gracefully polished skill with words. He recalled every bit of worldly success he could muster and even reminisced about being awarded the title of nobility. He then went down to the dining room and ate lunch at his small table. Getting into the elevator after the meal, Aschenbach was pushed to the back of the suspended little cubicle by a crowd of young people, who had also just finished eating. Tadzio was among them. He was standing quite close to Aschenbach, closer than ever before, so that the latter, looking for the first time from a vantage other than that of picturesque distance, could see and observe him precisely, in human detail. Someone spoke to the boy as they reached the second floor, and although he was already getting off, he responded with an indescribably charming smile, stepping out backwards from the elevator and batting his eyes. Beauty makes bashful, Aschenbach thought, probing the question of why that should be the case. On the other hand, he had also noticed that Tadzio did not have the best of teeth: they were rather jagged and pale, lacking healthy luster and of that peculiar brittle translucence common among anemics. He's quite delicate, even sickly, thought Aschenbach. He's probably not long for this world. And he refused to analyze a certain feeling of satisfaction, or reassurance, which accompanied this thought.

He spent two hours in his room that afternoon before taking the *vaporetto* across the foul-smelling Lagoon to Venice. He disembarked at San Marco, drank a cup of tea on the Piazza, then set off on a stroll through the streets, as he had done whenever he was there before. However, it was this routine walk that completely changed his mood and his plans.

A repulsive humidity pervaded the narrow streets. The air was so thick that the smells from apartments, shops, food stands—the stench of oil and sprayed perfume among other things—collected in great hovering clouds. Cigarette smoke lingered, taking forever to disperse. The push and shove of people in such tight quarters did not amuse the strolling tourist. On the contrary, he found it merely oppressive. The further Aschenbach went on, the more he was plagued, indeed overcome by that atrocious condition of simultaneous nervousness and exhaustion which can arise from the combination of salt air and the sirocco. He broke out in an embarrassing sweat. His vision blurred, his chest constricted, he felt feverish and a vein began to throb in his head. He fled the crowded streets of the shopping district, crossing over bridges into the alleyways of the poorer quarters, where beggars molested him, and the foul canal vapors made breathing difficult. Resting on the edge of a fountain in a quiet square, one of those forgotten and seemingly accursed localities in the interior of Venice, he wiped the sweat from his brow and realized that he would have to travel on.

Twice, and now definitively, it had been demonstrated that this city could be quite harmful to him in this weather. Obstinately sticking it out seemed irrational—

there was no guarantee the wind would shift. A quick decision was required. To go home so soon was out of the question. Neither his summer nor his winter quarters stood ready to receive him. But there were other beaches on the sea, and elsewhere they came without the harmful additives of the Lagoon and its febrile vapors. He remembered the name of a small seaside spa not far from Trieste that had been recommended to him. Why not go there? Yes, indeed, without delay, while the repeated change of locale still made sense. He told himself his mind was made up and rose to his feet. At the next stop, he hired a gondola to ferry him through the gloomy labyrinth of canals back toward the Piazza San Marco. It took him under ornate marble balconies flanked by sculpted lions, around corners of slimy stone walls and past mournful facades of *pallazi* topped by giant advertising signs that were reflected in the rippling bilge water. He had difficulty reaching his destination, for the gondolier was in league with various lace factories and glassworks and kept trying to drop him off to see and buy things. Thus, whenever the bizarre excursion through Venice began to cast a magic spell, the cutthroat commercialism of this sunken queen of cities did its irritating best to restore his senses to sobriety.

Back in the hotel before dinner, he notified the office that unforeseen circumstances had forced his departure early the next morning. Regret was expressed; his bill was settled. He ate, then spent the lukewarm evening on the back terrace reading periodicals in a rocking chair. Before going to bed, he finished packing for his departure.

Nervous at the prospect of another change of location, he didn't sleep all that well. In the morning, when he opened his windows, the skies were still overcast, but the air did seem a bit fresher. And regret, too, had already set in. Was it not a hasty and premature step to announce his departure, the result of the exceptional circumstance of feeling a bit ill? If only he had held off and not given up so quickly, waited to see whether he might not have acclimated himself to the Venetian air, or whether the weather itself might not have changed, he could right now be looking forward to another morning on the beach like yesterday, instead of having to hustle and bustle around. Too late. Now he had no choice but to carry on wanting what he had wanted the day before. He got dressed and went down at eight to the ground floor for breakfast.

On his arrival the buffet room was entirely empty, although a few people did straggle in while he sat waiting for his order. Sipping his tea, he watched as the Polish girls turned up together with their governess. Severe and morning fresh with their bloodshot eyes, they walked over to their corner table by the window. Immediately afterward the porter approached, cap in hand, to remind him that it was time to leave. The car was waiting to take him and other departing guests to the Hotel Excelsior, where a motorboat would convey them to the train station via a private company canal. Time was of the essence. — Aschenbach, however, did not think it was so at all. Over an hour remained until his train was scheduled to depart. He was irritated by this old hotel trick for getting rid of guests early and told the porter he wished to eat his breakfast in peace. The man hesitated, then withdrew, only to reappear five minutes later. The car wouldn't wait any longer. Then let it go, Aschenbach responded with exasperation, and send my bags along with it—he himself would take the *vaporetto* when it was time. Would they please let him worry about his own departure? The hotel employee bowed. Aschenbach, glad to have fended off such bothersome reminders, lingered over breakfast and even had the waiter bring him a newspaper. It was quite late when he finally did get up. As it so happened, that was the very moment Tadzio entered through the glass door.

On his way over to his family's table, the boy crossed the departing Aschenbach's path. He modestly lowered his eyes before the man with the gray hair and the lofty brow, only to raise them again immediately, gentle and wide, in signature charming manner toward the observer's own. Then he was past. Adieu Tadzio! Aschenbach thought. I saw you briefly. And with his lips, contrary to habit, literally forming and mouthing words for his thoughts, he added: "Bless you, dear boy." — He then commenced his departure, doling out gratuities, seeing himself escorted out by the small, soft-spoken manager in the French frock coat, leaving the hotel as he had come, on foot, followed by a servant carrying his hand luggage, retracing his steps across the island along that white-blossomed avenue toward the *vaporetto* landing. He arrives there, he takes his seat—and what followed was the journey of a grief-stricken man, a journey of sorrow, through the very depths of regret.

It was the familiar trip across the Lagoon, past the Piazza San Marco and up the Grand Canal. Aschenbach sat on the curved bench in the bow, his elbow on the rail, shading his eyes with his hand. The public gardens were quickly left behind. The Piazetta again opened up in all its princely grace and was abandoned. Then came the great flight of *palazzi,* and, as the canal snaked around in the opposite direction, the splendidly spanned marble arch of the Rialto appeared. The travelling Aschenbach took everything in, and his heart was torn. The air in the city, the slightly rotten smell of sea and swamp, which he had been in such a hurry to flee—he now inhaled it with deep, bittersweet breaths. Was it possible for him not to have known, not to have considered how much this all meant to him? What this morning had been a partial regret, a slight doubt as to the wisdom of his actions, now became wound, physical pain, an anguish of the soul so bitter that his eyes repeatedly welled over with tears. He told himself he could not possibly have anticipated this pain. As far as he was aware what he found so trying, indeed at times utterly unbearable, was the thought of never again seeing Venice, the thought that this time, it was goodbye for good. Having twice been shown that the city made him sick, having again been forced to flee it headlong, it would have to be regarded from now on as off limits, as a place that was beyond his capacities and that it would be senseless to revisit. Indeed, he realized that, if he left now, shame and bitter pride would surely keep him from ever seeing this beloved city again, where he had twice failed physically. This conflict between the inclinations of the soul and the capabilities of the flesh suddenly seemed so profound and weighty—the prospect of physical defeat so humiliating, so crucial to avoid at all cost—that the aging Aschenbach could no longer comprehend his easy capitulation of yesterday, when, without any significant struggle, he had decided simply to give up and accept the consequences.

Meanwhile, the *vaporetto* approaches the train station, and pain and helplessness intensify to the point of bewilderment. Departure seems impossible, turning back equally so. The poor tortured man enters the station utterly torn in this way. It is quite late. He has not a moment to lose if he wants to catch his train. He wants to and yet doesn't want to. But the clock beckons, drives him forward. He hurriedly buys his ticket and peers into the tumult of the great hall for the hotel representative, who is supposed to be stationed here. The man appears and reports that his large suitcase has already been checked through. Already checked through? Yes, with pleasure, sir—checked through to Como. To Como? And it turns out in the ensuing rapid-fire exchange of angry questions and embarrassed answers that, no sooner had his suitcase arrived in the luggage office of the Hotel Excelsior, than it was forwarded, along with some other outside baggage, in the entirely wrong direction.

Aschenbach had difficulty maintaining the only sort of facial expression that made sense under such circumstances. An adventurous joy, a glee transcending belief, suddenly seized his heart from deep within, almost convulsively. The hotel employee rushed off to see if he could re-collect the errant suitcase and returned, as expected, empty-handed. At that, Aschenbach declared himself unwilling to travel on without his luggage and stated his decision to go back to the beach hotel to await its reappearance. Was the company motorboat still at the train station? The man assured him it was waiting right outside. With typical Italian eloquence he persuaded the counter attendant to refund the price of Aschenbach's ticket, pledging all the while that telegrams would be sent and no effort spared to get the suitcase back very soon. Thus the unlikely happened, and the traveler, twenty minutes after arriving at the train station, found himself once more upon the Grand Canal, heading back to the Lido.

An unbelievably strange, humbling adventure! An absurd interlude from a dream! To stand again before the very stations from which you have just parted forever, in the deepest of sorrow! To stand there less than an hour later, because fate has turned you round and sent you back! Dodging gondola and *vaporetti* in a series of amusingly nimble back-and-forth tacks, the eager little boat proceeded toward its destination, spray before its bow, its lone passenger concealing the anxious exuberance of a truant schoolboy under a mask of irritated resignation. Now and then, his sides still shook with laughter at his mishap, which, as he told himself, couldn't have come at a more opportune time. Explanations would have to be given, surprised looks endured—but then, as he told himself, everything would be put right, a disaster averted, a serious mistake rectified, and all that he thought he had left behind would open up once more before him, to be had at his leisure. What's more, did the speed of the motorboat deceive him, or was the wind now, to top it all off, indeed really blowing in from the sea?

The ship's wake broke against the concrete walls of that narrow canal which cuts across the island to the Hotel Excelsior. A motorbus was waiting there above the rippling ocean water to take the returning guest directly back to the beach hotel. The small manager with the moustache and the frock coat and tails came down the front steps to greet him.

In soft-spoken sycophantic words he expressed his regret over the incident, calling it extremely embarrassing both for himself and his establishment, although he emphatically endorsed Aschenbach's decision to remain there to await his luggage. His room had admittedly been given away, but another, just as good, was at his immediate disposal. *"Pas de chance, monsieur,"* said the Swiss elevator boy with a smile as they were swept upstairs. Thus the refugee was reinstalled in the hotel, in a room whose location and furnishings were almost identical to his earlier one.

He distributed the contents of his hand luggage about the room and then sank, exhausted and numb from the whirlwind of activity on this extraordinary morning, into an easy chair near the window. The sea had taken on a pale green tint, the air seemed fresher and less thick, and the beach with its huts and boats looked more colorful, even though the sky was still gray. Aschenbach gazed out, his hands folded in his lap, content to be there once more, shaking his head at having been so fickle, at not having known what he really wanted. Thus he sat for at least an hour, resting and daydreaming, undisturbed by any real thoughts. Around noon he caught sight of Tadzio in the striped linen outfit with the red breast-knot, emerging from the sea, exiting the beach, then coming up the boardwalk back to the hotel. From his elevated vantage point, Aschenbach recognized him at once, before the boy had actually become fully visible, and was about to think something like: why, Tadzio, there you are again, too! But in that very instant he felt the flippant greeting die on his lips, sinking down before the truth in his heart. He felt the quickening of his blood, the joy and pain within his soul, and he realized that Tadzio was the reason it had been so difficult to leave.

He sat quite still, quite out of sight, high on his perch, and scrutinized what was going on inside him. His features came alive, he raised his brows and an alert smile of intellectual curiosity crossed his lips. Then he raised his head and, with his arms hanging limply from the armrests of his chair, began to describe a slow upward circular motion, simultaneously extending his palms, as though to suggest that those arms might fully open and spread. It was a gesture of eager welcoming, of calm acceptance.

Chapter Four

Every day now, the bare-skinned, fiery-cheeked god piloted his heat-breathing chariot across the sky's expanse, his golden locks waving in the simultaneously storming east wind. Silky-white radiance hung over the slow swells of the *pontos*. The sand was glowing hot. Before the changing huts, rust-colored canvas awnings were unfurled beneath the silvery glimmering blue of the ether, and the morning hours were passed in the sharply defined patches of shade they provided. Exquisite, too, was the night, when the park flora gave off soothing fragrances, the stars above danced in lines and the softly insistent murmur of the darkened sea conjured over the soul. Each evening contained the joyful promise of another sunny day of easily disposed leisure, a day made more attractive still by sweet fortune's dense and infinite assortment of possibilities.

The guest so conveniently detained by mishap was not at all inclined to see the restoration of his possessions as a reason for resuming his departure. For two long days, he had endured no small privation and had been forced to wear his traveling clothes to meals in the large dining room. So when his misdirected baggage was finally deposited back in his room, he unpacked completely, filling the closet and bureau with his things, set for now on an unrestricted stay, content to be able again to pass the hours on the beach in his silk suit and appear for dinner at his small table in appropriate evening attire.

The comfortably constant rhythm of this existence had put him under its spell, and he was quickly captivated by the soft luxurious ease of his newfound way of life. And what a place it is that combines the charms of a cultivated Southern European seaside resort with the constant proximity of such a strange and wonderful city! Aschenbach was no great fun lover. Whenever and wherever it was necessary to stop working, recover his peace of mind and take a few days off, restlessness and dissatisfaction would soon compel him to resume his noble toil and devoutly austere daily routine. This had been especially true of him as a young man. Venice alone had enchanted him, relaxed his ambition and made him feel happy. There were times when he thought back: in the morning, as he sat before his hut in the shadow of the awning dreaming off into the blue of the southern sea, or on mild nights under the great starry sky, as he leaned back into the cushions of the gondola ferrying him home after a long evening on the Piazza, the bright lights and fluid melodies of serenades receding behind him. He thought back to his country house in the mountains, the site of his annual summer battles. He remembered the low drifting of the clouds over the yard, the power outages in the house after violent evening thunderstorms and the flight of the ravens he fed into the tops of the pines. And it seemed to him in such moments that he had been transported to Elysium, to the very end of the earth, where mortal men were blessed with lives of utmost ease, where, instead of snow and winter, storms and pounding rain, Oceanus forever blew his gentle cooling breath and the days trickled away in blissful indolence, effortlessly, without struggle, entirely given over to the sun and its rituals.

Aschenbach saw the boy Tadzio frequently, almost constantly. A small radius of activity and commonly assigned routines preordained that, with only brief interruptions, the beautiful boy would be in his vicinity throughout the day. He saw, indeed met him everywhere: downstairs in the hotel, on the refreshing boat rides to the city and back, amidst the splendor of the Piazza, and often high and low and in between if he was lucky. Above all, however, it was mornings on the beach that provided him with regular opportunity to appreciate and study the fair vision. Indeed, it was exactly this happy arrangement—the daily recreation of such favorable circumstances—that filled Aschenbach with joyful satisfaction and caused him to savor his stay as it stretched on and on so pleasantly, one sunny day after the next.

He would get up early, as though still driven by his compulsive work habits, and arrive at the beach before most of the others, when the sun was still mild and the sea dazzlingly white in morning dreams. He would amiably greet the attendant at the gate and would also exchange familiar hellos with the barefoot old-timer, who always had his spot well-prepared—brown awning unfurled, beach furniture removed and set up on deck—before settling into his chair. The next three or four hours would then be his, hours in which the sun climbed in the sky and took on a terrible intensity, in which the ocean turned a deeper and deeper blue and in which he was permitted to watch Tadzio.

He would see him approaching from the left along the edge of the sea. He would suddenly spy his back emerging from between the huts or sometimes he would discover, not without joyous alarm, that he had missed the boy's arrival, that he was already there and had already resumed, in the blue-and-white-striped swimsuit that had become his exclusive beach attire, his usual sun-and-sand activities—that delightfully trivial, idly restless life of play and relaxation, one long span of strolling, wading, digging, chasing, lying and swimming, watched over and summoned by the women on the deck, who kept shouting his name "Tadziu! Tadziu!" in falsetto and to whom he came running, gesturing with excitement, to tell of his adventures and show his various finds and catches: mussels, tiny sea horses, jellyfish, sideways scuttling crabs. Aschenbach didn't understand a single word of what he said, but however commonplace it might have been, the sounds were a lovely warm blur in his ear. The impenetrability of the foreign tongue turned the boy's speech to music, an irrepressible sun bathed him in luxuriant glow and the sublimely deep view of the sea provided a constant backdrop and background against which he appeared.

Soon the observant Aschenbach knew every line and pose of this so superior, uninhibited body, joyously welcoming each feature of its already familiar beauty anew and knowing no end for either his admiration or the gentle desire of his senses. A voice might summon the boy to greet a guest waiting upon the women at their hut. He would run by, perhaps wet from the sea, tossing his locks, and as he shook hands, he would rotate his body in a most charming way, in one graceful taut twist—one leg bearing his full weight, the other extending its toes—embarrassed at being so adorable, anxious to fulfill his aristocratic duty and please the visitor. Or he might lie outstretched, a beach towel wrapped around his chest, his finely sculpted arm braced in the sand, his hand cupping his chin. The one called "Yashu" would squat to the side, doting on him, and nothing could have been more enchanting than the chosen one, with a smile in his eyes and on his lips, looking up at his vassal, his servant. Or he might stand there at the edge of the sea, alone, away from his family, quite near Aschenbach, tall, slowly rocking back and forth on the balls of his feet, his hands clasped behind his neck, dreaming off into the blue, while tiny in-rolling waves bathed his toes. His honey-colored hair curled in ringlets around his temples and neck, the down on his upper spine gleamed in the sun, the fine contours of his ribs and his even chest emerged through the thin wrapping around his torso, his armpits ran smooth as a statue's, the hollows of his knees glistened and, thanks to their bluish veins, his entire body appeared to be made of some more translucent material. What discipline, what precision of thought was expressed in this youthful body, stretched out in all its perfection! The strength and purity of that will, whose obscure activity had succeeded in realizing this divine sculpture—did not he, as artist, know it through and through? Was it not also at work within him, as he chipped away, full of sober passion, at the marble block of language to release that sleek form glimpsed in his imagination, which he then presented to his fellow man as a model and mirror of sublime beauty?

A model and mirror! His eyes took in the exquisite figure there at the edge of the blue, and in his mounting rapture he was convinced that, with this sight, he had apprehended beauty itself, form as divine thought, the one true, absolute perfection, which resides in the realm of the sublime and whose representation and reflection in human form had been placed here, light and fair, to be worshipped. Such was his intoxication, and the aging artist invited it upon himself heedlessly, even greedily. His imagination went into labor, his learning came to a boil and his memory dredged up ancient thoughts that had been preserved since childhood but had never before been animated with any fire of their own. Was it not written somewhere that exposure to the sun turns the attention from intellectual to sensory perception? Accordingly, it numbs, indeed bewitches reason and memory in such a way that the soul, overwhelmed by happiness, entirely forgets its actual state and clings in dumbstruck awe to that which is most beautiful amidst whatever is illuminated. In fact, it is only with the help of a bodily presence that the over-exposed soul can succeed in elevating itself to a higher level of contemplation. The god Amor, forsooth, was like those mathematicians who introduce slow pupils to abstract shapes via specific images. In order that we might know the sublime, he gladly availed himself of the form and hue of human youth, embellishing them with the reflected light of beauty into a kind of mnemonic device, the sight of which literally inflames us with anguish and hope.

Such were the enraptured Aschenbach's thoughts; such were the feelings of which he had become capable. A charming scene materialized before him that was put together from the rushing sea and glittering sunlight. It was the ancient plane tree, not far from the walls of Athens—that place of holy shadows and scents of *agnus castus*, adorned by sacred statues and pious tributes in honor of the waters of the Achelous and its nymphs. The river ran crystal clear over the smooth pebbles at the foot of the broad tree. Crickets chirped. On the meadow, which sloped gently so as to allow both the body to recline and the head to be held upright, two people were taking shelter from the midday heat: one older and the other young, one ugly and the other beautiful, the wise man with the adorable boy. Paying compliments all the while, couching his overtures in witty remarks, Socrates instructed Phaedrus as to the nature of desire and virtue. He told him of the searing panic of the passionate soul upon glimpsing a likeness of eternal beauty, told him of the envy felt by the profane, base soul, unable to conceive of beauty even while viewing its image and thus incapable of awe, told him of the divine terror of the noble soul before the sight of a godlike countenance or a perfect body—told him how that soul starts to tremble and lose composure, hardly daring to look, yet reveres the individual who possesses beauty almost to the point of offering up sacrifices, as though to an idol, were it not for the fear of appearing foolish before other men. For beauty, good Phaedrus, and beauty alone is both visible to the human eye and worthy of adoration: it is—mark my word!—the only form of the sublime that our senses can both perceive and endure. What would become of us if other divine ideals, if reason and virtue and truth were to reveal themselves to our senses? Would we not perish, burn up with love just as Semele once did before Zeus? Beauty is thus the path of the passionate toward divine spirit—yet only the path, only a means, young Phaedrus. . . . Then he made his subtlest pronouncement, that sly suitor, namely that the lover is more blessed than the beloved because God resides in the former, not the latter—probably the most tender and mocking of thoughts that has ever been conceived and one that still spawns all the mischievous and most secret lusting of the human heart.

The writer's greatest joy is thought become feeling, feeling become thought. At this moment, just such a pulsating thought, just such a precise feeling was in the solitary writer's power and possession, namely, that nature itself shudders with delight whenever the human mind bows to honor beauty. He suddenly longed to write. The god Eros may love idle hands, as it's said. He may even exist especially for them. Nonetheless, the restlessness of the haunted Aschenbach in this his moment of crisis ran toward productivity. It was almost inconsequential what the occasion was. A call had gone out into the educated world for closely scrutinized debate on a certain great burning question of culture and taste and had caught up with the traveling writer. He knew the subject—he had indeed experienced it firsthand—and all of a sudden his craving to illuminate it in the light of his own words was irresistible. In fact, what he longed for was to work on it in Tadzio's presence, to use the boy's appearance as a model while writing, to let his style follow the contours of this body, which seemed to be so divine, transporting its physical beauty into the realm of the sublime imagination as the mythical eagle had once transported the Trojan shepherd into the ether. Never had he known the desire for language to be more sweet, never had he been so certain that the god of love resided in the written word, as during the perilously delicious hours at his makeshift desk under the awning, in full view of his sacred image, the music of the boy's voice in his ears. He crafted his short essay on Tadzio's beauty, that page and a half of exquisite prose whose unalloyed purity, nobility and soaring emotional tautness were soon to win widespread admiration. It's a good thing the world knows only the finished work and not its origins or the circumstances of its creation, for knowing the sources from which inspiration comes to the artist would only create confusion and mistrust, thereby robbing excellence of its effect. What extraordinary hours! What extraordinarily nerve-racking labor! What exceptionally fertile intercourse between the mind and one individual body! As Aschenbach put away his work and left the beach, he felt exhausted, indeed shattered, as though from stirrings of conscience after a bout of excess.

It was on the following morning when, in the process of leaving the hotel, he noticed from atop the front steps that the already ocean-bound Tadzio was approaching—alone—the gate that led to the beach. He was seized by a wish, an ever so simple plan. He could exploit the opportunity and establish easy, friendly contact with the unwitting cause of his great inner uprising and turmoil. He could address the boy, then bask in the attention when he responded. The beautiful boy was ambling along, he was slow enough to be overtaken, and Aschenbach hurried his steps. He catches up with him on the wooden stairs to the rear of the huts, he's determined to lay a hand on the boy's head or clap him on the shoulders and say something; an amiable French phrase is on the tip of his tongue. But then he feels his heart beating like a hammer—perhaps this is also due to the physical exertion—and senses how panting and tremulous his voice will sound with him breathing so heavily. He hesitates, tries to regain composure and suddenly fears that he has trailed the boy for too long, that something will attract his attention and make him turn around. He begins another approach and breaks it off, before finally giving up and walking past his quarry with his head down.

Too late! he thought. Too late! But was it too late? The action he had just postponed taking might very well have had positive results, unburdening him and heartening him for a healthy sobering up. The truth was most likely that the aging Aschenbach didn't want sobriety, that his intoxication was just too precious. Who can solve the eternal riddle of that peculiar stamp of humanity, the artist? Who can fully comprehend the deep merging of instincts for discipline and abandon that makes artists what they are? For the inability to want sobriety and health is the very definition of abandon. Aschenbach was no longer in the mood for self-criticism; his tastes and his state of mind in his later years—dignity, maturity and late-found directness—left him disinclined to dissect his motives and examine whether it was conscience, or dissipation and weakness, that lay behind his failure to carry out his plan. He was agitated, afraid that someone, if only the lifeguard, might have seen his hasty approach and capitulation. He was very afraid indeed of appearing ridiculous. On the other hand, he looked upon his comically devout fears with a sense of humor. Felled, he thought, felled like a gamecock too scared to raise its wings during a fight. This is the true face of the god who breaks our courage at the very moment we catch sight of the one we adore, leaving our pride trampled in the dust. Aschenbach toyed with this thought, became rhapsodic and was far too full of himself to fear an emotion.

Already he no longer registered the dwindling of his self-allotted time off, and the thought of returning home never occurred to him even once. He had withdrawn ample money from his accounts. His only worry was the possible departure of the Polish family, although from a casually dropped question he had found out from the hotel coiffeur that these excellent guests had settled in there only just prior to his own arrival. Meanwhile his hands and face grew brown in the sun, and the salty air invigorated him to further emotion. But whereas he usually expended any energy recuperated from sleep, nourishment or the outdoors on some great work, he now gleefully squandered all the strength he gathered from his daily relaxation in the sun and salt air on intoxicated feelings.

He slept in short bursts, his exquisitely uniform days broken up by short nights of happy restlessness. Although he always retired early—for him, the day seemed over by nine o'clock, when Tadzio disappeared—he awoke suddenly, as though from a light shock, at the break of dawn. His heart recalled its ongoing adventure, it drove him from his pillows, and he got up, wrapped in a light robe against the morning chill, to sit by his open window waiting for sunrise. That miraculous event filled his soul, still solemn from sleep, with pious reverence. Sky, earth and sea lay motionless behind a ghostly, glassy pale; one dying star still floated visible against the void. Then a breeze came up, a giddy harbinger from unapproachable domains, announcing Eos' imminent rise from her husband's side, and that first sweet blush of the furthest stretches of sea and sky began, indicating that things were to become knowable to the senses. The goddess approached, that seductress of young men, that thief of Cleitus and Cephalus, who, braving the envy of all Olympus, had reveled in the love of beautiful Orion. Roses were strewn at the edge of the world. There was a shining and blossoming too fair for words. Infant clouds, transfigured and illuminated, hovered like attending *amoretti* in the pinkish blue haze. Crimson descended over the sea, whose waves seemed to wash it shoreward. Golden spears shot from below toward the highest reaches of heaven, their radiance igniting. Silent, driven by a superior force of divinity, heat and fire and burning flames surged upward, and the heavenly coursers of brother Apollo tucked their hooves and ascended over the surface of the earth. Basking in the god's splendor, Aschenbach sat alone and awake, his eyes shut, letting glory kiss his lids. Emotions once felt—precious heartaches from the past that had perished before his life's strict sense of duty—now returned, strangely transformed. He recognized them with a smile of confusion and astonishment. He pondered, he daydreamed, slowly a name formed on his lips, and, still smiling, with his face upturned and his hands folded in his lap, he fell asleep again in his armchair.

But the day that began with such fiery ceremony continued on strangely exalted, mythically transformed. Where did that breeze come from, which played, all at once, like a higher intimation, so gently yet so significantly around his temples and ears? Bands of feathery white clouds stood scattered across the sky like the grazing herds of the gods. The wind increased, and the steeds of Poseidon reared up and ran, bulls, no doubt, too, also property of the blue-haired god, which lowered their horns and bellowed as they charged. On the other hand, among the scree of the more distant beach, the waves sprang in the air like mountain goats. A world full of Panically driven life enveloped the captivated Aschenbach, and his heart dreamt tender fables. More than once, as the sun set behind Venice, he sat on a bench in the hotel park and watched as Tadzio played happily with a ball on the rolled gravel courtyard in a white outfit with a colorful belt. He could have sworn he was watching Hyacinth, who was fated to die young because a pair of gods loved him. He could literally feel Zephyr's agonized jealousy at how his competitor neglected oracle, bow and zither in order to play endlessly with the beautiful boy. He could see the discus, directed by terrible envy, strike the boy's adorable head. Turning pale himself, he caught the twisted body, and the flower that bloomed from the boy's sweet blood was inscribed with his never-ending lament. . . .

Nothing is more bizarre and uncomfortable than the relationship between people acquainted only by sight—people who come face to face on a daily, even hourly basis yet feel compelled by etiquette or foolish obstinacy to forgo all words of greeting, each maintaining a pretense of blithe unawareness of the other's existence. Unease and overworked curiosity hang in the air between them, the neurotic expression of an unsatisfied, unnaturally repressed need for recognition and interaction, along with a kind of tense respect. People, after all, only love and respect other people so long as they remain unable to judge them. Longing is a child of ignorance.

It was inevitable that some sort of relationship and acquaintance would develop between Aschenbach and young Tadzio, and the older man was delighted to discover that his interest and attention did not go wholly unreciprocated. What, for example, had motivated the beautiful boy to stop using the wooden stairs in the back for his morning walk to the beach and to take to strolling via the sand to join his family, passing sometimes so unnecessarily close to Aschenbach's domain that he would nearly brush up against his table or chair? Was it an attraction, a fascination exercised by a superior emotion on its delicate and unthinking object? Aschenbach awaited Tadzio's arrival every day. Sometimes he pretended to be busy when the actual event took place and let the beautiful boy pass seemingly unnoticed. But other times, he glanced up and their eyes met. Both parties turned deeply solemn whenever that happened. Nothing in the cultured and dignified expression of the older man betrayed any inner turmoil. There was, however, an inquisitive look in Tadzio's eyes, a look of reflective questioning. A moment's hesitation would often break his stride, he would bat his eyes charmingly, and after he had passed, something in his posture would seem to indicate that only his proper upbringing kept him from looking back.

On one occasion, however, in the evening, things turned out differently. The Polish children and their governess had been absent from dinner in the main dining room—a fact that Aschenbach had noted with great concern. He was getting some fresh air after the meal, strolling in formal evening attire and a straw hat at the foot of the hotel's front terrace, feeling quite uneasy about their whereabouts, when he suddenly saw the nunlike sisters and their tutor appear in the light of the arc lamps. Tadzio was four steps behind. They were obviously returning from the *vaporetto* landing, having dined, for whatever reason, in the city. It must have been cool out on the water. Tadzio wore a dark blue seaman's jacket with gold buttons and a matching cap on his head. He seemed to be impervious to the burning sun and the harsh sea air—his skin retained its original marble-yellow—but today he appeared even paler than usual, either because of the chill or the bleaching effect of the artificial moonlight. His even brows emerged more sharply, and his eyes shone deep and black. He was more beautiful than words can express, and Aschenbach was painfully aware, as so often before, that words can only praise physical beauty, not reproduce it.

He was unprepared for this priceless apparition. It came unannounced, leaving him no time to assume an expression of composed dignity. Joy, surprise and wonder must have been splashed across his face as his eye met that of the missing boy, for at precisely that second it happened that Tadzio smiled, smiled *at* him with an insinuating, familiar, charming and unabashed smile, his lips parting only slowly at the end. It was the smile of Narcissus bending down over his reflection in the water, that deep, mesmerized, prolonged smile with which he reaches out toward the reflection of his own beauty—an ever so slightly off-kilter smile, distorted by the futility of wanting to kiss the fair lips of his own shadow, coquettish, curious and a bit troubled, enthralled and enthralling.

The man on the receiving end of this smile spirited it away like a fatal gift. He was shaken so profoundly that he felt compelled to flee the light of the terrace and the front garden and sought out the darkness of the park in the back. Strangely indignant protestations of delicacy escaped his lips: "You shouldn't smile that way! No one, do you hear, should be allowed to smile at a person that way!" He threw himself upon a bench and inhaled the night fragrance of the park flora, completely beside himself. And leaning back with his arms at his sides, stunned and overwhelmed, shuddering, he whispered that standing formula of human longing, impossible in this case, ridiculous and nonetheless still sacred, still worthy of respect even here: "I love you!"

Chapter Five

During the fourth week of his stay on the Lido, Gustav von Aschenbach made several troubling realizations concerning the world at large. To begin with, it seemed to him as if, with the height of the tourist season approaching, the number of guests were actually on the decline, and in particular as if the German language were fading into silence around him, to the point where, whether at his table or on the beach, only foreign sounds reached his ear. Then one day in conversation with the coiffeur, to whom he was now paying regular visits, he seized upon a word that aroused his suspicions. The man mentioned a German family who had departed suddenly after a short stay, adding as a bit of conversational flattery: "But you're staying, sir. You're not scared of any affliction." Aschenbach looked at him. "Affliction," he repeated. The gossip fell silent, fiddled with something, ignored the question. Then, when Aschenbach posed it again, more forcefully, he declared he knew nothing and tried with sheepish eloquence to change the subject.

That was around twelve. That afternoon in the dead calm and burning sun Aschenbach took the ferry over to Venice. He was now driven by a mania for following the Polish children, whom he had seen start for the *vaporetto* landing with their governess. He failed to find his demigod at the Piazza San Marco. But over tea, sitting at a round iron table on the shadowy side of the square, he suddenly detected a peculiar aroma in the air, which all at once seemed as though it had been present in his senses for days without ever penetrating his consciousness—a sweet antiseptic smell reminiscent of suffering and wounds and dubious hygiene. Pensive, he pondered it until he knew what it was, then finished his tea and exited the Piazza on the end opposite the Basilica. The smell was stronger in the narrow streets. On every corner hung printed notices from the city council reporting the occurrence of certain gastric ailments, not uncommon in such weather, and warning the public against the consumption of oysters or mussels, as well as any contact with canal water. The euphemistic nature of this announcement was obvious. People congregated silently on bridges and in squares, and the foreigner stood among them, taking things in and brooding.

He went up to a shopkeeper who was leaning amidst coral necklaces and fake amethyst jewelry in his arched doorway and asked for information about the ominous smell. The man quickly perked up and his heavy-lidded eyes looked him over. "A preventive measure, sir!" he answered, gesticulating. "A police ordinance deserving our support. This is oppressive sort of weather. The sirocco makes people feel sick and exhausted. In short—you understand—probably an exaggerated precaution. . . ." Aschenbach thanked him and moved on. Even on board the *vaporetto* to the Lido, he could now detect the smell of the antibacterial agent.

Back at the hotel he went straight to the reading table in the lobby with the newspapers and flipped through several of them. He found nothing in the non-German ones. Those from home, however, offered up rumors, cited contradictory statistics, quoted official denials and questioned their veracity. That explained the sudden disappearance of the German and Austrian contingents. The guests of other nationalities apparently knew nothing; unsuspecting, they felt no need for alarm. This is supposed to be a secret, the excited Aschenbach thought, tossing the papers back on the table. It's being kept quiet. But at the same time his heart was filled with happiness at the adventure the outside world was getting into, for passion, like criminality, cannot abide the security and welfare of everyday proceedings. It welcomes any relaxation of bourgeois law and order, any chaos and disruption in the world at large, cherishing the nebulous hope of finding some advantage. Thus Aschenbach felt a vague satisfaction at what was going on under the cover of official silence in the squalid alleys of Venice—at the merger of this terrible citywide secret with his own most personal one, which had been so important for him to protect. Being in love, he worried only that Tadzio might leave, recognizing with a trace of horror that he might not know how to go on living if that should happen.

By now, he was no longer content to trust daily routine and luck to put the beautiful boy within visible proximity. He had taken to following him, even shadowing him. On Sundays, for example, the Polish family never appeared on the beach. Having guessed that they attended mass at San Marco, he had rushed over and, escaping the Piazza's midday heat into the golden dusk of that holy shrine, had found the sorely missed Tadzio kneeling over a prie-dieu saying his prayers. Now every week he stood at the rear on the cracked mosaic floor amidst a crowd of kneeling, murmuring and cross-making worshippers, the solid grandeur of the Oriental basilica impressing itself upon him in all its opulence. Up front the ornately vested priest walked back and forth, handling objects and singing, billowing incense enshrouded the tiny hapless flames of the votive candles, and another faint scent seemed to mingle with the musty, sweety sacrificial air: the odor of the contaminated city. But through the smoke and twinkling lights Aschenbach could see the beautiful boy up in front turn his head and search him out.

Then, when the giant doors opened and the crowds streamed out onto the bright Piazza, aswarm with pigeons, the enthralled Aschenbach hid in the vestibule, lying in wait. He watched the Polish family depart from church, watched the children take ceremonious leave of their mother, who turned into the Piazetta toward home. He confirmed that the beautiful boy, the cloistral sisters and their governess had turned right through the gateway of the clock tower into the Merceria; and, after letting them get a head start, he followed them, followed them surreptitiously as they strolled through Venice. He had to stop whenever they lingered, had to duck into snack shops and courtyards every time they changed direction; he would lose them and search in frantic exhaustion, over bridges and in dirty dead-end alleys, only to endure minutes of mortal agony whenever he suddenly spotted them coming toward him in a narrow passage with no possible escape. Nonetheless, you couldn't say that he suffered. His head and his heart were drunk, and his steps were directed by that demon who takes pleasure at trampling man's reason and dignity underfoot.

Usually Tadzio and his family took a gondola. Aschenbach, who had been protected from discovery by a protruding structure or fountain while they got in and pushed away, always did the same. He spoke quickly and in hushed tones as he promised the gondolier a nice tip to follow at an inconspicuous distance the vehicle just turning the corner up there, and a shiver ran down his spine when the man, illicit and obliging as a panderer, assured him in the same tone that his wishes would be carried out, carried out to the letter.

Thus, reclining in soft black cushions, he glided and swayed along in pursuit of the other long-beaked black vessel, to whose wake passion held him chained. Ever so often it pulled away, leaving him worried and restless. But his gondolier, who always seemed to have had a lot of experience with such requests, never failed, thanks to some clever maneuvers, quick crossings and short cuts, to put Aschenbach back within eyeshot of that which he coveted. The air was stagnant and smelly; the burning sun cut through the fog, which had turned the sky slate-gray. Water gurgled against wood and stone. The gondolier's call—part warning, part greeting—was returned in the otherwise silent labyrinth as if by some strange prior arrangement. Umbelliferous blossoms hung down white and purple and almond-scented from the tiny elevated gardens over the crumbling stone walls. Reflections of Moorish window frames appeared in the bracken. The marble steps of a church descended into the water. A beggar who squatted upon them protesting his misery held out his hat and displayed the whites of his eyes as if blind. An antiquities dealer in front of his cellar shop beckoned the passer-by with a crawling gesture in hopes he would stop and be swindled. That was Venice in all its alluring and deeply dubious beauty, the city—part fairy tale, part tourist trap—in whose putrid air the arts had once flourished with such prodigious rampancy and which had fed musicians with seductively lulling, soothing tones. To the ongoing adventurer, it seemed as if his eyes were literally drinking in that opulence, his ears being wooed by the same such melodies. Moreover, whenever he recalled that the city had taken ill and was concealing that fact out of greed, he peered with even greater abandon at the gondola bobbing up and down in front of him.

The distracted Aschenbach could neither conceive of nor want anything else than to pursue that creature that held him so inflamed, to dream about him in his absence and to whisper sweet nothings to his mere silhouette, as lovers do. Solitude, foreignness and the blessing of such a profound intoxication late in life pushed him further and further, convincing him to risk even potential humiliation without scruple or shame. Late one evening, for instance, upon returning from Venice, he had paused on the second floor in front of the beautiful boy's room, his head leaned against the door frame in utter bliss, unable for a long time to tear himself away despite the danger of being caught by surprise in such an irrational position and thus found out.

Nonetheless, he did have moments of introspection and partial consideration of potential consequences. How far! he would think at such moments, crestfallen. How far he'd come! Like any man in whom natural merit has instilled an aristocratic interest in personal ancestry, Aschenbach often thought about his forefathers in times of achievement and triumph, assuring himself of their imagined approval, their satisfaction and hard-won respect. He thought of them also here and now, entangled as he was in such an unseemly adventure, in the grip of such exotic emotional extravagance. He recalled their dignified severity, the respectable masculinity that was their very essence, and smiled gravely. What would they say? But then again, what would they have said about his whole life, which deviated from theirs to the point of degeneracy, this life under the spell of art, which he himself, speaking from his ancestors' perspective of civic responsibility, had once publicly ridiculed in a youthful polemic and which nonetheless had been so fundamentally similar to their own? He, too, had served. He, too, had been a soldier and a warrior like many of them—for art was war, a gritty struggle full of wear and tear to which these days it was hard to stay long equal. A life of self-conquest, a life "in spite of," dry, steadfast and abstinent, which he had transformed into a model for the frail heroism of the times—he was well entitled to call it masculine, to call it courageous. It seemed to him that the Eros that had overcome him was somehow especially suited and inclined to this sort of life. Hadn't the god enjoyed an excellent reputation among the bravest of peoples? Indeed, was it not written that he had thrived in their cities on account of his courage? Various heroic warriors of yore had willingly borne his yoke, for nothing ordained by God could bring disgrace, and actions that would have been castigated as signs of cowardice, had one engaged in them for other reasons—kneeling, oaths, desperate pleading and slavish protestation—such things brought no shame to the lover. On the contrary, one reaped great praise for them.

Such was the thinking of the enthralled Aschenbach; such did he try to prop himself up and preserve his dignity. But meanwhile, he also turned his inquisitive and determined attention to the shady events in the city center, to that adventure in the world at large that had obscurely merged with the one in his heart, stoking his passion with nebulous and lawless hopes. Obsessed with finding reliable information about the current status of the affliction and the prognosis for the future, he scoured his home papers in the city cafés—they had vanished several days ago from the reading table in the hotel lobby. Claims and denials vied for space on their pages. The number of the infected and the dead was believed to run as high as twenty, forty, even a hundred or more, while every instance of the epidemic, if not flatly denied, was dismissed in response as a completely isolated case imported from abroad. Interspersed were cautionary editorials, protests against the dangerous game being played by the foreign authorities. Certainty was not to be had.

Nevertheless, the solitary Aschenbach felt a special personal entitlement to share in the secret and, being kept in the dark, took a perverse pleasure in entrapping those in the know with loaded questions, forcing the conspirators into out-and-out lies. One day at breakfast in the main dining room, he conducted such an interrogation with the hotel manager, the small soft-spoken man in the French frock coat, who was moving around greeting the guests and supervising the service and had stopped at Aschenbach's table to exchange a few idle words. Why, the guest asked in passing, why on earth had they recently begun spreading disinfectant in Venice? — "It's just official precaution," answered the slippery fellow. "It's the authorities' duty to take such measures in advance to prevent any disruptions or other breakdowns in public health that might result from the unusual heat and humidity." — "The authorities are to be commended," responded Aschenbach, and after the exchange of a few meteorological observations, the manager took his leave.

After dinner that very same day, in the evening, a small group of street musicians from the city happened to give a performance in the hotel's front garden. They stood, two men and two women, by the iron stanchion of an arc lamp, their faces bathed in white light, looking up toward the main terrace, where the guests had come out to drink coffee and cool drinks and enjoy this local cultural offering. The hotel staff, elevator boys, waiters and front office clerks appeared in the lobby doors to eavesdrop. The Russian family, eager and exacting in matters of entertainment, promptly had wicker chairs arranged in the garden to be nearer the performers and sat gratefully in a semicircle. The old serf stood in the back, a kerchief wrapping her head like a turban.

Mandolin, guitar, harmonica and a squawking violin began to sound under the hands of the busker virtuosi. Vocal numbers alternated with elaborate instrumentals, the younger woman, for instance, lending her sharp squeak to the tenor's sweet falsetto in a searching love ballad. The main talent and leader of the ensemble, however, proved to be without doubt the other man, the one with the guitar, a baritone-buffo of a character. He had hardly any voice at all but was a highly skilled mimic and possessed a remarkable comic energy. Often he would detach himself from the others, his giant instrument in his arms, to advance demonstratively toward the sloping terrace wall, where his machinations were rewarded with encouraging laughter. Particularly the Russians in their orchestra seats showed delight at such displays of Mediterranean inventiveness, bolstering his courage and self-confidence with applause and shouts, urging him on to make an even greater spectacle of himself.

Aschenbach sat by the balustrade, wetting his lips now and then with a mix of pomegranate juice and soda, which sparkled before him amethyst-red in its glass. His nerves lapped up the tooting and jangling, the vulgar pining melodies, for passion cripples taste, solemnly following the lure of pleasures that sobriety would either laugh at or reject altogether. His features were contorted by the trickster's antics into a frozen, already painful smile. He sat there casually, but in the meantime extreme attentiveness had caused him to tense up inside. Six steps away Tadzio was leaning against the stone railing.

He stood there in the white belted outfit he occasionally wore to dinner with all his inevitable and inalienable grace—his left forearm on the parapet, his feet crossed, his right hand on a supporting hip—watching the street minstrels below with barely a smile, at most an expression of distant curiosity and polite indulgence. Several times he stood up straight, puffed out his chest and drew his white smock down through the leather belt with an elegant motion of his arms. Moreover, several times, to the older man's triumph and mental giddiness, not to mention horror, the boy turned his head, now shyly and cautiously, now suddenly and abruptly like a surprise attack, to stare over his left shoulder in the direction where his lover was seated. Their eyes never met, for an ignominious faintness of heart forced the errant Aschenbach to rein in his glances out of fear. Toward the back of the terrace sat the women who watched over Tadzio, and things had come so far that the love-struck Aschenbach had to worry about having become conspicuous and aroused suspicion. Indeed, on several occasions, on the beach, in the hotel lobby and at the Piazza San Marco, he had been forced to observe with a kind of paralyzed horror how they had summoned Tadzio from his vicinity and tried to keep the boy away from him. He couldn't help but take this as a terrible insult, one that had made his pride writhe in previously unknown coils of agony and that his conscience wouldn't allow him to dismiss.

In the meantime, to his own accompaniment, the guitarist had commenced a solo number, which could be heard right then on every Italian street corner and which he knew how to deliver with the necessary histrionics. It was a song of multiple verses with the ensemble joining in to sing and play the other instruments at each chorus. Slight of build, his features haggard and emaciated, a shabby felt hat tilted back over his neck so that a round patch of red hair stuck out from under its brim, he stood apart from his companions atop the gravel courtyard in a posture of arrogant bravado, aiming his jests, which were sung in an insistent half-spoken voice to the twang of guitar strings, up at the terrace, the veins on his forehead throbbing all the while with creative exertion. There was little of Venice about him. Much more he seemed to belong to that family of Neapolitan comics, part pimps, part comedians, who are both brutal and daring, dangerous and entertaining. The song itself—from the sound of the words, merely silly—took on an ambiguous, even vaguely offensive quality thanks to the faces he made, the way he moved and his habit of winking suggestively and lewdly licking at the corner of his mouth with his tongue. A wiry neck protruded from the soft collar of the white tennis shirt he wore despite being otherwise dressed for the city, revealing a remarkably large Adam's apple. His pale, snub-nosed face, whose clean-shaven features gave no clues as to his age, seemed to have been ploughed by constant grimacing and vice, and the grin on his rubbery lips oddly matched with the two deeply etched furrows that ran spitefully, imperiously, almost savagely between his reddish brows. Still, what really attracted the solitary Aschenbach's intense interest was the realization that this dubious figure seemed to carry his own dubious atmosphere. Every time the chorus was repeated, the singer would grotesquely make the rounds, clowning and shaking hands. This led him directly under Aschenbach's seat, and every time he arrived there, a cloud of strong phenol fumes would waft up from his clothes and body toward the terrace.

After the last couplet, he began collecting money. He started with the Russians, who gave with visible generosity, then proceeded up the steps. For all the insolence of his act, on the terrace he behaved humbly. Bowing and scraping, he shuffled among the tables, his powerful teeth exposed by a smile of calculated servility that contrasted with the two furrows still stretching ominously between his red brows. The spectators observed this strange creature collecting his income with curiosity and not a little revulsion, carefully throwing coins into his felt hat with their fingertips so as not to touch it. No matter how amusing the performance, the abolition of the physical distance between the comedian and his genteel audience always causes a certain discomfort. The man sensed this and tried to avert offense by sniveling. He was approaching Aschenbach, with him the smell, about which none in the circle seemed to think twice.

"Listen," the solitary Aschenbach said in a hushed, almost mechanical voice. "Disinfectant is being spread everywhere in Venice. Why?" — The jester answered hoarsely. "On account of the authorities! That is the procedure in the heat and sirocco. The sirocco makes the air heavy. It is too much for the constitution . . ." He spoke as though amazed that anyone could ask such a question, demonstrating with a flat, outstretched hand the pressure brought by the sirocco. — "So there's no affliction in Venice?" Aschenbach asked very softly between his teeth. — The clown's muscular features grimaced with comic helplessness. "Affliction? What affliction? Is the sirocco an affliction? Or maybe the authorities are an affliction? You must be joking! Affliction? Heaven forbid! A preventative measure, you understand, an official precaution against the heavy air in this weather . . ." He demonstrated with his hand. "Very well," Aschenbach said again in a clipped whisper as he dropped a coin of inordinate denomination into the man's hat. Then he motioned with his eyes for him to move on. He obeyed, grinning and bowing repeatedly. But before he had even reached the stairs, two hotel managers grabbed him and subjected him to a whispered cross-examination, their faces pressed close to his. He shrugged, protested his innocence, swore he hadn't said anything—all of it was clearly visible. When they let him go, he returned to the garden and, after briefly consulting with his companions under the arc lamp, stepped forward to play a final grateful encore.

It was a song the solitary Aschenbach could never remember having heard before, an audacious novelty number, sung in incomprehensible dialect and topped by a chorus in which the entire ensemble laughed as hard as it could. Each time that part came round, lyrics as well as accompaniment ceased, leaving nothing but laughing, which was somehow organized yet still performed quite naturally, especially by the soloist with his great talent for imitation. With the artistic distance between himself and his patrons now restored, he had rediscovered his former insolence, and the simulated laughter he directed unabashedly up at the terrace was that of mockery. Even before the end of every articulated verse, he seemed to be struggling against an irresistible tickle. He sobbed, his voice wavered, he pressed hand to mouth and coiled his shoulders, and at the proper moment unconstrained laughter burst, escaped and howled forth so true to life that it became infectious and spread among the audience, so that the terrace as well was seized by a hilarity without object, feeding only on itself. This just seemed to make the soloist doubly boisterous. He bent his knees, slapped his thighs, held his sides and generally split a gut, no longer laughing, but screaming. He pointed his finger in the air as if there were nothing more comical than the laughing audience above, and in the end everyone in the garden and on the veranda was laughing, right down to the waiters, elevator boys and servants in the doorways.

Aschenbach could no longer relax in his seat. He sat bolt upright as if about to commence some sort of defense or flight. But the laughter, the hospital smell wafting up to him and the beautiful boy's proximity combined to mesmerize his head and senses in an unbreakable, unescapable dream spell. In the general bustle and confusion, he found the courage to glance over at Tadzio, and as he did, he could see that the beautiful boy, on returning his look, also kept a straight face, as if he were patterning his own behavior and expression after Aschenbach's, as if the general merriment could have no power over him as long as the older man didn't join in. This childlike and insinuating imitativeness had something so disarming, indeed overwhelming about it that the gray-haired Aschenbach had to force himself not to bury his face in his hands. It also dawned on him that Tadzio's habit of getting up and taking in air might actually be a kind of gasp, perhaps a constriction in the chest. "He's sickly, he's probably not long for the world," Aschenbach thought again in that matter-of-fact way that is sometimes the strange product of emancipated intoxication and longing. And pure protective love, along with a certain extravagant satisfaction, filled his heart.

In the meantime the Venetians had finished and were withdrawing. Applause followed them, and their leader did not neglect to embellish his exit with various little tricks. His bows and mockly blown kisses provoked further titters, and he intensified his efforts. His companions had already gone, but he pretended to back painfully into a lamppost, then limped away toward the front gate, doubled over in pantomime agony. There, all at once, he finally discarded the mask of the schlemiel, straightened, indeed snapped bolt upright, insolently stuck his tongue out at the guests on the terrace and then slipped back into darkness. The hotel guests dispersed. Tadzio had left the balustrade some time ago. Yet the solitary Aschenbach, to the dismay of the staff, remained seated at his table over his pomegranate drink. The night progressed; time disintegrated. In his parents' house, years ago, there had been an hourglass. Suddenly he could see the fragile, symbolic little timepiece again as though it were standing in front of him. Silently and gradually, the rust-colored sand ran through the narrow aperture, and there where the sand in the upper glass was draining down, a tiny but torrential vortex had formed.

The very next day, during the afternoon, the stubborn Aschenbach made another attempt at provoking the world at large, this time with complete success. Specifically, he paid a visit to the English travel agency located on the Piazza San Marco, where, after changing money at the counter, he assumed the expression of a mistrustful foreigner, posing his fateful question to the clerk who had waited on him. It was a cardigan-wearing Englishman, still young, with middle-parted hair and closely set eyes, who was surrounded by that air of solid fidelity that seems so alien and misplaced amidst the mischievous cleverness of the Mediterranean. "Nothing to be concerned about, sir," he began. "Official policy, nothing serious. Such measures are often taken to prevent unhealthy effects from the heat and the sirocco . . ." But when he raised his blue eyes, he was met by a stare from the foreign tourist, a tired and rather sad stare with a trace of contempt, which was directed at his own lips. At this the Englishman blushed. "At least," he said in a whisper, visibly agitated, "that's the official explanation people here see fit to stick by. I can tell you, though, that there's more to it than that." And then, in his frank and easy language, he revealed the truth.

For many years, Asiatic cholera had been both on the increase and on the move. Originating in the humid swamps of the Ganges delta, carried by the mephitic breath of that haughty and untameable primeval island jungle shunned by man, where the tiger crouches in his bamboo thicket, the epidemic had raged long and with unusual intensity throughout Hindustan, spreading east into China and west into Afghanistan and Persia. There, following the main caravan routes, it had brought its horrors as far as Astrakhan, even as far as Moscow. But while all of Europe watched with fearful eyes lest this specter continue its invasion by land, Syrian traders were already carrying it by sea. It appeared almost simultaneously in several Mediterranean ports, raising its head in Toulon and Málaga, showing its face in Palermo and Naples and digging in its heels throughout Calibri and Apulia. The northern half of the peninsula had been spared. But in mid-May of this year, the terrible vibrio bacilli had been discovered twice on the same day, in the emaciated, blackened corpses of a ship's hand and a fruit-and-vegetable girl. Their cases were covered up. But within a week, there were ten, twenty, thirty of them, and worse still in various neighborhoods. A vacationer from provincial Austria who had spent several days in Venice died upon returning home, his symptoms unmistakable. That was why the first rumors of an outbreak in the lagoon city had made their way into German newspapers. Venetian officials declared in response that health conditions in the city had never been better and ordered the most necessary precautionary measures. But apparently something in the food supply had been contaminated—vegetables, meat or milk—for, under the official silence of a cover-up, death had begun to eat its way out amidst the narrow alleyways. The premature summer heat, which raised the canal water to lukewarm temperatures, had proven especially conducive to spreading the disease, and it seemed as though the epidemic had in fact been reinvigorated, as if its bacteria had been made doubly tenacious and fertile. Instances of recovery were few. Eighty out of every hundred victims died, and indeed in terrible fashion, for the disease attacked with extreme ferocity, often in its most deadly form, known as the "dry type." It left the body unable to evacuate the massive amounts of fluid sucked from the circulatory system, so that within a few hours, its victims became dehydrated, screaming in pain with cramps, and ultimately suffocated, their blood as thick as pitch. They could count themselves lucky if, as sometimes happened, they only felt slightly ill before the actual outbreak, lapsing into a coma from which they never or only very briefly awoke. By the beginning of June, the quarantine wards of the Ospedale Civile were quietly filling up, both orphanages had begun to run out of space, and traffic was becoming horrifically constant between the quay at the Fundamente Nuove and San Michele, the cemetery island. Nonetheless, fear about general detriment to the city, concern for the recently opened art exhibition in the public gardens and the serious losses facing hotels, shops and the whole diverse tourist trade, should people panic and word get out, had outweighed the city's love of truth and respect for international treaties. The stubborn authorities were thus able to maintain their policies of silence and denial. Venice's senior health official, a man of many years' service, had resigned his post in indignation and had been quietly replaced by a more easily manipulated person. The public knew about it, and the corruption of their leaders, along with the prevalent uncertainty of the emergency situation in which the string of deaths had placed the city, had decidedly weakened moral standards among the lower classes, encouraging their darker, antisocial impulses. This had led to intemperance, licentiousness and increasing contempt for law and order. An unusual number of drunks could be seen every evening; vicious riffraff, it was said, had made the streets unsafe at night; and there were a rash of muggings and even murders, for twice already it had turned out that supposed victims of the epidemic had actually been dispatched with poison by their own relatives. Moreover commercial vice had taken on obtrusive and excessive forms that was previously unknown in the area, being usually found only in the Italian South and the Orient.

The Englishman told him the substance of all this. "You would do well," he concluded, "to leave sooner rather than later. The imposition of a general quarantine cannot be more than a few days away." — "I'm very grateful to you," said Aschenbach and left the office.

The Piazza San Marco lay in overcast humidity. Oblivious foreigners sat in the cafes or stood literally covered by pigeons in front of the cathedral, watching the swarming birds beat their wings and jostle each other to peck at the cupped hands offering corn seed. Feverish with excitement, triumphant in possession of the truth, but also with a disgusting taste on his tongue and an uncanny horror in his heart, the solitary Aschenbach paced up and down the tiles of that splendid square. He was considering an action of cleansing decency. This evening after dinner he would approach the lady with the pearls and deliver the speech he was already rehearsing: "Please permit a stranger to be of service, Madame, and pass along a piece of advice, a warning, about something which is being kept from you out of self-interest. Leave here at once with Tadzio and your daughters! Venice is in the throes of the plague." Then, as a gesture of farewell, he could lay his hand on the head of that instrument of a scornful divinity and turn around and flee this miserable swamp himself. At the same time, however, he sensed how infinitely far he was from any genuine desire to take such a step. It would lead him back, restore him to himself, but when you're beside yourself, the last thing you want is come to in this way. He recalled a white building adorned with inscriptions glinting in the twilight in whose radiant mysticism his mind's eye had wandered about. He remembered the strange traveler who had awakened in him at his advanced age an errant youthful desire for distance and exotic surroundings. And the thought of returning home—of self-control, sobriety, labor and expertise—revolted him so deeply that his face took on a look of physical illness. "It's to be kept quiet!" he whispered vehemently. "Then I'll keep it quiet." Consciousness of his shared knowledge, shared guilt, intoxicated him in precisely the way that small quantities of wine can intoxicate a tired mind. The image of the disease-stricken, decimated city suspended desolate in his imagination raised hopes that were incomprehensible, beyond all rational understanding, abominably sweet. What was the delicate happiness of which he had just now dreamt for an instant, measured against prospects like these? What good were art and virtue to him, he who enjoyed the prospects of chaos? He kept quiet and stayed on.

That night he had a terrible dream—if that is the right word for an experience of body and soul that befell him in the depths of sleep as an absolutely autonomous sensory reality, but that did not permit him to see himself moving and existing in space, discrete from the dream events. Instead, his own soul was the setting. Events broke in on him from the outside, overcoming his resistance—a deep, mental resistance—with great violence; then they passed through him, leaving his entire self, his life's culture, devastated and destroyed.

Fear was the beginning, fear and desire and a horrified

curiosity about what was about to transpire. Night had descended, and his senses were alert, for, from far away, came turbulence, turmoil, a terrible violent racket—rustling, smashing and dull rumbling, shrill cheering, too, and a certain howl like a drawn-out *u*—all permeated and at times drowned out by the deep warbling of a gruesomely sweet, ruthlessly insistent flute, which mesmerized his very innards with its shamelessly cloying tone. Still he knew a phrase, albeit obscure, to describe what was approaching: *the Other God!* Smoky flames began to glow: he could make out mountainous land, similar to that around his country house. And in this refracted light, through the branches and the mossy boulders, something began to thrash and spin its way down from the wooded peak—humans, animals, a swarm, a raging herd. The slope was inundated with bodies, flames, tumult and frenzied circles of dance. Wailing women stumbled over clumsily long animal hides secured by belts and shook tambourines over each other's upturned, moaning heads, swung spark-laden torches and unsheathed daggers, carried fork-tongued snakes coiled around their waists and clutched at their breasts with both hands. Men—with horns above their brows, animal-hide loincloths and hairy skin—bowed their heads, exposed their necks, lifted their arms and thighs in the air, banged iron cymbals and furiously pounded drums, while smooth-skinned boys prodded goats with leaf-wound staffs, clinging to the animals' antlers and crying out with joy as they were dragged around in leaps. What's more, the revellers were all howling out that word with the soft consonants and the drawn-out *u* at the end, simultaneously sweet and wild, like nothing ever heard. It sounded first here, bellowed into the air as though by rutting stags, then there, a chorus of voices adopting it as a rowdy chant of triumph, inciting each other to dance and flail their limbs, never letting it fade. Meanwhile the low seductive sounds of the flute ran through and above it all. Was it not also trying to seduce him, the reluctant spectator, enticing him with shameless tenacity to join in the wanton festivity of utmost sacrifice? His revulsion was great, great, too, his fear, and he was sincerely determined to defend what was his to the last against the Other God, the enemy of his composed and dignified intellect. But the noise and the howling kept increasing, amplified by the echoing mountainside, drowning out everything else, swelling into irresistible insanity. Odors assaulted his nose: the bitter stench of the goats, excrescent bodily scents, a whiff of something like stagnant waters, and, along with them, yet another familiar smell—that of wounds and rampant disease. His heart pounded to the drumbeats, his mind whirled, rage seized him, blindness, numbing lust, and his soul craved to join the dancing circle of the god. The obscene symbol, a giant piece of wood, was unveiled and raised, at which the revelers all began to howl their battle cry with greater abandon. Frothing at the mouth, they raged, clawing with lurid expressions and ravenous hands, laughing and moaning, stabbing each other with prods and licking the blood from each other's limbs. But now, with them, among them, was the dreaming Aschenbach. He had given himself over to the Other God. Yes, he was one of them as they attacked and slaughtered the animals, tearing them to dripping shreds and devouring the remains, and again, as free and open copulation in honor of the god began everywhere on the mossy ground. And his soul tasted descent's orgiastic fury.

The stricken Aschenbach awoke from this dream unnerved and shattered, delivered up helplessly to the demon. He no longer avoided the observant eyes of others; whether he exposed himself to their suspicions was now entirely irrelevant. In any case, they were taking flight, traveling on. Many of the changing huts now stood unoccupied, larger gaps had opened up between patrons in the dining room, and foreigners were a rare sight in the city. The truth seemed to have seeped out, and despite the dogged solidarity of the interested parties, panic could no longer be averted. Yet the lady with the pearl necklace stayed on with her family. Perhaps she didn't hear the rumors, perhaps she was too proud and fearless to budge. In any case Tadzio remained, and to Aschenbach in his rapture, it sometimes seemed as if departure and death might remove all other disturbing presences from their midst, leaving him alone on the island with the beautiful boy. Indeed, every morning by the sea, as his eye dwelt with a hard, reckless, fixed stare on the object of his desire, or at sunset, as he ignobly followed that object through the alleys where the progress of the vile plague was being concealed, monstrosities began to seem propitious, moral law invalid.

Like any lover, Aschenbach wished to please and was bitterly afraid of rejection. He livened up his attire with youthful little touches, he wore jewelry and used cologne, he fussed over his appearance repeatedly during the day and always turned up at dinner well dressed, jittery and anxious. In the presence of that sweet youth that had so taken possession of him, he found his own body repugnant: the sight of his graying hair, his pinched features, plunged him into shame and despair. He felt he had to spruce up and restore his looks. He paid frequent visits to the gossipy hotel coiffeur.

With a hairdressing gown draped over him, he leaned back in the chair under the latter's soothing hands and stared at his reflection in a hand mirror, looking pained.

"Gray," he said, scowling.

"A touch," the man answered. "And where does the fault lie? A minor lapse, a neglect of external matters. Understandable, though hardly commendable, among persons of importance. Especially since they are precisely the ones who should be above little prejudices about what is natural and what is not. Some of these people and their moral objections to the art of cosmetics—if you extend the same logic to teeth, you see how offensive it is. Ultimately we are only as old as we feel in our hearts and minds. In certain cases keeping your hair gray actually involves more of a deception than the corrective some people see fit to scorn. A man in your position has a right to his natural hair color. Will you permit me simply to give you back what is yours?"

"How so?" asked Aschenbach.

The eloquent coiffeur washed the customer's hair in

two different liquids, one clear, one dark, and once more it was as black as it had been in his youth. The man then curled it with heated tongs into soft waves, took a step back and examined his work.

"The only thing left," he said, "would be to put a little color in your complexion."

And like the perfectionist who can never leave well enough alone, he scurried around, indefatigably, and fiddled with this and that. The comfortably reclining Aschenbach, incapable of defending himself, indeed suffused with sudden hope at what was transpiring, watched in the mirror as his brows grew starker and more evenly arched, as the shape of his eyes was elongated, their green enhanced with some faint liner, watched further down as a delicate, gently applied pink was awakened where his skin had turned leathery brown, as his ever pallid lips turned plump and raspberry-red, and as the lines on his cheeks and mouth, the wrinkles around his eyes disappeared under skin cream and "Breath of Youth." With his heart beating wildly, he beheld a young man in first bloom. The cosmetician finally declared himself satisfied, as people like that often do, by sycophantically thanking the person upon whom he had just waited. "A minor adjustment," he said, touching Aschenbach's skin for the last time. "Now, sir, you can safely fall in love." The spellbound Aschenbach left, dreamily happy, a bit confused and timid. His tie was red; his wide-brimmed straw hat had a rainbow-colored band.

A tepid storm wind had come up. The rain was infrequent and light, but the air hung humid, thick with odors of decay. Fluttering, clapping and whistling could be heard all around, and to the feverish Aschenbach under his makeup it seemed that an evil race of harpies was at work in the sky, fiendish sea birds who would ruin the condemned man's last meal, leaving it half-chewed and soiled with dung. The humidity had robbed him of all appetite, and he couldn't help but imagine that his food had been contaminated with infectious material.

One afternoon while on the beautiful boy's trail,

Aschenbach penetrated deep into the internal maze of the ailing city. Although he had lost his bearings in the labyrinth of indistinguishable alleys, canals, bridges and city squares and wasn't even sure in which direction he was headed, he was determined not to lose sight of his hotly pursued vision. Forced to proceed with humiliating caution, pressing up against walls and hiding behind the backs of pedestrians, he was unaware for quite some time of the fatigue, indeed exhaustion that emotion and constant strain had wreaked upon his body and mind. Tadzio was walking to the rear of his family, letting the governess and his nunlike sisters proceed ahead in narrow passages, so that, strolling by himself, he could occasionally glance back over his shoulder with his peculiar twilight-gray eyes to make sure his lover was still following. He saw him, and he didn't betray him. Intoxicated by this realization, lured on by those eyes like a puppet on passion's strings, the love-struck Aschenbach stole along in pursuit of his unseemly hope, only to find himself cheated in the end. The Polish family crossed a slightly arched bridge, the height of whose curvature obscured them from the view of their pursuer. Once on top of it himself, however, he could no longer spot them. He peered around in three directions, straight ahead and off to the sides along the narrow, dirty canal, but it was no use. Frustration and weakness finally made him abandon his search.

His head was on fire, his body was covered in feverish sweat, the nape of his neck tingled, a no longer bearable thirst now tortured him, and he looked around for anything that would bring instantaneous relief. From a tiny vegetable stand he bought some fruit, strawberries, soft and overripe, which he ate as he walked. A small square, forgotten and seemingly accursed, opened up before him. He recognized it. It had been here, weeks ago, that he had decided upon his unrealized plan to leave. He collapsed on the steps of the cistern in the middle of this space, resting his head against its stone rim. All was silent, grass was growing between the cobblestones and garbage was strewn everywhere. Among the weather-beaten, unevenly tall surrounding houses, one stood out like a palace with its lion-flanked balconies and arched windows, behind which dwelt only emptiness. Located on the ground floor of another house was a pharmacy. Warm gusts carried over occasional smells of phenol.

He sat there. The great master, the artist grown dignified, the author of "A True Wretch," the writer who had dismissed everything vagabond and every gloomily plumbed depth in such exemplary pure form, the intellectual who had rejected sympathy with the abyss and disdained dissipation, the climber of such heights, the transcender of personal knowledge who had outgrown irony and accustomed himself to the amenities and obligations of mass public trust, the celebrity whose fame had been officially sanctioned, whose name had been ennobled and whose style served as the model by which schoolboys were taught to write—he sat there. He held his eyes shut, casting only the occasional short glance down to one side with an expression of scorn and embarrassment, while his slack, cosmetically enhanced smile formed isolated words taken from the strange dream logic produced in his half-conscious brain.

"For beauty, Phaedrus—mark my words!—only beauty is both divine and visible to the human eye. Therefore it represents the path of the sensual man, young Phaedrus, the artist, to the sublime. Do you really think, dear boy, that he whose path to the sublime passes through the senses can ever attain wisdom and true dignity as a man? Or do you think that this is a dangerously enticing path, one of falsehood and sin, which necessarily leads us astray? I leave it up to you to decide. For you must know that we artists cannot follow the path of beauty without the accompaniment and guidance of Eros. Indeed, though we may be heroes in our own way, trained warriors, we are also like women, for passion is our inspiration, and our true longing must always remain a desire for love. That is our desire and shame. Do you see now that we artists can be neither wise nor dignified? That we necessarily go astray, that we can never be anything but disreputable soldiers of emotional fortune?

Our mastery of style is nothing but a foolish little lie, our fame and glory a farce, the public's faith in us a joke, the idea of educating youth or the masses with art a risky practice that should be outlawed. What use is a teacher born with a natural, incorrigible tendency toward the abyss? We may deny it and acquire dignity, but no matter which way we turn, it attracts us. We renounce all-unravelling intellect, for intellect, Phaedrus, possesses neither dignity nor rigor. It knows, understands, forgives, but without any fixed position or form. It lives in sympathetic attraction to the abyss—it *is* the abyss. This we ultimately reject, to strive from then on only for beauty, that is to say, for simplicity, greatness and renewed rigor, second unfettered innocence and form. But form and unfettered innocence, Phaedrus, lead to intoxication and lust. They may even lead the noble mind into some awful emotional sacrilege, which his own aesthetic rigor rejects as unspeakable. They lead to the abyss, they, too, to the abyss. This, I tell you, is where we artists are led, for we are incapable of soaring on high, only of running riot. And now I must go, Phaedrus. You stay here, and only when you see me no more, are you to go, too."

Several days later Gustav von Aschenbach, feeling sick, left the beach hotel later than usual in the morning. He had been forced to battle against definite, if only semiphysical attacks of nausea, which were accompanied by an acute mounting anxiety, a feeling of hopelessness and futility impossible to pinpoint either to the world at large or to his own personal life. In the lobby he noticed a great many bags standing ready for departure. He asked a doorman who was travelling on and received as an answer the aristocratic Polish family name he had secretly been expecting. He took in the information without a flinch of his sunken features, curtly raising his chin as people do to acknowledge learning something they didn't need to know, and added: "When?" The answer came: "After lunch." He nodded and walked down to the sea.

There, shop had been closed up. On the wide shallows

separating the beach from the first stretch of sandbar, rippling shudders of water ran back out to sea. An autumnal, out-of-favor atmosphere seemed to have descended over this once so colorful and crowded, but now almost deserted resort, whose sand was no longer kept clean. A camera, apparently abandoned, stood on its tripod at the edge of the sea, its draped black cloth flapping in the breeze, which was cooler than before.

Tadzio, along with three or four remaining playmates, was running around to the right in front of his family's hut. Aschenbach sat in a chair approximately halfway between the sea and the row of huts with a blanket over his knees and watched Tadzio one more time. The game was unsupervised (the women were apparently preparing for departure), seemed to have no rules and quickly got out of control. The strapping lad with the belted jumpsuit and the black pomaded hair called "Yashu," enraged by some blinding sand thrown in his face, challenged Tadzio to a wrestling match. This soon ended with the beautiful but weaker combatant being pinned. Nevertheless, as though in this final hour the servile vassal had been transformed into a terrible brute who now sought revenge for his long subordination, the victorious "Yashu" refused to stop attacking his vanquished foe and instead kept one knee on his back, pressing his face into the sand. Tadzio, who was already out of breath from the fight, was near suffocation. His efforts to shake off the weight on top of him were convulsive, ceasing entirely for moments at a time, to return as mere twitching. Horrified, Aschenbach wanted to leap to the rescue, but just then the bully finally released his victim. Very pale, Tadzio got halfway up and sat motionless for several minutes, leaning on one arm, his hair mussed and his eyes glowering. Then he took to his feet and walked slowly off. His name was called, at first playfully, then apologetically and urgently, but he turned a deaf ear. The dark-haired boy, no doubt overcome with immediate regret at having gone too far, ran after him and tried to patch things up. A shoulder motioned for him to stay back. Tadzio walked diagonally down to the water. He was barefoot and wore his striped linen outfit with the red bow.

At the water's edge he paused, head down, to draw some shapes in the sand with his toes, then continued out into the shallows, which even at their deepest didn't come up over his knee, leisurely making his way through them until he reached the sandbar. There he stood for a moment, his face turned toward the open sea, before walking slowly leftward over the long strip of narrow exposed land. Cut off from the beach by the wide stretch of water, cut off from his playmates by his own proud moodiness, he paced back and forth, an utterly isolated and disconnected figure with disheveled hair out there in the sea and the wind, against a backdrop of hazy infinity. Once more he paused to gaze into the distance. And suddenly, as if remembering something or following some other such impulse, he rotated his upper body, one hand on his hip, in an elegant twist from his basic position and looked back over his shoulder toward shore. There on the beach, the watching Aschenbach sat as he had sat once before, when those twilight-gray eyes had first glanced back over that fateful threshold and met his own. His head, resting on the beach chair, had slowly turned to follow the boy's movements as he paced in the distance. Now it lifted level with the boy's gaze, before suddenly slumping down over his chest. His eyes rolled and his face took on the slack, sunken expression of deep slumber. It seemed to him, however, as if the pale and lovely shepherd of souls out there smiled at him, beckoning, as if he took his hand from his hip and pointed, indeed himself glided ahead into the looming immensity, full of promise and portent. And as he had so often before, Aschenbach got up to follow.

Minutes passed before help arrived for the man slumped over sideways in his chair. He was brought to his room. And that very same day a respectfully shaken world received the news of his death.

Man and Dog: An Idyll

He Comes around the Corner.

Whenever spring lives up to its lovely reputation, and the twittering of the birds has—thanks to my having ended the previous day at a proper juncture—sufficed to awaken me in time, I quite enjoy a half-an-hour stroll before breakfast. Not bothering with my hat, I start along the suburban lane by my house, sometimes continuing into the parks further out, in order to catch a few breaths of fresh morning air and to savor for a bit—before I'm spirited away by my work—the joys of the sheer earliness of hour. On my front steps I let out a whistle consisting of two notes, tonic and lower fourth, as in the beginning melody of the second movement of Schubert's *Unfinished Symphony*. It is a signal, something like a two-syllable name set to music. The very next instant, as I continue toward the front gate, a sound can be heard in the distance, barely audible at first but quickly growing closer and more distinct, a delicate tinkling of the sort produced by a license medallion hitting the metal clasp of a dog collar. Glancing back, I see Baushan coming at full speed round the rear corner of the house straight for me, as though planning to run me over. His lower lip is retracted slightly in exertion, exposing two or three front teeth that gleam white and majestic in the early morning sun.

He comes from his house, there on the ground under the elevated veranda in the backyard, where, before my two-syllable whistle brought him so vividly to life, he was most probably taking a short nap after a night of varied activity. His house is equipped with a curtain made of coarse material and is strewn, which explains why one or two pieces of straw are to be found in Baushan's somewhat sleep-tousled fur and sometimes in his paws. The sight always reminds me of a very accurately realized production of Schiller's *The Robbers* I once saw, in which the old Count Moor climbed down from his tower of starvation with a piece of straw sticking up from between two of his poor toes. I wheel instinctively away from my attacker and adopt a posture of defense, for his seeming intent—to undercut my feet and make me fall—never fails to deceive. At the last second, though, just before the crash, he's always able to put on the brakes and bring himself round with a great display of both physical and mental self-control. Then, without a sound (for he makes only sparing use of his rich, expressive voice), he commences a bewilderingly intricate salutary dance in circles around me. It consists of stamps, aerial leaps in which he curls up and then releases his coiled body like a spring, uncontrolled wags of not only the appointed expressive instrument for this sort of thing—his tail—but his whole body from the ribs down, and revolutions around his own axis. For some strange reason he endeavors to hide all these maneuvers from me by switching sides every time I turn to watch. No sooner do I bend down and extend a hand, though, than he leaps to my side, where he stands with his shoulder pressed against my shin. Leaning diagonally against me, he stands there as motionless as a pillar, his strong paws braced against the ground, his face turned up toward mine, staring upside down and from below into my eyes. And his utter immobility, as I pat his shoulder blades and mutter a few words of praise, radiates the same intense concentration and passion as his previous frenzy.

He's a short-haired German pointer, at least insofar as one isn't too severe or strict with this classification. One has to take it with a grain of salt, since on close inspection and if one goes by the book, Baushan isn't really a pointer at all. In the first place he's probably a bit too small: he falls, let's be clear about this, somewhat *below* average height for a game dog. Likewise, his front legs aren't straight but have a slight outward bow, which also deviates somewhat from the purebred ideal. His hint of dewlap—i.e. the wrinkled skin around the neck that can give such a regal appearance—looks quite good on him. It, too, however, would be regarded as a flaw by unforgiving breeders, for with a true pointer, I'm told, the skin around the neck should stretch smoothly over the throat. Baushan's color is quite handsome. His fur is basically reddish-brown with black stripes, yet there's also a lot of white mixed in. The latter especially predominates on his chest, his paws and his belly, while the entirety of his pug nose looks as if it had been dipped in black. Atop his broad head, as well as on his cool drooping ears, the black combines with the auburn in a lovely, velvetesque pattern, and he has a white cowlick, or knot, or tuft, that weaves itself together on his chest and that projects out horizontally like the spike on an antique breastplate. The cowlick is one of his best features. Nonetheless, the somewhat random splendor of his fur color would likewise probably be deemed "invalid" by anyone who emphasizes breeding conventions over personal idiosyncrasy, for the classic pointer may be monochrome or variously spotted, but never striped. The definitive indication, however, that Baushan cannot be classified according to some rigid paradigm is the hair that hangs from the corners of his mouth and the underside of his muzzle, which one could, with at least a semblance of justification, call a Van Dyck, and which on first glance, both from a distance and closer up, is reminiscent of a pinscher or a schnauzer.

Pointer or pinscher—he's a fine, handsome animal, standing stiff and slanted against my knee, looking up at me with the profoundest devotion! His eye is particularly handsome, gentle and wise, if also perhaps a bit distended and glassy. Its iris is reddish-brown, the same color as his fur, although, owing to the considerable dilation of the mirror-black pupil, it actually only makes up a thin ring, drops of which seep out into and float upon the surrounding white of his eyeball. The expression on his face—that of carefully considered middle-class common sense—affirms the masculinity of his life ethos, which his body in turn manifests physically. His arched chest, with its ribs powerfully outlined against his smooth, supple skin, his inwardly drawn hips, his nerve-veined legs, his rugged but well-formed feet . . . they all bespeak steadfastness and robust integrity, peasant stock and hunting blood. Both the hunter and the game dog predominate in Baushan, and this, if you ask me, qualifies him as a pointer, even if he doesn't owe his existence to some act of snobbish incest. That may well be the gist of the otherwise so confusing, logically disjointed words I address to him while I pat his shoulder.

He stands and stares, ears pricked to the tone of my voice, searching for accents of unmitigated approval, with which I try to speckle my speech. Then, suddenly, jerking his neck forward and quickly opening and closing his jaws, he snaps up at my face as though trying to bite off my nose. This is a pantomime apparently intended to answer my friendly words, and it often makes me recoil, laughing, as Baushan knows it will. It's a kind of make-believe kiss, half-tender, half-teasing, a signature maneuver of his ever since he was a puppy and one that I never observed in any of his predecessors. In any case he immediately apologizes with tail-wags, brief bows and an expression of embarrassed glee at the small liberty he's taken. After this we proceed through the front gate out into the open.

A roaring like that of the sea surrounds us, for my house sits practically on the river, where the strong current kicks up froth as it rushes over the flat terraces of its bed. The only things separating my house from the water are the poplar-lined lane, a fenced-in stretch of grass planted with young maples and an elevated path bordered by aspens—bizarre willow-emulating giants—whose white, seed-bearing down snows in the entire neighborhood every year in early June. Upriver, toward the city, military engineers are busy building a floating bridge. The thumping of their heavy boots on the planks and the bosses' shouted commands carry downstream.

From the opposite bank come sounds of industry, for over there, a bit downstream from where I live, there is a locomotive factory with the expanded industrial grounds customary these days and tall windows shining out into the darkness the whole night through. Brand-new, freshly painted machines get test-driven back and forth, once in a while a steam whistle howls, and muffled thuds of indeterminate origin occasionally shake the air. Rows of chimneys exhale columns of smoke, which is usually driven off by a felicitous wind over the woodlands and has a hard time making its way across the river. Such it is that in the suburban, semirural isolation of this area the sounds of solipsistic nature combine with those of human activity, with the bright-eyed freshness of the morning hour above them all.

It may well be seven-thirty, standard time, when I set out—thus in real time it is six-thirty. Walking with my arms behind my back through the mild sunshine, I proceed down the lane, which is hatched by long shadows from the poplars. Although the river isn't visible from here, I can hear its broad, regular current. The wind whispers gently in the trees, the chirping, piping, twittering and sorrowful warbling of songbirds permeate the air, and in the damp-blue skies an airplane—a stiff mechanical bird with an ever so slightly oscillating drone—appears from the east, following its autonomous route far above land and river. Meanwhile Baushan delights my eye with a series of nimble, fully outstretched jumps over the short fence bordering the grassy area to our left. Over and back he goes. He does this because he knows I find it pleasing, for I have often encouraged him by clapping my hands and tapping on the fence, showering him with praise whenever he does as I wish. Even now, he still trots over after almost every jump to hear me say what a clever and elegant hurdler he is, after which he snaps at my face and beslobbers my protectively raised arm. At the same time, however, these exercises also serve as a kind of morning routine of gymnastic hygiene that he puts himself through in order to smooth his sleep-tousled fur and rid it of the offending pieces of straw that make him resemble old Count Moor.

It's good to take a morning stroll, your mind rejuvenated, your spirit cleansed after a night of bathing in sleep, of imbibing Lethe's waters. Brimming with confidence, you can look forward to the coming day even as you revel in the luxury of putting off its official start, master of an uncommon, unoccupied and unmolested period between dreams and daytime, which is your reward for having been sensible in your ways. The illusion of a steady, simple, undistracted existence of inwardly directed contemplation, the illusion that your time belongs to you alone, brings great happiness, for man tends to assume that his state of mind at any given moment (be it that of good cheer or anxiety, peace or passion) is his true, natural and permanent one. He immediately transforms every happy feeling of *ex tempore* into his golden rule and inviolable practice, whereas in reality he is condemned to live by improvisation and, in terms of life ethos, from hand to mouth. Breathing in the morning air, you can truly believe in your own sovereign virtuousness, even though by now you should—and in fact do—know that the world has its nets ready and waits to catch you. Tomorrow, in all probability, it will be nine o'clock by the time you find your way out of bed, having first found your way *in* there—flushed and foggy-headed, excited and amused—at two the previous morning . . . Be that as it may. For now you're still a man of sobriety, an early riser, the legitimate master of that young huntsman springing once more over his short fence, overjoyed that today you seem to want to spend time with him, not with the world at your back.

We usually walk about five minutes down the lane until it turns into an ungroomed gravel wasteland along the riverbank. This we then leave behind as we make our way down a broad, as yet undeveloped street of finer gravel, which is replete, as is the lane, with a bicycle path. This street veers off to the right between two low-lying parcels of woodland toward the slope forming the eastern border of our riverbank locale and the end of the world, as Baushan knows it. We cross another still-to-be-developed street running open between the woods and field. It, however, is hemmed in by apartment houses further along toward the city and the streetcar station. A path of downward-sloping gravel then takes us to a nicely laid plot of land, much like a sanitarium garden in appearance. It's deserted at this hour. So, too, is the entire surrounding area, its park benches squatting alongside curved paths that often widen into circular flowerbeds and well-groomed play areas. Groups of lovely old trees—elms, beeches, lindens and silver willows with drooping crowns and trunks barely visible above the grass—stand arranged on expansive lawns as though in a park. I thoroughly enjoy these carefully groomed grounds and couldn't roam with any greater contentment in them if they were my own personal property. Nothing has been neglected. The gravel paths that gently descend the surrounding grass hillsides have even been fitted with cement gutters. Moreover, there are charming, expansive views through the greenery, distant points of closure being provided in both directions by the architecture of the in-looking villas at either end of the park.

Here I indulge in a short stroll along the paths, while Baushan covers every inch of grass with crisscross gallops and leaning turns, overjoyed at so much level space. Or sometimes he pursues—barking with a mixture of disappointment and delight—a bird that, whether spellbound by fear or determined to tease him, flits away barely in front of his jaws. If I sit down on a bench, though, he immediately sprints to my side to take up position atop my foot, for one of the iron laws of his existence is that he may only run around as long as I too am in motion. As soon as I am seated, he also must come to rest. There's no obvious reason for this rule, but Baushan sticks to it nonetheless.

It's a strange feeling, intimate and comical, to have Baushan sitting on my foot, warming it with the feverish heat of his body. Good cheer and collegiality stir within me, as they almost always do in his presence and company. There's something rather peasantlike about the way he sits, shoulder blades turned outward and paws facing in unevenly. His body seems smaller and fatter in this position than it really is, and to great comic effect, the knot of white fur on his chest is thrust out even further. The dignified rigidity of his head and neck, however, compensates for his lack of postural elegance in the extreme attentiveness it expresses . . . Neither of us makes a sound, and, with the rush of the river thoroughly muffled by the time it gets here, everything is quite still. Every furtive little noise around us seems significant and alerts our senses: the brief rustle of a lizard, the song of a bird, the burrowing of a mole in the earth. Baushan pricks his ears—at least to the extent that their droopy musculature permits it. He cocks his head to train his hearing, and his wet black nostrils remain in constant motion, sniffing out the slightest scents.

Then he lies down, careful never to lose contact with my foot. He lies there, perpendicular to me, in that age-old posture of animal idolatry typified by the Sphinx: head and chest held high, limbs tucked underneath his body, paws extended parallel. Having gotten a bit overheated, he opens his jaws, and in the process all cleverness of countenance dissolves into bestiality, his rapidly blinking eyes narrow to slits, and from between his powerful white canine teeth a long rosy tongue flops forth.

How We Obtained Baushan

It was through a sympathetically stout, dark-eyed woman—who, with only the help of an almost grown-up, likewise dark-eyed daughter, runs an inn in the mountains near Tölz—that we made Baushan's acquaintance and acquisition. That was two years ago, when he was only six months old. Anastasia (the woman's name) no doubt knew that we had to have our Percy, a Scottish sheep dog and harmlessly loony aristocrat, put down in his old age after he had contracted a painful and disfiguring skin disease, and that we had done without a watchdog ever since. With this in mind, she telephoned from her mountain abode to inform us that a dog, as fine as any we could ever want, was presently in her care and commission and could be viewed at our convenience.

The very next afternoon, the children having pleaded with a curiosity that was shared almost as much by the adults in the family, we trekked up to Anastasia's inn. We found the proprietress amidst the warm nutritious smells of her spacious kitchen, where, red-faced and sweaty, sleeves rolled back from her round arms, dress open at the neck, she was preparing supper for her guests, her calm industrious daughter moving about to and fro lending a hand. We were greeted warmly: to our credit it was noted that we hadn't put things off but had immediately made our way there. And in response to our inquisitive glances, Resi, the daughter, took us around to the kitchen table, put her hands on her knees and directed some flattering words of encouragement under its surface. There, tied to the table leg with a worn rope, stood a creature whose presence we hadn't noticed in the smoldering dusk of the room, but at whose sight, however, we couldn't help but break out in pitying laughter.

He stood there on long spindles of legs, his tail between his thighs, his four feet close together and his back hunched, and shivered. He may well have been shivering with fear, but it seemed that a more likely cause was lack of warming bodily insulation, for the poor creature was hardly more than a skeleton—a rib cage and backbone on four stilts—over which some ragged fur had been stretched. His ears were flat—a pose that never fails to extinguish all glimmers of intelligence and spirit in a dog's face and that indeed rendered his otherwise quite puppylike countenance inexpressive of anything but stupidity, hopelessness and an urgent appeal for understanding. To make matters worse, what might today be called his Van Dyck seemed much larger back then in proportion to the rest of him, injecting a hue of sour melancholy into the overall wretchedness of his appearance.

All present bent down to offer this picture of misery some words of encouragement and reassurance. Over by the stove, Anastasia added to the expressions of sympathetic glee from the children with a series of personal footnotes concerning her boarder's personal history. His name for the time being was Lux, she said in her pleasant, matter-of-fact tone, and he was the son of good parents—she had been personally acquainted with the mother and had heard only good things about the father. Lux had been born on an agricultural conservatory in Huglfing, and it was only because of unavoidable circumstances that his owners had decided to put him up for sale at such a bargain price and had brought him to her, thinking of the profuse traffic at the inn. They had come in their little cart, Lux running undaunted all twenty kilometers between its rear wheels. She had thought of us immediately as people looking for a good dog and was almost positive that we would decide in his favor. Should we be agreed, all parties would benefit. We would certainly receive great enjoyment from him, he in turn would no longer be alone in the world and would have found a nice home, and she, Anastasia, could rest easy knowing he was in good hands. We shouldn't let ourselves be deterred by the face he was making. He was just feeling uneasy and uncertain of himself on account of his strange surroundings. In no time at all, it would be evident that he came from parents of exceptional stock.

—Yes, but apparently somewhat ill matched.

—Not at all, insofar as they had been truly exceptional animals. He possessed the best attributes of both—that much she, Anastasia, could guarantee. What's more, he was unspoiled, moderate in his requirements, which was important nowadays. Until now, potato peelings had been his exclusive diet. She suggested that we take him home for a few days to start out, on a trial basis with no commitments. If we found our hearts hadn't warmed to him, she would take him back and refund the small asking price. She made this offer without hesitation since she wasn't worried about our taking her up on it. From what she knew about him and about us—i.e. both parties—she was convinced that we would come to love him and would never think of parting from him.

She made many such arguments in her calm, fluid, pleasant voice, as she went about her business at the stove, every once in a while rekindling the flames before her face like a witch. She even came over and opened Lux's jaws with both hands to show us his beautiful teeth and, for some reason, the pink-channeled roof of his mouth. To the expert query of whether he had already had distemper, she replied somewhat brusquely that she didn't know. To the question of size, her quick-witted response was that he would get about as big as our dearly departed Percy. There was much discussion back and forth, much warmhearted recommendation on Anastasia's part, which found support in the children's entreaties, much half-convinced uncertainty on our own. Finally we asked for some time to think things over, which she gladly granted, then made the pensive trip back down to the valley, examining and evaluating our impressions along the way.

Naturally the four-legged wretch under the table had gotten to the children, and all our adult pretense toward laughing at their lack of discrimination was in vain. We, too, felt a pang in our hearts and realized how difficult it would be to erase the image of poor Lux from our memories. What would become of him if we rejected him? Into whose hands would he fall? A mysterious and terrible figure took form in our imaginations: the knacker, from whose horrible clutches we had previously rescued Percy with a couple of genteel gunsmith's bullets and a proper grave at the edge of our yard. If we had wanted to abandon Lux to his uncertain, probably gruesome destiny, we should have taken care in the first place not to make his acquaintance and to study his puppy's face with its Van Dyck. Now that we were aware of his existence, a responsibility seemed to lay upon us, which we could only disavow with heart-wrenching difficulty. — The third day after our initial meeting saw us once again making our way up that gentle Alpine foothill. We hadn't exactly decided upon his acquisition. But we saw only too clearly that the matter as it stood could hardly have any other outcome.

This time Anastasia and her daughter were sitting on either end of the near side of the kitchen table drinking coffee. He who was for the time being called Lux sat in front of them—sat then just as he sits now, his shoulder blades twisted like a peasant's, his paws pointed inward—with a little corsage of wildflowers stuck behind his shabby leather collar. This gave him a decidedly more festive look, something of a village lad in his Sunday best or a hillbilly bridegroom. The younger woman, herself looking quite done up in her traditional dirndl and bodice, said that she had put it there in honor of his new home. Both mother and daughter assured us that they had never been so certain of anything as that we would return to pick up our Lux, and what's more, that it would be this very day.

Thus, from the moment we walked in, any further debate proved impossible and superfluous. Anastasia thanked us in her pleasant way for the nominal price we handed over, which totaled ten marks. It was clear that she had asked it of us more for our own benefit than hers or the conservatory owners', so that Lux might have a positive monetary value in our eyes. We understood this and gladly concluded the transaction. Lux was untied from the table leg, I was handed the end of the rope, and best wishes and friendly promises accompanied us as we made our way back across Anastasia's kitchen doorstep.

The approximately hour-long trek home we made with our new cohabitant was no victory parade. The bridegroom soon lost his corsage in the general bustle, we could read the reactions in the faces of the people we met, and the instances in which we were confronted with not only congenial amusement, but mocking contempt multiplied as our route home passed through the marketplace, indeed through the entire marketplace. To top matters off, it turned out that Lux had apparently been suffering for some time now from a diarrhea that required us to linger for long intervals under the eyes of the townspeople. We stood in a protective circle around him in his most intimate misery wondering whether this was not, in fact, distemper announcing its first symptoms. However, our fear was unwarranted, for it emerged in time that we were dealing with a fundamentally sound and durable constitution, one that to this day has proved immune to every plague and pestilence.

As soon as we got home, the maids were ordered to appear so that they, too, could meet the newest member of the family and offer their modest opinion. One could see them preparing to be amazed. Once they had gotten a look at him and read the dubious expressions on our faces, however, they let out a harsh laugh, turned their backs on the sad staring creature and dismissed him with a wave of their hands. This strengthened our doubts about their capacity to understand the benevolent rationale behind the small sum Anastasia had charged us, so we told them we'd gotten the dog for free and took Lux out to the veranda for a welcoming dinner of nutritious scraps.

In his timidity he rejected the meal. Though he sniffed at the individual morsels on offer, he shied away, not daring to believe cheese rinds and chicken legs could be meant for him. He didn't, however, turn down the cushion—a potato sack filled with sea grass—that had been placed for his comfort in the hall: he settled down upon it, paws tucked underneath, while, inside, a debate ensued and a decision was reached as to the future name he would bear.

He still refused to eat the following day. Then came a period when he devoured everything that came in the vicinity of his muzzle, gorging himself indiscriminately, until finally his nutritional habits grew more moderate, his taste more discerning. His progressive familiarization with and initiation into bourgeois life is thus described in a single stroke, so I won't lose myself in an overly exact depiction of this process. Only once was it briefly interrupted—Baushan got misplaced. The children had brought him into the backyard and undone his leash to allow him greater freedom of movement, whereupon in an unwatched moment, he had slipped through the narrow gap between the gate and the ground and got out into the open. His disappearance caused considerable consternation and sadness in our household, at least among its principal members, the servants being inclined either to shrug off the loss of a dog that had been given away for free or to discount it entirely as a loss. A flurry of telephoning broke out between our house and Anastasia's inn, where we hoped and suspected him, in vain, for he never showed his face there. Two whole days passed before her daughter called with word from Huglfing that an hour and a half earlier Lux had turned up at his original home, the conservatory. So that was where he was: pure force of instinct had summoned him back to the land of potato peelings, had driven him to march for days, alone, through wind and weather, retracing the same twenty kilometers he had last covered between the wheels of a wagon! As a result, his former owners once more had to span their little wagon so that he might be placed in Anastasia's temporary custody. After two more days, we again set out to pick up our little Odysseus, whom we found, as before, tied to the table leg, run-down and dishevelled, covered with the muck of the country road. He even showed signs of joyful recognition when he first caught sight of us! Why, then, had he run off in the first place?

A period then ensued in which he had obviously forgotten all about the conservatory but had yet to put down any roots with us, so that in his soul he was without master and thus like a leaf scattered by the wind. In those days we had to keep a sharp eye out whenever we took him for a walk, since the weak bond of sympathy between himself and us tended to tear without warning, causing him to stray into the woods, where, if allowed a life of independent roaming, he would clearly have reverted to the condition of his undomesticated ancestors. Only our careful attention saved him from this dire fate, holding him securely at that high level of civilization that his species has achieved during its several millennia at man's side. Then, in one fell swoop, a dramatic change of scenery—our relocation to this city, or better yet, to this suburb—did much to reorient him toward us and establish firm ties with our household.

Some Information Concerning Baushan's Life and Character

A fellow from the Isar valley once told me that this breed of dog could easily become a nuisance, since pointers always stick to their masters' sides. Thus I knew better than to interpret all too personally the obstinate loyalty Baushan soon began to show toward me, and as a result I found it easier to restrain and, when necessary, fend off his expressions of fidelity. There's an age-old patriarchal instinct in all canines that causes them—especially the more masculine, sport-loving breeds—to regard the male head of the family as their primary master, as the guardian of the hearth and the provider. They seek a life of dignity via a special relationship of congenial servitude with him, while maintaining much greater independence from the rest of the family. From day one Baushan held to me in this spirit, gazing at me with eyes manly and true, soliciting commands—which I preferred to withhold since it soon became apparent that obedience wasn't one of his strengths—and attaching himself to my heels in the visible conviction that his inseparability from me was part of the world's divine order. It went without question in the family circle that he would sit at my feet and no one else's. It also went without question on walks that, whenever I broke off from the group to go my own way, he would follow in my footsteps. He also insisted on my company when I was working, and if he found the back door closed, he would take a startlingly sudden leap and spring into the room through the open window, strewing dirt all over and plopping down with a heavy sigh under my desk.

But there is an awareness of other living creatures too active for even the presence of a dog not to become bothersome in times when solitude is required, and Baushan also disturbed my work in a more concrete sense. He would come over to me where I sat, wag his tail, muster me with searing looks and stamp his paws to attract my attention. The slightest acknowledgment would make him put his front legs on my armrest, press his head against my chest and kiss in the air at me until I burst out laughing. Thereupon he would proceed to conduct an examination of the tabletop—no doubt under the assumption of finding something edible there since I hovered so urgently over it—and invariably smudged my drying ink with his big, hairy game dog's paws. Sharply ordered to sit, he would lie down and go to sleep. But no sooner would he fall asleep than he would begin to dream, setting all four of his outstretched paws in motion and emitting a high-pitched yet muffled howl that seemed to come alternately from a ventriloquist and from another world entirely. It was no wonder I found this both irritating and distracting, since it was uncanny, for one, and stirred, indeed weighed upon my conscience, for another. This dream life was an all too obvious compensation for actual running and hunting, invented by nature out of necessity, for as long as he lived with me he would never be blessed with the amount of outdoor exercise his blood and sensibilities demanded. I felt badly, but since there was nothing I could do about it, I gave in to more pressing concerns and rid myself of the disturbance, my justification being that in bad weather he tramped too much mud into the study and that his claws were destroying the carpet.

Thus he came to be banished from our living quarters and generally forbidden from my presence as long as I was inside, although occasional exceptions to this rule were allowed. He quickly understood and submitted to this unnatural prohibition since it was nothing less than the inscrutable will of his landlord and master. The forced absences from my side, which often extend over long parts of the day, especially in winter, are only a question of spatial distance and don't amount to a separation or severance of our bond *per se*. He is not at my side, at my command, but that in itself is the execution of a command, a negative form of being-at-my-side, so that there can be no talk of Baushan's leading an autonomous existence during the hours when we're apart. Through the glass door of my study I can see him on the small lawn in front of the house playing like an avuncular buffoon with the children. Yet amidst all the horsing around, he still regularly trots over to my door, sniffs at the crack to make sure I'm still there (the tulle curtain obstructs his view), sits down on the steps with his back to my study and keeps watch. From my desk I can also see him meandering around aimlessly and pensively on the raised path between the old aspen trees. Such back-and-forth parading, however, is nothing but a way of killing time, devoid of pride, enthusiasm or life. It's utterly inconceivable that Baushan might simply decide on his own to indulge in the splendid art of the hunt, although no one would stop him, and my presence, as we shall see, is actually somewhat superfluous.

Life begins for him when I leave the house—though, alas, even then it often doesn't actually begin! Every time I walk out the door, the question presents itself whether I will turn right, down the lane toward the wide open spaces and solitude of our hunting ground, or left, toward the streetcar stop on my way into the city. Only in the former case does it make any sense for Baushan to accompany me. In the beginning he did join me when I opted for the world, experiencing to his amazement the streetcar thundering toward him, whereupon he followed me, violently suppressing his fear, in one blind loyal leap up onto the platform amidst the throng of people. A storm of public indignation always swept him back down, and he would run full tilt alongside the roaring vehicle that was so unlike the little wagon between whose wheels he had run of yore. True of heart, he always kept pace as long as possible, and his wind never entirely deserted him. But the urban hustle and bustle always got the better of this conservatory son. He got entangled in people's legs, strange dogs snapped at his side, a hodgepodge of exotic smells such as he had never known excited and addled his wits, the lure of corners drenched in the perfume of past adventures attracted him irresistibly, and he hesitated. He could catch up with the tram as it thundered along the rails, but, unfortunately, he usually attached himself to an impostor that, as it happened, was absolutely identical to the one he sought. Baushan would then run in entirely the wrong direction, straying ever further into this strange, insane world, and it would be two days before he found his way, famished and limping, back to the peace and quiet of the last house by the river, to which his master in the meantime had also been sensible enough to return.

That happened two or three times, before Baushan finally had enough and ceased accompanying me when I turned left. He can tell the instant I walk out the door what I have in mind: our hunting grounds or the world. He jumps up from the mat under the arched doorway where he awaits my departure. He jumps up, and at that very moment he can guess my intentions. My attire gives it away, the type of walking stick I'm carrying, no doubt also my expression and carriage, the look I merely graze him with, cold and distracted, or direct invitingly *at* him. He understands. He flings himself head over heels down the front steps and does a whirling dance of mute excitement all the way before me to the gate, whenever a positive outcome seems assured. He cringes and flattens his ears, on the other hand, the light in his face sputtering, dying out in sorrow and ruination, whenever his hopes are dashed, and his eyes well over with the sort of meek wretchedness that misfortune calls forth in the faces of both man and beast.

There are times when he refuses to accept the sad truth before his eyes, namely that, for now, hunting is out of the question. His desire proves too powerful: he will ignore the external indicators, try not to notice the decidedly urban walking stick, the elevated bourgeois attire of my person. He pushes up beside me on my way through the gate, spins around one hundred and eighty degrees and tries to lure me to the right by taking off at full speed in that direction, looking back at me, forcing himself to disregard the fateful "No" with which I greet his efforts. As soon as I do turn left, he runs back, loudly snorting and emitting weird little squeaks that vent the extraordinary tension within him. He accompanies me to the end of our front fence and starts jumping back and forth over the railing of the adjacent public grounds by the road, even though that impediment is quite high and he must groan with exertion or risk incurring injury. What motivates him is a kind of desperate gaiety in the face of facts, part of an attempt to bribe me, to win me over with a demonstration of eager skill. Though unlikely, it isn't impossible, at least not utterly, that at the end of the grassy median I might nonetheless depart the city road, turn left and lead him, after a short detour past the mailbox to drop off a letter, into the wide open spaces of the park. This has been known to happen, but not often, and when this hope, too, is extinguished, Baushan sits back down and lets me go.

He sits in the posture of an oafish peasant in the middle of the road, eyes following me down the entire long prospect of the lane. If I look back at him, he pricks up his ears but doesn't run after. Even if I were to whistle and call his name, he wouldn't come, for he knows it's useless. At the end of the lane I can still see him sitting there—a tiny, dark, oafish dot in the middle of the road—and something stings at my heart. I board the tram with nothing less than a pang of conscience. He has waited so long, and we all know what torture that can be! His whole life consists of waiting, waiting for our next walk in the outdoors; no sooner is he rested up from our last one than he begins to wait once more. Even at night he waits, for his sleep is spread over all twenty-four hours of the solar cycle. Little naps on the blanket of grass in our backyard with the sun warming his fur or behind the curtains of his doghouse are absolutely required in order to shorten the many idle intervals in his day. Consequently, his sleep at night is sporadic and fitful. In the darkness he is variously driven over lawn and yard, so that he flings himself first here, then there, waiting. He waits for the night patrolman with the lantern to come by on his rounds, accompanying, despite knowing better, the man's heavy footsteps with a mournful watchdog howl. He waits for the sky to grow pale, for the rooster to crow from a distant garden, for the morning breeze to stir in the trees and for the kitchen door to open and allow him to slip inside and warm himself by the stove.

However, Baushan's nocturnal torment is mild compared to what he must endure by the light of day, especially in nice weather, winter as well as summer, whenever the sun beckons with thoughts of the outdoors. The need for exercise tugs at his muscles, and his master, without whom nothing can be undertaken, simply refuses to budge from his post behind the glass door. Baushan's nimble little body, so alive with feverish pulse, is completely, indeed overly rested—sleep is out of the question. He climbs the steps of the terrace to my door, plops down with a sigh that seems to issue from his very depths and lays his head on his paws, gazing up at the heavens with a look of martyrdom. This only lasts a few seconds, and then he has had all, indeed more than he can take and begins to find his situation unbearable. There's still something he can do. He can go back down the steps and lift his leg toward one of the little pyramid-shaped evergreens that flank my rose beds, always the one on the right, which over the years has been corroded by Baushan's proclivities and needs to be replaced. He descends the steps and does that which he has no need of doing but which does serve to pass the time temporarily. For quite a while, despite the ultimate fruitlessness of this activity, he stands on three legs. He stands there until his fourth leg begins to quiver in the air, and he must hop from side to side to maintain his balance. Then he returns to all fours and is no better off. He gazes dully up at two songbirds flitting around in the cluster of aspens, watches the feathered creatures darting rapidly through the branches as though shot from a bow, then turns his back on them with what looks like a shrug at their childish tomfoolery. He stretches and stretches until it seems he's intent on tearing himself to shreds.

For thoroughness's sake he divides this activity into two segments—first extending his front legs with his rear suspended in air, then *vice versa,* his hind legs splayed—and his mouth gapes open the whole time in a wide animal yawn. Then that, too, is over and done with and can't be prolonged. Once one has stretched every muscle, nothing more can be stretched for a while. He stands and stares at the ground, depressed. Then he begins to spin round in slow, searching circles, as though wanting to lie down but not knowing how. In the end he changes his mind and moves off lethargically to the middle of the lawn, where he flings himself down with a sudden, almost violent motion, vigorously scrubbing his back to and fro on the freshly mown grass, cooling it. This must produce a powerful feeling of ecstasy, for he rolls around with paws clenched, snapping up in all directions at the air in a frenzy of fulfilled passion. Indeed, he tastes all the more eagerly of this pleasure, drinking it to the dregs, because he knows that it won't last. One can only roll around like that for ten seconds at most, and he knows that what follows is not the beneficial exhaustion one gets from joyful exercise, but the disillusionment and double emptiness with which one pays for intoxication and numbing excess. He lies there on his side like a corpse, with eyes rolled. Then he gets up and shakes himself off, shakes himself off as only a dog can, without fear of concussion, every part of him rattling and clattering, his ears slapping against the underside of his chin and his lips flanging out from his gleaming white teeth. And what then? He stands motionless on the scene, lost to the world, and has no idea at all what to do with himself. Under these circumstances he resorts to a desperate measure. He climbs the terrace steps, approaches the glass door, and, ears flat, a truly beggarly expression on his face, lifts one tentative paw to scratch. He scratches only once, quite softly. Nonetheless, his demurely lifted paw touches my heart, for he has only decided upon this single gentle scratch after reaching his wits' end. I get up to open the door and let him in, though I know that it will come to no good. And sure enough, right away he starts jumping around in dances of exhortation to manly sporting endeavor, completely disarranging the rug and messing up the study. With that my concentration is gone.

Now judge for yourself how easy it is for me, having seen how Baushan has waited, to ride off in my tram and leave him sitting there, a sad little dot all the way at the other end of the lane! In summer, when the days are long, his misfortune is hardly so great, since my evening walk may at least take me into the open fields, so that despite a most difficult wait, Baushan will reap the reward of his patience and, hunter's luck willing, get to chase a hare after all. In winter, though, the game is up if I take the noon train, and he must bury all hope for another twenty-four hours. For then, by the time I take my second walk, night has long since fallen, our hunting ground lies shrouded in inhospitable darkness, and my only remaining route takes me through the artificially lit areas upstream, the streets and grounds maintained by the city, which are hardly the thing for Baushan's instincts and simple sensibilities. In the beginning he came along but soon gave up and remained at home. It wasn't just that he couldn't see far enough to romp around—the contrast between light and dark made him skittish. Every person, every shrub startled his muddled wits. A night watchman's cape billowing in the wind would make him leap aside and start howling, whereupon, with a courage born of sheer terror, he would take a run at the likewise deathly frightened officer, who would try to compensate for the shock he had suffered by dispatching a streak of crudely threatening invectives in Baushan's and my direction. And that's nothing compared to the unfortunate incidents we've had on nights of fog. — Apropos the night watchman, I'd like to add here that there are three types of people to which Baushan is absolutely averse: policemen, monks and chimney sweeps. He simply can't abide them and will bark furiously when one or the other passes by our house or any other time that they somehow come into view.

But let me return to the topic at hand. Winter is the

season when the world most perniciously undermines our autonomous virtue, when it least permits a well-regulated life, that is, a life of seclusion and contemplation. All too often the city draws me back for a second evening visit. Social obligations fall due, and it's late—around midnight if I can catch the train to its penultimate stop out here, or still later if I miss my last chance at public transit and have to walk—before I get home, distracted and buoyed by wine, smoking cigarettes, beyond natural exhaustion, with a false nonchalance toward everything. Often at such times it happens that my home, the quiet life I call my own, rushes up and greets me, not only without recrimination or hurt feelings, but with the greatest joy, bidding me welcome and reintroducing itself—all in the form of Baushan. Surrounded by complete darkness, with the rush of the river in my ears, I turn into the poplar lane, and after a couple of steps I can sense silent dancing and jostling around me. Early on it took me several minutes to figure out what was happening. "Baushan?" I asked the first time it happened, directing my question out into the darkness . . . The dancing and jostling grow faster and faster, ultimately degenerating into something like the wild frenzy of a dervish or berserker, always without a sound. The instant I stop walking, I have those trusty, if damp and dirty paws all over the lapel of my overcoat, and there'll be a snapping and lapping at my face, forcing me to lean backward as I pat a bony shoulder blade that is also damp from the snow or rain . . . He has picked me up from the tram, the fine fellow. As sensitive as ever to my comings and goings, he set off for the stop when it seemed about time and has been waiting here—probably for quite a while in the snow and rain. And his joy at finally seeing me again knows no ill-will on account of my coldhearted neglect, though I may have utterly ignored him that day and crushed all his hopes and dreams. I shower him with praise as I pat him on our way home. I tell him he did a good job and give him my word of honor for the morrow, assuring him (and myself) that at noon we'll definitely go hunting, no matter what the weather. Under the force of such a resolution all my worldly preoccupation dissipates like smoke, my mood once more turns serious and sober, and the prospect of our hunting grounds in their seclusion merges with the thought of more elevated, obscure, preternatural incumbencies . . .

I would like to flesh out my sketch of Baushan's character with some of his other traits, so that interested readers can visualize him as vividly as possible. Perhaps the best way to proceed is to invoke our dearly departed Percy as a counter-example, since a more dramatic contrast between types within a single species is hardly conceivable. For starters we must consider the fact that Baushan is in full possession of his wits, whereas Percy, as mentioned and as is often the case with aristocratic animals, was a blathering idiot his entire life, insane, the very personification of overbred eccentricity. This has already been pointed out earlier in a more general context, and it is only mentioned here to highlight Baushan's earthy common sense. The difference becomes most apparent upon the announcement of walks and during greetings. Baushan's methods of communicating his emotional dispositions on such occasions remain well within the norms of reason and healthy enthusiasm, never even approaching the borders of hysteria that Percy's behavior crossed every time and usually with quite outrageous results.

Yet there's more to the contrast between the two creatures than just this. In reality, each case is more complicated and complex. Baushan is as rugged as the common man, but also just as prone to whining, whereas his aristocratic predecessor combined an infinitely more resolute and prouder spirit with far greater delicacy and tolerance of pain, so that, despite being insane, he utterly surpassed his little peasant counterpart in self-discipline. Not to advance some pro-aristocratic doctrine, but only for the sake of truthfulness, do I underscore the antitheses of coarse but soft, delicate but steadfast. Baushan, for example, is absolutely the one to spend even the coldest winter's night outside on the straw bed behind the Hessian curtains of his doghouse. Because of a weak bladder, which renders him unable to spend seven consecutive hours inside, we ultimately had no choice but to put him out even in inhospitable weather, rightly trusting his robust good health. After an especially frigid, damp night he may come in with not only a whimsical frosted Van Dyck but a slight cough—one of the abrupt, monosyllabic variety dogs tend to get—but within a few hours he has overcome the affliction and suffers no lasting harm. No one would have even considered exposing silken-haired Percy to the wrath of such a night. On the other hand, however, Baushan is terrified of even the slightest pain and responds with a self-pitying pathos that would be repugnant, if naive rusticity didn't disarm the observer with its humorous appeal. Every time he goes creeping through the underbrush I can hear him break out in loud squeals at a scratching thorn or a flying branch in his face. And if he scrapes his belly or twists an ankle even slightly while jumping over the rail, you get an outcry worthy of Greek tragedy: three-legged hobbling, unrestrained yowls and lamentations of fate. These are all the more piercing the more sympathy you show him, even though after fifteen minutes he is running and jumping just as before.

It was altogether different with Percival. He gritted his teeth through everything. Like Baushan, he feared the leather strap and had the misfortune of tasting its wrath far more often. Not only was I younger and more hot-tempered during his lifetime than I am now, there was also something insolent and malicious about his foolishness that cried out for and indeed provoked disciplinary measures. Whenever he pushed me too far, so that I had no choice but to take down the lash from its hook, he slunk under table and chair and hid there cringing. Yet no cry of pain ever escaped his lips as first one blow, then the next came whistling down upon him. At most he let out a grave sigh if some blow struck him too directly. Old Baushan, on the other hand, starts squealing and howling in rank cowardice as soon as I raise my arm. In short, Baushan has no sense of honor, no mastery of self. Happily, his conduct hardly ever gives occasion for such punitive measures, especially since I forgot long ago about demanding a level of performance from him that isn't in his nature and would lead to conflict if I insisted upon it.

Tricks, for example, are something I don't ask him to perform—it would be pointless. He's no scholar, no sideshow genius or silly court poodle: he's an athletic young hunter, not a professor. Earlier I stressed the fact that he's an accomplished jumper. When it's really necessary, he can overcome any obstacle—if it's too high to be surmounted with a single continuous leap, he clambers up one side and drops himself down the other. In any case he conquers it. But the obstacle must be genuine, that is, one that cannot be slipped through or ducked under. In that case Baushan finds jumping irrational. A wall, a ditch, a gate, a solid fence—these are genuine obstacles. A horizontal pole or an outstretched stick is *not*, and one cannot jump over them without lapsing into ridiculous inconsistency vis-à-vis oneself and the world. Baushan refuses to do this. He simply refuses. Just try to make him jump over such imaginary barriers! In your anger you would have no choice but to grab the squealing animal by the scruff of the neck and toss him over the pole or stick, whereupon he would behave as if your command had been carried out and celebrate the occasion with dances and enthusiastic barks. Cajole him, beat him. A well-reasoned antipathy to all purely artificial tricks holds the reins here, and you will never break it. It's not that he doesn't want to oblige. As his master, my satisfaction is indeed of paramount importance to him: he will jump a hedge, for instance, not only at his own whim, but also on command, then bask in my praise and expressions of gratitude. But before he'd jump over a pole or a stick, instead of just crawling under it, I'd have to beat him to death. Thousandfold he would plead for forgiveness, understanding, even mercy, since he fears pain to the point of being a sissy, but no amount of fear or pain can compel him to perform a trick that, physically, would be child's play, but for which, in mind and soul, he lacks the necessary capacity. To demand such a trick of him is not to confront him with the question of whether he will jump or not—that is a foregone conclusion. The command itself is tantamount to a beating, for to demand something incomprehensible and—in its incomprehensibility—impossible from him is the same in his eyes as to seek pretense for a conflict, a disruption of friendship, a thrashing. Such a command is, in fact, the first step toward all the above. This is Baushan's perspective, as far as I can tell, and I doubt we can speak of obstinacy in his case. Obstinacy must, indeed demands to be broken. His antipathy to all purely artificial tricks, however, would be sealed with his death if need be.

What a strange soul! So intimate a friend, yet so alien, so different in some respects that our language cannot adequately express his logic. What relation have words, for example, to that laborious ceremony, so unnerving for participants and observers alike, by which two dogs exchange greetings, introduce themselves or perhaps do little more than register each other's presence? A hundred times over, my walks with Baushan have made me witness—unwilling witness—to such encounters, and every time, for the duration of the scene, Baushan's otherwise so familiar behavior becomes utterly inscrutable. I have found it impossible to penetrate with any sympathy the sensibilities, rules and customs that underlie this ceremony. The meeting of two unacquainted dogs out in the open is truly one of the most embarrassing, tense, dire spectacles that can be imagined: it's surrounded by an aura of the diabolical and the weird. There's a connection at work there for which no exact names exist. Two creatures are simply unable to pass one another by—what could be more disconcerting?

What I'm saying hardly applies when one of the parties finds itself confined to its estate, restricted by a fence or a hedge. Even then, it's difficult to comprehend both sides' motivation, but at least the whole situation is less inflammatory. They catch scent of one another from afar, long in advance of making eye contact. Baushan hurries over to me as though seeking protection and lets out a whimper to articulate some obscure, utterly ineffable sense of pain and urgency deep within, while the other, incarcerated party sends up a sudden flurry of barks, probably intended to sound like energetic watchfulness but lapsing every so often into tones similar to Baushan's, into the same ardent, simpering, jealous, immensely needful whimper. We draw closer, approach the spot. The other dog sits waiting behind the fence, cursing and lamenting his helplessness, lunging wildly at the barrier and acting—one can't tell if he's serious—as though he would rip Baushan to shreds right then and there, if only he could get at him. Nonetheless Baushan, though he could just as well remain by my side and keep walking, always approaches the fence. He has to, he would even if I ordered him not to, for to keep his distance would be to transgress against internal laws far more basic and inviolable than my restraining authority. He approaches and, assuming an attitude of humility and placid reserve, makes that special offering which, as he well knows, will serve to end the standoff and effect a temporary and conditional truce, his adversary doing the same, albeit under the odd curse and whine. They then start to chase each other, one here, one there, keeping pace in silence with one another. They turn simultaneously at the end of the stranger's estate and bolt back in the other direction, turn round again and take off once more. Then, suddenly, they stop and stand in the middle as though rooted, no longer parallel but perpendicular to the fence, through which their noses are pressed. They stand there like that for some time, only to resume their bizarre indecisive footrace, shoulder to shoulder, opposite one another. Finally mine avails himself of his freedom and breaks off. What a terrible moment for the one confined! He can't accept it—he sees it as an incomparable humiliation that his counterpart should simply decide to leave on a whim. He throws a fit, foams at the mouth, goes seemingly mad with rage, bolts back and forth over the entire length of his estate, threatens to jump the fence and strangle his betrayer, and hurls the most vulgar epithets at his back. Baushan hears this and takes it quite personally, as I can see from the stony yet insulted expression on his face, but makes no move to turn around. He goes on his merry way, while to his rear the terrible streak of cursing eventually subsides to a whimper and slowly ceases.

That's how the scene plays itself out whenever one of the parties finds itself in custody. Such encounters are only truly awkward when they take place out in the open and on equal terms—the results can be quite unpleasant to describe. It's the most oppressive, insidious and potentially explosive encounter in the entire world. Baushan, who until a moment ago has been frolicking carefree, runs to my side and forces himself against my leg with one of those sniffling whimpers from the depths of his soul, a whimper in which the specific emotional disposition to be conveyed remains unclear yet is nonetheless all too familiar. This leads me to conclude that another dog is headed our way. I may have to peer quite far into the distance, but, yes, I was right, here he comes, and even from here it's apparent from his tentative and tense posture that he, too, is aware of the other's presence. My own distress on such an occasion is hardly less than that of the two parties involved. The incident is most unfortunate. "Go away!" I tell Baushan. "Why always beside my leg? Can't you go somewhere on your own and do your business?" I try to shoo him off with my walking stick, for if it comes to a fight—always a possibility, whether or not I comprehend the reasons—the whole thing will take place at my feet and put me in a most unpleasant position. "Go away!" I repeat softly. But Baushan doesn't go anywhere. In his anxiety he sticks to my side, trotting off only for a moment to make his offering under a nearby tree, while his counterpart up ahead, as I can clearly see, does the same. Twenty paces are now all that separate us, and the suspense is frightful. The other dog starts crawling on his belly, crouched like a tiger, his neck craned, awaiting Baushan's approach in this highwayman's pose, seemingly intent upon going for the throat at the first opportunity. But this never happens, as Baushan seems to know it won't—at least he proceeds directly, if with trembling and heavy heart, toward the animal lurking up ahead. He would advance in this way no matter what, even if I were to disengage myself, turn down a side path and leave him to the difficulties of his situation. However tense the encounter may be for him—avoidance is out of the question. He approaches transfixed, bound to his counterpart; indeed, they are bound to each another in some obscure, volatile relationship they are not allowed to deny. Two steps are all that separate us.

At this point the other dog silently rises, as though never having intended to play the tiger, and stands exactly as Baushan does. Sheepish, miserable and deeply embarrassed, they both stand there, unable to pass. Both would probably like to do just that: they turn their heads, then steal sidelong glances at each other, and a mutual feeling of guilt seems to hang over them. They shove and sidle up to one another, nervous and grimly alert, flank on flank, to sniff each other's procreative privates. At this juncture they often start snarling, and I call out to Baushan in a low voice and admonish him, for this is the moment of truth that decides whether a fight is to erupt or whether I will be spared that trauma. There's no telling how and even less why it comes to a fight. All of a sudden, they're nothing but a ball, a raging turmoil, from which bestial growls and tearing noises issue. I have no choice but to intervene with my walking stick to prevent serious injury, trying at the same time to get my hands on either Baushan's collar or the scruff of the neck and lift him in the air, often with the other animal dangling by its jaws or enacting various other horrors that keep my teeth on edge for the better part of our walk. It can also happen that little or nothing comes of all the theatrics, but even then it's difficult to make an inch of progress. Even when they don't try to take a bite out of each other, the two animals are altogether too united by some unyielding internal bond. They may seem to have gotten past one another. They may be standing in a straight line instead of flank to flank, facing in opposite directions instead of staring each other down, scarcely turning their heads, only glancing back as far as their eyes alone allow. Nonetheless, despite their spatial separation, the unhappily stubborn bond refuses to break. Neither can tell whether the moment of freedom is truly at hand. Both would like to leave, but because of some obscure qualm of conscience, neither dares stir from the spot. Then, at long last, the spell is broken, the bond dissolves and Baushan goes hopping away, liberated, his heart unburdened, as though life itself had been restored to him.

I bring this up to illustrate how utterly foreign and strange to me such an intimate friend can become in certain circumstances. At such times his very nature is baffling and obscure. I shake my head every time and can only guess at what underlies this side of him. Otherwise, I know him through and through and have a sympathetic understanding of his mannerisms, his facial expressions and his physical behavior in general. I know only too well, for instance, that special squeaking yawn of his whenever one of our excursions has been too short to scare up any prey. I may have gotten off to a late start that morning so that I have only fifteen minutes to take some air, before being required to turn back. Disappointed, Baushan trots beside me and yawns. It is an unabashed, impolite, jaw-unhinging, bestial yawn accompanied by a guttural squeak and an insultingly bored expression. "A fine master I have," this yawn seems to say. "Here I picked him up from the bridge late last night and waited outside today while he sat behind his glass door, until I practically died of boredom, and when he does finally decide to go out, it's only to turn around again before I've caught a single scent. Woe is me. A fine master! A fraud, this master! A pathetic excuse for a master!"

His yawn expresses all this with an ill-mannered frankness impossible to misinterpret. And I have to grant that he has a point, that I owe him something, so I stretch my hand down to pat his head or shoulder in consolation. However, under these circumstances, he shows no gratitude and refuses to accept my endearments. He just yawns again—if possible, more rudely—and wriggles out from under my hand, even though unlike Percy, and in keeping with his commoner's sensitivity to physical pain and pleasure, he normally likes to be patted. (Above all, he loves having his throat rubbed and has developed a comically frantic technique of jerking his head so that one's hand is directed to the proper spot.) Disappointment is not the only reason for his temporary disinterest in my overtures. It also has to do with the fact that whenever he's in motion—that is to say, whenever I'm in motion—he feels no need to be patted. He finds himself in too masculine a state for physical endearments—a situation that changes as soon as we come to a stop. Once we do, he is again receptive to my affections and will requite them with clumsily fervent insistence.

Sometimes when I'm reading a book in the corner of my yard or under my favorite tree, I'm quite happy to interrupt my intellectual pursuits in order to talk or play some game with Baushan. What do I say, when I talk? Mostly I just call out his name, that sound which above all others is of particular interest to him because it designates himself, and which consequently has an electrifying effect on his whole being. By repeating the word with various intonations, I can rouse and ignite his ego, reminding him and making him ponder the fact that "Baushan" is what he's called and who he is. If I keep this up for a while, I can put him in a state of rapture, a kind of ego-intoxication, in which he will spin round his own bodily axis and, chest bursting with pride, bark loudly and jubilantly up toward the heavens. Otherwise we entertain ourselves with a game in which I tap him on the snout, and he responds by snapping at my hand as if it were a fly. This makes us both laugh—yes, Baushan, too, laughs, and to me in my laughter, the spectacle of his mirth is one of the strangest, most moving sights in the world. It touches my heart to see the corners of his mouth, his typically haggard animal cheeks, start to quake and quiver when I tease him, to see in his blackish animal face the physical manifestations of human laughter—or at least their pale, somewhat hapless, melancholy reflection. I watch them appear, then disappear, giving way to startled embarrassment, before returning once more to tug at his face . . .

Let me break off here before I lose myself any further in details. Despite my best intentions, this short description is already threatening to take on a distressing scope. I only want to sketch my hero in his full splendor, in his element, in that part of life in which he's most himself and his talents appear in their best light, namely, at hunt. Prior to this, however, I must acquaint my readership with the arena of these delights, our hunting ground, my stretch of land by the river, for this location is intimately bound up with Baushan's person and is as dear, as familiar and as significant to me as he is. So, without any further literary justification, the reader will allow me to introduce the hunting ground as the official heading and subject matter of my next portrait.

The Hunting Ground

In every backyard of our spaciously planned development, there is a sharp contrast between older, giant trees that loom over the rooftops and frailer, artificially planted young ones. Easily recognizable as the original vegetative inhabitants of the region, the former are the pride and joy of our still quite recent settlement, and extreme care has been taken to protect and preserve them wherever possible. If in the process of measuring and dividing the lots a conflict arose—that is, if some venerable trunk covered with silvery moss happened to fall on a demarcation line—a fence was made to bulge out slightly, thereby incorporating it into someone's yard, or a considerate gap was left in a concrete wall, where the old fellow still stands tall, half private, half public, its branches sometimes bare and snow-laden, sometimes adorned with tiny late-blossoming leaves.

They are all specimens of the aspen, a tree that thrives on dampness as few do—which tells you something definitive about the unusual character of this stretch of land. It wasn't long ago, no more than a decade and a half, that human ingenuity first reclaimed this area for habitation. Before that, it was only wild swampland, a real mosquito hole, where willows, dwarf poplars and other stunted growth cast their reflections in stagnant ponds. The region is alluvial, and a few meters below the earth's surface there lies a layer of impregnable rock. Therefore the soil here was naturally marshy, and water collected in every depression. The land only dried out when the river level was lowered. I'm no engineer, but basically the trick was to get the water that couldn't seep into the ground to run off laterally: in many places subterranean streams now feed into the river and the ground has firmed up. At least it has for the most part, for if you know the region as Baushan and I do, you can still find many a reed-overgrown hollow downstream that harkens back to the land's original condition, remote areas where the damp keeps everything cool in even the hottest weather and where one gladly lingers for a couple of minutes on a summer walk to catch one's breath.

The entire region possesses its own curious individual character, distinguishable at a glance from the landscape of pines and mossy fields you might expect on the banks of a mountain stream. It has retained, I say, its *original* character, despite coming into the hands of the development company. Everywhere, not just in people's backyards, the original, native vegetation has the clear upper hand over that introduced and cultivated by man. The horse chestnut, the fast-growing maple, even beeches and various other ornamental tree types occur along the esplanades and on the public grounds, but they are all cultivated, not natural, as are the Italian poplars that stand in rows of sterile masculinity. Earlier I identified the ash as aboriginal, and it's quite widespread. You can find examples of all ages everywhere, from hundred-year-old giants to tender saplings that shoot up in great numbers like weeds from the sandy soil. It's the ash—together with the white poplar, the aspen, the birch and the willow in both tree and shrub form—that puts a distinct stamp upon the landscape. These are all small-leaf trees, and small-leafiness—delicacy of foliage despite the often gigantic proportions of the trees themselves—is one of the regional flora's immediately striking features. An exception is the elm, with its broad serrated leaves, whose bright, sticky surfaces spread out toward the sun in large clusters. Great hordes of creeping vines also wind their way everywhere in the woods around the younger trees and confusingly introduce their own lush foliage in amongst that of their hosts. The trim figure of the alder may collect in little thickets wherever there's a hollow; the linden, however, seldom makes an appearance, the oak doesn't occur at all and neither does the spruce. Such varieties can be found on the slope bordering our grounds to the east, where, in different soil, more usual forms of vegetation take over. They tower there dark against the sky, keeping watch over our shallow valley.

No more than five hundred meters separate the slope and the river—I've paced them off myself. Although it may well be that the riverbanks fan out a bit upstream, the difference in breadth is insignificant, and it's therefore remarkable what a wide variety of landscape this narrow stretch of land has to offer. This holds true even if one makes only restricted use of the open space available along the length of the river, as Baushan and I do, hardly ever prolonging our excursions beyond two hours in total. The variety of scenery and the vast number of possible routes for walks—which keep one from getting bored or noticing the narrowness of the park—are directly attributable to the grounds themselves falling into three quite distinct realms or zones, which can be enjoyed one at a time or combined via sharply angled diagonal paths. These are the river and its immediate banks on one side, the opposite slope, and the forest in between.

Of the three, the widest is the forest, park, willow-thicket, or perhaps riverside-brush zone—I wish I could find a more accurate and vivid name for this extraordinary terrain than the word "forest," yet it seems I can't. In no way are we talking about a forest in the usual sense: a great cathedral with a floor of moss and straw and countless pillars of approximately equal dimensions. The trees in our hunting ground differ radically in age and size. Principally on the riverbanks but also deeper within, there are massive ancients of the willow and poplar families. Then there are others that are fully grown but only about ten or fifteen years old, and lastly there is a legion of tender saplings—naturally sown nurseries of wild ash, birch and alder that might seem haggard were they not, as pointed out earlier, shot through with winding creepers and thereby given an almost tropical lushness. Nonetheless, I suspect that these weeds actually retard the development of their hosts, for in all the years I've lived here I never observed any of these saplings to have made much progress.

The types of tree are few and closely related. The alder is a member of the birch family, and the poplar hardly differs from the willow. Moreover, you could even say that all of them tend to converge on the willow as a basic type, for as every forester knows, trees of various families tend to adapt together to an environment by imitating the lines and forms of the type originally predominant there. The lines that predominate here are those of the fantastically gnarled, witchlike willow, the faithful companion and neighbor of both running and standing water, whose sweeping limbs branch out in every direction like twisted fingers, and whose basic posture the other trees obviously attempt to emulate. The white poplar hunches over and can be quite difficult to distinguish from the birch, which, following the spirit of the place, also doubles up and grows extremely crooked—although I wouldn't deny the existence of numerous individual specimens of the latter, that, especially when lit by the colors of a flattering afternoon sun, appear quite well formed and are delightful to behold. The birch is well known in these parts as a thin silver stalk with a few scattered leaves at its crown—as a charmingly figured and neatly attired maiden with a pretty chalk-white trunk, whose leafy locks dangle in languid beauty. However, it also occurs in truly elephantine proportions, with a trunk far too thick for any man to get his arms around and a skin of true bark that turns white and smooth higher up while remaining rough, charred and cracked down below . . .

Nor does the ground, for its part, bear much resemblance to that of a forest. It consists of gravel, clay, even sand, and hardly seems arable. Within certain limits, however, it is arable to the point of lavishness. A lush carpet of tall grass thrives there, which sometimes takes on the dry, sharp-edged form of beach grass, lying flat against the ground in winter like hay. Sometimes it gives way to reeds, though elsewhere—interspersed with hemlock, nettles, coltsfoot, all manner of creeping flora, overgrown thistles and tender young shoots where pheasants and other wild fowl take cover—it swells in soft, thick, abundant waves to touch the knotted roots of the trees. Wild grape and vine-hop twist their way up from these swells of ground cover like broad-leafed spiral garlands, and even in winter their stems remain firmly wound round the tree trunks like tough, uncuttable wire.

The place is neither forest nor park—it's a magic garden, no more, no less. I will defend the appellation, even though what we're talking about is little more than a barren, constricted bit of nature conducive only to stunted growth, which could be summed up botanically with a few simple technical terms. The ground is rolling, constantly on the rise and fall, and as a result every vista it presents is pleasantly self-contained and sheltered on all sides. Were the woods miles wide—as wide as they are long—instead of only a hundred or so paces from middle to edge, you could hardly feel more hidden, enveloped and secluded. The ear alone is reminded, by the sound of running water from the west, of the proximity of the trusty river, which remains concealed from view . . . The ravines in that direction brim with elderberry, privet, jasmine and buckthorn underbrush, so that on humid June days one's lungs can hardly contain the scent. There are also hollows, mere gravel pits along whose sides and bottom nothing grows but a couple of willow saplings and a bit of dried-out sage.

The entire forest zone never ceases to have a peculiar effect on me, though I've visited it every day for a number of years. For some reason my fantasy is excited by the great number of ash trees that so remind me of giant ferns, by the twisting creepers and bedded reeds, by the dampness and aridity, by the scrawny jungle of underbrush. The ultimate impression is a bit like being transported to a landscape from another period of the earth's history or walking on the bottom of the sea—a comparison with a grain of truth to it, since many places around here were once covered by water, especially those hollows, now rectangular grass basins with naturally sown nurseries of wild ash, that serve as pastures for sheep. One such basin is located directly behind my house.

The wilderness is crisscrossed by paths, some mere stretches of trampled grass, others dirt trails clearly never planned but rather born of use, without any clear indication of who the people might have been who walked so often this way, for it is an unsettling rarity when Baushan and I do encounter anyone else. Whenever this happens, my companion will stop dead in his tracks and let out a single muffled yelp that quite accurately expresses my feelings about the intrusion as well. Even on beautiful Sunday afternoons in summer, when hordes of people come streaming from the city for a stroll (it's always a couple of degrees cooler in these parts than elsewhere), we can normally wander along these inner paths in complete solitude. The others don't know about the paths, and what's more, the water, the river, has its usual allure. Pressing as close as it can up to water's edge, up to the very edge if possible (i.e. if the river isn't flooded), the great mass of humanity hurries out into the landscape and returns again at nightfall. At most we'll stumble across a pair of lovers camped out in the bushes, their defiant yet timid animal eyes staring out from their nest, as though challenging us to raise some objection to their going about their business in this out-of-the-way spot. This we silently decline to do by turning off to one side, Baushan with his characteristic indifference toward everything that doesn't bring with it the scent of game, I with an utterly blank expression that withholds judgement and never betrays the slightest indication of either approval or reproach.

The paths are not my only means for conveying myself through my little park. Said location also has *streets*, or to be more precise, provisions for streets, which either previously were streets or were to have been streets and which—God willing—may yet still become streets. The explanation is this. Traces of a groundbreaking shovel and an idealistic entrepreneurial spirit make themselves felt far beyond the developed portion of our area, the little villa colony. The ambition was broad, the planning bold. The corporation that acquired the property ten or fifteen years ago intended something different—namely, bigger—for both the land and themselves than the handful of villas to which the settlement would eventually be restricted. Scores of building lots were made available, and one kilometer further downstream everything stood ready—as indeed it still does—to accommodate purchasers, enthusiasts of the sedentary life. Extravagance obviously ruled those initial board meetings. Not content with shoring up the riverbanks, constructing an adjacent boardwalk and planting a few trees, the planners extended their cultivating hand deep into the forest, clearing land, laying down gravel and partitioning the wilderness with streets—a few running lengthwise, more laterally—grandly envisioned streets of splendor, or at least the outlines of such streets in coarse gravel with indications of curbs and broad public sidewalks. Upon them, however, no public ever treads save Baushan and me, he on the sturdy leather of his four paws, I in my hobnailed boots to combat the gravel. The villas that according to the development corporation's calculations and hopes were to be crowding these streets have refused to materialize, despite my setting good example and building my house here early on. The additional villas have refused, I say, to materialize at any time during the ten or fifteen intervening years, and thus it's no wonder that a certain malaise has settled over the region and that steadfast resistance toward further expenditures or even the completion of the original grand designs now holds sway in the company bosom.

Nonetheless, enough progress *was* made for these uninhabited streets to have been given proper names, just like any within the city limits or suburbs, and I would love to know who the dreamer and historically minded literary connoisseur was among the developers who thought them up. There's a *Gellert-*, an *Opitz-*, a *Fleming-*, a *Bürger-* and even an *Adalbert-Stifter-Straße*, upon which it seems especially fitting for me to walk in my hobnailed boots. Signposts, similar to those one might find in suburbs, have been stuck in the ground at every intersection, and attached to them are the signs themselves, blue enamel signs with white letters, as is customary in these parts. Alas, they aren't in very good condition. Too long they've designated mere sketches of streets where no one actually wants to live, so that they, as much as anything, now embody the local atmosphere of malaise, fiasco and arrested development. Neglected, with no one bearing responsibility for their maintenance or replacement, they stand in disrepair, and the rain and the sun have taken a heavy toll. Much of their enamel is cracked, and rust has eaten away the white letters, often leaving nothing but brown flecks or yawning gaps with unpleasantly jagged edges, so that the street names are difficult to read. One of them in particular presented a puzzle when I first came here and began to explore the area. It was an exceptionally long sign on which the word *Straße* was undamaged. In the name itself, however, which (as I said) was, or rather had been, quite long, most of the letters were illegible. The number of rust spots revealed how many of them there were supposed to be, but nothing could be made out beside half of an *S* at the beginning, an *e* somewhere in the middle and another *e* at the end. That was too little for my wits to go on; the equation had too many variables. For quite a while I stood, hands behind my back, staring up, studying this long sign. Then I continued with Baushan along the sidewalk. Yet even as I imagined I was thinking about something else entirely, my subconscious was working, searching for the mystery name, and suddenly it hit me—I stopped dead in my tracks, then hurried back and repositioned myself before the sign, testing my hypothesis. Yes, indeed, it fit. That was the solution. I was walking down *Shakespearestraße*.

These are the perfect signs for such streets and the perfect streets for such signs—dreamlike and fantastically dilapidated. The streets run in every direction through the forest they've invaded, but the forest doesn't stand idly by for decades, allowing them to remain untouched until the settlers finally arrive. Instead it prepares to *close*, since anything hardy enough to grow here isn't afraid of a little gravel. Accustomed to such soil, purple-headed thistles, blue sage, white willow bushes and young ash seedlings have sprouted up undaunted over every surface, even the sidewalks. There's no doubt about it. The park streets with the poetic names are being overrun by weeds and reclaimed by the brush so that, lamentably or not, in another ten years an *Opitz-* or *Flemingstraße* will have become impassable and will have for all practical purposes ceased to exist. For the time being, though, there's no reason to complain, since, in the eyes of a painter, or at least a romantic, no streets in the world could be more beautiful than these in their current state. There's nothing so delightful—so long as you have a sturdy pair of shoes against the gravel—as to amble through the solitude of this unfinished place or to let your eye wander from the wild brush at its bottom to the small-leafed, damp-loving trees that frame its horizons. These are trees as painted by a certain master from Alsace three hundred years ago . . . What am I saying? *As* painted? They are the very trees. He was here, he knew this area, no doubt he made studies of it, and if the romantic developer who named my park streets hadn't restricted himself exclusively to literature, one of the rusty signs might well have been deciphered with the name Claude Lorraine.

With that my description of the middle forest realm is complete. The eastern slope realm, too, possesses considerable appeal, not only for me, but Baushan as well, for reasons that will follow shortly. You might call it the brook zone, since that body of water lends the area a pastoral charm and, with its picturesque beds of forget-me-nots, makes a nice contrast to the opposite zone of the river, whose rush is also faintly audible here whenever there's a west wind. At the end of the first of the manmade streets, which run from the poplar lane to the slope like breakwaters between grassy hollows and parcels of forest, there's a steep path, used by the children in winter for sledding, down into the lower-lying areas. The brook begins where it levels off, and both man and dog enjoy walking along the surrounding slope with its varied terrain, either on the right or left bank, depending on our mood. To the left there is an expanse of pasture dotted with trees. A subsistence farm as in the country is located there, the backs of its agricultural buildings looking out at us. Sheep graze and tear at the clay ground, tended by a none-too-clever young girl in a red skirt who screams harsh commands at the top of her lungs, hands braced against her knees, enraged at her charges' disobedience yet scared to death of the large, majestically thick-seeming ram with his great wool coat. He does as he pleases, taking orders from no one. The child saves her most blood-curdling shrieks, however, for those occasions when Baushan's appearance panics the flock. This happens regularly, despite Baushan's innocent intentions, sheep being a matter of profound indifference to him. Indeed, he takes no more notice of them than of the air. Sometimes he even tries to forestall new outbreaks of foolishness by exaggerating his disdain and contemptuously skirting their territory, for although to my nose their smell is strong enough (though not unpleasant), theirs is not the scent of game. As a result Baushan has no interest whatsoever in chasing them. Nonetheless, all he has to do is make a sudden movement or simply appear on the scene, and in a flash the entire flock—whose individual members were theretofore spread out grazing and bleating peacefully in voices of various pitch—dashes off *en masse* in one direction, back to back, leaving the dimwitted girl to cry out after them, alone, bent over at the knees, until her voice cracks and her eyes bulge. At this, Baushan will only look up at me as though to say: "You tell me whether I'm at fault or in any way responsible."

Once, however, something different happened, something far more disconcerting and far stranger than panic. One of the sheep—an ordinary specimen of medium size and average appearance for a sheep, with thin upturned lips, reminiscent of a smile, which gave it a look of malicious stupidity—apparently fell head over heels in love with Baushan and refused to budge from his side. It simply followed him: it broke from the flock, left the pasture and, with its silent idiotic smile, stuck to Baushan no matter which way he turned. Whenever he left the path, it followed; whenever he started to run, it took off too; whenever he stopped short, it did the same, directly behind him, always with that same inscrutable smile. Dismay and embarrassed confusion spread across Baushan's face: his position was not at all enviable, for there was no rhyme or reason, no better or worse, to it. It was just absurd, and neither he nor I had ever experienced the like of it. The sheep strayed further and further from the fold, seemingly without concern. It kept following the exasperated Baushan, visibly determined not to leave his vicinity no matter how far he went or where. Not making a sound, Baushan clung to my leg, less afraid—there was no reason to be—than ashamed of the indignity of his position. Finally, as though he had had enough, he stopped, looked back and growled menacingly. The sheep then let out a bleat that sounded like malicious human laughter, and this so terrified poor Baushan that he ran away with his tail between his legs, the sheep bounding comically behind.

In the meantime we had come quite a way from the flock, and the dimwitted little girl was screaming bloody murder, bending not only her hands but sometimes her face to her knees, looking in the distance like some sort of hunchbacked lunatic. At that point a milkmaid came running up in an apron, having either heard the screaming or been otherwise alerted to the situation. With one hand carrying a pitchfork and the other restraining an unfettered breast that flopped back and forth with every stride, she ran breathlessly up to us and set about trying to herd the sheep, which had slowed down to keep pace with Baushan, back where it belonged. Her efforts met with no success. Although the sheep did have to spring sideways to avoid her pitchfork, with a single pivot it was again on Baushan's trail, and no power in the world seemed sufficient to make it desist. Thus, seeing that only one thing would help, I reversed direction. We all went back together, I with Baushan at my side, then the sheep, followed by the milkmaid with the pitchfork, while the hunchbacked little girl in the red skirt stamped her feet and screamed at us across the way. But it wasn't enough to return to the flock—we had to see the job through to completion. We had to go back to the farm itself, to the sheep pen, whose broad door the milkmaid rolled back before us with a great display of strength. We filed in, and once we all were safely inside, the three of us had to slip nimbly back out and slam the pen door in the gullible sheep's face so that it couldn't escape. Only then could Baushan and I take leave of the grateful milkmaid and resume our walk—although Baushan continued to sulk and act humiliated the whole way home.

So much for the sheep. To the left of the agricultural buildings is an extensive *Schrebergarten* colony, reminiscent of a cemetery, with pergolas, chapel-shaped sheds and tiny private garden lots. As a whole, it's quite secluded. Only gardeners who own lots can gain entrance through the lattice gate that serves as an entrance, but every so often I get a glimpse of some fellow with his sleeves rolled up digging around in a nine-pace-square vegetable patch, looking for all the world as though he were digging his own grave. Further along there are more open fields, which extend to the edge of the middle forest region and are shot through with molehills, although they play home not only to moles but field mice—a fact I note with an eye toward Baushan and his various hunting predilections.

On the other side—that is, to the right—brook and

slope stretch out as far as the eye can see, the terrain of the latter, as mentioned, changing constantly. Initially, it tends toward gloominess, rarely getting any sun through its cover of spruce trees. A bit further on, it becomes a sandlot that reflects the sun's warm rays, then a pit of gravel, and finally an avalanche of bricks, as though somewhere higher up a house had been demolished and the worthless remains simply tossed down the hillside to form a temporary impediment to the brook's natural flow. The brook, however, won't be impeded for long; its waters collect and spill over the top, tinted red by brick dust, dyeing the grass on the surrounding banks red as well. They then flow on clearer and brighter for this interruption, sunlight glimmering here and there over their surface.

I love brooks as much as I do all bodies of water, from the ocean to the tiniest reed-overgrown puddle. If my ear happens to catch the hushed splash and babble of a brook in the distance—for example, in the mountains during summertime—I will follow the liquid sounds a long way if necessary in order to find the source, to see the sequestered yet talkative son of the hills and make his acquaintance face to face. Especially beautiful are the mountain brooks that thunder down brightly between pine trees and cliff terraces and form ice-green pools, before dissolving into whiteness and plummeting straight down to the next level. I also like the sight of flatland brooks, whether they be so shallow as barely to cover their bed of slick-polished silver pebbles or as deep as small rivers, swelling to full strength under the protection of the overhanging willows on their banks, their current quicker in the middle than on the sides. What stroller wouldn't follow running water if given the choice? The attraction of water to the human animal is a kind of natural and sympathetic affinity. After all, man is a child of water: nine-tenths of our bodies consist of it, and at a certain stage in our prenatal development we too possess gills. As far as my person is concerned, I can say that the sight of water in all its forms represents by far and away the most immediate and moving way of enjoying nature. Indeed, for me it's the only occasion of true contemplation and self-forgetting in which my own limited existence actually dissolves into the universal. The sight of it—the sight of the sea, for example, either at rest or battering the coast—transports me into a state of such profound organic dreaming, such utter remoteness from self that I lose all sense of time, and the concept of boredom ceases to have any meaning, as hours of unity in and company with it pass in what seems like minutes. I can stand for as long as you want leaning over the rail of a bridge spanning a brook, lost in the sight of the stream, the foam and the current, never letting that other stream flowing around and within me—that of rapidly elapsing time—make me anxious or impatient. In light of this aquatic affinity, it's important that the narrow area where I live is surrounded on two sides by water.

The brook at hand is one of the simple, truehearted kind, nothing special, cheerfully average in character. Naive and bright as glass it flows, incapable of falsehood or duplicity, far removed from any murky pretense toward depth. It is shallow and clear and makes no attempt in its innocence to hide the discarded tin cans or the remains of a tennis shoe imbedded in the green slime at its bottom. It is deep enough anyway to harbor cute, extraordinarily nimble silver-gray fish that flee in broad zigzags at our approach. In many places it swells out to form small pools, and lovely willow trees line its heel, one of which I especially enjoy looking at as I pass by. This particular willow is actually located on the slope, that is, at some distance from the water, but one of its branches reaches down longingly toward the brook, which it has succeeded in reaching, so that the flowing water gently encircles the silvery leaves at its very tip. There it stands enjoying the physical contact.

It's nice to walk here, gently kissed by the warm summer breeze. On hot days Baushan usually wades into the brook to cool his belly (he never allows the water to get any higher if he can help it). He will stand there, ears flat, an expression of pure virtue on his face, letting the water flow by and around him. Then he will trot back to me to shake himself off—an activity that some obscure conviction insists must take place in my vicinity, even though the vigor of his shaking splatters me with water and mud. It does no good to shoo him away with harsh words or my walking stick. There's no dissuading him from what he considers natural, proper and necessary.

The brook flows on toward the setting sun in the direction of a small village that dominates the landscape between the forest and the northern slope, at whose entrance is an inn. There, the brook again forms a pond, in which kneeling village women wash their laundry. There's a bridge, and crossing it, you come to a road that cuts from the village to the city between the edge of the forest and the outer fields. If you veer off to the right, however, you can return in no time via a likewise well-trodden route through the trees to the river.

With that we've come to the river zone, since the river itself now lies, green and foaming white, before us. It's really nothing more than a mountain stream, but its perpetual rush—more or less audible throughout the region and here absolutely dominant—fills the ear and provides an acceptable substitute for the sublime crash of the ocean surf, which just isn't available here. It is often joined by the incessant squawking of countless gulls that circle around the drainpipes in search of food throughout the fall, winter and first part of spring, until the season allows them to resume residence on the lakes higher up. The same is true of wild and semidomesticated ducks, which also spend the colder months here in the vicinity of the city. They float on the swells, yielding to the river's drop, spinning round, rocking back and forth, taking flight only at the last second to escape the rapids by gliding back into the water further upstream . . .

The riverbank is divided into the following segments. Along the edge of the forest, there is a wide gravel surface extending the oft-mentioned poplar lane approximately one kilometer further downstream to the ferry house, which will be discussed shortly and beyond which the riverbank is totally overgrown with brush. There's no mystery as to the story behind this desolate stretch of gravel. It's the first and foremost of the manmade boulevards, grandiosely conceived by the development corporation as a most scenically landscaped esplanade, an elegant carriage route where gentlemen on horseback were to approach the doors of spit-polished landau coaches and exchange dalliances with smiling ladies leaning back into cushions. That much is announced in dilapidated fashion by a large, crooked board of wood at the landing, the ultimate destination of such carriage processions. It makes known in thick letters that this corner lot, a prime location for a park café or better-class establishment, is up for sale . . . That it is and always will be, for instead of a park café with tables, scurrying waiters and drink-slurping patrons, a crooked wooden sign looms there—a gradually and dishearteningly sinking offer with no takers—while the promenade remains nothing but a desolate stretch of the coarsest gravel, almost as thickly overgrown with brush willow and purple sage as *Opitz-* or *Flemingstraße*.

Parallel to the promenade, closer to the river, runs a narrow gravel ridge with overgrown grassy embankments. Telegraph poles stick up everywhere out of it, but nonetheless I sometimes enjoy walking up there, first because it offers a change of pace and also because the gravel offers a relatively clean, if arduous route in rainy weather, when the clay path below looks unpassable. This path—the actual promenade—continues for hours downstream before finally terminating in numerous little unmaintained forest trails. It is planted with young trees, maple and birch, toward the water and is lined on the other side by the mighty natives of the region—willows, aspens and white poplars of colossal dimension. The river embankment is steep, dropping off considerably toward the water, and is protected with ingenious withe fortifications, as well as concrete reinforcements below, against the floodwaters that encroach upon it once or twice a year, when the mountain snows melt or heavy rains pour down for several consecutive days. Here and there it's outfitted with wooden steps, almost ladders, so that you can climb down quite easily to the riverbed proper, that is, to the mostly dry, approximately six-meter-wide secondary gravel riverbed, for this relatively large stream changes size like many smaller examples of its kind. Sometimes, depending on the water levels further upstream, it consists of little more than a greenish trickle—barely covering the stones on which gulls stand as though on the water's surface itself—only to turn, under other conditions, almost dangerous, becoming a torrent. It then swells out to flood its entire secondary bed, raising a terrible din, sweeping away in tight spirals all sorts of foreign material—wicker baskets, shrubbery, even dead cats—and constantly threatening to break its banks and go on a rampage. Thus, even the secondary riverbed is protected against flooding by a series of diagonally positioned breakwaters of woven withe. It is covered with reeds, marram and the region's premier form of plant life, purple sage, and is always passable, thanks to a strip of flat stone that forms a quay at the river's extreme outermost edge and affords still another possibility—indeed my one of choice—for injecting variety into my walks. Its hard stone may not be all that pleasant a surface for the foot, but the immediate proximity of the water more than compensates, and occasionally beyond the quay one can even walk on sand. Yes, there's sand between the gravel and the reeds, a bit muddy perhaps, not so sublimely pure as the ocean variety, but genuine sand nonetheless. You can take a walk on the beach—down here by the edge of the river, completely hidden from view—and lack nothing, neither the rushing of the waves nor the cry of gulls nor that intoxicating uniformity that swallows both time and space and that is the very opposite of boredom. Everywhere you can hear the rush of horizontal rapids, and halfway toward the ferry house this is joined by the splash of a waterfall from a diagonally terminating feeder canal on the opposite bank. That mass of falling water is convex, clear and glassy, like the body of a fish, and its foot is constantly boiling and bubbling.

The spot is truly lovely. When the skies are clear, the skiff that serves as a ferry will fly a decorative banner—be it to celebrate the weather or some other festive occasion. There's more than one skiff here, but only the ferry is attached to a wire cable connected by pulley to a second, thicker one stretched across the river. The current itself is what pushes the vessel, the ferryman's hand on the tiller doing the rest. The ferryman lives a short distance to the rear of the upper path with his wife and child in the ferry house, which has a vegetable garden and a chicken coop and which, no doubt, comes with the job. It's a kind of dwarf villa, a cheap and capricious construction with little oriels and balconies and what appear to be two rooms in both the up- and downstairs. I quite enjoy sitting on the bench between the upper path and the ferryman's yard, with Baushan squatting on my foot and his chickens scurrying around me, jerking their heads forward with every step. More often than not, his rooster will perch next to me on the backrest, its green *bersaglieri* tail feathers hanging down behind us, one of its red eyes mustering me from the side. I watch the activity of the ferry, which can't exactly be called feverish, or even lively, taking place only between long stretches of idleness. Therefore I enjoy it all the more when I spy a man here or a basket-carrying woman there who needs to be brought across. The poetic "Ahoy there!" remains as humanly compelling today as in olden times, even when it, as here, takes on more modern, technologically advanced forms. On both sides of the river, a pair of wooden staircases—one for arrivals, one for departures—curves around the embankments down to the landings, and there is an electric bell beside each of the entrances. Hence, when someone appears on the opposite bank and stands there peering over the water, he no longer cups his hands and calls out, as he once did, but merely approaches the bell, stretches out an arm and presses the button. It then rings shrilly in the ferryman's villa. That's today's "Ahoy there!" but even so, there's something poetic about it. The man stands there waiting and peering; immediately after the bell commences its shrill ringing, the ferryman emerges from his official house, as though he had been doing nothing but standing or sitting in a chair by the door, poised for the signal. He emerges, and something in his walk makes it seem as though the pressing of the button itself has wound up the machinery within him, as in a shooting gallery, where a direct hit will cause the door of some little house to spring open and a figure—a shepherd girl or a sentry—to pop out. Without haste, swinging his arms in an even rhythm, the ferryman walks through his yard, over the path and down the steps to the river; he pushes the ferry off and steers while the little pulley runs along the wire and the boat is drawn cross-stream. On the other side he holds the vessel steady for the stranger who, having safely navigated the current, hands him a small coin, happily bounds up the steps and disappears to the right or left. Sometimes when the ferryman is indisposed or otherwise detained by urgent household business, his wife or even his child will come and pick up the stranger, for they can do his job as well he can. So, for that matter, could I, for the office of the ferryman is easy and requires no special skill or training. He should count himself double blessed to call this sinecure with its dwarf villa his own. Any idiot could replace him, and he knows it, always behaving with corresponding humility and gratitude. On the way back to his house, he never forgets to greet me, sitting there between my dog and his rooster, with a well-mannered provincial *Grüß Gott*, from which one can tell he has no desire to make enemies.

Smells of tar, wind on the water—and water lapping muffled against the side of the boats. What more could I want? Sometimes I'm overcome by a different feeling of familiarity: the water is deep, its smells rotten. That is the Lagoon; that is Venice. Everything is different during flood season, when the rains pour down without end. Dressed in my slicker, with water streaming down my face, I must brace myself on the upper path against the west wind that tears up the young poplars on the lane by their roots—you can see then why the trees here tend to slant in one direction and have lopsided crowns—and Baushan frequently stops on the path to shake himself off, spraying water everywhere. The river is no longer what it was. Swollen and dark-yellow, it rushes along with apocalyptic mien. It pitches, rolls and surges forward in belabored haste like a genuine torrent, its dirty swells covering the entire secondary riverbank up to the edge of the embankment and crashing against the concrete and withe reinforcements, so that one thanks God for the foresight that installed them. The uncanny thing is that the river in this condition turns *quiet,* much quieter than usual, almost silent in fact. It no longer forms rapids, its level being too high, although the places where it usually does are recognizable from the comparatively deep troughs and higher crests of the swells, which break against and not with the current like regular surf. The waterfall practically vanishes: its drop is pathetically flat, and the boiling at its foot ceases. Baushan is completely dumbfounded by the drastic change in scenery. He can't get over it, can't comprehend that the dry land where he usually runs has today disappeared under water. Frightened, he flees up the embankment away from the rising waves. He wags his tail, glances back at me, then stares again at the water, letting his mouth gape crookedly open, somewhat haplessly, his tongue lolling in its corner. It is a face both human and animal, too crude and primitive to be truly expressive, yet thoroughly comprehensible as the sort of face a somewhat simple-minded person of low birth might make when confronted with a tricky situation, no doubt while also scratching the back of his neck.

Now that I've also gone into the river zone in some detail, I've covered the entire area and done everything possible, as far as I can see, to give a vivid picture of it. I'm quite pleased with the description, although of course it doesn't compare to the real thing in nature, just as the real-life Baushan is warmer, livelier and more amusing than the image I've conjured up. I'm quite devoted, indeed grateful to this landscape—which is why I wished to make this portrait. It's my playground, my retreat. My thoughts and dreams are intermingled and bound up with its scenes like the leaves of the creepers that are entwined with those of the trees. I've observed it at every time of day and year. In the fall, the chemical smell of decaying foliage fills the air, hordes of thistle blossoms shed their down, the giant beeches in the "sanitarium garden" spread a rusty carpet of leaves over the surrounding meadow, and golden afternoons fade into dramatic early evenings, a crescent moon floating in the sky, an opaque fog clinging to the lowlands and a red sunset smoldering amidst the dark silhouettes of the trees . . . That's the fall. In winter, snow covers the gravel and provides a smooth, soft surface passable in galoshes, while the river flows black between its pale, frozen banks and the cries of a hundred gulls fill the air from morning until night. Still, the most casual, intimate contact with this landscape occurs during the milder months, when no preparations are required if I want to dash out for a quarter of an hour between rainstorms, stick my face through the branches of an alder bush and take a peep at the wandering waves. Perhaps guests were there, and now they've gone. Exhausted by conversation, I sit within my four walls, a foreign presence still lingering in the air. At such moments it helps to amble out for a little while to *Gellert-* or *Stifterstraße*, take in some fresh air and recuperate. I look up at the sky or peer into the depths of the delicate foliage, my nerves settle down, and once more I grow calm and sober.

But Baushan is always there, too. He was unable to prevent the outside world from invading the house: he may have raised a terrible howl in protest and complaint, but it was no use, and he had to retreat. Now he's happy that we are once more together in our hunting ground. With one ear casually flopping back, he trots before me on the gravel, waddling the way all dogs do by setting his hind paws somewhat laterally to, not directly behind his front ones. And I watch as something suddenly seizes him in body and soul and sets his stiffly outstretched stump of a tail in furious motion. He cocks his head forward and sideways; his body tenses and stretches out lengthwise; he hops around, first here, then there, then takes off like a flash, nose to the ground, in a specific direction. He's got a scent. He's after a hare.

The Hunt

Our region teems with wild game to hunt, and that is precisely what we do, which is to say, Baushan gives chase and I watch. Our labor thus divided, we hunt hares, partridges, field mice, moles, ducks and gulls. Nor do we shy away from big game: we gladly go after pheasant, even deer if one of their numbers happens our way. This is most often the case in winter, and it's thrilling to watch the long-legged, delicately built deer, yellow against the snow, its white tail bobbing up and down, fleeing before little Baushan, who strains with all his might in pursuit. I follow the chase with the most intense interest and excitement. Not that anything will come of it: nothing ever has and it never will. Yet the lack of tangible results doesn't dampen Baushan's passionate desire or disrupt my enjoyment in the slightest. We practise the hunt for its own sake, not for the purpose of the catch or any material benefit, Baushan, as I said, being the active party. He requires nothing more from me than moral support, for he knows of no other form of cooperation, no more efficient or scientific methodology for going about the task at hand—at least not from direct personal experience. I wish to emphasize the words "direct" and "personal" because in all probability his ancestors, insofar as they were indeed pointers, did know a more genuine form of hunting, and now and again I wonder whether he has inherited any memories that might be stirred up by some chance stimulus. At his evolutionary level, the life of the individual is no doubt far less thoroughly differentiated from that of the species than at ours. Birth and death amount to a more superficial fluctuation of being, and blood inheritances are probably better preserved over generations, so that it's only an apparent contradiction to talk about congenital experiences or innate memories, which, if activated, might well contradict the animal's own individual experience and lead to conflict. There was a time when this unsettling thought took hold of me, but I quickly put it from my mind, just as Baushan apparently put from his mind the violent incident to which he was witness and which gave rise to these hypotheses.

By the time I take him out hunting, it's usually around noon, eleven-thirty or twelve, though occasionally on hot summer days it can be put off until or repeated at six or even later in the evening. Whatever the hour, my mood is another one entirely than that of our first casual morning stroll. The fresh, carefree spirit of the early hours is gone. In the meantime I've fretted and struggled, overcome obstacles and hammered out details, gritting my teeth and keeping sight at the same time of the broader and more intricate context, whose remotest implications need to be thought through with a clear mind. Invariably my head is tired, and hunting with Baushan provides a necessary diversion. It cheers me up, revitalizes my creative energies and enables me to get through the rest of the day, during which there is still much to be done. I therefore offer this portrait in the spirit of gratitude.

Naturally we don't single out any one of the aforementioned types of game—hare or duck, for example—as the day's exclusive quarry. Instead we hunt anything and everything that comes . . . I almost want to say, before our sights. We don't have to go far to find it. The hunt literally begins as soon as we set foot outside the front yard, for the grassy hollow behind the house contains hordes of field mice and moles. Strictly speaking, these furry creatures aren't wild game at all, but their secretive burrowing—especially the conspiratorial dexterity of the field mice, which, unlike the more subterranean moles, aren't blinded by sunlight and often dawdle near the surface, darting back down their black holes so quickly at the approach of danger that their legs become a blur of motion—excites Baushan's instinct for the chase nonetheless. Moreover, they are the only game

Baushan ever catches: a field mouse or a mole is also a *snack*, not to be snubbed in days as lean as these, when he often finds nothing more by his doghouse than a small bowl of tasteless barley gruel.

My walking stick has hardly touched the ground two or three steps down the lane, Baushan having kicked off our outing with a brief leaping romp, than I see him off to my right engaged in the strangest caprioles. The passion of the hunt already has him in its grasp, and he no longer sees or hears anything but the infuriatingly concealed activity of the surrounding wildlife. Muscles tensed, tail wagging, he creeps on tiptoed paws through the grass. He halts in mid-step, one front and one hind leg raised, and peers down his snout at the ground, his head cocked and the flaps of his pricked ears hanging down on either side of his eyes. He hops forward, gropes with his paws, once, twice, then stares suspiciously at the spot where something just was but isn't anymore. Then he starts to dig . . . I feel a powerful urge to wait beside him until he achieves success, but we'd never make any progress, and he would squander all his pent-up desire for today's hunt on this one meadow. So I continue on, not worrying about leaving him behind. Even if he lingers for some time and doesn't see which way I've turned, my scent is no less clear to him than that of the wild game. He tracks me down with his head between his front paws, if he's lost sight of me. Soon I hear the tinkling of his license medallion and his regular running footsteps to my rear; he shoots past, then turns round and reports back to me, wagging his tail.

Nonetheless, sometimes in the forest or in the open fields near the brook I do stop and watch him dig for a mouse, even if it's late and watching him wastes time allotted for my walk. His passionate labor is simply so captivating, his intense eagerness so contagious, that I can't help but wish him success and gladly accept a certain sacrifice to be present when he achieves it. Externally there's never anything special about the spot he's chosen—perhaps some moss-covered mound shot through with birch roots. That, however, was where he heard, smelled, probably even saw something as it scurried away. He's positive that it's sitting in one of its underground tunnels or bunkers—he only has to find it. So he digs as fast as he can, abandoning himself to his task, utterly oblivious to the world, though his is more the precise passion of a sportsman than the frenzy of an amateur. It's a splendid sight: his striped little body, arched in the middle, ribs clearly defined and muscles working away under smooth skin, his hindquarters stuck stiffly in the air, his stump of a tail oscillating at full tempo, his head buried between his front paws in the diagonally excavated hole. Face averted, he tears up the soil, turning it over as fast as his iron claws will go, sending clods of earth, little stones, clumps of grass and bits of root flying up under the brim of my hat. Meanwhile his snorts sound in the still air as his muzzle burrows further and further into the ground, besieging the clever, motionless, frightened creature underneath with his sense of smell. There are muffled, abrupt exhalations to clear the lungs and inhale, inhale the delicate, pungent, if also distant and hidden scent of the mouse. What must the little creature down there feel when it hears these dull snorts? That's the mouse's problem. Or better still, it's between him and God, for it was God who made Baushan into the archenemy of field mice. On the other hand, fear enhances the sense of being alive, and the little mouse might be bored if Baushan weren't around. If not for Baushan, there'd be no point to its beady-eyed cleverness and deft mining skill, for they ensure an extremely fair contest in which the attacker's chances for victory remain decidedly bleak. In short, I feel no pity at all for the mouse and root wholeheartedly for Baushan. Often I cannot content myself with the role of mere spectator, intervening with my walking stick whenever a firmly imbedded stone or obstinate root impedes his progress, helping him in my prying, levering way to remove the obstacle. At such moments, he glances briefly up from his work with a harried and excitable look of approval. Plunging his beard back into the obstinate, root-infested soil, he bites and tears, shovels aside clods of earth, snorts once more into the depths and, fired by the scent, resumes his claws' fast and furious labor . . .

In the great majority of cases all this effort is fruitless. With a nose full of soil, mud splattered up to his shoulders, Baushan takes one last cursory sniff at the spot before giving up and indifferently moving on. "It was nothing, Baushan," I tell him as he looks up at me. "It was nothing," I repeat, shaking my head and shrugging to communicate the gist of what I'm saying. Yet there's no need to console him: his lack of success doesn't depress him in the slightest. The hunt is the important thing, not the feast. Anyway, it was a splendid bit of exercise, he thinks, that is, insofar as he thinks back at all upon the activity in which he was just now so fervently engaged, for in no time he will have found some new pursuit—opportunities for such positively abounding in all three zones.

But sometimes he does catch the mouse, to my distress, since as soon as he gets hold of his prey, he's merciless, eating it alive, fur and bones and all. Perhaps the unlucky creature was betrayed by its instincts and chose a spot for his hole that was too soft, too easily exposed and unearthed. Perhaps it didn't tunnel far enough down and then was too scared to correct its mistake. Perhaps it lost its head and tried to hide a few inches below the surface, its beady eyes bulging in horror as the terrible snorting drew near. Whatever the reason, the iron claws ultimately uncover it and toss it in the air—up into the light of day, you hapless little mouse! You were right to be afraid, and it's a good thing that your overwhelming, fully justified fear seems to have left you only half-conscious, for you're about to be ground into meal. By now he's got it by the tail. He dashes it against the ground two or three times, and a faint squeak—the last sound this godforsaken mouse is destined ever to make—can be heard. Then Baushan snaps it up between his jaws and into his white teeth. Legs spread wide, front paws braced outward and neck inclined, he jerks his head forward as he chews, shifting his grip on his prey with every bite and moving it around in his mouth. The little bones crack, and for a second a scrap of fur hangs from the corner of his mouth, to be licked away. Then the whole business is over, and Baushan takes up a joyous victory dance around me as I stand leaning on my cane in the very spot from where I've watched the whole proceeding. "Well you're a fine one!" I tell him, nodding in horrified recognition of his achievement. "You murderer, you cannibal!" He dances in double-time at these words—he does everything but laugh out loud. I continue on my way down the path, somewhat chilled by what I've witnessed yet also inwardly bemused by life's crude sense of humor. It's part of the natural order of things that mice with faulty instincts get pulverized. Nonetheless, I prefer it in such instances if I've only been a spectator and haven't actually assisted the natural order of things with my walking stick.

It's a shock when the pheasant suddenly bursts from the bushes where it had been asleep or, if awake, hiding, and from where it has been flushed out, after a bit of sniffing, by Baushan's game-dog nose. Flapping and beating, crying and clucking in terrified outrage, the great rust-colored bird takes to the air with its long tail feathers. Dropping its dung onto the woods below, as fearful as a silly chicken, it flees into a nearby tree and continues making a racket, while Baushan, braced against the tree trunk, barks furiously up at it. "Up and off!" his barking says. "Keep flying, you silly object of desire, so that I can chase you." And the pheasant cannot withstand this powerful voice. With a rustle it forsakes its perch and continues its arduous flight through the treetops, squawking and carping all the while, with the stoic and silent Baushan giving hot pursuit at ground level.

This is Baushan's idea of bliss—he wants and knows no other. What would happen if he ever caught one of these birds? There's no need to speculate. Once I actually saw him stumble across a pheasant—it must have been fast asleep, its heavy wings unable to lift it in time.

He got hold of it between his claws, then stood there as the discouraged victor and had no idea what to do. One wing splayed out, its neck craned sideways, the creature lay in the grass, shrieking and shrieking, sounding for all the world like a little old lady being murdered in the bushes, which foul deed I came running to prevent. But I was soon convinced that no one was in any danger: Baushan's transparent helplessness—his half-curious, half-disgusted expression as he looked sideways down upon his prisoner—assured me of that. The womanly screeching at his feet seemed to grate on his nerves, and the entire incident was more a source of embarrassment than triumph. Was it just his concern for honor and a bit of *schadenfreude* that made him pick at his prey? I think I saw him pluck out a couple of feathers—using his lips, not his teeth—and toss them aside with a contemptuous jerk of his head. Then he walked off, letting the bird go, not out of pride, but boredom, because the situation as it stood seemed to him to have nothing more to do with the joyful art of the hunt. Never have I seen such an astonished bird! It had no doubt bid farewell to life, and for a while it apparently no longer knew what to make of its own continuing existence, lying there as though dead for quite some time. After that, it reeled a bit on the ground, swooped up into a tree, seemed about to fall back to earth, then finally came to and made for the horizon on its arduously flapping wings. It was no longer shrieking; its beak was shut. Silently, it flew over the park, the river and the woods beyond, on and on, as far as it could, and I'm sure it has never returned.

But there are many more like it in these parts, and Baushan hunts them in the best sporting tradition. The only blood he sheds is that of the mice he eats, and this is but a superficial by-product of his real activity—the finding of scents, the flushing of game, the running and the chasing—as anyone who witnessed him during this splendid game could attest. How handsome he becomes! How idealized, how perfect! Thus the young hayseed from the highlands becomes perfect and exemplary. Thus the Alpine deerhunter comes into his own. Everything fine, authentic and superlative in him rises to the surface during these hunting hours and is displayed in all its glory. That's why he insists so vehemently on our hunts and suffers so deeply if they pass without turning up anything. He's no pinscher, he's a game dog and tracker, as good as any in the book, and self-satisfaction speaks from every one of the masculine and primal warrior poses he strikes in rapid succession. There's little I find so delightful as to see him trotting jauntily through the brush, then suddenly stopping as though chained to the spot, one paw delicately raised and inwardly bowed, clever, alert, all his features beautifully taut! He's whimpering. He's stepped on something like a thorn and is crying out. But that, too, is nature, that, too, the appealing license of handsome simplicity, which can only momentarily undermine his dignity. A second later his full glory has been restored.

I look at him and recall a time when he in fact did lose all his pride and dignity, sinking back into the physical and emotional depths of our first encounter in the innkeeper's kitchen, which it had cost him such struggle to overcome and replace with confidence in himself and the world. I don't know what was wrong with him—to this day it remains a mystery—but he was bleeding, sometimes from the mouth, sometimes from the nose or the throat. He left behind drops of blood wherever he went: on the grass of our hunting ground, the straw in his doghouse, the floor of whatever rooms he was in. Although he didn't appear to be injured in any way, his muzzle often looked as though it had been smeared with red paint. When he sneezed, blood would shoot from his nostrils, and he would walk through it, leaving behind brick-red paw prints at every step. Careful examination yielded no answer, only multiplied worries. Was he consumptive? Or afflicted with some other unknown ailment, to which his breed was susceptible? When this unsettling, as well as unclean, symptom didn't go away after a few days, it was decided to take him to the veterinary clinic.

The next day around noon, in a friendly but firm manner, I as master forced him into his muzzle, that mask of leather straps he so singularly abhors and always tries to remove by shaking his head and scraping with his paw. I put him on his woven leash and led him down the lane to the left, through the *Englischer Garten* and along another street to the university, where we walked through the main gate and crossed the campus. We were received in a waiting room, where a number of people sat along the walls, each of them holding a dog on a leash, just as I was, dogs of various sizes and breeds, all looking depressed as they measured one another through their leather visors. There was a granny with her distemperate pug, a servant in a livery with a tall, snow-white Afghan that from time to time let out an aristocratically hoarse cough, a rural-looking man with a dachshund that must have been headed for some sort of orthopedic exhibition, since the attachment of his feet to his body was utterly deviant, twisted and cockeyed, and many others. One by one they were all admitted by the busy veterinary assistant into the adjacent examination room, whose door was finally opened for Baushan and me as well.

The professor was a white-lab-coated man well on in years, with gold-rimmed glasses, curly hair and a manner so expert, friendly and mild that in a medical emergency I would have entrusted myself or any of my family to him without hesitation. He smiled paternally at the patient, who sat before him gazing up sideways with a trusting look, and listened to me recount his symptoms. "He has handsome eyes," the doctor said, neglecting to pay tribute to Baushan's beard, then declared himself ready to undertake an on-the-spot examination. With the help of the assistant, Baushan, too astonished to resist, was spread out atop a table. I was moved to see the doctor applying his black stethoscope and conscientiously subjecting the striped little body to auscultation, just as I have had done to me on more than one occasion. He listened to Baushan's rapidly beating canine heart, listened to the activity of his internal organs from various positions. Then, putting his stethoscope under his arm so as to free his hands, he examined Baushan's eyes, nose and oral cavity, whereupon he made his preliminary diagnosis. The dog was somewhat tense and anemic, he said, but otherwise in good health. The source of the bleeding was uncertain. The problem might be epistaxis or hematemesis. At the same time he couldn't rule out tracheal or pharyngeal hemorrhage. For now it was probably most accurate to speak of a case of hemoptysis. It would be best to keep the animal under close observation. I was to leave him behind and check back in a week.

Enlightened, I thanked the doctor and gave Baushan a farewell pat on the shoulder. I watched the attendant lead the latest admittee across the courtyard toward the entrance of the opposite building and noticed how Baushan looked back at me, confused and frightened. He should have felt flattered, as I couldn't help but feel, that the doctor had pronounced him tense and anemic. Who would have believed when he was born that he would ever receive such a diagnosis or be the object of such educated, exact scrutiny?

From this point on, though, my walks were like food without spice, and I hardly enjoyed them at all. No storm of mute joy enveloped me when I left the house, no proud eagerness for the hunt as I went on my way. The park seemed desolate. I was bored. I couldn't refrain from interrupting the observation week by making telephone inquiries. The answer, communicated by a subordinate, was that the patient was doing well under the circumstances—but for better or worse those circumstances were left unspecified. And when the weekday on which I had delivered Baushan came round once more, I set out again for the clinic.

With the help of many ornately lettered signs and pointing fingers, I found my way without getting lost directly to the entrance of the department where Baushan was being kept, and, heeding the instructions on the door, walked in without knocking. The medium-size room that received me was reminiscent of the predators' house at the zoo, as was the general atmosphere, although the odor of wild beasts mingled with those of various sweet-smelling medicines—an oppressive and unsettling perfume. Cages, almost all occupied, ran along the walls. Deeply pitched barking greeted me from one of them, at whose open door a man stood, apparently an attendant, going about his work with a rake and a shovel. Not wanting to interrupt his labor, he was content to exchange greetings and left me to my own devices.

Having spotted Baushan at first glance through the open door, I walked over to him. He lay there behind kennel bars on a bed consisting of ground-up bark or something similar, which contributed its own peculiar aroma to the pervasive animal odors and various chemical smells. He lay there like a leopard, a very tired, disinterested and morose leopard. I was taken aback by the sullen indifference with which he met my arrival. He thumped his tail once or twice weakly on the floor, his head only lifting from his paws at my first words, before immediately drooping back down to stare gloomily off to one side. An earthenware bowl full of water had been set out for him at the back of his cage. Attached to the outside was a partially pretyped, partially handwritten chart in a frame that, in addition to Baushan's name, breed, sex and age, contained a graph of his daily temperature. "Bastard pointer," it said. "Name: Baushan. Male. Two years old. Brought in on this and that date for observation. Symptoms: occult hemorrhaging." Then came the pen-drawn graph of his temperature, whose oscillations were minimal, and numerical entries reflecting his heart rate. That meant the doctors were taking his temperature and pulse—in this respect, at least, he was getting the attention he required. His spirits, however, worried me.

"Is that one yours?" asked the attendant, who had walked over in the meantime, tools in hand. He wore a gardener's apron and was a stocky fellow with a full beard, red sideburns and moist, rather bloodshot brown eyes, in whose loyal glassy stare there was something itself decidedly doglike.

I answered in the affirmative, referring him to my initial instructions and the information I'd received by telephone, and then declared that I'd come to find out how things stood. The man glanced at the chart. Yes, indeed, the dog was suffering from occult hemorrhages, he said, and it was always a lengthy process to determine where they came from.

Then that still hadn't been settled?

No, they still didn't know anything definite. But the dog was being kept under observation, as prescribed.

And the hemorrhages were continuing?

Yes, they occurred every now and again.

And when they did, they were observed?

Exactly.

Did he have a fever? I asked, trying to decipher the chart on the cage.

No, he had no fever. The dog's body temperature was normal, as was his pulse, ninety beats per minute, just right—any slower would be problematic, and if they were much slower, he would have to be put under closer observation. Except for the occult hemorrhages the dog was in great shape. For the first twenty-four hours or so, he'd howled a lot, but afterward he'd adapted. Of course he wasn't eating much, but then again he wasn't getting any exercise, and loss of appetite was, of course, relative to how much he usually ate.

What were they feeding him?

Gruel, said the man. But as he said, Baushan never ate much of it.

"He looks depressed," I said, feigning expertise.

Yes, he sure did, but that didn't mean anything. After all, it wasn't much fun for a dog to be cooped in there under observation. All of them were depressed to varying degrees—at least those that were well behaved. Some turned mean and took to biting. But he couldn't say that about that one there. He was well behaved: he'd never take to biting, not if you kept him under observation until the end of his days.

I agreed with the man on this point, but with a worried and indignant heart. How long, I asked, did they mean to keep Baushan here?

The man glanced back down at the chart. Another week for further observation, he said, was what the professor had indicated. In a week I could come back and ask again. That would make two weeks in total: by then they should be able to tell me something concrete about the dog's condition and suggest a cure for the occult hemorrhages.

I left, after trying once more to revive Baushan's spirits by calling out his name. My departure affected him as little as my arrival. Loathing and bitter despair seemed to have descended upon him. "Since you proved capable," his behavior seemed to say, "of putting me in this cage, I see I can no longer count on you." Was it not inevitable that he should become deluded and lose faith in reason and justice? What had he done to deserve that I should not only consent to his fate but also actively bring it about? My intentions had been only the best. The bleeding hadn't stopped, and while that didn't seem to have bothered him, I had thought it wise for the appropriate branch of medicine to have a look at him, a dog of good house, and had been proud to hear him pronounced tense and anemic like some adolescent count. And this was how it had to end! How could I make him understand that it was an honor to be the object of such attention, to be treated like a jaguar and be deprived of fresh air, sunshine and freedom behind the bars of a cage, to be plagued by a thermometer day in, day out?

Thus I questioned myself on my way home, and whereas I had theretofore only regretted Baushan's absence, I now experienced both anxiety about him, about his state of mind, and nebulous feelings of guilt. Was it ultimately just proud, selfish snobbery that had made me bring him to the university clinic? And was that not also perhaps bound up with the secret wish to get rid of him for a while, an inquisitive craving to be liberated from his constant watchful eye, to see how it would feel simply to turn right or left, with utter peace of mind, exciting neither joy nor bitter disappointment in the living world around me? Indeed, ever since Baushan had been interned, I had enjoyed an undeniable and almost forgotten feeling of inner freedom. No one intruded upon me through the glass door with a martyred expression of waiting. No one approached with a timidly raised paw designed to touch my heart, draw a sympathetic smile and move me to immediate departure. Whether I went to the park or remained in my study was of interest to no one. It was easy, relaxing, and had the charm of novelty. Without the usual prodding, however, I seldom took my habitual walks. I felt less healthy, and as my own condition noticeably began to resemble Baushan's in his cage, I concluded that the bonds of sympathetic affinity were more conducive to my well-being than the egocentric freedom for which I had longed.

The second week too ran its course, and I stood again on the appointed day with the round-bearded attendant before Baushan's cage. Its occupant lay on his side, stretched out in some arbitrary position on his bed of crushed bark, pieces of which clung to his fur. His head was slung back, and he was staring at the limestone wall at the rear of his cell, his eyes glassy and dull. He didn't move. He could hardly be seen to breathe. Only intermittently did his chest heave in a sigh that revealed every one of his ribs, to fall again with a low, heartrending whimper resonating from his vocal cords. His legs seemed to have grown too long for his body, his paws disproportionately large—the result of his terrible emaciation. His fur was rumpled, extremely dishevelled and, as previously mentioned, dirty from rolling around on the crushed bark. He took no notice of me, indeed seemed unwilling ever again to take notice of anything.

The hemorrhages, said the attendant, weren't completely gone. Every once in a while there was still an outbreak. Where they came from was still an open question, but in any case they were harmless. If I wanted to be doubly sure, I could leave the dog here for further observation, or I could take him home, where the ailment would probably fade away with time. I took the woven leash from my pocket—I had deliberately brought it along—and said I would take Baushan with me. The attendant found that sensible. He opened the cage door, and we called Baushan's name—alone and in unison—but he didn't come. He just kept staring straight ahead at the limestone wall. On the other hand, he didn't resist when I stuck my arm in the cage and dragged him out by the collar. With a hop he landed on his feet back at ground level and stood there, tail between his legs, ears flat, the very picture of misery. I collected him, gave the attendant a tip and went to the front office to settle the bill: at the rate of seventy-five pfennig a day plus a flat fee for the doctor's initial examination, it came to twelve marks fifty. Then I led Baushan back home, enveloped by the sweet chemical-animal aromas of the clinic that clung to my companion's fur.

He was broken in body and soul. Animals are less inhibited, more primal, thus in a sense more human about the physical expression of their emotional states than we are. Phrases that, for us humans, refer only to our morale in a metaphorical sense remain true of them in their original, literal meaning, without simile or allegory—something refreshingly visual, in any case, for the eye. Baushan "went," to use such a phrase, "with his head down"—that is, he actually hung his head for all to see, just as a worn-out workhorse stands at a carriage stop, with scabby legs and nervously twitching skin, his poor fly-besieged nose seemingly pulled down by some unseen anchor to the cobblestones. It was exactly as I said before: his two weeks at the university had returned him to that condition in which I found him the first day at the mountain inn. He was only a shadow of himself, I'd say, if that weren't an insult to the shadow of the previously proud and happy Baushan. Except for the occasional whiff, the hospital odor he had brought back home yielded to repeated baths in the washtub, but, while baths may have a symbolic effect on human psychology, no amount of physical cleansing could restore poor Baushan's spirits. On his very first day home I took him out to our hunting ground, but he just skulked along at my feet, his tongue hanging out like an idiot, and the pheasants enjoyed an extended holiday. At home he lay around for days just as in his cell, staring glassy-eyed into the distance, inwardly listless, lacking his former healthy impatience, not once begging me for a walk. On the contrary it was I who had to go find him and prod him from his spot by the doghouse door. Even his wild, indiscriminate devouring of food was reminiscent of his early days of ignominy. It was thus all the more gratifying to see how he later came to himself, how his greetings regained their devotedly playful fervor, how he once more came bolting from his house at my first morning whistle instead of trudging glumly forward, how he put his paws to my chest and snapped up at my face, how, once outdoors, his pride and enthusiasm in his own sporting prowess returned, how those gracefully adept postures and precipitous, taut-muscled pounces onto unseen creatures in the tall grass reappeared before my eyes . . . He forgot. The ugly and—for Baushan—so senseless incident receded into the past, and though he was incapable of resolution or true comprehension, time buried it, the same as must occasionally happen in relations between humans. Our lives went on, and the unspeakable incident fell deeper and deeper into oblivion . . . For several weeks, there were occasional outbreaks of redness around Baushan's nose, but they became less and less frequent. Finally the strange symptom disappeared. It was gone, and no one cared anymore whether it was epistaxis or hematemesis . . .

There I go again. I never intended to tell the clinic story. The reader must forgive my digression and return with me to the park, to the hunt we were enjoying before we were interrupted. Is the reader familiar with the whining howl a dog lets out when he summons his utmost energies in pursuit of a fleeing hare, this mix of rage and bliss, desire and ecstatic desperation? How often have I heard it from Baushan! It is passion—pure passion, hoarded, pent up, then savored in intoxicated joy—that echoes shrill over the landscape, and every time its frenzied cry reaches my ear, from near or far, a pleasant shiver runs down my spine. Happy that today Baushan is getting his full due, I hurry forward or off to one side to follow the chase, if possible, and as it flashes past, I stand, transported and transfixed, despite the inevitably negligible result of the adventure, and watch, a smile of excitement tugging at my face.

The hare? A dime a dozen. Scared of its shadow. Dragging its ears through the air, its head pressed into its neck, it runs for its life, scampering away from the soulfully howling Baushan in long leaps, kicking its hind legs and light yellow bottom into the air. And yet at the core of its fearful, flight-inclined soul, it must know that it's in no serious danger, that it will surely escape, just as all of its brothers and sisters have previously in this situation—perhaps as it itself has once or twice already. Baushan has never caught a hare in his life and won't either, since it's practically impossible. A pack of dogs may be a hare's death, as they say, but one alone will never get the job done, even one with much better speed and endurance than Baushan. For the hare can always resort to "doubling," which Baushan cannot, and with that the outcome of the contest is preordained. It is the infallible weapon and talent of a creature born to flee, an ever available escape route that it keeps in reserve and knows how to use at the very moment when Baushan's hopes are highest. And when it is used, Baushan and all his hopes are sunk.

Here they come, angling through the brush, across the path before me toward the river, the hare silent in the knowledge of his inborn trick, Baushan howling his high-pitched whine. Don't howl, I think. You're expending energy, lungpower, breath you should conserve and use all at once to catch up! So I think because in my heart I'm involved in the chase, because I'm on Baushan's side, because I too feel his passion and am anxiously rooting for him, even at the risk of having to watch him dismember the hare before my eyes. How he runs! It's beautiful and gratifying to see a creature exercising every muscle to its fullest. He can run faster than the hare, having the stronger musculature, and the distance between the two has shrunk noticeably when I lose sight of them. I hurry behind, without clear direction, turning left through the park toward the riverbank, arriving on the gravel path just in time to see the chase flash by from the right. It's an exciting chase, full of promise, with Baushan at the hare's heels. He's ceased howling; he's running with clenched teeth, the proximity of the scent bringing out his best effort. One last leap forward, Baushan! I think. And I want to shout: "Steady now! Take good aim, and watch out for doubling!" But the doubling has already occurred: the worst has happened. In the very instant Baushan makes his decisive leap, the hare veers off at a short, mischievous right angle from his line, sending Baushan flying straight past its rear end, howling helplessly and kicking up gravel and mud as he tries to apply the brakes. By the time he sets off in the new direction—I should say, by the time this somehow comes about under his plaintive howls of torment—the hare gets a considerable head start toward the woods and in most cases loses its pursuer entirely, for during his futile attempt at braking, the latter can't see in which direction his quarry is turning.

It's no use, I think, as the frenzied chase continues in the opposite direction through the park and then disappears. It's beautiful, but fruitless. You need more dogs, five or six at least, a true pack. Others have to attack from the flanks, cut him off in front and make him pull up, then grab him by the neck . . . And my overheated imagination envisions a throng of thoroughbreds with outstretched tongues pouncing on a hare in its midst.

It must be my own hunting impulse that makes me daydream of such things. After all, what has the hare ever done to me that I should wish upon it such a horrible end? The reason is that Baushan is more like me, and therefore I sympathize with and root for him. On the other hand, the hare is a living creature too. It's not personal malice that makes it frustrate my hunter, merely the fervent desire to continue nibbling tender young leaves and reproducing itself a little while longer.

Nonetheless, I can't help thinking—with a glance down at my walking stick—that everything would be different if I weren't just holding my harmless cane, but an implement of graver intent, lightning quick and effective at a distance, which I could use to aid Baushan's valiant effort, *dropping* the hare, so that it halted in its tracks with a final airborne somersault. No other dogs would be needed then: Baushan's work would be done as soon as he flushed his prey. As things stand, however, it's Baushan who does somersaults when he tries to follow the cursed "double." Sometimes the hare does the same, but for it, somersaulting through the air is just a minor stumble, a trivial, even expected setback that in no way shakes the little creature, whereas it not only deflates Baushan's morale but puts him at risk of a broken neck.

Most of these chases are over in a few minutes, as soon as the hare puts on a burst of speed and succeeds in ducking under the cover of the brush or loses its pursuer with doubling and feinting, so that he stops short in uncertainty, springing this way and that, while I yell to him in futile blood lust and use my stick to point him in the direction I saw the hare jump away. Often, though, the chase extends far and wide across the land, Baushan's soulful yowl like a hunting bugle in the distance, sometimes nearer, sometimes farther off again, while I go silently on my way, knowing he'll return. And Good Lord, the shape he's in when he does finally turn up! Foam drips from his mouth, his chest heaves, his legs bow and his tongue hangs down from his jaws, which gape crooked and wide. His watery, intoxicated eyes are distorted into a Mongolian slant as he stands huffing and puffing like a steam engine. "Lie down and rest, Baushan, or you'll die of a lung seizure!" I tell him, pausing so that he has time to recover. In winter, when the weather is frosty, I worry about him sucking great gulps of icy air into his overheated insides and belching out clouds of steam as he wolfs down whole mouthfuls of snow to quench his thirst. Yet as he lies there looking up wild-eyed at me, lapping now and then at the foam on his lips, I can't resist the temptation to tease him a bit about the invariable futility of his efforts. "What about the hare, Baushan?" I ask him sometimes. "So you're not bringing me a hare?" And he thumps his tail on the ground, suppressing the rapid pumping of his chest for a moment at the sound of my voice and lapping sheepishly with his tongue. He doesn't understand that my teasing is intended to conceal, from both of us, my shame and guilty conscience at my failure to assist him during this exchange, at my not being the man to "drop" the hare like a real master. He doesn't understand, so I tease him and pretend *he's* somehow to blame for everything . . .

Strange things happen on these hunts. Never will I forget the time a hare ran into my arms . . . It was by the river, on the narrow and muddy upper promenade, to be exact. Baushan was flushing game, and I came running from the brush toward the riverbank, beating my way through the thistles of the gravel embankment and springing down the grassy slope onto the path. At precisely that moment the hare appeared, about fifteen paces in front of Baushan, fleeing in long hops from the ferry house, in whose direction I was facing, straight down the middle of the path toward me. My initial violent huntsman's impulse was to seize the opportunity of blocking the hare's escape and to drive it back, if possible, into the jaws of its torturously yelping pursuer. Thus I stood, rooted to the spot, gripped with excitement, moving not a muscle except to weigh my walking stick in my hands, as the hare approached. I knew it would have poor eyesight; hares rely on sound and smell to warn them of danger. Perhaps it would mistake me for a tree—that was my strategy—and I desperately hoped it would fall into this fatal trap, whose possible consequences I had hardly thought out but intended nonetheless to exploit. Whether the hare did at any time actually make this mistake is uncertain. Personally I think it only noticed me at the last second; but what it did then was so unexpected that in a flash all my schemes and plans were undermined, and I felt a devastatingly sudden change of heart. Was it crazy with fear? Whatever the case, it jumped up toward me just like a lap dog, scrambled up my overcoat with its front paws and buried its outstretched head in my lap, in the horrible lap of the huntsman himself! Bent back at the waist, arms raised, I stood there staring down at the hare, who gazed back up at me, blinking. It may have only lasted a second, or perhaps a fraction of a second, but the result was that I got an extraordinarily close look at my adversary. I saw its long ears, one sticking up while the other hung down, its large, bright, myopically bulging eyes, its cleft lip and long whiskers, the white on its breast and its tiny paws. I felt, or thought I could feel, its frantic little heart trembling. It was strange to see it in such detail and have it so close to me, the little demon of the region, the heartbeat within the landscape, the eternally fleeing creature I had only ever glimpsed for brief comical moments turning tail over hollows and fields. This same creature was now huddled against me in its moment of greatest need and despair, clinging to my knees, clinging to the knees of the man who was not only Baushan's master but the master of hares as well, i.e. its own master as much as Baushan's. As I said, this lasted but a second; then the hare let go. It stood once more on its own dissimilar legs and sprang up the embankment to the left. Meanwhile, taking its place, Baushan approached with his hunter's halloo and all the other headnotes of passion. These, however, were cut abruptly short once he arrived, for a well-aimed, clearly intentional cane blow from the master of the hare sent him whimpering and stumbling on temporarily lame hindquarters down the right slope of the path, which he had to limp back up before he could resume late pursuit of his no longer visible prey. —

Finally, I would also like to address a few words to the hunting of one last sort of game, aquatic fowl. This only takes place in winter and in the colder months of spring—before the birds relocate from their provisional stop in the city on behalf of their stomachs to the mountain lakes—and isn't as exciting as chasing hares can be. It does, however, have its own appeal for both hunter and dog, or rather, for hunter and master. The appeal for me is largely scenic, since hunting fowl entails immediate proximity to running water, but it also entertains and amuses me to observe the subsistence routines of these amphibious creatures, forgetting in the process my own, to take imaginative part in theirs.

Ducks enjoy an easier, more stolidly bourgeois existence than gulls. They almost always look full and seem to worry little about getting food, for what they require will most probably be there for the taking, and thus their table is always set. As far as I can see, they will eat just about anything: worms, snails, insects, even mouthfuls of pure slime. This leaves them plenty of time to sit on the stone riverbanks in the sun—bills tucked under their wings, napping and greasing their feathers, so that the water practically never touches them but rather beads up and runs off the surface—or just to swim around for fun on the rapid current, their tails in the air, spinning and turning with complacently shrugged shoulders.

In contrast, there's something wild, ragged, bleak and drearily monotonous about the gulls' existence. An aura of coarseness that only comes from a life of hunger and theft surrounds the great cawing flocks of them that circle the waterfall nearly all day, their flight paths crisscrossing that spot where the brown runoff from distant sources gushes from a drainpipe into the river. Diving for fish, as this or that one does from time to time, never yields enough to satisfy their roving mass hunger. Often, even if their crooked beaks are able to snatch something from the river and carry it to shore, they must content themselves with nothing more than some unappetizing tidbit. The gulls aren't especially fond of the riverbank. But they do huddle in dense packs on the outcroppings that protrude from the river during the low-water season, so that these are blanketed by their whiteness, just as the rocks and small islands of the northern seas are often covered with white swarms of nesting eider geese. It's splendid to see how they start cawing and take to the air *en masse* when frightened by the menacing barks that Baushan directs from the riverbank across the intervening water. They needn't feel threatened—there's no real danger. His natural aversion to water notwithstanding, Baushan wisely and understandably exercises caution around the river's current, to which his strengths would never be equal and which would sweep him off downstream to God knows where, perhaps all the way to the Danube, leaving him in certainly rather grotesque shape by the time he arrived. The bloated corpses of the cats we always see after winter storms are sufficient proof of that, and he never wades past the point where the water washes over the first rocks. Though he may be tantalized by the impulse to give chase and indeed acts as if he were about to plunge into the river swells, the very next instant, without a second to spare, you can count on good judgement asserting itself over passion. The attack goes no further than a pantomime running start and some extreme-looking preparations—nothing but bluff, not dictated by passion, but rather cold-bloodedly calculated to scare his web-footed adversaries.

And in the end, the gulls have too few brains and too little spine to laugh off his machinations. There's no way Baushan can get at them, but he can send his threatening bark across the water in their direction. It makes contact, being also a kind of physical presence, and the attack is too frightening for them to withstand for long. No doubt they try to maintain their position, but a nervous shudder runs through the group. They look over their shoulders; first one, then the other lifts its wings just in case; and then suddenly the whole congregation takes to the air under bitter and dire squawking like an opaque cloud. Back on the rocks, Baushan jumps this way and that in order to disperse them and keep them in motion, for movement is all he cares about: they can't be allowed just to sit there—they have to fly, either up- or downstream, so that he can give chase.

He sweeps along the strand, dashing its entire length, far and wide, and everywhere he goes, disdainfully relaxed ducks, their beaks under their wings, take flight before him. Thus he does indeed sweep this stretch of sand and stir up an amusing cloud of dust. With a splash, though, the ducks glide back down to the water, in whose safety they rock back and forth and spin round; or, alternately, they fly away with outstretched beaks above Baushan's head, while he runs along the bank measuring his honorable legs against their wings.

He's overjoyed and grateful as long as they fly and provide him with the opportunity for a grand old race up and down the river, whereas they, in turn, are familiar with his desires and can exploit them, if that seems advisable. Once I saw a mother duck with her brood—although it was spring and the river was empty of fowl, she had stayed behind, watching over her little ones, who weren't yet able to migrate—in a slimy puddle left over from the last flood in a hollow of the otherwise dry river bed. Baushan stumbled across them there—I watched the scene from the path above. He jumped into the puddle and started barking as though wild, which sent the duck family scurrying. Naturally he did no harm, but he did throw an immeasurable scare into its members so that the ducklings fled in every direction, flapping their stumpy wings. The mother was then seized by that maternal heroism which blinds her kind to all risk, inspires it to defend the brood against even the fiercest enemy and often succeeds with a preternatural, trance-like display of courage in chasing off the intimidated adversary. With outspread wings and hideously gaping beak, she counterattacked, flying at Baushan's face, throwing herself heroically upon him again and again, hissing all the while. But though the perverse spectacle of such fanaticism indeed caused her enemy to retreat, dumfounded, she was never able to make him withdraw once and for all. He kept on barking and advancing anew, so the mother duck changed tactics and tried guile where bravery had failed. Perhaps she was acquainted with Baushan from before and knew his weaknesses, his childish susceptibilities. In any case, she abandoned her offspring—or rather, she gave the *impression* of abandoning them. She fled to create a diversion, flying off over the river, "driven" by Baushan (as he probably thought, though he was actually being led by his own hyperactive nose). She flew first with, then against the current, farther and farther, while Baushan raced down below in leaps and bounds, until finally both dog and duck had travelled so far from the puddle with the ducklings that I lost sight of them. Only later did the fool find his way back, absolutely frantic and breathless, to me. But the previously besieged puddle, by the time we passed it again, was deserted . . .

That was what the mother duck did, and Baushan counted himself grateful to her for it. Normally, he hates ducks with their bourgeois complacency who refuse to play along with the hunt, who simply slip from the riverbank into the water whenever he comes storming up and sit rocking back and forth in disdainful safety directly before his nose, unperturbed by his mighty voice and, unlike the nervous gulls, not fooled by his pantomime running starts. We stand side by side on the rocky riverside, Baushan and I. Two steps before us the duck bobs up and down in the insolent security of the waves, its beak pressed to its breast with affected dignity, reasonable and sober, utterly indifferent to Baushan's enraged voice assaulting its ears. It paddles against the current, more or less holding its position, but nonetheless drifting downstream little by little. One meter off to the side is whitewater, one of those lovely frothing eddies, toward which it turns its smugly uplifted tail. Baushan braces his front paws against the rocks and barks, and I bark inwardly with him, for I can't help but share to an extent his hatred toward such insolent rationality and wish the ducks ill. Concentrate on our barking, I think, and not on the cataract, so that you get sucked down into the whirlpool. We'll see then how you deal with a truly humiliating and dangerous situation. But this malicious hope, too, remains unfulfilled, for the very second it reaches the brink of the cataract, the impertinent creature flies a short distance into the air, flutters a few yards upstream and glides back down.

When I think of our irritation with the ducks in such situations, I always remember one adventure in particular, which I would like to relate in conclusion to this report. It was an occasion of undeniable satisfaction for my companion and me. However, it also raised a delicate, disruptive and perplexing issue; indeed it even led to a temporary chill in my relationship with Baushan, and if I had been able to see it coming, I would certainly have avoided the spot where it awaited us.

It happened quite far downstream, beyond the ferry house, where the riverside wilderness meets the upper path. We were walking, I in full march, Baushan trotting along lopsidedly a little bit ahead. Having already tormented a hare that day—or if you want, having already *been* tormented by a hare—and having flushed out three or four pheasant, he was now sticking relatively close so as not to neglect his master entirely. A small group of ducks, necks outstretched, flew in wedge formation above the river, too high and too near the other bank to qualify as possible game. They flew along in our direction, paying us no mind, not even noticing our presence, and only now and then did either of us cast a deliberately indifferent glance up at them.

Then it happened. Suddenly, on the equally steep opposite riverbank, a man emerged from the brush and struck a pose that made both Baushan and me halt and close ranks, our eyes upon him the entire time. It was a fine enough figure of a man, somewhat rough on the exterior, with a droopy mustache, square gaiters and a loden hat slanted over his forehead. His billowy trousers were probably of that coarse material known as Manchester velvet, and his matching jacket boasted various leather belts and straps, for he wore a knapsack and carried a rifle slung over his shoulder. Better yet, he *had* carried it slung over his shoulder, since no sooner did he appear on the scene than he took his weapon in his hands and, with his cheek pressed flat against the butt, aimed it sideways up at the sky. With one square-gaitered leg in front of the other, the gun barrel resting in the hollow of his outstretched left hand, his left elbow drawn in underneath, his right elbow, right hand on the trigger, splayed sideways, and his face angled boldly toward the sky, he took aim. There was something decidedly operatic about the man's sudden appearance there above the river scree, towering against the natural backdrop of the brush, the river and the open sky. Yet we could only admire this picturesque image for a second—for from across the water came the dull crack of the gunshot that I had awaited with bated breath, so that I flinched when it occurred. At the same time a tiny flame shot up, pale in the light of day, followed by a puff of smoke. The man took one giant operatic step forward, his chest and face arched toward the sky, his right fist firmly gripping the strap of the rifle, while up above, where both his and our eyes were trained, brief aerial pandemonium broke out. The group of ducks scattered, there was a wild flapping like that of loose sails in a gusty wind and an attempt at gliding, then suddenly a form coalesced, the victim's body, plummeting like a rock into the water near the opposite bank.

But that was only half of it. Here I must interrupt my account to train the living gaze of my memory upon Baushan. Many familiar sayings—perennial currency for great events—leap to mind as possible descriptions for his behavior. I might say, for instance, that he'd been hit by lightning. Yet that strikes a false chord and leaves me dissatisfied. Great words, being worn out, do a poor job of expressing the extraordinary. This is better accomplished by using ordinary words to the uttermost extent of their meaning. Therefore let me just say that at the rifle shot, the attendant context and everything that followed, Baushan *stopped short.* It was typical for him to do so whenever something unusual occurred, that I knew. Only this time the arrest of motion was intensified *ad infinitum.* He did a veritable double take that propelled his whole body a step backward, shook him from right to left and jerked his head into his chest with such force that it was practically torn from his shoulders on the rebound. It was like a cry from deep within: "What? What? What was that? Wait one minute! *What was that all about?"* His eyes and ears took everything in with the sort of indignation caused by great amazement, yet despite the novelty of it all, everything was already present somehow, just as it always had been. Indeed, gripped by uncertainty, jerking in great spasms to the right and to the left, halfway around his own axis, he could well have been trying to examine himself from behind, asking all the while: "What am I? Who am I? Is that me?" The moment the duck hit the water, Baushan sprang forward to the edge of the embankment as though about to jump down to the riverbank and plunge in. But then he remembered the current, checked this impulse and, ashamed, resumed the role of mere spectator.

I looked on uneasily. Once the duck had fallen from the sky, I was of the opinion that we'd seen enough and should now move on. He, however, had settled down on his haunches, ears pricked, facing the other bank, and to my question "Shall we be on our way, Baushan?" he barely turned his head in response—not unlike someone answering in a peremptory tone, "Please leave me in peace"—and kept on watching. Thus I resigned myself, crossed my legs, leaned against my walking stick and watched as things unfolded.

The duck—one of those that always bobbed up and down before our noses in insolent safety—was floating face down in the water, a shipwreck whose front could no longer be distinguished from its tail. The river is calmer down here, its drop less drastic than further upstream. Nonetheless the dead bird was immediately seized, spun round and carried off by the current. If the man had something more practical in mind than just killing his mark for sport, he had to make haste. That he did, without losing a moment, so that everything transpired with the greatest speed. Hardly had the duck broken the water's surface before he came storming down the embankment, jumping, stumbling and almost falling. He held his rifle outstretched in his arms, and once again the scene had all the romance of an opera, with him springing down over the ornamental-seeming backdrop of the river scree like some thief or clever smuggler of melodrama. He struck out a bit to the left, cleverly, for the duck threatened to float away before he could catch it. And stretching out the butt of his rifle and leaning forward with his feet in the water, he actually succeeded in putting a stop to its drift and bringing it under control. Carefully and with considerable difficulty, he managed to nudge it tugboatlike against the rocks and up onto land.

That was the end of the business, and the man could once more breathe easily. He laid his weapon down beside him on the bank, took his knapsack from his shoulders, stuffed his kill inside, strapped it on again and, happy with the additional weight, climbed peacefully back up the scree toward the brush, using his rifle as a walking stick.

Well, he's got something for tomorrow's grill, I thought with a mixture of approval and resentment. "Come, Baushan! Let's go now. It's all over."

Baushan got up. But after turning completely around, he sat back down again and continued to stare at the opposite bank, even though the man had already made his exit and disappeared through the bushes. I wasn't about to call him twice. He knew where we lived, and he could sit there for hours gawking after the show was over and there was nothing more to see, if that was what he wanted. It was a long way home, and I for one meant to get going and put it behind me. With that he followed.

He clung to my heels for the whole uncomfortable walk home, not once giving chase. Instead of running ahead at an angle as was his wont whenever he wasn't rummaging around and tracking some scent, he trotted to my rear and put on the kind of face I couldn't help noticing when I happened to glance back. I might well have let that go: it's not so easy to get to me. On the contrary, I was much more inclined to laugh and shrug the whole thing off. But every forty or fifty steps he *yawned*. That was what enraged me. It was that unabashedly rude, jaw-unhinging yawn of boredom, with the guttural squeak that clearly expressed the following sentiment: "A fine master I have! A fraud, this master! A pathetic excuse for a master!" I can never hear this sound without taking it personally, but this time it was enough to shake the very foundations of our friendship.

"Go on then!" I said. "Go! Go and join your master over there with the blunderbuss. He seems not to be in possession of a dog, and maybe he can use you in his sporting endeavors. He's just some common fellow in Manchester, not a gentleman, but in your eyes he probably is a gentleman, just the sort to be your master. So I sincerely advise you to go follow him, since he seems to have set ideas nagging at your flea-bitten head. Not that you could tell the difference."

Having gone that far, I continued: "We won't ask for his hunting license. It might well cause trouble if one day someone catches you two at your respectable sport, but that's your business and I repeat, I mean my advice sincerely. You, a hunter! Of all the hares I let you chase, did you ever bring one back for my kitchen? It's not my fault you don't know how to double and end up plowing the ground with your nose like a fool precisely when you need to be clever! Or a pheasant—that would be no less welcome in these lean days! And you yawn! Go, I tell you. Go follow your master with the square gaiters. Go and see whether he's the man to stroke your neck and make you laugh—I bet he hardly knows how to laugh, and if so, only at coarse jokes! If you think *he* will submit you to medical observation, whenever you decide to have occult hemorrhages, or that *his* dog will be pronounced tense and anemic, then go follow him! Maybe you overestimate the regard such a master would have for you. There are things for which such rifle-toting types have a fine sense of distinction and a sharp eye. Just so there's no misunderstanding: I mean inborn qualities and flaws, ticklish matters of genealogy and pedigree, which not everyone has the compassion and humanity to overlook. I hope I've made myself *clear*. So the first time you fall out with your exciting new master, and he reproaches you with your beard and calls you all sorts of ugly names, I hope you think about me and what I've said today . . ."

Such were the cutting words I addressed to Baushan on the way home as he slunk along behind me. And though I only spoke them silently to myself, so as not to be overly dramatic, I'm convinced that he understood exactly what I meant and was able to follow my line of thinking. The long and short of it was that we were profoundly at odds, and when we arrived home, I deliberately let the front gate fall into its latch before he could slip through, making him jump up and climb over it. Without even a glance back, I went into the house, and when I heard him whimper at the scrape on his belly, I just shrugged my shoulders in spite. —

However, that was a long time, more than six months, ago, and the whole thing passed just like the clinic incident. Time and forgetting have covered it over, and our lives go on atop their swampy ground, which is the ground of all life. Baushan, after a few days' moping, regained his innocent enthusiasm for hunting mice, pheasants, hares and aquatic fowl and anxiously awaits our next walk as soon as we return home from the previous one. On my front-door landing, I always glance back at him one last time. This is his signal to take the steps in two great leaps and stand upright with his front paws against the door, so that I can give him a farewell pat on the shoulder. "'Til tomorrow, Baushan," I tell him, "assuming I don't have to go out into the world." And then I hasten to slip out of my hobnailed boots, for supper is on the table.

Suggestions for Further Reading

Cohn, Dorrit. *Transparent Minds: Narrative Modes for Presenting Consciousness in Fiction.* Princeton: Princeton University Press, 1992.

Corngold, Stanley. *The Fate of the Self: German Writers and French Theory.* Paperback reprint of 1986 original. Durham, NC: Duke University Press, 1994.

Gay, Peter. *Weimar Culture: The Outsider as Insider.* New York: Harper & Row, 1968.

Hatfield, Henry. *Thomas Mann: A Collection of Critical Essays.* Englewood Cliffs, NJ: Prentice-Hall, 1964.

Hayman, Raymond. *Thomas Mann: A Biography.* New York: Simon & Schuster, 1995.

Heilbut, Anthony. *Thomas Mann: Eros and Literature.* Paperback reprint of 1995 original. Berkeley: University of California Press, 1997.

Heller, Erich. *Thomas Mann.* Cambridge: Cambridge University Press, 1981.

Hollingdale, R. J. *Thomas Mann: A Critical Study.* Lewisburg, PA: Bucknell University Press, 1971.

Lukács, Georg. *Essays on Thomas Mann.* North Woodbridge, UK: Merlin Press, 1964.

Minden, Michael, ed. *Thomas Mann.* Harlow, UK: Addison Wesley Longman Higher Education, 1995.

Mosse, George L. *Nationalism and Sexuality: Middle-*

Class Morality and Sexual Norms in Modern Europe. Madison: University of Wisconsin Press, 1991.

Prater, Donald A. *Thomas Mann: A Life.* Oxford: Oxford University Press, 1995.

Reed, T. J. *Thomas Mann: The Uses of Tradition.* Revised edition. Oxford: Clarendon Press, 1996.

Swales, Martin A. *Thomas Mann: A Study.* Totowa, NJ: Rowman and Littlefield, 1980.

Travers, Martin. *Thomas Mann.* New York: St. Martin's Press, 1992.

Wysling, Hans, ed.; Heilbut, Anthony, tr. *Letters of Heinrich and Thomas Mann, 1900–1949.* Berkeley: University of California Press, 1998.

Young, Frank W. *Montage and Motif in Thomas Mann's* Tristan. Bonn: Bouvier, 1975.

Thomas Mann's Major Works

Little Herr Friedemann (1898).
The Buddenbrooks: Decline of a Family (1901).
Tristan/Tonio Kröger (1903).
Fiorenza (1906).
Royal Highness (1909).
Little Herr Friedemann and Other Stories (1909).
Death in Venice (1912).
Observations of a Non-Political Man (1918).
Man and Dog (1919).
The Magic Mountain (1924).
Disorder and Early Sorrow (1926).
Mario and the Magician (1930).
Joseph and His Brothers (Vol. 1: 1933; Vol. 2: 1934; Vol. 3: 1936; Vol. 4: 1943).
Doctor Faustus (1947).
The Confessions of Felix Krull, Confidence Man (1954).